CATALINA;

OR,

THE SPANIARD'S REVENGE.

A Romance.

BY

WILLIAM HILLYARD.

WITH BEAUTIFUL WOOD ENGRAVINGS,

DRAWN BY F. SKILL, JUN.

LONDON:

PUBLISHED, FOR THE PROPRIETOR, BY JOHN DICKS,

AT THE OFFICE OF "REYNOLDS'S MISCELLANY,"

No. 7, WELLINGTON STREET NORTH, STRAND.

———

1848.

CATALINA;

OR, THE SPANIARD'S REVENGE.

INTRODUCTION.

NEAR the City of Soria, in Northern Spain, and almost on the site of the once populous Numantia of the Romans, there stood in the 16th Century a stately castle, the noble

1

residence of family not less renowned for arms in the field than celebrated for their wisdom in the council. Of this almost palatial abode, time, desolation, and the fount of war, has scarcely left a relic to denote to the present day its former proud and extensive magnificence.

A strange and mysterious fatality attended its last lineal possessor, Don Ferdinand De Almazuma, who, with his young and beautiful wife, had suddenly and for ever disappeared from the midst of their household, from their friends, and as it was believed, in the full plenitude of their happiness; no cause assigned, no motive, by time revealed, ever threw light or prospect on this dark and singular disappearance.

In vain the lady's relatives sought, examined, threatened; neither friend, priest, vassal, or domestic, knew, or could reveal ought to dissipate the veil that shrouded a circumstance so fraught with mystery and alarm.

Years rolled away; and as no heirs remained to claim the titles or estate of Almazuma, the entire feofdom merged in the crown, which, satisfied with the ample rental of the extensive possessions, permitted the mansion to remain uninhabited and disregarded, Indeed, it would have been a matter of no inconsiderable difficulty to have induced any domestic to remain in the house for an hour after the singular disappearance of its former master; so much were the minds of the ignorant impressed with the conviction, that to supernatural agency alone was to be attributed a calamity that affected alike friend and vassal with grief and wonder. The revolution of years at length brought on the sure decay that perishes the works of art equally with the productions of nature; and in the year 1692, exactly a century after the fatal event narrated, nothing but roofless chambers and desolated vaults remained to testify what was once the sumptuous palace of one of Spain's proudest and noblest chieftains.

Tradition still kept alive the memory of the past, and credulity, feeding on the terrors of superstition, failed not to magnify former events into acts of necromancy and witchcraft; and there were few, however well informed, for miles around the scene of that catastrophe, who could disabuse their minds of the impression early imbibed and still kept alive by the rumours of the unhallowed deeds of its former possessor, and the supernatural appearances and unearthly sounds that still visited the lone and ruined castle; and that peasant was considered hardy indeed, who at mid-day would approach, within a furlong, a place visited by the wrath of heaven; and for more than three generations, no living thing, save the bat, owl, and lizard, had crossed its threshold, or disturbed, by human sound, those precincts given up to solitude and desolation.

A few years before the end of the 17th Century, when the Duke of Anjou, under the title of Philip the V, ascended the throne of Spain, he found it necessary to confer favours, and bestow benefits, upon some of those adherents by whose intrigues, in the court of the irresolute Charles, his elevation to that dignity had been mainly owing; and among other boons, disposed this estate of Almazuma upon a devoted follower and youthful companion, named Don Juan de Estivan. This g--- young hidalgo,

charmed with the richness and surprising beauty of his new estate, resolved to repair the neglected mansion, and lavish on its adornment all the splendour refined taste could devise, or unbounded affluence achieve, and spare no cost to make the home of his future mistress the most magnificent in Spain. In vain the traditions of the place, its horrid solitude, the fearful sounds said at times to issue from its dreary vaults, were represented to him with all the force of fear and eloquence of belief; but these tales fell upon an ear dead to the idle phantoms of superstition, and to his lively and instructed mind, served only as themes of mirth, or, at best, subjects for his commiseration or ridicule: and determined to fulfil his purpose, swayed by a powerful desire to fathom the mystery that involved the fate of its last owner,—not doubting but by a steady investigation of the entire building, to find a clue which would lead him to unravel this long buried subject; and that the castle itself would reveal better than lips or tradition, the secrets of a tragedy so fearful and ominous. Accordingly, upon an appointed day, Don Juan, accompanied by about a dozen retainers, well supplied with implements to prosecute their search, proceeded to explore the secret apartments and subterranean labyrinths of the uninhabited castle. Damp, gloomy, and desolate were the once sumptuous chambers, along whose green decaying walls, hung disfigured tapestry, in long and waving shreds, flitting in the wind, like sombre plumage over the solitude and death around; the battered casement, the roofless halls, the mouldering floors, the crumbling stone, all spoke to the heart in accents deep and sorrowful; filling the reflective mind with saddest images, gloomy and consonant; and Juan felt a tremor of the heart, a mysterious dread creep on his soul as he surveyed the desertion that surrounded him, and contemplated the unhappy end of the last lord of all this ruined grandeur. By a powerful effort the youth shook off the palsying dread that began to chill his blood, and with awakened vigour and new alacrity, addressed himself to the object before him. It would be unnecessary to record, step by step, the plodding and unwearied investigation pursued by Juan and his domestics; but neither subterranean passage, secret chamber, or hollow panel, rewarded their indefatigable search; and as the deep shadows of evening fell through the dilapidated windows and stained glass, Estivan turned away chagrined and vexed that all his labour would be profitless, and that ignorance, and superstition would claim from his defeat, a double influence to triumph over reason and reflection. But at the moment he was about to retire from the apartment he had last inspected, his eye fell upon a portrait over the lofty oaken fire place, and which appeared in infinitely better preservation than any of the numerous pictures that in the galleries and bed chambers hung tattered and dropping from their frames. Juan's curiosity was excited by the freshness and integrity of the painting, and returning to the apartment, discovered that the portrait was executed upon one of the sunken panels of the wainscot, which formed a rude convenient frame to the severe head of a martyr that adorned it. Estivan drew his sword, and with the hilt struck the panel several smart, quick blows: the hollow sound that followed the strokes, plainly indicated the presence of a cavity, and with increased delight and alacrity, Juan examined the picture again, minutely sounding the panels around, and at length was rewarded by discovering a secret spring, upon pressing which the portrait flew suddenly open, revealing a cavity about four feet square, in the recess of which was stretched a broad metallic sheet, having a wooden mallet suspended on a pivot in front, to which was attached several small wires, that seemed to be conducted through some hollow tubing to a remote portion of the castle. For some moments the young noble stood gaping on the revelation before him in silent speculation; every possible or likely purpose for which such machinery could be applied, passed through his vivid and active mind; but each hypothesis was rejected as soon as conceived, till at length stretching forward his sword, and moving the mallet with its point, there issued from the struck plate a sound so deep, reverberatory, and mournful, that every hearer's heart felt chilled, while a vague fear pervaded each breast as the decaying notes trembled through the lonely chambers and vaulted passages, and died in echoing whispers in the far-off galleries. There was something so sad, unearthly, and supernatural in that one note of prolonged and solemn music, that out of all the band who heard it, but two remained with Juan when its last tremor vibrated on the ear; the rest had fled, hoping to find in the open fields more safety than their fears permitted them to believe it possible to be obtained within the house itself.

At length by threats, by promises, and persuasions, Estivan induced his servants to return; and by ridiculing their fears, and threatening their timidity, ultimately compelled them, though with an ill-concealed alarm, to break down the panelling in the direction of the secreted wires.

Chamber after chamber, wall succeeding wall, now rising, now descending, they followed this singular clue, till having traced it to the remotest angle of the spacious building, it seemed to bury itself in a mass of masonry that formed the foundation of the castle, and appeared to defy their implements and industry to follow farther; but difficulties to Juan's disposition served but as spurs to the furtherance of his purposes; and what his vassals manual strength failed to effect, he achieved by blasting the foundation with gunpowder, and to his unspeakable delight, beheld the massive wall rent for the space of several feet at the very spot where the wires had been made to enter, what, through the darkness beneath, appeared an extensive vault. Having ordered his servants to procure a ladder and flambeaux, Juan instantly descended into the gloom, succeeded, but most reluctantly, by his followers with torches. After a momentary pause to familiarize his eye to the red resinous glare of a dozen flaring torches, the young nobleman looked around him, and surveyed a picture that might have struck a bolder heart than his, with horror and amazement. His servants no sooner beheld the awful scene, than with a simultaneous cry of terror, they rushed precipitately to the ladder, impelled by an apprehension that almost destroyed their reason,—breaking down in their eagerness to escape, the only means of exit from this abode of fear, and extinguishing many of their lights in their anxiety to fly from horrors more terrible than death. Juan, though himself appalled by what his sight beheld, drew his sword, and rushing among his half-maddened domestics, swore to cut the first man to the ground who offered to quit the spot till he had investigated the bloody tragedy before them. So bold and determined was his speech and manner, that their supernatural dread gave way, for a time, to the closer danger menaced by their master's sword; though it was not without a cold shudder and a palpitating heart that they re-lighted their torches, and followed, trembling, their young lord to the centre of that fatal apartment.

Having contemplated the objects before him, Juan discovered himself to be in an extensive and lofty vault, fitted up as a chapel, or oratory, the circumference of the walls being hung with ample draperies of black cloth, dependent from the ceiling, and sweeping in their broad folds some distance over the ground. The upper part of the floor was covered by a rich matting of sombre and subdued dye; all the lower portion, on which Juan and his followers stood, was the bare hard earth, upon which, and only a few paces from his feet, extended on its left side, lay the body of a murdered man, dressed in the costume of a noble of the previous century. From a deep wound in the throat the blood had issued in vast quantities, and lay congealed in pools around him; the eyes were closed, the hands relaxed, and the visage white and marbly, evincing that death had only followed the last drop of blood. The corpse was that of a man in the prime of life, of robust and well knit stature, and appeared but to have just expired. On the ground, at a short distance, lay a long, small lady's poniard, coated with blood, the instrument of the murder. Sad and harrowing as this object was, it was far out-matched by the sight that lay beyond it, and next engaged the attention of the annoyed group. Stepping over the body, Juan advanced a few steps, and beheld a sight that entranced his gaze, and despite its horror, spell-bound him to peruse the fearful lineaments. Extended on the carpeted earth, lay the body of a woman of commanding presence and noble features, habited in a gown and robe of dark purple; the arms bare and beautifully white, were adorned with bracelets of diamonds; while in each convulsively rigid hand was clenched the extremities of a small cord, that had been twice circled round her beautiful neck, and drawn with all the tension of desperation. The tumid, black, and livid face, formed a hideous contrast to the snowy neck and fair developed breast beneath; the eyes were open, widely distended, blood-shot, and protruding; and as the ruddy flame of the torches fell on them, they seemed to flash a vitality of beam, that Juan, for the moment believing that life and consciousness still played on the expanded orbs, sprang forward to sever the fatal instrument of suicide, but recoiled aghast at the chilling icy touch that pervaded, with a freezing dread, the blood within his heart.

The sculptor's effigy of hardest stone was not more rigid, cold, insensible, than the disfigured and habited statue that lay in the sleep of death, supine along the floor. Beside the body was an empty antique phial, on which was a label bearing the single word, "stabium." It was evident, then, that the cord had anticipated the slower-footed and tardy poison, and that fearing the solitude and the action of the incertain potion, she had in desperation forestalled the less immediate death.

But the secrets of this grave were not yet all explored; a new sight awaited them, of equal, if not, from its situation, of paramount interest. Passing by the body of the strangled beauty, Juan approached the upper extremity of the vault, where, in a deep recess, was erected an altar of carved oak, while on either side of the opening, hung in deep festoons, curtains of crimson cloth, suspended by rings from a brass rod that traversed the entire width of the vaulted chamber. The youth drew near the steps of the edifice, and bowed in reverence to the displayed symbols of his faith; but instantly recoiled before the new object of wonder that solicited his attention. Upon the table of the holy altar lay, what at first appeared an effigy, but which on closer inspection proved, too terribly, to be the body of a man, a youth,—and like its silent companions of this fatal spot, untimely ended. Two deep and still red gashes on either breast, bespoke the foulness of the death. The features, like the first found body, were pale to whiteness, but chiselled in a style so exquisitely handsome, frank, and manly, that sorrow filled each gazer's eye to see such noble manhood so untimely nipt. His long rich hair flowed to his shoulders, and in its dark and massy waves, contrasted strongly with the light silk embroidered tunic, puffed trunks, and silken hose of a bye-gone century.

Festering death had not yet made an inroad on the dead carcase, that, for a hundred years, had lain in the still attitude of eternal sleep. The other forms bore trace of suffering,—one of agony; but this was calm repose. The weapon by his side, the glove upon his hand, and but for the deep broaches in his heart, you might have thought the youthful gallant only slept, and paused to hear the breath, and watched to note the slumberer awake,—so placid, natural and undisturbed the body lay; while above and around the murdered man, stood the bold evidences of a creed of mercy, and on the very table of the Lord lay bleeding sacrilege! and by its side, the tabernacle, crucifix, and chalice, with six massive candlesticks of silver, whose waxen tapers had burnt to their sconces: and over the body itself lay the notted scourge. Sad picture!—murder and mercy,—penitence and guilt!

Resolving to inspect each particular in this cave of horror, Juan ascended the steps of the altar, to examine if the lose drapery that half screened the sacred place, and which was but partly withdrawn, concealed more terrors,—was witness to further guilt; but scarcely had his foot pressed the first step, when a tremor pervaded his whole frame, and a quick vibratory motion trembled under his feet, instantly followed by a deep sonorous boom, like the far-off sound of a cathedral bell. Amazement seized on each hearer, and terror again began to usurp the place of awe, which hitherto had held them mute. The young lord beheld their alarmed looks, and slow digression from his side; and assuming a courage which at the moment he hardly felt,—

"Come back!" he cried. "Base cowards, return! draw back those curtains! Do you hear me, slaves? Return! for by the God in heaven I swear I will unravel this mystery that shakes your souls with fear! Fling back those folds! Am I obeyed?"

Slowly and trembling, two of his domestics approached, one on each side of the recess, and with agitated hands and averted eyes, drew suddenly back the rich pendant drapery, that before only half disclosed this outraged temple of the Lord; but scarcely had the sharp jar of the rattling rings subsided, when there pealed upon their ears a deep sonorous strain of notes in grand, solemn, and measured sequence. The hollow tones echoed through the distant and deserted halls, trembled in the dense masonry, and reverberated in deep boomings through the vaulted chamber above them, and ultimately died in faint and mournful tremors in the empty courts and dilapidated towers.

One! two! three! four! till the tones had measured twenty distinct and regulated strokes! The grand solemnity of the sound seemed to captivate the mind and pervade the soul with a holy dread, a religious awe, that took from each frightened hearer the very power to move—the wish to fly. Its grandeur charmed the ear, and its deep sepulchral tongue struck a fascination on every throbbing heart; and when the last faint concussion of the air faded to silence, each expectant ear was bent in eager listening, and hoping to hear again music so solemn, strange, and grand.

"Count the rings on those curtains!" suddenly exclaimed Juan, to his attendants. Half hesitating, two of the most courageous obeyed, and with their eyes numbered the circles. "Ten on either side," was the response. "And there were twenty strokes on that strange instrument," Juan musingly continued. "'Tis so then," he exclaimed aloud. "This is some cruel tyranny to watch from afar the punctual vigils of some victim at this shrine of blood; those wires are all connected with these rings; I read a part of this sad tragedy, and by our sainted mother I will be master of it all! Let us examine further: attend!"

So saying, he descended the steps of the altar, and again vigilantly searched the vault. The only furniture it contained beyond what has been described, was a small antique table, with a purple velvet cover, and a curious high backed chair carved into grotesque and hideous features, whose grim and distorted lineaments seemed to mock those who approached or used it. On the table were implements for writing, and a packet of papers firmly tied with the silken cord, at that time in use, to secure the lips of the folded letter. Juan instantly took up the documents, and examining the bundle by the torch-light; read in a small, quaint, but distinctly legible hand, this superscription:—"Atonement,—Blood for Blood, and Life for Life! Junius 15th, 1592. Midnight." The young nobleman stood amazed as he perused the date. Could it be possible, he thought, that a hundred years, to the very day and hour, had passed since such a scene as this had been enacted? All above was decay and ruin; yet here each act seemed just performed: all was perfect as at the day committed,—the very drapery that shrouded in this hearse and cave of death, bore evidence of fresh integrity, unstained by time, uninjured by decay. No foul or noxious air pervaded this long closed tomb,—nay, it was elastic, healthy, and vigorous, filling the breather's veins with pulsing action. "Can it be possible," Juan exclaimed, "that this buried chamber, gives from its womb preserving vapours, such as distil within the wondrous vault at Bremen, where I have seen the corpse of ages dead, sleeping as though just parted from the world? Great heaven! it must be so! each circumstance denotes it; but this—this perhaps will solve it all. Let us away my friends, I long to read this legacy of woe, and, doubtless, guilt,—for this must be the testament of Almazuma's last unhappy lord. Come: follow me!"

The following day the Holy Office investigated the subterranean chapel, and behind the black tapestry discovered a curiously secreted door, which conducted them through a long and irregular labyrinth, constructed between the walls of the outward building, and terminating at the foot of a lofty, narrow, and winding stair, which conducted at length to a bed chamber in the right wing of the castle; but both entrances had been so artfully concealed, that nothing but resolute perseverance could have discovered them. The three bodies were without rite or ceremony committed to one grave; no stone raised, or memorial placed, to note where rested the once proud Almazuma, or his ill-fated wife. The plough passed over the ruins, and even tradition forgot, in time, alike the spot and history of their crimes.

The papers found by Don Juan de Estivan proved, as he expected, the recital of a tale of woe, written by the Donna Catalina, the proud, guilty, but miserable wife. Many circumstances not recorded in her mournful journal, were still remembered by the descendants of her father's house; and with such traditionary facts to fill up the detail of her narrative, and condensing the daily occurrences and immaterial subjects, Juan arranged the whole into a brief, regular, and sequent chronicle, expunging nothing revelant, or adding aught that could diminish the interest of the lady's record, but leaving in her own terse, bold language, the events and characters, to stand the pity or censure of the world.

The tale so told will be found in the ensuing chapters.

CHAPTER I.

About three leagues South of the City of Soria, and situated on the western tributary of the Duoro, stood the hereditary mansion of the Marquis of Alfendera, a nobleman blest with all the gifts that enhance existence, and give to the hopes and expectations of life, a conscious felicity that knows no check from doubt, apprehends no alarm from adversity. Noble, rich, and prosperous; not less happy in the estimation of his people, than beloved and valued by his friends and family, Alfendera felt himself the happiest of men as he surveyed his two noble sons, and contemplated the matchless beauties of his idolized daughter. His boys had honour, wealth, and reputation; to them the busy world should be a school, to learn to guard and play the chequered game of life fearlessly,—for they were men; but her,—his beautiful, his prized, and peerless daughter, where should he find a sea so tranquil, a haven so provided against all storms, that not a chilling blast or angry wave might shake the steady current of its tide, to harbour in so fair, so rich an argosy? These, and such provident and watchful thoughts engrossed, for many years, the mind and heart of the affectionate and doting parent. He knew too well how little man, in his best nature, estimates the fond being who has devoted life and toil to minister to him; who sacrifices home, parents, friends, and tried affections, for the unproved heart of a professing love; and knew how the forbidding look and chilling word can poison peace, and kill effectually as knife or bowl,—and as the tender father thought on all the ills of life, and man's ingratitude to woman, a sadness crept upon his heart, a mournful sorrow settled on his mind, and in the bitterness of his thought he cursed his callous sex, who lock their bosoms to nature's holiest, noblest impulses, till frosty age, or the paternity of blood, too lately makes them sensible to all the love they missed, to all the happiness their selfish feelings killed.

"No!" he would exclaim, "no—my beloved; better, yes,—infinitely better the dull pallor of the peaceful cloister, than those dark looks, and those carroding cares, my anxious fears presage within this selfish, cankering world."

But all these strong evidences of affection were expended upon a being more calculated by nature to breast the dangers of life's perilous voyage, than sink resistless under the waves of oppression; for Donna Catalina was the very opposite in person and disposition to the timid creature her father's excessive fondness and blind partiality represented her,—more suited, by temperament and physical ability, to govern—not submit; and it is questionable whether the ardent solicitude evinced by the marquis for his only daughter, was not, in secret, treated by the proud beauty more as the dotage of age than the result of that healthy anxiety which, ever watchful, ever prudent, characterises paternal love and fatherly affection. For Catalina was not the beauty that at one gaze enchants the eye and captivates the heart, filling the beholder's soul with a quick consummate love, and diffusing through the mind pleasurable contemplations drawn from the perfected excellence of nature; nor was hers the soft and timid shrinking beauty, that fond and tendril-like, puts forth its twining arms for shelter and support; and where it loves it clings, fondly depending alike through shade and sunshine, prosperity or decay, till death, or the unfeeling hand, severs the embrace. No, not such as these, was Catalina's; but a beauty bold, proud, and majestic, the contour of her mind, if it may be so expressed, giving a twin-like stamp of character to the expresive features which, classically regular and faultlessly beautiful, acquired, from their very order, a dignity as far removed from the soft amenities of love, as the cold effulgencies of night is to the rich, warm glow of morning. Above the ordinary height, with a stature graceful and full of flowing lines, a look commanding, and a step firm and decisive;

while her round, polished arms, adorned with hands of most bewitching whiteness, to which the rosy tips of the tapering fingers lent an uncommon charm, and made the picture faultless. It was impossible that a form so perfect and queen-like, could be seen and not admired. Every eye, indeed, performed instinctive homage; each tongue confessed her beauty, but *one* heart alone fell captive to her charms. Whether the contemplation of her own perfections had insensibly given a corresponding complexion to her disposition, and made her reserved, proud, and haughty; or the increasing consciousness that she was but admired, viewed as a gorgeous picture, to be priced, but not beloved, had its influence in forming her character, is uncertain; for friendship never spreads a net to mesh her straying thoughts or confident desires. Her heart was cold, dead, or seemingly dead to all humanities that knit congenial souls; and those excellencies mankind call virtues, compassion, tenderness, the sympathy of love, she either felt them not, or buried them beneath such icy coldness, that none felt courage or desire to warm such passionless and freezing statuary.

In all the accomplishments that made the education of the period, Catalina excelled, gracefully surpassed all competition; and this was fame, and served to fill the void in her unloving heart; and this thirst for praise grew, day by day, more powerful, till it fixed its seat within her heart, formed her whole governing influence, until at length it reigned in the full arrogance of haughty pride: to bear in the world's opinion a fame so pure, so high, that scandal dare not threaten, nor malevolence malign it, became the one ambition of her life. The very grace and gentleness of woman was lost behind this watchful armour and vigilant defence in which her pride was wrapt; and we shall see hereafter how the very virtue of her object became her cause of misery.

It is not to be supposed that the daughter of one of the oldest families in Spain, rich, young, and beautiful, had remained to her eighteenth summer unwooed or unsolicited: such was not the case.

About two leagues from the palace of Alfendera was situated the proud castle and wide domains of the young and affluent Almazuma, the last heir to a long line of noble ancestry; and though the marquis and Almazuma's father had been staunch and long tried friends, yet, at his death, a coldness had gradually grown up between the proud and haughty son and the open, generous, and confiding marquis; and for many years no intercourse had taken place between the neighbouring families; and it was only accident that, at the opening of our story, produced an unwished-for return of courtesies, and a reciprocity of those acts of neighbourhood and friendship, that had for several years been allowed to slumber into almost extinctive oblivion. It was upon one of these renewed visits, more of form than compliment, that Almazuma first beheld the beauteous Catalina, then in the full burst of feminine grace and bewitching womanhood. The young Spaniard gazed in amazement on her perfected beauty, and felt awed by her majestic mien and queenly dignity; and though his cold and callous nature could not feel the warm and vivifying power of love,

his eye was captivated by the matchless elegance of her form and symmetry of feature, and his ambition fired by the vain glory of calling such transcendant charms his own; and for the first moment in his morose and selfish life, the young hidalgo felt an instant glory in contemplating such a splendid prize *his* only. His jealousy and envious soul was roused by apprehension, lest another, and more welcome suitor, might in the interval step in and bear away the gorgeous beauty from his very eyes, and every hope of competition; and he resolved to make a special embassy, and on the morrow claim, undowered, the spotless hand and regal heart of the imperious Catalina.

But we must here pause, and for a brief space endeavour to make our readers understand something more of the new and important character introduced to their notice.

Don Ferdinand de Almazuma was the last lineal heir of a revered and ancient family; but unlike his ancestors, who, for four hundred years had flourished on that spot, he was neither endeared by his virtues, or reverenced for his generosity. Early deprived of his mother, and too maturely thrown on the world by the death of his father, Almazuma found himself, at twenty, the lord of large possessions, a numerous tenantry, and undisputed master of the vast wealth which had accumulated in the family for ages; pouring at the feet of the last heir a prodigal fortune, that gave no pleasure by its possession, and afforded no consolation in its magnitude.

From his earliest years reserved and distant, his manners, as he advanced in life, became more morose, more haughty, till at length the few who had grown up together in his society, one by one, fell from his company, chilled by his hauter, or repulsed by his indifference, till, finally deserted by the disinterested few, who from early association felt some esteem, and ridiculed by the crowd that ever surrounds the atmosphere of affluence,—the needy and the prodigal,—he retired to his country estate near Soria, some two leagues from Alfendera's palace, and excluded himself, at six-and-twenty, from society and the world.

It was not from meanness, or the estimation of his wealth, that Almazuma closed his doors and heart to all appeals of charity, and lived an anchorite while his menials feasted. No; he had not the soul to be generous; liberality had no share in his composition; and if his hand was closed, it was from the infirmity of his nature. He knew not how to give; his life was purposeless; he lived, moved, acted, and performed each duty, but without a heart. Selfishness,—that deadly phase of selfishness that knows no happiness itself, and detests the show of it in others,—was his ruling passion, hating what he did not possess, and with all the malignity of a fiend, tyrannizing where tyranny was most cruel,—on the weak, unresisting, and oppressed. Coward he was not; but craven from the very direction of his vice.

In person Don Ferdinand possessed all those outward attributes of manhood and marks of favour that please the eye, and too often captivate the sense of the more fickle. grave in deportment, serious in speech, his bearing and his whole demeanour seemed to give the lie to falsity or weak pretence; and when he unbent the native gravity of his soul to love, soft, persuasive, and fascinating strains fell from his utterance, holding the captive ear a pleased and willing prisoner, while over every sense stole the seductive accents to the heart, winning the fancy ere judgment woke the citadel to arms against the lodged and treacherous foe. Nor lacked he solid eloquence to sway men's judgments, or the more specious arts,—handmaids of oratory,—dissimulation, craft, and cunning, and all the tortuous paths of dark intrigue, were to his mind familiar and consonant to his thoughts. Human hypocrisy never yet assumed the badge of truth so fatally, as when from his assuming lips the delusive accents fell; for he could wind and twine around the heart, till every pulse and fibre to its core, was all his own; and yet so truthfully could play the sycophant, so boldly vindicate the virtue he despised, that reason fell and prudence self shrunk back abashed before his conquering speech and virtuous indignation.

Such was the dangerous, subtle, and designing man who now addressed him to the self-sufficient and strong-souled woman, who held her very beauty as a shield before the strong rampart of her entrenched and haughty honour. Not one,—the semblance of the dark passion which licentious profligacy calls love; not admiration for her talents, reverence for her virtue, esteem for her high name, nor pleasure for her all-conquering charms, stirred Don Ferdinand's dull soul to win this trophy of her lovely sex. No: it was cold and selfish heartlessness to fetter to the lingering prison of his unloving self, the qualities that, to an admiring heart and consonant affection, would swell each day into a life of mutual love and soft endearing happiness.

Such were the unexpressed, but inward sentiments that swayed Don Almazuma, and induced him somewhat precipitately, on the following day, to propose to the marquis for the honour of his daughter's hand. To the anxious father such an offer could not but be distressing; for though in a worldly view the match was more affluent than he could expect, yet, to the solicitous parent, a more objectionable espousal could not have been propounded; for Almazuma's cold, stern look, monotonous life, and deep seclusion, with the accredited rumours of his cruelty and oppression, made him the very last person he could have desired to be addressed by on so momentous and enduring a matter. The marquis, however, evaded a direct reply, and with much courtesy, referred the suitor to his daughter for a decision, the result of which so materially affected herself,—not doubting, from his knowledge of her nature, but that her manner would be sufficiently chilling and repulsive to destroy every prospect of a repetition to the subject.

Whether influenced by the advice of her father in his brief absence to apprise his daughter of the solicited alliance, and to summon her to the tarrying suitor; or piqued that after three years sojourn in the vicinity, he had not sooner paid her charms the homage of their worth; or from a detestation of his character; or a mysterious and expulsive antipathy that she entertained to the name and person of Almazuma,

is uncertain; but in the interview that took place, her conduct and bearing was haughty and contemptuous, not confined to looks alone, but, by her sharp and insulting words, expressing how low she held all his boasted love and speechless admiration.

"I am come, fair excellence," exclaimed the specious lover, as he bent lowly, and with a studied ease, at the feet of the tall, swan-like beauty, who, with a half-averted head and drooping lids, looked scornfully upon the kneeling suppliant to her shrine. "I am come, not with the honied words and silver accents of professing love, for I am poor in the mellifluous gift that sounds like sweetest incense in the approving ear of those who feel affection's power; barren and ignorant in the arts of speech men use to captivate and blind thy gentle and confiding sex; I come armed but with my honest homage, and the heart's true rhetoric,—holy devotion, constancy of faith, and life-performing deeds. Let these, fair lady, be my speech and tongue, and let them mutely plead my cause better than the eager words and rapid gesture or redundant oratory of the confident and practised gallant, on whose glib lips love finds a thousand attributes. Thus, poor in my expression, but prodigal in the deep sense of all thy perfect beauty, permit me, thou chaste and spotless image of thy sexes virtues, here at thy feet, to which I bow in full humility, to make a tender of my heart, my hand, my life, my wealth, and all the attributes and rites pertaining to my lineage and my name."

"Arise, Don Ferdinand," replied Catalina, with a dignified wave of her white hand; "your supple knee is as your quick affection, something pliant, and methinks rather too prone and instant in its professed and ardent constancy. Arise! you wrong your manhood, sir, by so much debasement."

"He were debased indeed," added Almazuma, not marking the bitter sarcasm of her tone and words, and still preserving his attitude of deep respect, "who would not bow him to the earth to court a solitary beam of that bright planet that is the sunshine to his heart,—the fire that thaws and animates his blood. Oh! let me kneel, if but to borrow grace from the blest shrine on whose pure altar I offer up my humble sacrifice. There's more virtue, lady, in my devotions *here*, than ever cowled monk or mitred abbot drew from this sealed, and till now, obdurate heart."

"Arise! you do offend me," exclaimed the Donna, as she glided in slow stateliness by him. "While I thought you did but jest, I was content to give your humour play, but when you offend me by your assumed affection——"

"Lady! Madam! I swear!" cried Almazuma, eagerly interrupting her. "You do my love a grievous wrong to doubt its constancy or truth. Never did man so bless the teeming earth that gave him food, as I that barren spot of which thy treading foot has made a paradise. I love you, lady, with every sinew of my heart, and all the capacity of my new-inspired and awakening soul. For years I've dreamed in apathetic sleep: the world, no picture to my eye—nor life a purpose to my thought; dragging out my time in dull satiety; but, seeing you, my mind new inspiration takes, and fires my dormant energies; thy beauty and perfection, like the cloud of night before the morning sun, lifts up the curtain from my soul, and gives me back to life, that I may bask me in the summer of thy charms."

"Don Almazuma," cried the lady scornfully, "I will end this scene of studied compliment, and fulsome adulation. If your purpose here is but to seek my love and know my mind, I'll answer both in one: arise—and leave me, sir!"

"I will obey," replied Almazuma, rising slowly, and answering in a subdued, desponding voice; "yet ere I leave to seek again my condemned and lowly solitude, tell me, fair madam, is every hope extinct? may I not in my sad retreat harbour one stray beam of coming pardon?"

"I am not wont to answer twice," added Catalina. "There is no participation in our thoughts, and never can: we stand as much antagonised as earth to heaven."

"And must I never hope?"

"When Spain has lost all gentle suitors, and I am still unwed, I will condescend to give you privilege to woo."

A slight start of the body, and a hectic flush of the cheek and brow, passed for an instant over Almazuma's features, as the taunting words of the arrogant beauty fell on his ears;—but quickly subduing the feelings they gave rise to, and assuming his former deferential and modest bearing, and bowing low as he crossed the chamber, said,—"You have mistaken both of us, fair lady—deeply mistaken both, but I will offend no more, but fill each void and lonely chamber of my heart with thy undying image, and live again through the long dreary years of life these blest moments spent with thee—though crushed in spirit by your stern rejection. Madame, I go," he added, sorrowfully, as with a mute action of her raised arm she pointed to the portal; "may that peace dwell with thee, for ever banished from my despairing breast," and with a low obeisance he quitted her presence,—then bidding the marquis a hasty farewell, left the palace and mounted his horse, under all the outward show of spiritless dejection; but when in the seclusion of his home, a change passed over him, sudden and threatening; and as the folds of the gathering clouds are broke by the lightning, even such a change, ominous and bright, settled on the gloomy features of the rejected suitor, as striding with impatient steps his spacious chamber, he muttered deep-mouthed curses, and then a dark, unpleasant-meaning smile played on his thin lips, giving a malign expression to the stern character of his face, as halting in his eager strides a sudden thought woke in his plotting mind.

"What! am I despised?" he at length exclaimed, stamping fiercely on the floor in the bitterness of humiliation. "Contemned, insulted, scorned by this overweening piece of womanhood? Rejected? I, Almazuma! who never yet to mortal being bent the knee or cringed, but, cased in his panoply of haughty pride, made princes sue respectfully! Damnation! she will hold me forth to her levéed throng in pictured abjectness and boyish whining! Curse on her stubborn heart! but hold—is this scolding passion—this bitter impotency of railing words, worthy of me, or my high name

of stern resolve?—No! my part is action, and I will win her yet—yes, hear it, recording heaven! she shall—she shall be mine! not for the idle sport of pleasing dalliance, or ·* eak trifling of debasing love, but for the more glorious purpose of revenge,—yes, I will make her stubborn nature yield; that pride succumb to my dominion; bow down her soul to the humiliating earth, and crush and trample on that pride, that in its lofty arrogance o'ermated me! Hear it, ye saints!" he cried in an impassioned voice of deep intensity; "hear, thou peopled heaven! that I, from henceforth, dedicate my life to this one purpose: vice, sin, and murder, shall not stop me; I will not budge at outrage, ere so damned, to win this now insatiate object of my strong desire,—yes! from this hour forth I live for a purpose—a glorious, though a deadly one! In that short interview I have read, as in a book, the full development of her nature, each stray line, perused her very soul, clearly defined each working thought, and scanned my way through all the sinuosities of her mind; and against this vaunted strength of hers, this bulwark pride, I will bring the full force and undiverted tide of my strong muscular conception. I will arrange each circumstance, plan every passage of our after-life, leave nothing that can be done—undone, but slowly and methodically tread on my way, to its accomplishment, and take the flood when fortune favours me—— 'Tis all down, here—here in my brain," he continued with a faint and satisfied smile; "all plotted, typed, and ready for an immediate impress;—then look thee to thy peace, proud woman! for on this track stalks damned malice, resolute revenge, that never from this hour can know satiety, till in the full humility of abject sufferance, thy majesty of beauty grovels in crushed abasement at my triumphant feet!" And with this swelling and engrossing thought prompting his malevolent heart to the instant furtherance of his revengeful views, the roused and imperious Almazuma quitted the chamber to put in practice the first step of his remorseless scheme!

CHAPTER II.

WITHIN a week of the events of the last chapter, the spacious castle of Almazuma was closed; the numerous retinue that usually filled its halls, more from pride of ancestry and custom than in the bachelorhood of its lord was needful, was dismissed; the huge and stately portals shut, and silence, that fearful agent of superstition, reigned undisturbed in the deserted chambers and the vast solitude of the neglected mansion.

Rumour, with her thousand tongues, had spread as many vague reports. Some said that its morose and discontented lord had fled to Palestine, there at the holy sepulchre to seek for absolution for committed crimes; some, that the Inquisition, in its watchful care of the true church, had seized a dangerous heretic; others, more charitable, professed a knowledge that the gallant Ferdinand had gone to lay his sword and fortune at the feet of his good king, to swell the armament of the now far completed and invincible armada; and that in this new

A. MILES

crusade, against the heretic and scoffing Briton, he was assigned a post of high and trusty honour.

But none for certainty could tell. That he was gone—was sure, but beyond the knowledge of that fact all was wide conjecture. The Donna Catalina was the only one who seemed to know the cause; and as the idle rumours fell on her ear, and ignorance filled its vague-told tale with dark surmise and visionary fears, she felt a secret pleasure at her heart, and deemed the sudden absence of their neighbouring lord, as sure testimony of her great power and his affection; and the consciousness, added to her over-weening heart, served still farther to augment her self-sufficiency and cold hauteur. Though inwardly she felt a deep contempt for Almazuma's love, and in her soul instinctively believed him base and treacherous, yet in her mind the thought was not unpleasant to her

pride, that he, the misanthrope, had fled from the too potent influence of her charms.

But as it is not our intention to deal in needless mystery, we will follow the steps of Almazuma, and reveal to the reader his present pursuits, which, at first sight, may appear at variance with the strong purpose we have seen him resolve to execute.

It was towards evening, at the end of June, and about a month subsequent to his sudden departure from his paternal residence, that Almazuma, mounted on a strong black horse, descended one of those long and intricate defiles that lead from the Pyrenees into the wooded vales of Navarre. Already had the sun sunk below the lofty ridge of the distant mountains of Burgos; and spurring his horse as he reached the level plain, he was about to urge him to his full speed, in hopes of reaching the town of Majera ere darkness rendered his further journey impracticable, when his horse's head was suddenly seized by two brigands, as a third, mounted on a powerful Andalusian steed, rode up to his side, and brandishing a broad toledo, ordered him, in an imperious voice, instantly to surrender both his steed and purse. But Almazuma was not a character to be intimidated either by force or numbers; and though generally of a tame and less military disposition than was the fashion of the day, yet when once roused, and the full energy of his passion excited, he became not only a determined, but a dangerous foe. Drawing in his bridle rein with a sudden and violent jerk, he compelled his strong chested charger to rear high on his haunches, then goading him with the sharp rowel, made him plunge out with a bound that hurled his two assailants to the earth; while Almazuma, bending his head as he passed, evaded the well-directed stroke of the mounted bandit, who hoped to cut off his retreat by the quick passage of his sword. In the meantime Don Ferdinand drew his long rapier, and wheeling round his horse, made a furious charge on his assailant, who, finding himself attacked with such fury, called on his companions, who had risen from the ground, to dispatch him in the back. At this moment, and while one of the banditti shortened his sword to plunge it in the unprotected flank of the averted Almazuma, a fifth personage suddenly made his appearance, and leaping quickly from a rocky bank above, drove a thick, short hanger, that was unsheathed in his hand, up to the hilt in the brigand's breast, who fell dead without a groan. A back-handed stroke of Almazuma's blade cleft the skull of the other pedestrian, and giving his horse the rein and spur, dashed him with terrible concussion upon the mounted robber, and hurled him, bleeding and insensible, from his unsteady saddle.

"I claim the captured horse as my share of this day's spoil," exclaimed the stranger, who had so opportunely arrived to his succour, at the same time leaping like an agile Indian upon the still terrified beast, and with admirable manage and skill, soothing the irritated and still prancing animal.

"By our lady, he's a true Andalusian! I have not felt such a seat these ten years!" continued the stranger, as he caressed and brought his curvetting steed abreast of Almazuma, who, for the first time, had leisure to survey his new companion, whom he perceived to be a man of tall and robust stature, habited in the picturesque garb of the Bohemian gipsy; his long dark hair set off to much advantage, his dusky features, on which, though cunning and dissimulation might be detected by the shrewd eye, lacked not altogether a pleasing jollity, that though it could not inspire confidence, was not deficient in a certain manliness, that from the very hardihood and boldness of their character, lent a zest to curiosity.

Almazuma perused every lineament of his companion's face with that keen instinct into character that was peculiar to his nature, and with strict scrutiny investigated all the phases of his disposition; nor once removed his steady gaze, or paused in his examination, till he unravelled all the debasing springs that took their source from his corrupted soul. At length

satisfied in his mute scrutiny, and apparently finding something congenial in the other's bearing or aspect, Almazuma threw off his usual reserve, and in a frank and generous strain addressed his new associate.

"Many thanks, kind friend, for thy most timely succour. The steed is thine by right of arms, and worthily hast thou won him. But thou art no Gitano? How comes it that I find a Spaniard in the quaint garb of a Zingari?"

"Nay, senhor, you ask too much for a mere stranger," replied the other, with more respect than he had at first evinced; for the man felt awed by the firm glance of Almazuma's steady eye; and unaccountable as the feeling seemed to himself, he felt insensibly that the person before whom he stood was one of no ordinary mould, and could command, and would compel obedience and respect in those whom he addressed or held communion with.

"But how," he continued, after a pause, "you should find out that I am a Spaniard, and not what I would seem to be, by the foul fiend! I know not;—though I'll not deny the justness of your guess. But, by your leave, my lord, we'll see what spoil the enemy has left. I've been a soldier, and pillage is a natural as well as an acquired propensity." So saying, the seeming Gitano sprang lightly to the ground, and throwing the rein of his steed over his arm, addressed himself in earnest to rifle the pockets of the two dead brigands; and having obtained all the effects of their ill-supplied pouches, approached the wounded and overthrown leader, where the plunder was infinitely more to his taste, and estimable in value. Having secured the whole on his person, he re-mounted his horse, observing to his companion, who had silently, but with observant eye, watched all his motions, "I never spill unnecessary blood, though pretty well seasoned in crime. I therefore let that rascal live,—not that there is much chance of his recovering. for he has an ugly fracture on his scull,—but still I like to give even the enemy a chance. The night dew will perhaps revive him,—and now, senhor, talking of night, which way lies your road? For I take it you must ride hard to reach an inn ere midnight. Where lies your course?" inquired the gipsy.

"Where your road lies, there, for the present, shall mine be," replied Almazuma, as he turned his horse's head in the direction of his companion.

"The devil you will!" ejaculated the other. "There may be more danger than you wot of, senhor."

"No matter: lead on."

"Well, you take it cool, cavaliero! Would you run your head into the lion's mouth?"

"Ay! into twenty, were they all such lions as thou art!" replied Almazuma, with slight disdain.

"I know not what you imply by that, senhor, but I would fain know the cause of your confidence. Certes, it is not every one who would be so bold."

"I'll tell you, friend:—had plunder been your object, you would rather have taken the part of my assailants than have risked your life in my defence; and the impulse that caused a generous action, would be disgraced if it used treachery to reward it."

"Granting that true," answered the other, "I might have aided you then to sacrifice you after, and so enhance my own booty."

"Such a thought has not entered your mind, and had it, you would not dare to put it into practice."

"Not dare?" rejoined the other, in a fierce tone.

"Not dare!" repeated Almazuma, as he gazed fixedly in the fellow's eyes, till his defying look sank abashed before the intimidating sternness of his keen survey.

"Well, you are a strange gallant," replied the other, in a gentler tone, and with an averted look. "I never yet was bearded as by you to-night; but come your ways, my lord, for of noble blood, I feel assured you are;—you'll find us but a rough, rude set, but you'll be welcome, and a piece of that gold you carry so openly in your girdle, will ensure you safety. Nay, nay,—you need not touch your hilt; brave as you are, one arm could do but little against a palisade of fifty swords. Come, I'll be your surety, and you may trust me, for I'm in the humour to be generous. Its a new passion that has grown upon me of late, and if I stay with the tribe much longer, I shall lose my very nature. Come, let us ride, and as we move along I'll tell you of our horde:" so saying, they both pricked their horses' flanks, and at an easy pace quitted the scene of their late encounter with the robbers.

"Well, cavaliero!" resumed his new acquaintance to Almazuma, when they had ridden a short distance, "how you had the penetration to see through this gipsy dress of mine, and tell Spanish from Egyptian blood, something perplexes me! Are you a magician? for, by my faith! to read men's thoughts is something harder, I take it, than detecting national differences. How comes it, senhor?"

"It little matters by what means I can detect imposture, and read men's hearts: it is sufficient for thee to know that I have an intimate and thorough knowledge of thy feelings and propensities. Thou art cunning, avaricious, deceitful,—shall I go on?"

"I know not, senhor, what power withholds my hand," replied the other, half jesting, half in earnest, "and that I do not cleave you to the chin for such bold speech;—but, certes, I will not deny my character, though you do paint my features somewhat harshly,—but no matter, I have ceased long since to blush either at my virtues or my vices."

"Your virtues!" cried Almazuma, scornfully. "Were you ever troubled with such reproachful visitors?"

"Faith! but little. But I pray you finish my fascinating portrait: you paint, senhor, to the life. Let me hear the final qualities."

"By nature false," resumed Don Ferdinand; "by inclination robber. Gold is thy idol, and to win the precarious ore, murder and thou have been familiar; and, I should say, to sum up thy attributes, thou art not devoid of genius."

"By the mass, I'll not deny I have been all you say! but I am leading now an honest life, that is, for me an honest one. Some day, perchance,—that is, if we remain in company as I believe we shall, for it appears to me you have

an object in bearing company with such an one as me,—I'll tell you all my history."

"You shall," replied Almazuma, with a distinct emphasis. The man turned round in his saddle, and stared inquiringly in the face of the person who seemed to decide and govern his very will, but the calm dilated eye that returned the glance, checked the angry answer on his lip, and shrugging his shoulders, he merely replied, "We shall see."

"We shall. But tell me, what lights are those that flash and blaze through the far vistas of that deep wood?"

"'Tis our encampment, senhor; the fraternity, to which, for a time, I have attached myself;" an emigrant tribe from Bohemia."

"To which you have fled for safety?"

"You must either be an Inquisitor or the devil incarnate," rejoined his companion, casting an amazed and angry look on Almazuma. "But I have promised you safe conduct for the night, and were you the arch fiend, this time I will not baulk my word."

"You dare not!" added Don Ferdinand, calmly.

"Dare, again? Senhor you press too hardly."

"No; mark me!" continued Almazuma, in a steady and impressive tone—"mark me: there is a destiny in each man's life no human power can thwart—no virtuous resolve overcome; there is a sympathetic chain between thy fate and mine—an influence from the stars; thy life has been a record of dark deeds, and justice dogs thy steps. Reform is from thy heart as far removed as the supporting poles of earth. Guilty thou art, and guilty wilt thou die. I'll give thee work and occupation, pay thee with liberal hand, and when we part, give thee that which shall, for thy remaining days, abundantly supply thy utmost need:—but we are in the wood, and among your friends,—answer me anon."

By this time the two horsemen had entered an extensive glade in the tall pine wood, to which they had for some time been directing their steps. The high overhanging branches formed an impervious canopy above, while the straight lofty trunks of the trees, like double rows of tapering pillars, diminishing in symmetrical harmony in the distance, gave the long vista that extended nearly half a league through the heart of the wood, the appearance of a grand aisle in nature's true primeval temple. On either side of this wide avenue, suspended from tree to tree, was arranged a series of full twenty tents, round which were grouped a heterogeneous crowd of swarthy men, women, and half-clad children, some poultry, dogs of the hound and lurcher breed, and here and there, tied to some low drooping branch, were knots of horses, or groups of shaggy mules. Four or five large fires, fed by the resinous branches of the larch and fir, burnt bright and genially in the open space, on which large cauldrons, containing the evening meal, were suspended from a tripod, sending forth a savoury steam to the hungry nostrils of the impatient tribe. The night had closed in dark and still; and as the red light from the fires fell on the swarthy features of the group, revealing their dark, flashing eyes and picturesque costume, set off by the looped and long-leaved hat; the twinkling foliage, that here and there spangled by the stray fire-beams that lit the green leaves as with an edge of gold; the impenetrable shade beyond, and the deep gloom above, gave to the living picture a character of bold simplicity, and of natural grandeur.

A few words from his guide, and the liberal distribution of some pistoles, procured for Almazuma a cordial welcome, and assurances of protection from all the band. But there was one individual, however, who took no part in the free welcome given by the rest to the new comer. This was an old man, of harsh and forbidding aspect, and one of an authority in the tribe, who, sheltered from observation behind the folds of his tent, beheld with greedy and rivetted eyes, the full and weighty purse that hung so temptingly at Almazuma's girdle, and which had before drawn the notice of his companion and guide. This man, with a species of reasoning not unusual in human nature, believed,—by artfully avoiding to compromise himself personally by pledges of welcome, and not sharing in the divided gold,—that he was absolved from the obligation that bound the rest, and had already in his mind resolved to make himself master of the stranger's purse, and for that purpose, cautiously withdrew from the now deserted tents,—for the band was already at their evening meal,—and secreted himself in the dense shadow of the thick underwood. As soon as they had made an end of their repast, Almazuma's companion conducted him to the mouth of his tent, before which one of the fires was still burning, and sitting down upon some folded skins, pointed to a corresponding seat for his guest, and drawing from out the seat a box, opened the lid, and taking out several small instruments and some unfinished work, addressed himself to the completion of his ingenious task.

"What! are you a mechanic?" inquired Almazuma, in some surprise, as he surveyed the elaborate piece of minute mechanism on which his companion was employed, and contemplated the artful arrangements of wheels and levers, and the consummate skill displayed by the rude artist. "Are you familiar with such devices?" he inquired, with evident interest and gratification.

"I am such as you see," observed the other. "I have always had a natural taste for works of skill and ingenuity; besides, it was once my trade. I should grow maudlin and mad in this dull life I lead, had I not some such recreation. This is a clock, senhor, that at any given hour shall ring such a peal, that I'll warrant it shall rouse the heaviest sleeper that ever snored out a weary watch; besides, it will detect, when placed and fitted, if any one has crossed, within a certain boundary, its lawful precincts."

"Ha! indeed!" exclaimed Almazuma, with increased pleasure and vivid curiosity. "The plan is admirable, and could, no doubt, be much extended."

"To any distance. A league," rejoined the other.

"Good! admirable! Yes, such—such was my thought: it will do," he half-musingly exclaimed.

"What will do?"

"No matter now. For what sum would'st thou devote a year of thy life in working out so great a scheme?"

"What,—a league?"

"Not so far. Say from a vault to the extremity of a large pile. I say a *detective* property —ha!"

"On a large scale? The plan were easy."

"Aye, it shall be large. Your price?"

"Why, a pistole a-day would not be bad reward, and sooth to say, I am tired of my dull life. I am not a vegetable, and I grow sick of the green wood."

"I'll give thee six pistoles a-day; and, as I said before, when the need for thy service is past, I'll give thee affluence for life. Will this suffice?"

"I'd cut all my kindreds' throats for half the sum."

"I shall not require such proof of thy ability."

"Well, senhor, I am not scrupulous, but if a friend is in the way, I'll throw a life or two into the bargain, to show I am not covetous. Hush! keep still,—move not a muscle," cried his companion, in a low whisper, as he carefully put down his work, and looked carelessly around.

The Zingari had all retired to rest. The fires, all save the one round which they sat, had sunk to ashes, and a profound silence reigned on the spot,—so lately the scene of so much life and animation. Almazuma followed his companion's eye in some surprise at the implied caution, but saw nothing in the dim surrounding objects to cause alarm; but his host, though he affected an indifference in his look, nevertheless kept his moving eye on an object, that, snake-like, wormed along the ground, wriggling its long, emaciated length over the mossy earth skirting the sheltering trees, and sometimes pausing in its course, looking in repose like the withering pole of some felled pine.

"'Tis that old villain, Zelmar. I marvelled why he did not come to bid you welcome, and claim his share of the initiatory bribe. Keep still, senhor, and speak loud," continued he, as he threw himself back against a supporting tree. "The night is so mild I'll e'en sleep where I am: good night;" and folding his arms and closing his eyes, he appeared in a few moments, by his action and deep inspiration, to be in profound repose.

That there was danger at hand Almazuma felt assured; but trusting in his acquired influence over his companion, and confident that his vigilance was on the watch, he adopted the same precaution as the other, and leaning against a corresponding tree, appeared to sleep. So quiet and undisturbed was all around, not broken even by the note of a solitary bird, and so genially warm the bland air in that sheltered spot, that from sembling sleep, Almazuma's senses were quickly wrapt in soft and hushing slumber, from which, however, he was suddenly aroused by the bounding of a heavy substance on his chest, and then hurled backward, as a second weight fell on both, pinning him to the ground. In another moment two men in deadly struggle rolled off his oppressed chest; and opening his eyes, Almazuma saw his host kneeling on the body of a man whose throat he had just divided to the bone. He sprang instantly to his feet, and laid his hand on his rapier, as his friend joined him, saying, in a low hurried voice,—

"It is not needed: I was obliged to cut the

hoary villain's throat to keep him quiet. We must be off, for he is an especial favourite with the tribe. I will go seek our horses. So, senhor, I am at your service, and shall account myself in your pay."

"Agreed!" cried Almazuma; "and we will settle the particulars of our compact as we ride along. But tell me by what name I am to call you?"

"Call me Garcia," replied the other. "I have as good a right to that as any for the present;—and yours, my lord?——"

"You shall know that when our treaty is ratified. Now, quick!—the horses," exclaimed Almazuma.

The other staid not to reply, but disengaging the two animals from amidst a troop that was tethered to a tree, shortly made his re-appearance; and each leading his animal slowly by the bridle, threaded their way through the obscurity of the wood, till reaching its extended confines, they both mounted, and giving free rein to their beasts, dashed into the dim and level country, keeping due south; and long ere the hills of Burgos were blushing in the rising sun, the horsemen had placed five leagues between themselves and the wild Zingari.

CHAPTER III.

THE left wing of the magnificent palace of Alfendera was allotted exclusively to the use of the Donna Catalina and her attendant women, while the spare apartments of that spacious division of the mansion, were kept in readiness for those female visitors who occasionally honoured the marquis's residence with their company.

It is to one of these sumptuous chambers that we now beg the attentive reader to permit us to conduct him. The apartment was spacious, and lighted by three lofty windows, extending from the corniced ceiling to the floor, and from their lower halves, opening with glass doors upon an extensive verandah, that, running the whole length of the room, formed, during the day, when screened by their green jalousies, a cool and agreeable retreat, and as the balcony looked on the lawn that skirted the ample and varied garden, it constituted a convenient auditory at evening, from which to hear the deep rich music of the serenade that nightly greeted the fair inhabitant, or to note, in the calm hour of midnight, the liquid tones of the nightingale, that from the populous groves kept up a ceaseless concert of richest harmony.

The apartment within was adorned with all the elegance and grace that wealth and art conspiring could achieve. The ottomans, fauteuils, and sofas, with their rich satin hangings, might have embellished the palace of the Cid himself, from whose near neighbourhood the luxurious innovation formerly came. The costly mirrors, the exquisite vases, filled to repletion with many coloured and odoriferous flowers; the sumptuous carpets from the Venetian isles; the arabesque and inlaid tables; the light, rich, fringed drapery, that in graceful silken folds drooped over the casements; the florid and gilt architecture, and embossed gold painting of the walls, with the diamond crucifix, that catching the oblique rays of the evening sun, shone with a thousand brilliant dyes, formed on the whole a portraiture of luxurious ease and prodigal splendour.

Seated on a low voluptuous ottoman, near one of the open windows, through which the beams of the setting sun poured warm and mellow, gilding each point upon which they fell with a transparent flood of golden light, sat two females, young and beautiful, but as opposite in feature, form, and disposition, as youth, loveliness, and breathing nature can be. Tall, symmetrical, and gracefully developed, with her dark expressive eyes and luxuriant locks of raven brilliancy, sat Catalina, now in her twentieth summer, the stateliness of woman, and the full consciousness of her well-instructed mind, evinced in her erect deportment and sober gaiety; while beside her, in playful ease, half sitting, half reclining on the heaped cushions, that hardly seemed to yield the elastic surface to her slight and fairy form, reclined the happy, joyous Amina de Alvarey, the affianced bride of Catalina's youngest brother. A soft and loving being, just eighteen, that but to see woke pleasure in the eye and rapture in the heart; whose voice of touching gentleness, and words of sweetest harmony, sounded like silvery music in the listener's ear, and in her witching laugh, that dimpled all her face in smiles, the delighted hearer stood entranced at the soul-infectious mirth; yet, when a sudden feeling touched her heart, her low, soft utterance, like an Æolian harp, fell on the sense thrillingly musical, while the confiding glance that from her liquid orbs beamed forth, played o'er the beholder's heart like summer sunshine. She was so fair, so beautiful, as curtained in the abundant tresses of her chesnut hair, that, flowing to her neck, drooped over her polished shoulders in many a wanton curl, that never man had truer cause to worship female excellence, than the sunny picture Amina's joyous face and graceful form inspired, as in her light and happy mood she jested playfully with her grave friend's sedate and queenly mien.

"Thou art too gay, giddy, and too full of girlhood yet to be a wife, Amina," observed Catalina, in reply to some mirthful sally of her fair friend.

"And thou, too sober, grave, and womanly, to be a bride, my most severe and serious sister," rejoined Amina, in laughing mockery.

"Not so. Father Eustatius, our confessor, says, that women should not wed till they have buried all youthful follies in the grave of sober prudence."

"I'll not believe his maxim," replied the volatile maiden. "I would not cheat my husband out of all my mirth, my unpruned levities, and young heart's feelings, for all the confessors upon earth. What! take to the lover of your choice a melancholy smile, a serious face, a staid demeanour, and, on the threshold of your future hope and bliss, shake hands and bid farewell to the young hilarity of nature! No. I will go to mine with the green freshness on my heart, with all that pleased him in our early days, and banish only that which his experienced hand shall cull from out the wild flowers of my too fond love."

"I would, Amina, that I could love and feel like you, or own part of that enthusiasm that makes up your life," observed Catalina, with a pensive sigh.

"And can you not?" inquired her friend, much surprised.

"No."

"Not love? not feel a tranquil joy in the anticipated blending of your heart, your thoughts, your future life, with one to whom you stand bound, pledged, affianced, with every tie but holy church to make you wife? Alas! my brother then has pressed an empty shadow to his breast, and for two years lived in a false delusive dream. Nay, thou art but in jest, my dearest Catalina. Did we not, at the same shrine, record our mutual obligation,—thou to my brother, I to thy dear Felix? and shall we not, at the same altar, ratify with hands the promise made by our full concurring hearts?"

"Yes: and I shall fulfil the contract with my holiest thoughts; perform with constancy and truth the utmost duties of a faithful wife; but in my nature, love has no power to stir the deeper fountains of the soul above the staid and equal course of smooth tranquillity. I could not die for love, or break my heart, or blanch the native health from off my cheek, with sighs, with tears, or weak laments. Love is not within my breast a passion steadfast or absorbing; yet, from my very pride, as you are pleased to term my natural reserve, I should be as constant to the man to whom I pledged my faith, as the most professing and devoted maid who ever worshipped Venus' boy. I tell thee this in sisterly regard and confidence; yet will I own, that never gallant to my eye had more attractive charms, more manly grace, more like to win upon my good esteem, than my plighted husband, thy Alonzo."

"Oh! you have made me happy once again, for my dear brother loves you with the full vigour of his noble heart. You have two loved objects on which to lavish all your fond affection,—Sebastian, and my true, devoted Felix; but I am poor and rich in having only one, my friend, my playmate, and my brother. I, in my sisterly regard and partial eyes, picture Alonzo peerless,—first in renown, affection, honour, truth, and constancy, and deem him fitted most of all mankind, to make my friend, my sister, joyously happy. But yet I do not envy you your stoical disposition, sweet Catalina. I'd rather feel the impulse in my soul, full to the swelling; luxuriate in the consciousness of love, however brief or evanescent; feel the decaying life-strings fade, day after day, from my deserted heart; weep o'er the image of my faithless lord, till the exhausted brain refused its springs, and the worn channels in my cheeks were dry and cracked, and die at length, as I had lived, sensible of grief as of my love. Oh! no. Let my brief life be filled with sympathies, though living but an hour; let my felicity be real and complete, though in the lapse of the enduring time the shooting star, that from the fornix to the belted earth travels in countless space, longer sustains identity and engrossing sight. Oh! what were the ennoblement of love, the pleasure of our life, to feel affection but as the homely housewife does her daily task of needful drudgery, a thing of law and custom, a

conned, a tedious lesson, duly repeated without note or emphasis, without a throb or impulse from the cold heart to give a sentiment—a soul, to the dull, stale, and apathetic peace of such unloving, uncongenial love?"

Then checking herself, in the full volubility of her exuberant heart, she rose, and approaching Catalina, bent over her fair neck, to kiss from her smooth brow the apparent shadow that her quick words seemed gathering on that stately front. And as the young, affectionate, and joyous Amina, gracefully inclined and passed her dimpled arms around her waist, and her light hair mingled with the dark tresses of Catalina's abundant locks, a stray sunbeam fell full on her blond features, dyeing her bosom, neck, and face, with the soft tint of blushing roses; and as she twined round the tall, majestic beauty, who rose to her embrace, circling her neck with her proud arm, that pair,—of nature's most perfect graceful handiwork,—looked not unaptly like the imperial lily, round whose tall stem a gentle rose had twined dependingly for shelter and support, while over all, the rich, warm sun cast a transparent mantle soft and heavenly, bathing in a flood of golden light the lovely and embracing pair.

"And can you forgive my unruly tongue, that, hurting thee, wounded myself?" cried Amina, kissing her friend's lips as they took their places in a recess of the open verandah.

"Yes, thou too-sensitive plant, I can!" replied Catalina. "But tell me, what news of our coming bridegrooms?"

"Oh! they will be here to-morrow, or the following day at farthest. They were to rest last night at Burgos," replied Amina, with enthusiasm. "The campaign is over, and they have both,—thy brother and my own,—obtained a respite from their weary duty for three months. And we must go, dear Catalina, to Brussels with our husbands when they return to camp. Ah! Catalina, what would your former suitor, that grim recluse you told me of, that Almazuma, say, did he but know the lovely queen who drove him from his home two years ago, was within a month upon the eve of wedlock? ay! and with the familiar brother of his boyhood?"

"His sentiments on such a theme," replied Catalina, "were to me of little consequence. He is a man that from my soul I most sincerely hate, nor would I call him master for the wealth of Crœsus joined to that Lydian Pythius who offered millions to his king. No; not to sate my ambitious heart with purchased sceptres, had I to call him consort to the diadems! Do you know him, Amina?"

"Nay; I never saw him, but I have heard my brother, dear Alonzo, speak of him with many marks of commendation. Where is the moody anchorite?"

"I know not. It is two years since he profaned my ears with his revolting love. And shortly after, while Alonzo and yourself paid our poor house a visit, and——"

"And Catalina lost her heart to that same youth, Alonzo," laughingly interrupted her companion, as a slight flush passed over the marble features of her friend at the implied consequence of the visit.

"And when the good and venerable Condé, your esteemed father," resumed Catalina, unheeding the badinage of Amina, "proposed an alliance of mutual interest between our houses—it was then, I was about to say, that Almazuma suddenly withdrew from our vicinity, shut up his inhospitable home, and wandered no one knew whither."

"My women tell me that the place is haunted, and that unquiet ghosts make nightly rounds of the vast pile; that flames and smoke are seen, and horrid groans, and deep-mouthed solemn bells, are heard at midnight-hours to sound and rumble through the vaulted domes, filling the hearers with amaze and horror."

"Marvel and fear are handmaids. And that which ignorance does not understand, it magnifies to acts of magic horror, or imputes to supernatural agency. Some three months after the lord's departure, two Benedictine monks arrived at the castle, followed by several wains of heavy-chested goods. They bore a letter from Don Ferdinand himself—a mandate, ordering his steward to insist upon a strict privacy being observed towards the two holy men to whom he willed the castle should be surrendered. That once a-week a due supply of wine and meat should be deposited at the great gate; but none on pain of high displeasure were to presume to cross the outward moat, or pry with idle scrutiny into the devotion and deep study of the two professing brothers. These are the simple facts from which the credulous and gaping throng have built a structure full of ghastly fears and wondrous marvel."

"And are these monks then never seen?" inquired Amina, with much curiosity.

"Sometimes at night, with their heads deep hooded in their cowls, they glide along the tangled paths of the rank, deserted garden, but never by the day. The lights and sounds said to be seen and heard, are doubtless emanations from some forge or crucible,—for better-formed belief has set them down as visionary alchemists, searching in their hot alembics for the nectar of eternal life,—that elixir to the festering grave! —medicine of perpetual youth!"

"Hast thou no curiosity, Catalina," asked her friend, "to investigate these secret men's pursuits, and see if they be really what they seem?"

"It is a vice I am not guilty of."

"Thou art too hard, my sister. A vice! Oh! fie on thee, thou art a railer on thy sex, and, next to love, woman's most ardent passion."

"A weakness then," rejoined Catalina, amending the phrase, "that I am not conscious of possessing. But what pleasure could be gained in watching two dull, old men, supposing you could gain an entrance, busied in some obtuse research?"

"Perhaps they are not what they seem."

"Why not?"

"Might they not be some skilful limners, or other cunning traders, employed to render quaint and rare the spacious dwelling before its lord's return?"

"Oh! most unlikely. They are, depend on it, what they seem. Then plague thy truant fancy with no more conceits on so worthless a pursuit. But tell me, have our good fathers, in their wisdom, settled the day on which we are, s custom orders, to render up our freedom and allegiance at the shrine of sacred wedlock? Where is the Condé and my father?"

"Oh! doubtless busy planning and settling that knotty point, our dowries," laughed out the gay, sprightly girl, in answer to her expected sister's question.

"I would my brother, Don Sebastian, were returned, that he might glad us with his presence at our coming nuptials," observed Catalina.

"Where is Don Sebastian?"

"Serving with his regiment in Peru; for as you know my brothers, both by election and hereditary custom of remote ancestry, are soldiers," replied Catalina. "He has won high honour in those delightful realms, and seems but little prone to leave their golden sands. His time of service will expire twelve months from this, and we shall have him back, never, I trust, to quit us more. How now, Benina?" inquired the Donna, as her waiting-woman entered the apartment and approached the open verandah.

"The marquis, madam, attended by the Donna Amina's father, the Condé de Alvares, craves the honour of an audience with my lady."

"Oh! let them come," exclaimed Amina, springing lightly into the room. "You'll not refuse?"

"No, not to pleasure you,—though it is against my customary rule to permit any man to cross this section of the house, except my father, and he but seldom craves the privilege."

"I know you are most scrupulous, but I have so often pictured to my father's mind this graceful room, that he has begged me hard to ask permission that he might view it, so he might take the image in his eye and form another such for me. That's a dear girl;" and bounding on her more stately friend, as with a measured step she left the balcony, she threw her arms round Catalina's neck, and pressed a kiss upon her brow, then, turning to the respectful attendant, she cried with the pleased accents of a happy child,—

"Run, run! Benina, dear, and tell my honoured father that he may come." With a low courtesy the maid retired, and in a few moments the two aged noblemen entered the sacred precincts of that strongly guarded shrine.

The Marquis of Alfendera was a tall, portly Spaniard, of a chivalrous and commanding front, with all the urbanity and polished elegance of the noble soldier, and though advanced in years and constitutionally impaired from long and arduous wars (for he had fleshed his maiden sword at Pavia, and through all the busy times of Charles and Philip, shared in every danger that menaced his country, and closed his long military career, and fought his last field on the plains of the revolted Netherlands), still bore an erect carriage, and supported his years with firm and elastic steps, his hair hung thin and scattered over a high commanding forehead, while his full bushy brows of grisly grey, corresponded to his aged locks, and gave a fullness to his face, and stamp of vigorous health unusual to his years.

The Condé de Alvares was a nobleman of a very different character, something under the middle size, of a slight and manly build, possessing neither the dignity of expression, or the commanding presence of his friend the marquis, he seemed as evidently the man of peace as the other was of war. His features small but regular, bore in their bland arrangement an impress of a mild and generous heart; his forehead bare, and benevolently high, was shaded by hair of snowy whiteness, that fell in soft straight filaments far down his neck, while from his meek, kind eyes, a forgiving love streamed forth, that on the whole, lent to his aged and patrician form a character of meek and venerable reverence, that in one look inspired esteem and grateful love. Though only a few years older than the marquis, he seemed, when contrasted with the firm figure of his friend, to have long passed the allotted bourne of human life; and though in reality hale and strong, the sensibility of his nature had made greater inroads on his external than on his inward constitution. Married late in life to a woman long sought, but deeply loved, his felicity would have been complete in the possession of his noble son Alonzo, and his fair, beautiful Amina, had not the broken health and long sickness of his dear partner, shadowed his happiness, and clouded all the pleasures of his life; for to his feeling soul life's best gifts, nature's richest boon, lost half their charms, not being shared by her he loved,—for unparticipated joy held no seat in his affectionate and tender heart,—and though he doted on his son with all the pride of fond paternity; watched with delighted eyes his bright career, and viewed his chivalrous soul expand with bounding ecstacy, yet would his delight have been almost measureless, had his beloved wife enjoyed the healthy frame of mind, to mix and share in all the hopes, and fears, and trembling sympathy, that watch, like angel guards, around the objects of our deeper love.

Such was the tender father round whom Amina wound her delicate, taper arms in all the confidence of true affection, as the venerable Condé crossed his threshold; while Catalina, with a stately reverence, saluted the marquis and the Condé with a low obeisance.

"We are come, fair ladies," cried Alfendera, with a courteous ceremony, "to inform you that a courier from the two happy bridegrooms, Don Alonzo and Don Felix, has arrived, bringing us the welcome news, that we may anticipate their early coming on the morrow, and that my worthy and gallant friend, the Condé de Alvares, and myself, have definitively settled the auspicious day,—and that a month from to-morrow the happy consummation of our hopes and wishes shall be fulfilled, and on that day your mutual nuptials shall be solemnized with every show and demonstration of respect and honour."

"Ah! do you blush my shrinking, timid flower," cried the Condé, in a soft tender voice pressing his lovely child fondly to his heart, as the more formal marquis made an end of his announcement. "Thy beauteous friend, the Donna Catalina, hears her gentle doom pronounced with an unflushed brow, but thou, more prodigal of blood, show in thy tell-tale face the truant feelings of thy heart,—nay, I will not shelter thy revealing blushes," he cried, as gently disengaging the clinging girl from his protecting breast, he compelled her to raise her suffused and crimson cheek,—then gazing earnestly in her countenance, the affectionate father clasped her to his breast, and blessed her fervently; but Amina, suddenly extricating herself from his embrace, drew off the attentive eyes of Catalina and her father, by compelling the Condé to take cognizance of all the rare articles of art and genius that so liberally bestrewed the apartment,—pointing like a delighted child, to each adornment of that chaste sanctuary, and pressing on her pleased parent's mind the full details of each, so that he might well remember how to build a tower as fair as rich, and chaste, for his own delighted bird.

In such conversation we must leave this happy group, as events of more consequence to our tale, and new actors in this life's history, call on us for notice and review; and we shall proceed at once to introduce our readers into scenes of graver import, and more momentous consequence.

CHAPTER IV.

IT was on a bright, warm day, early in the month of August, in the year 1588, that two youthful cavaliers, mounted on strong war-steeds, somewhat distressed by their long journey, were seen winding down a steep defile in that chain of lofty mountains that forms the south-eastern boundary of the kingdom of Navarre, separating it from the fertile province of Soria. About five hundred yards in the rear of the travellers, and completely out of the hearing of their master's conversation, followed about twenty varlets, horse-boys, and muleteers, each conducting by the bridle a heavy loaded mule, whose heterogeneous freightage of panniers, cases, armour, and instruments of defence, formed, with the irregularly accoutred servitors and fanciful dress of the mule-drivers, a peculiar charm, and lent an animation to the dull back-ground of rock and shadowy wood, as, in single file, they cautiously descended the rude pathway, dotting the long line of their extended column with points of warm and varied lights. Having gained the level plain, the little troop formed itself into four lines, and putting their well-trained animals into a smart pace, followed in close order,—the two cavaliers observing the same respectful distance.

The two youthful travellers, whom we must now proceed to describe, were Don Felix, the younger brother of Catalina, the betrothed husband of the lovely Amina; his companion was the gallant Don Alonzo, the only son of the Condé de Alvares, descended from one of the noblest houses in Castile,—young, handsome, rich, with a reputation far spread and honourable for his gallant service in the field,—frank, generous, open, and confiding. In all the dangerous actions of the period, he had, with his friend Don Felix, borne a foremost and an arduous part; and with some regret, even at the sacrifice of their expected happiness in their coming union, they had been refused to bear their share in the honourable post assigned to the land forces embarked on board that mighty fleet, whose size and numbers had filled the wondering populace with awe. As every hope of Spain was centred in this expedition, all minor circumstances were, for the time, suspended in the precarious interval between the armada's sail and ultimate success, and they

A. MILES

had obtained leave to visit their long left home, and devote to love those brief days of respite, ere more stirring news recalled the youths to action and to arms.

From the first hour Alonzo had beheld Catalina he had loved her with all the deep devotion of his impassioned soul, fervently—truly; and when he poured out his feelings with the force and honourable impulse of his heart before the stately beauty, even her cold nature felt a sympathy, and for a moment took a livelier hue, and as far as she was capable to feel reciprocal affection and the power of love, she loved him. Though her reserve, and formal ceremony, and distant manner, disguised even the little that she felt, and though Alonzo's was the only heart that ever yet had bowed submissive to her will, that loved her for the very state and haughtiness of mien, and in her proud unbending nature, found material for his ardent and devoted passion, she never once relaxed her distant and cold form, but seemed with scrupulous exaction to her heart, to keep subdued, and in a constant check, all evidence of her feelings. But of this her lover seemed insensible; he was supremely blest—felt fully happy; he saw no coldness in her look, no reservation in her love; he felt no apathy in her mien, no ice within her blood; he viewed her by the transports of his heart, and felt her truth in his own excess of joy.

Even the watchful and ever solicitous father was happy in the purposed union. Young Alvares was all his vigilant care could desire to make his daughter blest; and he banished for ever from his mind those parental and misplaced fears, that had, for many years, impaired his peace for Catalina's welfare, and he believed that he could now part with his beloved child to such a protector, without one grief, one doubting pang; and time, the probationer of

3

Don Alonzo's love, had now flown by, and brought, within a month, the long anticipated day, when with princely splendour the double nuptials were to be solemnized.

Don Felix had just completed his six-and-twentieth year, being some eighteen months the junior of Alonzo, his companion and brother-in-arms. He had already served with distinction in two campaigns in Flanders, and taken an active part in that brilliant series of skirmishings before Sluys, where the unprincipled and vascillating Leicester had his pride humbled, and his gallant troops defeated, in their daily conflicts with the Spanish infantry,—at that time, and long before, esteemed the flower of European armies, and considered invincible till on the fatal field of Rocroy, half a century posterior, they were annihilated by the victorious Condé.

Never, to the ardent minds and youth-inspiring thoughts of the two lovers, had life assumed so gay, so prosperous a happiness. Each grave or trivial circumstance on their march, each hazard of the way, took from their jocund hearts the hue and bright complexion of their own felicity, covering the toilsome road with pleasurable objects.

As the small cavalcade approached the borders of a deep extended forest, through which the main road from Bayonne to Soria lay, and where the high track was intersected by numerous diverging bye-roads and bridle-paths, they were encountered by two meanly-clad Franciscan friars, mounted on sorry mules of a lean and hungry aspect, one of whom addressing the young cavaliers, requested, in a meek and submissive tone, to be permitted to join their company, should their route lie in the direction of the city, as the forest was reported to be beset with brigands and wandering tribes of emigrant Bohemians, to whom the small collection they had amassed in alms for their poor chauntry, would fall as lawful booty.

"Such unbelievers and scoffing men of war and plunder," continued the speaker, "deeming the unworthy servants of the holy Catholic Church fit and estimable objects whereon to wreak their indignation and abuse,—not always sated in their rage with plunder, but too often putting the followers of the blessed cross to cruel deaths."

"You are right welcome to such safe conduct as our small troop can grant, holy fathers," replied Don Alonzo; "but methinks if the forest bears so ill a reputation as you imply, our own baggage runs a harder risk than your lean purses;—however, it may be as well to take precaution:" and halting till the little band had come up, he ordered the men to put on their arms, laid aside during the heat of the day, and to proceed in closer and more regular array. Then placing the two friars in the centre of the front line, Don Felix took his station on one side of them, while Alonzo occupied the corresponding position on the other,—and, thus arranged, they all set forward through the forest at a quick steady pace.

"What is the latest news, good father?" inquired Don Felix, of his nearest companion. "In your wandering lives you hear much gossip. What business stirs most the idle tongues of the ever-hungry crowd?—for we are almost strangers on our native soil."

"That in lastest fashion yesterday," replied the friar addressed, in a deep studied voice, as he more carefully drew down the ample hood that enveloped his head and face, giving to his utterance a subdued and smothered sound, "was the rife report of the quick return of two young nobles from the seat of war, and the great state and preparation made at the Alfendera palace for the nuptials of one Don Alonzo, the second son of the proud marquis. The province rings with rumour of the sumptuous pageantry. It is said, the throne itself will be nigh eclipsed in the coming splendour! Doubtless you've heard of this?"

"Aye! holy father, as far as being principals, we have."

"I ask forgiveness in all humility for my presumption," replied the friar, bowing stiffly his cowled head.

"It is not needed," observed Don Felix. "'Twere hard to put a curb on public tongue, or dictate to the world how it shall speak of us. But is thy news so scanty? Is there nothing further to record?"

"My brother gleaned, in his morning's elemosynary walk, something touching the Don Almazuma,—but what, I did not hear."

"Ha! what of my noble friend—my old companion—fellow schoolboy?" exclaimed Alonzo, eagerly.

"Brother Antonius will inform my lord of what he has heard;—myself am ignorant."

"Speak, good father," cried Alonzo, turning to his next companion, designated as brother Antonius,—a man of tall and robust habit, clothed, like the other, in the coarse garb of the mendicant fraternity, and equally shielded from observation in the full hood of his large frock.

"Two days since," replied the friar, "I met a train of many wagons, filled, 'twas said, with all the sumptuous elegance that the rifled stores in the capital could supply. There was a host of servitors, and all the vain and needless adjuncts to a princely residence. 'Twas said the absent lord had just returned from a weary pilgrimage, and was about to wed, and would be down to take possession of his home soon as the busy hands of his large retinue could make the neglected castle habitable. All this I gleaned from an Italian valet, who claimed my spiritual benison, being sore hurt in conscience for faults committed on his way. And holy Saint Francis be praised for his great mercies! for he, working our cause, opened the menials' hearts to our poor order, and raised among their troop a sum of twelve ryals,—a great blessing!—twelve ryals!"

"When did they say Don Ferdinand would return?" inquired Alonzo, when the friar had ended his prosy and begging speech.

"Nay,—I know not, worthy lord."

"Didst thou not say, brother, when thou didst rejoin my company, that the lord of Almazuma was for certain expected home to-morrow?" observed the first-mentioned friar; "and that 'twas said he had returned so suddenly to grace some dear friend's nuptials?"

"Ay, truly! I do now remember, good Philip," replied Antonius, reminded of the circumstance, "such was the tenour of my communication, but wrapt in the rich largesse acquired for our suffering house, the fact had left my memory. Twelve ryal's—'tis above a ducat!"

"I will visit him to-morrow, Felix, and thou shalt bear me company. You will grow to like him. Though something cold, stately, and reserved, he had, when young, great qualities. 'Twas kind, noble of him to return purposely to honour me. I long once more to greet him: it is more than ten years since we last met. Oh! he shall join our company, and fill the measure of our happiness to overflowing. And you, holy men, if you will come with us, shall, for this good news, have an ample guerdon, and make a harvest for your house out of the full purses of the collected guests."

"We thank you humbly, senhor, but our vow forbids it;—besides, we are allotted heavy penance, weary masses, fasting and discipline, to avert the anger of incensed heaven against the dreadful scism and heresy that has brought Divine punishment so heavily upon our nation, in this great calamity sprung from the spread of such a damnatory doctrine."

"What calamity do you mean?" inquired Don Felix.

"What, senhor! dost thou not know that for our sins, in judgment for our crimes in fostering and permitting heretics, the Lord hath taken his face from us, and scourged us with defeat?"

"Defeat! what mean you?" exclaimed Alonzo, eagerly. "We have been three weeks on sea and land, travelling from the low countries to Bayonne, and since we sailed from Sluys till now, have heard no tidings of the expedition."

"Ay!" cried Father Antonius, with more energy perhaps than became his holy calling. "Ay! such a defeat as never yet disgraced the annals of a mighty kingdom or a gallant nation! Call it ruin—not defeat. Twenty lepantos cannot wipe away the stain of such a dismal overthrow. Our fleet, that armament, which in arrogance of pride we called invincible, is swept from the sea that groaned beneath its weight; and what the scoffing heretic spared, or his red shot escaped, the stormy sky has scattered, and the devouring ocean swallowed up."

"This is disastrous news indeed!" replied Alonzo, "and casts a cloud upon our happiness. But what better could have been expected of such an admiral as Medina Sidonia? But see! we are through the forest. Our way is to the east;—how travel you, good fathers?"

"A league farther westward. Many thanks, good senhors, for your safe conduct. Benedicite!" observed Father Philip, crossing himself, and with his companion,—drawing aside as the party defiled off.

"Should you pass the castle of Almazuma, bear my hearty greeting to my worthy friend—its lord, and say, that I will visit his noble seat to-morrow. Adieu!" cried Don Alonzo, waving his hand.

"He shall not fail to hear the message," replied the friar. "I will myself convey it to his ear."

"Here, good father, are two ducats for thy perishing house," cried Felix, laughing, and putting the money into Father Antonius' hand, while at the same time Alonzo presented the delighted monk with a doubloon.

"Heaven open her gates for you, fair senhors! You have absolution for a month. Your souls are safe—Pax vobiscum:" and the parties then separated in opposite directions.

When the two itinerant priests had ridden for about an hour in the same course on which they had started on parting with their late companions, they suddenly turned their mules, and putting them into a rapid pace, pursued a direction parallel to that taken by the cavaliers, —nor once drew bridle till the tall towers, massive grandeur, and extensive buildings of the half-castlellated palace of Almazuma broke upon their view. Seated like a proud monarch on an eminence, surrounded by a wide wooded park, that here and there diversified by level plains or swelling undulations, gave the domain the picture of exquisite beauty.

Dismounting in one of the long chesnut avenues, that, like arteries, in all directions, converged to the castle as to a centre, they unsaddled their animals, and depositing the harness in the hollow of a withered elm that had grown to a gigantic size, and turning the mules loose to seek new masters, the two friars struck into a low, narrow path, almost hid by the dense foliage, that like walls, shut out light and observation, and followed its course till it terminated abruptly at a low door-way that seemed cut out of the green hill, on which the stately pile rose towering above. Drawing back the wild briars and rank luxuriance that nearly concealed this apparently dungeon entrance, and applying a key to the small secreted lock, the door opened and admitted the two mysterious individuals into a low, rocky passage, along which they had to bend as they proceeded through its devious track, enveloped in the profoundest darkness.

CHAPTER V.

ON the second story, in one of the wings of the Castle of Almazuma, was situated a suite of three rooms,—the only apartments in the now re-inhabited and newly furnished mansion that remained undecorated. The first of the range, was a large reception, or ante-room, containing a long, coarse oak-table, and two antique armchairs and implements for writing. Several beakers of walnut tree, hooped and tipped with gold, with cups of the same material, stood on the table; and in a recess of one of the deep-sunk windows, was placed two large gilt stoups, —not unlike in shape the "amphord" of the ancients,—filled with rich wine.

Seated in one of the chairs, his dark brows knit, his eyes fixed on the ground, with arms folded over his chest, and his countenance bearing the stamp of deep resolve and deadly malice, reclined Don Ferdinand de Almazuma, wrapt in cogitations ominous as his features. The next chamber was something smaller in size, but like the first, from which it entered, destitute of furniture. Passing through this deserted room, and opening from it was a third, much smaller than the preceding ones, and formerly used as an oratory, and which was panelled from its vaulted roof to the floor, in long narrow compartments of wainscot. It is necessary for the reader to bear in mind, that these three apartments had but one common outlet, through the lofty portal in the first chamber, as the subsequent events will be rendered more comprehensive and clear by the knowledge of their situation, and this particular. On the floor, opposite the only window, in the small oak-panelled oratory, was a low truckle-bed, and beside it a strong, square, girded trunk, on which stood an iron lamp. A common deal stool, and a pitcher of water, constituted all the contents of this gloomy abode. The room at the time, was untenanted, and the door locked and doubly secured by means of a wooden bar that fitted into staples in the supporting posts. Presently one of the long panels in the centre of the wainscot was gently pushed back, and the cowled head of a monk was protruded cautiously from the opening,—first, with a hurried glance looking to the door, then with a longer and more earnest inspection, examining with his eye the strong-bound chest. Having at length satisfied himself that all was safe, the monk stepped out of the recess, and closing the sliding panel, threw back the enveloping hood from his head, and exposed the sunburnt features of the quondam Gitano, Garcia.

"It is all safe!" he remarked, as he approached and unfastened the box. "All as I left it, and as it has always been. Why should I doubt it? He has given me no cause for my mistrust. He pays more like a prince than a noble. Let me see!—let me see! Yes, I will once more feed my eyes with the bright pieces;" and sitting down on his bed, he drew the weighty chest between his knees, and throwing back the lid, luxuriated in the gold and silver that sparkled beneath his eyes; and burying his hands in the heaped treasure, drew out handfuls of the bright coins, allowing them to fall slowly and deliberately through his fingers, enjoying the melody of their chinking sound, while his eyes glittered with unutterable glee, and his mouth curled into a selfish, gloating smile of ecstasy as he exclaimed, "Oh! exquisite delight! beautiful picture! All mine!—mine! —mine! Here are ducats of Castile, Arragon, and Navarre; nobles of Flanders, Utrecht and Holland; guilders of Charles and Philip; ryals of all nations; pistoles, double and single pieces of eight, doubloons and——Ha! how came these cursed profaning carnadoes and maravedies here?" he cried, passionately, throwing out a few wretched decimal fractions of farthings. "Out of my sight, base copper! Ho! but this is a glorious sight! And here—here too!" he exclaimed, taking out and perusing a parchment, "here is the deed and title of the fine house in Madrid that Almazuma gave me to spend my days in,—here it is signed and attested by the corregidor, and the first lawyer in Spain. All fair—all clear—distinct and equitable;—no subterfuge—no evasion. Made out in my own name: here it is—'Antonio Garcia.' The house, even in a marketable sense, is a fortune. Yes, he has paid me well;— given me his black charger too, and a valued mule, to carry myself and treasury to my new abode. Another month,—another month, and I shall be free—yes free! What have I to fear? I have done my duty to him freely, honestly for two years; brought my great achievement to an end, and made it work to admiration; and he has doubled every promise on me; loaded me with wealth,—and here—here it is! no deception! Coin—coin—tangible coin!" And he plunged his arms into the heap again, and stirred it up, and rolled it over, and seemed to revel and wanton in the sound and quantity of his stored specie.

"Why should I doubt him?" he resumed, musingly. "'Tis true, he is a villain, and playing a villain's part,—a damnable one! And am not I a villain, too? Yes,—but a poor, contemptible, and abject one to him. Oh! he is a great master—a transcendent villain!—above the gusts, and storms, and petty weaknesses of passion,— bold, deliberate, steady. Why,—I would, in the anger of my hate, have killed, and there have done; but he—this earthly devil—I speak it in commendation—will expend a fortune and consume a lifetime to wither a frail woman into the grave! Well, that's his taste. 'Tis true he exerts an influence over me more than man ever yet acquired; keeps me under the vigilant watch of his fascinating eye, and sometimes cows my very soul with his prolonged, determined gaze. How is it I cannot shake it off? But, but did I not twice save his life, and is he not grateful? Aye! life is a boon the basest heart is grateful for:—then, hence all lingering doubts, I have no cause to fear him;—besides, did he not tell me to take my gold and put it out to usury, and make cent. per cent. upon it? Is that not proof of honesty? It is. But I would rather keep it in my eye—to gloat my heart on; to kiss, and hug, and feel, and see, and dream, and wake, and dream again upon my hoarded affluence! Another month—but thirty days— and I am free! Oh! how I shall riot then. Yes, let me finish my next performance but as well as that completed, and I am a made man; yes—provided for the longest day man can cheat from nature. All is swimmingly fair;— yes,—yes.——Ha! he calls," he cried, suddenly, as a small bell rang faintly over his head.

Garcia instantly withdrew his hands from the gold, closed the lid of his chest, and placing it again beside his bed, rose, and drawing the hood over his face, unlocked his door, and securely closing it after him, crossed the middle room, and with a staid and sober step entered the first chamber, where we have already described Almazuma as seated.

"See that the portal to the corridor is closed, good Garcia, and then return, for I have much to ask and tell," observed Almazuma, as he entered the apartment, with a quiet tone, and a countenance from which every trace of the dark passions that so lately disfigured it had been obliterated.

The assumed monk quitted the room to comply with his lord's injunctions, and, returning in a few minutes, reported that everything was safe.

"You have this day, Garcia," said Don Ferdinand, addressing his confederate, "brought to completion the tedious labour of two years. You have, in the skill, contrivance, and ability of your mind, exceeded my most prodigal expectancy. Here is your daily hire;" and he placed on the table twelve pistoles,—a sum not far short of five pounds. "And here, as a slight premium on your labour past, is a bag of a hundred gold doubloons: I said I would not be a niggard master. Take it, for you have earned it well."

As Almazuma placed the money before him, Garcia, with a deep, suffused face, and a convulsive twitching of the fingers, approached the table; and though gold, as Almazuma had truly prophesied, was his idol, yet the man felt abashed at the excessive liberality of his employer; and though his fingers bent instinctively to clutch the tempting heap, the better feeling of his heart kept him modestly aloof, and with a not ungraceful bow, he said,—

"No, Don Almazuma, no; you have paid me already far too liberally. I will take the twelve pistoles, but for the doubloons,—no, it is too much—no!"

"'Take it!" was the only answer made by Don Ferdinand; but it was expressed in that quiet, determined tone, that Garcia knew was not to be disputed; so taking up the bag of gold and the loose coin, he threw back his monkish garb, revealing beneath the habit of the Zingari, in which we first beheld him, and deposited the money in the leathern pouch that hung on his left hip above the short, strong, and slightly bent hanger, or falchion, that, under every disguise, he never for a moment permitted te leave his side.

"Our fortunate, though planned encounter, yesterday, with Don Alonzo and his friend, has answered all my expectation," remarked Almazuma, when Garcia had complied with his will, and secured the gold on his person, and enveloped himself again in his cassock. "He has visited me to-day, and afforded me all I sought,—free access to the palace of Alfendera. Our first disguise as Benedictines, and our last as begging friars, will serve effectually to quell suspicion of identity, should such be dreamed of. And now, what of your morning's mission, —for our time for mutual converse is drawing to an end,—how sped you?"

"I disguised me as you directed," replied Garcia, "as a poor servitor, without a place, and went to the marquis's palace, saw Don Alonzo, urged my piteous tale, and, to make the matter short, he took me to his service, and this night I take up my residence at the marquis's as one of the gay bridegroom's chambervalets."

"That is well—very good! You are too apt of thought, too quick of comprehension, Garcia, not to perceive my deep-staked play—part of my intricate and double-handed game?"

"So please you, senhor, I see it all," replied the accomplice.

"All?" resumed Almazuma, with his steady eye fixed on Garcia.

"Yes, my lord,—all."

"No, Garcia, not all—not all!" replied Don Ferdinand, with a tranquil, meaning smile of deep and serious import. "Not all yet; but you shall know all my plans, each particular, as time and place gives it development. You shall, before we part, have my bosom confidence, and I will prove to thee, in a way thou little thinkest of, how I will reward thy vigilance and bind thee to me for ever. Another month, good Garcia, and thou shalt be free as air,—no mortal power shall harm thee: believe me, I will provide for that especially.

"Senhor, you are too generous."

"Not a whit; you have deserved my utmost care,—but to other matters. You understand, good friend, all the subtle plans I have arranged and noted down for you to act,—the dress, the letter, the trinkets to be dropped, the place of nightly meeting, your total ignorance of me and every circumstance I have recorded to you. I would not have the most trivial item lost or omitted in the prosecuted scheme; no," he exclaimed, rising and striding the apartment, "not for the wealth of the teeming Indies! She shall fall by such full, constructive, damnatory evidence; so perfect in its tissue, so complex in device, that not the upholding angels should redeem her from the implication wrought by my attesting proof!"

"Fear nothing, senhor, from my vigilance and care. My heart is in the cause, and I am yours —soul and body—for the work."

"I do believe you, and will recompense you to the utmost bent of your desire. Take thy gold with thee,—but keep it from the prying eyes of thy observant fellows, or it will betray us."

"Nay, by your leave, my lord, I'll leave it here; 'tis safer where it is."

"As thou wilt. Lock up thy door, and take the key thyself,—I shall not visit the subterranean chapel before the hour of consummation,—then look heedful to thy treasure's safety."

"Aye, marry! I trust the foul fiend will not jilt me now, and leave me beggar once again. Curses on the Inquisition!"

"You do remember me of thy promise; and as we may not have the time for conference when next we meet, you shall recount the promised history of your life. See! the wine stands tempting,—fill the stoups, and give a confidence to thy lagging memory with a brimmed beaker,—drink!"

Garcia approached the recess in the window, and took up the two full stoups of wine, and setting one of them with an empty drinking cup before Almazuma, filled his own beaker out of the other, and drinking the measure off at a draught, replenished his cup, and taking the chair at the extremity of the long table, began a record of his life in the following manner:—

GARCIA'S TALE.

"You have witnessed, me Don Almazuma, in moments of danger and positions of some peril; and I have had my share of buffets from the rough hand of war, and have taken my degree from that irascible and strict schoolmaster— the world; and I have had work to do in which I jeopardized my life in no considerate measure, in places too, where no mortal eye was near to look a confidence upon my deeds, or give a spur to flagging resolution; and not a witness, but the recording heaven, attesting what I did. And I can truly say, I never yet failed or shrunk from the full hazard of the dangerous enterprise, but followed up, for ill or good, the subtle work or bloody deed entrusted to my skill, staunch as the sleuth-hound. I tell you this not boastingly, but to check your marvel at what I shall reveal in sequence. You have ever found me brave, that is, what is called in men of my condition—insensibility to pain and hardihood,—for I am neither Don nor Duke,—and what is only nature, instinct, or brute courage in the debased and lowly serf, is valour, enterprise, and heroism when coupled with a Count or Marquis,—ha! ha! Such is society's law,—a very just and nice distinction, is it not, Don Ferdinand? Well, well, let that pass; and to return: I am now, and have been for many years, indifferent to death, and therefore men have called me brave; and with this present character I can afford to speak my former shame;—for you must know, senhor, that I was born a coward! and, up to manhood, was a creeping, timid, abject craven;—a thing without capacity to circumvent the butchery of a mouse,—a pigeon-livered hind, that smiled when he should have frowned, grew pale when other men were flushed, and chattered like a pie when noble hearts were up and did; forswore strong drink and abnegated oaths,—in fine, I was a skulking coward,—a despicable, weak poltroon,—the women's laughter and the men's contempt.

"You wonder, senhor, I have the courage to avouch this of my youth; and were I what I was, hell should not pluck the impeachment from my tongue, but you have asked the history of my life, and I will give it truthfully.

"My father, Antonio Garcia, was a man of substance, and in his native town Tortosa, of great repute for many skilful sciences of which he was the master; besides, he had a natural genius for mechanic arts, and no work, however elaborate, if once seen, but he could imitate. He made dials, designed and executed models of all kinds,—but these were merely recreation; his legitimate and usual work was graving golden crucifixes, polishing rare stones, and all the mystery of that earliest branch of human art—the goldsmith's trade.

I was the only child my parents ever had, and,—like all solitary pledges to the married pair,—a greater curse than blessing. I was lazy, idle, wilful, and though of quick and most retentive parts, would never take the toil to wade progressive through the dull labyrinths and drudgery of knowledge, but learnt the flourishes and gew-gaw parts of science, and left the hard and tasteless task for plodding minds and weak capacities; besides, I caught, intuitively, and with ease, whatever took my fancy, no matter how obtruse; and with my school, as with my father's trade, I sipped the honey from each work, and left the rifled petals to decay. My earliest youth can recollect no wish ungratified that liberal folly could bestow upon an only son; and long before the stage of boyhood passed, my heart was old in vice, hard as the rock, insensible as steel to all effects but fear. My compeers hated me,—for I was avaricious, mean, and full of guile. At home my wish was law. My father trembled, and my mother wept, as in my youthful heat I oft affronted them with stern commands; the servants feared; the world, that is, our neighbourhood disowned me, and fixed upon my name the brand of coward! I felt the deep indignity of the contempt eating day by day into my soul, and prayed in the full cowardice of my heart for courage to avenge the withering injuries I sustained. At length chance did what prayers had never done: it gave me resolution. I was one day, senhor, publicly whipped,—you may smile, Don Almazuma, and so can I do now; indeed, I have reason to be thankful for the

chastisement, for it was the making of me. A youth, something younger than myself, beat me in the streets, in the very eye and gaze of all the town, adding to every blow the bitter taunt of coward. Well,—I felt the shame like hell-fire scorching in my heart; but for my life I could not return one blow, but turned and fled, while the street shook with jeering laughter, nor stopped till I had buried the derisive sounds; and my hot shame, in the darkest corner of my father's house.

"That night I rose when all the rest were locked in sleep, and robbed my parents' coffers of a good round sum; left my home for ever, and, guided by the moon, directed my steps towards Valencia, where, after a week's hard walking, I arrived just in time to secure a passage on board one of three galleons bound for the new kingdom of Peru.

"I will not fatigue you by recounting the erratic fancies that filled my mind, or the prospects that opened to my imagination on entering that world of romance and gold—that land of exquisite peace and beauty, which such lawless ruffians as myself, urged by cupidity and lust, changed into a desert of ruin and bloodshed. You will deem it strange that entertaining such a craven spirit and so cowardly a soul, I should for a moment seriously contemplate adopting arms as a profession: indeed, it would be vain to analyze the feeling that prompted it,—but so it was; for scarcely had I landed in those regions of perpetual summer, before I embraced the occupation of a soldier, and for the first time in my life buckled on a cuirass, set a bascinet upon my head, with a good toledo by my side, a bandilier around my neck and a heavy arquebuse in my hand, took my place in the Spanish army of 500 foot; and, three days after landing in Peru, was on my march from Lima, with fifty comrades, to subdue a refractory cacique near the city of Cusco.

"On the fifth day of our expedition, we came suddenly on a large body of Peruvians, who had taken possession of a strong defile. Fortunately for me, our little band was marching in close order,—I say fortunately, for it prevented me putting into practice my first suggestion to run away, which, had I done, I should have remained a coward to the end of my life. But flight was out of the question, unless I had knocked down half-a-dozen comrades, right and left, rear and van; for I was wedged into the centre of our troops, and there was no alternative but to be shot by my friends as a coward, or transfixed with a poisoned javelin by the Peruvians, as a foe,—so I made a virtue of my dilemma, and strode manfully on with the company. The enemy disputed the ground for some time, foot by foot,—for our musketry had ceased to terrify them,—and they stood four vollies of our fire and smoke, as they called it, with veteran courage; and by the time we had driven them from their position, our band had lost its two front files; and as we issued upon the open plain beyond, I found myself unwillingly in the van of our reduced party,—and, as I believed at the moment, the butt and sole object of the Peruvians' darts and arrows. The word was given to charge, and our little company instantly separated; each man selecting his own quarry gave an immediate pursuit. The flight of the enemy gave me courage, and for the first time in my life I followed danger with a zest and appetite; and selecting a tall, powerful Indian as my prey, followed with all my energy. Throwing away my arquebuse, I drew my sword and taunted the Peruvian with cowardice. The cacique, for he was a chieftain, stung by my insulting words,—for he knew too much of Spaniards not to understand my Castilian,—turned suddenly rouud, and drawing his body to his full height, and covering his breast with his bright shield, confronted me with his drawn sword. I had pursued my foe with such speed, that the sudden check I received from the abrupt halt and defiance of the chief, threw me instantly on my knee defenceless, and in his power; but with a disdainful wave of his short falchion, and a contemptuous curl of his lip, the Peruvian declined to take advantage of my position, and bade me rise and meet a warrior! I will not describe what I felt at that moment. Fear and shame was struggling in my breast for mastery. I could not fly, my comrades were behind and around me, the Indian in front, and with a sort of delirious desperation, I sprang to my feet, and dealt a succession of quick, heavy blows at my antagonist, which he parried with admirable skill and coolness with his shield, watching with panther eyes, the moment to rush in and dispatch me with his strong manageable sword. The combat warmed me, and I felt passion rising in my heart; and as this feeling took possession of my breast, fear abated, and confidence sent new life into my veins. And at length, when my foe suddenly dashed aside my blade with his defensive buckler, and made a bound upon my body, I leaped backward, and with a quick downward impetus of my sword, cut through the feathered zone that crowned his head, driving the golden circlet to the brain, and ended the assay and maiden fleshment of my sword, by piercing his tawny bosom with my good toledo.

"A shout of praise burst from my comrades at my prowess, and fired my soul with a strange and novel impulse; and bounding forward on the hapless fugitives like the baulked wolf, whose lips have tasted blood, I sated my now thirsty appetite in many a gory wound and shrieking death.

"Within an hour, Don Ferdinand, I had become a warrior! 'Tis strange how quick, when once the hand is in, the heart participates in deeds of blood and outrage. Without initiation, step, or progress, I sprung at once from cowardice to valour; nor have I since disgraced the name I won in my first field, or tarnished the respect of soldier.

"I have often pondered on that day's work and consequence, and marvelled much on my sudden change of nature. Had the Peruvians stood their ground, I had been coward still; but in their fears I gained my courage. But, after all, 'tis circumstance that makes or mars us, and discipline and emulous desire makes brave men of cowards, and Hercules of timid fools. I know not whether it was inherent evil in my heart, destiny, or accident that developed all the vices of my disposition, but one by one the vicious traits broke out,—the plague spots on my soul. In boyhood I was wilful, greedy, and malicious; in youth, cunning and revengeful; and in my manhood, avaricious, savage, bloody. Each phase of deadly passion has had its ebb and flow within my heart in the brief lifetime I have run in sin; and if I judge aright of my own feelings, I shall sink at last to base and canting priestcraft.

"But to return: I gained high honour for my deeds that day, and so went on from year to year, accumulating praise for bloodhound slaugtering; for I can look upon it now with something like remorse, for it was a long tragedy of tedious iteration. Slaughter—slaughter, from the rising to the going down of each day's curtain!

"At length we quelled the fractious tribes and turbulent caciques; and we had stipulated the hard terms of peace to the rebellious hordes, and were cantoned at Cusco, waiting the gathering tribute. To facilitate this golden harvest, a comrade and myself were sent some thirty leagues to the north, to the banks of the fast flowing Ucayli, a powerful tributary of the mighty Amazon. Our duty here was light enough,—simply to give safe conduct, and ferry over the broad stream, those chiefs who came with tribute to purchase from their iron conquerors precarious life, with all their opulence. The last of the appointed days had arrived when submission could be tendered, and all, as we believed, had passed the watery boundary to lay their homage at Don Jose's feet, the governor of Cusco. When late that night my comrade and myself were roused from sleep by the hasty summons of an old cacique, who craved an instant passage, as he had barely six hours left to reach the nearest station, and bore with him a mine of wealth,—the ransom of six chiefs besides himself.

"The night was dark and painfully silent; a thick and heavy vapour spread like a pall over the wide river; not a breath of air stirred the dense foliage of the tall linchonas; not a frog from the marsh, nor a bird from the bush, gave utterance to break the stillness of the hour,— while an oppressive weight and ominous silence pervaded the entire atmosphere. As we loaded the boat by a pine torch, and stowed the rich freight of sparkling ingots that loosely packed in Indian matting glittered through the broad chinks temptingly brilliant. I had hitherto slain, in the heat of battle, hundreds, and called it glorious sport, and the excitement of war had grown into a passion; but now, another impulse rose up within my heart, and this desire begot another, and I felt them swelling in my throat, and mounting to my brain, seeking approval from my soul. How quick is mischief!—'twas robbery and murder! I looked into my fellow's face, and by the ruddy light of the solitary torch, read in his clenched teeth and his dilated eyes, a confirmation to my thoughts—an answer to my appeal.

"The old man dismissed his troop, and took his seat; and without a sound or word we dipped our oars; and like the ghostly bark that plies across the stygian wave, we glided noiseless, spectre-like and dim, into the hazy shroud, that with a heavy gloom encompassed land and stream; while from the shore, the fading torchlight shone through the dark mantle of the air like an expiring star,—then faded, and, in the thick obscurity, was lost to sight, and left us floating in profoundest night and solemn stillness.

When we had gained half-way across,—for here the river flowed a league from either bank, —we laid aside our oars, and with a mutual and instinctive act, as if one spirit swayed both breasts, seized the venerable and unresisting chief, and plunged his head and body in the stream, and held him by his feet immersed in the dark tide, until the gurgling in his throat, and the floating bubbles, charged with his last pants, no longer rose to let the soul loose from their inflated sides, and the last spasm of tenacious life had ceased to vibrate through the stiffening nerves. The man was old, died soon, and struggled little; and we had murdered him without a sound, save the dull gluck of the escaping air forcing its passage through the dense obstructing water. Some heavy stones, the ballast of our boat, tied to the cacique's feet, sent the mortality like a plummet to the deep, soft bottom, while we, resting on our oars, waited with longing minds the coming morning. And when at length the sun rose high above us, scattering the night fog, we told with trembling hands the sum of our possessions. The tale was vast, the half to each was a rich prince's ransome, and we hugged, and felt and kissed the sparkling ingots, and weighed them in our hands, and laughed, and smiled, and wept by turns with joy. And like two children with a novel toy, we piled the wedges up, and took them down, and packed them up in bales, then ripped up the new made seams, and spread them out before our sight, paving the rough bottom of our boat with a golden flooring, feasting our hungry eyes with the extended treasure.

"And when at length we equally partitioned our rich hoard, each wrapped up his weighty share, and placed his packages between his knees, dreading a moment's absence from those yellow bars, to which our very souls were held in bondage. And every now and then, as we bent our willing shoulders to the oars, we paused to jerk the packed gold nearer our encircling limbs, or pluck an ingot from the heap, and kiss and place it in our breast.

"At length we shot our bark across the stream, and gained the safe retreat of our secure and lonely hut,—planning a thousand wild conceits to revel in our plunder, when once escaped and back in sheltering Europe. That night we dug two holes and buried our easy booty till circumstance should aid our flight.

"But a new passion woke within my breast; or, rather, a dormant one, revived. Much coveted the more; and this feeling grew to agony in my heart, and I resolved to have the whole.

My comrade was a powerful man, a tried and practised soldier, and to assault and cut him off in fight were too much hazard, though my resolve was equal to the attempt. No! I would not try the risk—his stronger arm might in the end prevail, and I should lose, with life, my wealth. No, I said, cunning shall win the way, and I was match, much more than match for him in that.

"It was our daily custom to row or sail into the centre of the stream, and cast our lines and fish,—for the time was Lent,—and this, with dry ears of Indian corn, was all our food. That day we were too busy with our spoil to think of food or drink, and we consumed the day in feasting on our gold, and picturing scenes of future bliss; but on the next, I took the boat, and with the semblance of confiding confidence, left my whole wealth behind—risking my all to his cupidity in the hope of making more. But he was a Castilian, and too proud to be dishonest to the partner of his guilt. This I well knew, but could not altogether banish from my heart a sickening fear, and my very soul shrunk as I departed from the shore. But this my fellow saw not, for with an outward show of wild hilarity and careless ease, I sprang into the boat, and shot my little craft into the wide, deep river, and purposely delayed, till late, my usually brief return,—for I had much to plot, and it was my policy to find but little sport. And as the evening closed, and I returned upon my homeward voyage, I bored the rotten bottom of the crazy boat with numerous holes, and filled the apertures with masticated wheat, so that the night's soaking, and the washing tide, might, with ease, dissolve the vegetable glue. Then filed the oars and filled the indentations up with seeming substance, so that a vigorous strain would break each short. And next I artfully displaced a forward plank on which the coming navigator must set his foot when he stepped forward to draw in the baited line, or furl the latine sail. All these villanies, —for I have no pride in misapplying names,— had been of little use could my companion swim —though then the risk over such a space of water had been great; but he was as lead in the buoyant element, and would sink resistless like a stone. This fact was known to me, for I had saved him once before at the imminent jeopardy of my life; and the huge fool was grateful; and I do think upon his native earth that Lopez would have died for me,—and perhaps I would for him, had not the blasting gold stepped in to damn me.

"When I landed he reproached me for my long delay, for he was mad to talk about what he would do, and the bright schemes he had plotted to enact in Spain; and like a child full of the promised treat, could think or speak of nothing else. I told him what bad luck I'd had, took out a solitary fish, and wished him more success to-morrow. We made a scanty meal, and laid us down to sleep, and when the morning broke, we went at once and trimmed the boat, and made her taut for use. There was a curling breeze upon the water, and I helped to hoist the matting-sail, that he might take advantage of the wind to reach the middle stream before the sun was high to scare the finny prey, and as he left, I bade him not to stay, but be content with the first haul—and with a benison of God speed him, I saw him off.

"The freshening breeze caught the expanded sail, and the frail boat shot like a bolt from the small creek, and severed the limpid wave in her fast passage. I watched the lessening bark with every faculty of my soul, and when she distanced to a speck, my eyes, as if with telescopic power, could note each action of my condemned and fated comrade minutely, but distinct, and could perceive him with a hollow

A. MILES

gourd bailing out the fast making water, that through her sievy bottom, I felt, was pouring into the devoted vessel. Presently the sail was furled, and I beheld him make a bound forward to secure the fluttering sheet, and disappear; the plank had sunk beneath his feet, he rose again—seized the oars, and bending his broad chest, swept them through the water. The boat obeyed the sudden impulse, and turned its head to shore, but as he strained in the repeated strokes, the treacherous sculls broke in his hands;—and then a cry of horror, wild and shrill, rose from the river, as the encroaching tide climbed up the gunwale, and flowed over the low thwarts. I saw it all; each circumstance was magnified before my view as on a wall; the magic glass cast atoms big as mountains! I stood and viewed his wild dispair; saw his extended arms, and watched the rising water cover his chest, his head, his clasped and elevated hands, as in a vortex sinking down, the opening river swallowed all, sucking the freighted bark down to its oozy bottom, and leaving the smiling stream unconscious of a crime so black, so damned, and heartless! So deeply was I absorbed in the tragic picture that passed before my eyes, that mechanically, and unknowing to my mind, my body re-acted, from a sympathetic power, each action of the sinking man, following with strange precision every movement of my far-off comrade: now pulling down the sail with desperate haste, then springing back as my imagined foot sunk through the treacherous trap, and clinging hard, with frantic gripe, to the frail gunwale; then, madly seizing on the fancied oars, opened my chest, and strained my arms in vigorous strokes, propelling vainly on through the obstructing wave the foundering skiff, till, as she sank, I clasped my hands, and acted to the life the burst of agonised

4

dispair that floated to the bank from my beguiled and sinking friend: and when at length the sun shone tranquilly on the deserted stream, a copious, steaming sweat, rose on my flesh, bedewing all my shaking limbs, and my crisp hair, hung wet and straight down my blanched and ghastly cheeks, while terror, wild, unutterable, held me mute and spell-bound to the spot,—each sense merged, and my whole soul centred in my red and straining eyes!"

Garcia paused suddenly in his narrative, and drew his breath hard, as his bosom heaved and his thin, white lips quivered under the agitation of the remembered scene, that seemed indelibly fixed, brand-like, upon his brain. His fingers worked, and a convulsive starting of the fibres of his limbs, with a quick tremour of the bushy brows and pendant eyelids, gave to his working features a wild and horrible reality to the picture he had just described. After a moment's terrible indecision, that seemed to shake his very soul, Garcia gave a loud, hoarse laugh, and rubbing his damp head and bedewed face in the coarse serge of his friar's gown, cried with a harsh, grating voice, as he sprang forward to the table,—

"Some wine! my lord, some wine,—hot, drenching, memory-killing wine!" and seizing the large gold mounted stoup, placed the flagon to his parched mouth, and drank deep potations of the inspiring juice; then setting down the nearly emptied measure, exclaimed with a vulgar, brutal laugh,—

"Ha! ha! ha! ha! Ho! ho! Thou art the true elysium—life's nectar—memory's bane,—and only antidote to coward conscience! Ho! ho! Potent elixir! Well might man deify thy maker! Excellent invention! The true temperer of earth to heaven! Ha! 'tis good! 'tis good! Try it, my lord—drink my noble master—drink, and strangle recollection!"

Almazuma had sat erect, in his carved chair, in solemn stateliness, listening with unmoved feature, and a steady prescient eye, to every syllable of his creature's tale, never by an averted look, or action trivial, showing a loss of interest in the depravity of the tale he heard; and though he noted each particular, and his retentive mind took cognizance of every fact; he read the while, with artful skill, each subtlety and phase of the dark villain's character; deciphering familiarly his closest thoughts, and the yet unborn conceptions of his mind, and all the latent passions of his degraded, desperate helpmate.

"Do you repent you of your evil course?" inquired Almazuma, after a brief pause, and waving back the proffered goblet Garcia offered him. "Is your conscience still so prudish and effeminate as to blench at the mere recital of a tale of guilt? What! is thy soul so sensitive as to rear and plunge at the blunt spur of a stale memory? Do *you* repent?" cried Almazuma, in a cold, sarcastic strain of irony, to which his steady, placid smile gave all the edge of sharp contempt.

"Do I repent?" replied Garcia, almost fiercely. "No! it were a mockery to think so. The barren rock, the arid sand, can yield no fruit for sustenance, nor man's obdurate heart bring forth the blossomings of grace. No! 'tis not remorse that moves me: I am too much villain o repent—too hell-dyed to reform; but there's

a weeping fear comes over me at times, such as you witnessed now,—an agony of the mind, not personal or allied to the alarm of conscience, but a perturbing of the soul,—a delirious horror at my anticipated death;—for I have mysterious, strange surmises as to the process of my end; —nay, smile not, senhor,—I have a most revolting fear that I shall linger in my dying,—and then the frightful pictures that would rise before my glazing eyes of deeds committed, outrages achieved, that, on my soul! as I am a man, Don Ferdinand, the hideous horror of a reflecting and procrastinated death, fills we with wild alarm, and makes my matted hair stand bristling with dismay! No, no, no!—heaven avert that dread catastrophe, and let me die a sudden and immediate death. I care not how exquisite the expiring soul is racked with mortal sufferance, so that there be no lapse or pause for the busy, haunting, and convicting mind to frenzy me with buried and committed crimes;—for, oh! my God! it is a fearful thing to look into departed time; review our ruined hopes; scan o'er the recollections of our buoyant youth, and trace the passage of our life through all its devious ways, to the abrupt declivity of that devouring gulf that laves the shores of life and death. But how much more terrible that retrospect which tracks in every feature of its savage course, dark and consuming guilt, when on the recording page no generous deed, no hallowing tear, no virtuous act, stands registered to break the sheer damnation of the yawning hell that gapes for us beneath. Oh! this is terrible! 'Tis this affrights me. And Lopez's death e'en now awoke the dormant terror. Heavier guilt than his lies on my black heart; but his, by ever waking in my mind the fear I have of some dark lingering fate, unmans me more than my accumulated crimes, heaped tenfold on my head!"

"Question the wine again, and test its potency,—'twill sacrifice the latest scruple—try!" replied Almazuma, as he pointed to the other stoup of wine.

"No more, my lord, no more;—the qualm has left me,—I'll drink no more! Come, let me make a finish of my tale:—

"'Twere needless to recount the hourly jeopardy and the daily fear my ill-got wealth occasioned me; nor tread again the weary steps of my long pilgrimage,—the quick disguise—the cunning lie—the acts of turpitude and guilt, that tracked my lengthened travel through that drear wilderness of scorching plains, or benumbing frosts of ice-clad mountains, threading my painful way by the sun's light, or the north star to guide my lonely wanderings; exhorting my exhausted mule, that, fainting under my heaped treasure, filled me with ceaseless apprehensions for his enduring strength. At length, after six months of hard, incessant journeying, I saw beneath my feet the two vast oceans, washing on either hand that thread and span of earth, that seems in mockery to part their infinite embrace. I saw, but did not mark the glorious scene, nor the golden coloured sun, that bathed the grand Pacific as if in a flood of fire: my speculating sight but measured the vast leagues that parted me from happiness. I reached Panama, and on board a well-defended galleon (for the English were abroad like wasps to sting and rifle us, thrusting their adventurous prows wherever danger prowled or booty lurked) placed myself and seeming merchandise, and with a flowing sheet, and gladsome heart, bade a last farewell to the new world,—and in three months more anchored our brigantine in the bay of sunny, pleasant Cadiz.

"From Andalusia I soon set out for the gay capital; bought me a splendid mansion; filled it with useless lackeys, gorgeously trimmed; assumed another name; wrote Don upon my character; and let the world salute me Don Garcia De Rimero, and took a place with the nobility of nature; opened my house to all the profligacy of the town, and stood the foremost in Madrid for sensuality and riot. And with the splendour I begat and mingled in, a newer passion warmed in my unsated heart, which libertines call love, and women gallantry; but, with juster speech, plain-tongued honesty calls lust and debauchery.

"And this new impulse grew an insatiable disease, and mounted upwards till it pervaded all my frame, and formed my ruling passion, the guide and action of my fiery soul, the living appetite to my sensual will! And I would lavish wealth in fortunes, to compass my desire, and crown my conquests with success. And with a liberal purse, cunning, deceit, and treachery, with ready tools to back my profligate ambition, you need not marvel that my success was great; but like all my ignorant and headstrong passions, vulgar in conception, selfish in practice, it had its ebb and flow, and bloodily was the period written of that fierce fire. Mark you the episode, Don Almazuma.

"It was on a day in June,—for each circumstance of that event is stamped indelibly on my mind;—high in the sky the sun shone gloriously, earth smiled blushingly beautiful before the warm salute of heaven, and the dull earth, that day, seemed paradise. I was alone, slow pacing over the Prado, musing on my last achievement —a maiden ripe and beautiful—my houri Beatrice,—when chance, or fate, or that inscrutable decree that mocks all reason, threw upon my gaze a form so exquisite in mould and grace, and such transcendent charms, that I—the hard hypocrite, the unblushing libertine,—I stood abashed—amazed—at the excelling beauty; while full upon my view she cast those dazzling orbs, whose soft, yet speaking fire, seemed instinct with the soul of love. It was but an instant that we encountered looks, but one moment's space, that prelude to so much woe, ere in the deep folds of her mantilla she concealed those beaming eyes that had been life to gaze on, and veiled those suns that were my light and hope. From that moment all vulgar passion, all divided feeling, quitted my breast,—even my lately prized and conquered Beatrice was banished from her throne, and an undivided sentiment usurped the seat of my promiscuous loves. She passed,—that ravishing perfection, —that earth's angel left me, while I, fired with gross purpose, ungoverned by remorse, followed and following, vowed to achieve, and plotted to possess the peerless excellence!

"Who heeds the devious way or rugged path when on the hill of high expectancy he first sets foot triumphant? No matter how or what great dangers hedged the road to the accomplishment of my desire. We met,—ay, often met! Her heart was mine, indissolubly mine!—it poured forth in the first gush of maiden confidence and truth, pure, devoted, holy love. But what had I to do with hearts or love? That soft effeminacy was to me unknown. My love was a resistless wave of whelming, burning passion,—fierce as destructive; her's, the soft, devoted, clinging excellence, that worships where it loves, making a demi-god of the black heart of man!

"At first my rude and eager gaze, and fervent kiss, abashed the maid; but when more clear my words attested all my soul, she fled in terror from my polluting touch, evading all pursuit, excluding all redress, and left me foaming, furious, maddened in my disappointed rage.

"Days, weeks, months flew by;—a year elapsed. Theresea's form no more rejoiced my sight! Though in my breast my feelings grew in fury with my thwarted hopes, yet day and night around the mansion of her sire I kept unwearied watch—unbroken vigilance. The purchased and obsequious tool, the foul duenna, through whose ministry was planned our secret meetings, met me no more. Enraged at my defeat where I had sworn to win, I rashly scaled the garden wall, and aided by the branching sycamores that lined the wide enclosure, leaped fearlessly on the excluded ground. Scarcely had my foot touched the forbidden sward, when a hand firmly, but lightly, touched my arm, and an imperious voice cried, 'Follow me!' Turning with indignant look, I perceived the speaker moving rapidly from the ground. A long mantle enveloped his person, while his plumed hat was drawn down purposely over his eyes to conceal his features from my view. His mien was proud and noble, and he strode forward under the embowering trees, without deigning even to cast a look to observe whether I had obeyed his imperious mandate. Stung by his haughty bearing, and smarting under the implied censure of his tone, I eagerly followed my proud guide as he glided before me down the deep glades and vistas of the perfumed orange and myrtle, till, entering an open and retired space at the extremity of the princely domain, my mysterious companion disengaged himself of his hat and mantle, and, drawing his sword, turned suddenly into the moonlight and confronted me.

"I started back as the full refulgence of the night revealed to me the features of Theresea's brother, the heir to old Medina's dukedom.

"'Draw, base villain!' exclaimed Don Jose, with a disdainful wave of his sword. 'You have disgraced a noble house, and though the hangman's scourge were fitter than the blade of a nobleman to give thee chastisement, yet will I allow the degradation for the satisfaction of ridding the profaned earth of thy polluting presence. Come on!'

"'Willingly!' I replied, unsheathing my rapier, and half-choking with the indignity of his taunting words. 'Have at you, presumptuous boy! Thus, thus I pay thy officious tongue and damned intrusion!—thus, and thus!— and this—this be thy passport to the court of hell! This through thy heart!' The fight was brief, so fierce and sudden was my assault, so rapid every lounge that his defenceless breast lay open to my sword; and as I taunted him with every pass, I drove my weapon through the flesh and bone—through heart and spine, till my broad hilt rang sharp and hollow on his ribs. Life fled from his gaping breast, and, staggering back, without a groan or sigh, the youthful noble fell dead at my feet, covering my light hose with his spouting gore!

"Scarce was the deed performed when the tramp of feet, and the loud clamour of approaching tongues, warned me of danger,—and the furious father, with his armed myrmidons, rushed in the open space, as with a bound I leaped into the shade, and sought the shelter of the concealing wood; climbed the tall trees, and baffled in the purpose of my hope, leaped downwards from the high and dangerous wall. The cry was up, the hot pursuit begun. No time had I for lingering doubt. Life all depended on my speed. Homeward I bent my steps, and made such hasty disposition of my wealth as space permitted, then fled, and long ere morning broke, had placed a dozen leagues betwixt Madrid and me.

"I passed a year, a weary year, in bootless travel,—for my mind and passion still was wedded to the only object that had yet had power to bind my unstable fancy,—and I returned, driven and urged by destiny, to fill the measure of my deep damnation to the brim.

"It chanced, one day, that as I crossed the Prado, I was an unmarked listener to the conversation of a monk and woman; and as the voice of one sounded familiar to my ears, I drew me near to catch each particular of the muttered revelation; and then I heard that which a thousand daggers in my heart could not have made me feel so keen; I heard, the object of my love had taken the veil, and that the monk before me was the confessor of her strict nunnery, and the woman my former confidant, the old duenna. I followed them until they parted: she to the duke, to tell how wept the nun, how mourned some hidden sorrow, not even to mother church revealed;—he, to his college, whither I too now bent my exulting steps. As a heart-sick penitent, a life-weary sinner, I gained admission to the holy man,—be sure I was not tongue-tied;—cunning and damned hypocrisy was never gifted with such eloquence as I grew master of. My sins,—for I wept abundant tears of sharp contrition, and implored acceptance of my hated gold,—were soon forgiven, and, with each yellow ducat dropped, I was escorted higher up heaven's steep pathway. But why recount the easy conquest of a sensual monk! By deepest show of penitence, and weighty largesse to his house, I gained at length the wily Jesuit's belief and pity; won day by day upon his heart—if such a thing had heart, and by that key,—infallible, red, life-corrupting gold, I opened all the labyrinths of his dark mind, and traced the foul soul of this most saintly priest.

"Slowly I broke my purpose to him, veiled in the sophistry and deceit of his own school, each wish weighed, every project balanced with the bulky, soul destroying ore; and as I piled my barred ingots in his eye, the pitying monk wept for my errors, censured my love, but found counsel for my hopes! It were dull here to record each circumstance or step that led to the full accomplishment of my now pregnant purpose;—suffice it then to say, that he supplied me with a master-key to all the gates, dressed me in the grey frock and ample hood of his most austere and pliant order; made known to me each particular that lends an evidence to the priestly trade; and every point revealed to guide my doubtful steps. So armed, I passed the frowning and forbidding portals of the gloomy convent, ostensibly to visit a sick sister, under the specious plea that Father Philip was on a holy mission sent to Rome——"

"It was an excellent device," observed Almazuma, with his cold forbidding smile. "A choice expedient! How fared your mission?"

"You shall hear," resumed the confederate, and judge if I am wrong in deeming priestcraft my next best occupation. Methinks I played the whining, begging monk not badly yesterday;—but to resume: I reached in safety the long, low passage, where, on either hand, the close, damp cells branch off, where, shrouded as in a living tomb, the lovely sisterhood reposed! I found, and quickly shrived the meagre, sallow maid, whose feeling nipped in life's warm spring, had in revulsion fixed and curdled in her heart, stopping the healthy current of its stream, and clogging up the fountains of fresh life. Well, I shrived her, heaven knows how well! and purposely delayed the time till all the house had sought their beds, and silence dwelt a painful void upon the ear; then, with a benedicite and muttered prayer, I left this uncongenial cell, and bent my noiseless steps to my Theresea's couch. 'Twas easy to be found, for her dark crypt, stood last in that dim vault. Softly, and with a heaving breast, I undid the latch, and stole silently to where the shadow from a small lamp fell thick as night.

"There, innocently voluptuous, that white form and undulating bosom reposed upon a couch lowly and scant, contrasting hideously with her excessive beauty, as in the deep embrace of guileless sleep the spotless maiden lay in holy peace and blest security. Time, place, and circumstances so apt,—the danger half o'ercome, could man look there, upon that soft and palpitating loveliness, and not desire to gaze eternally,—or quit, untasted, all those beauties inviting spread to woo him to perdition? No! I was a man, and had I even, Don Ferdinand, been less, the sight I there beheld had roused me to overleap damnation for such a prize.

"As the hawk that swoops upon his prey,—all prudence merged in the close won quarry, I flung myself with boisterous force upon the sleeping maid, rudely rifling from her soft, full lips, eager and sensual kisses. Alarmed in horror, she awoke, and screamed but faintly,—for at first she seemed to dream, though native modesty, instinctive in her fear, prompted the act that drew the white limar more closely round the neck and crimsoning breast it had so late revealed. Anon, with misty and unsteady gaze, her eye vaguely perused my garb and lineaments, as if her reason and her fears in doubt conflicted,—then with a look as consciousness grew strong,—a look that petrified me with amaze to read the terror in her eye, she gave a smothered cry, and clasping both her hands, exclaimed, 'Blessed Maria! it was no dream—'Tis he!'

"Instant from my person I tore the hateful symbol of the monk, and stood confessed in the full affluence of my assumed and princely garb.

"'Ay, Theresea! it is I!' I exclaimed, approaching with extended arms, as she, with wild alarm, shrunk my polluting touch. ''Tis I, come to snatch thee from this living death—this stifling grave. Arise! and fly with me, my love! my life! my everlasting joy!'

"'Never!' she cried, indignantly. 'Hence, monster! and quit my sight; or, by my cries, I'll raise the sisterhood for help, and give thee to the inexorable judge of Holy Office, for thy profanity!'

"'Hear me, rash woman!' I replied, in a deep, low whisper: 'if you articulate a breath so loud as but to start the lizard from its slimy bed, by all the saints you hold as true, that moment you shall die! Mine you are—mine you shall be! Together we will quit this hateful gloom, and seek beneath other skies for mutual peace and measureless content!'

"'Away! Tempter begone!' she cried; then in a voice low and tremulous, as former love woke in her heart, she softly said, ' swear to me on yon blessed sign that thou wilt——' but here her tears opposed the further current of her speech; and I, with my quick words, barred all after progress of her tongue, and vowed by every sign to swear by all the oaths ere registered in heaven or sealed in hell, to pledge myself to aught;—but first I'd win the treasure that had cost so much to gain!

"'Mercy! mercy!' shrieked the terrified nun, as she buried her shrinking form beneath the meagre covering of her coarse pallet.

"'Mark me, Theresea,' I cried in a subdued and angry voice, as laying my rude hand on her sweet mouth, I continued in accents severe and deep, 'no power, earthly or divine, shall step between me and my purposed will. I hold the master-key to all the gates; my horse is saddled, waiting my return; my flight is safe and certain,—yield then at once, or by that Madonna to whom you supplicate, my dagger ends that life you value less than the weak bauble—honour! Hear then my sworn resolve, —for not thy heaven of saints——' I paused, and lifted up my hand from her compressed lips; for a distant shout rolled its swelling tumult even to that dark vault, while the deep convent bell rang out a peal of terrible alarm. Theresea marked my trepidation, and from her freed mouth poured forth loud and piercing shrieks and cries for help;—while, down the vaulted passage, I could hear the rushing feet of armed and hasty men. Enraged, frantic, heedless of all but quick escape and life, and furious at her still directing cries, and delirious at my baffled hopes, I drove my dagger in her heart, and, turning, fled, as her expiring groans rang in my ears!

"The danger was too imminent to pause. I drew my sword, and rousing every nerve to action, sprang to the passage. The upper end was filled with troops, each with a lighted torch waving above his head. I fled; and they pursued. Before me lay the wicket whose master-key was in my hand,—instant I turned the lock —damnation!—the door was chained and bolted from without. Shouts and exulting laughter burst from my foes, as, foiled in my attempt, I dashed the instrument to the earth, and turned to bay.

"'Perdition! death and hell! I was betrayed —trapped, taken in the mesh wove by myself —and by a priest,—a damned and wily monk! I cursed my confiding folly, gnashed my teeth in impotent rage, and beat the damp pavement with my impatient foot. My enemies were within six paces of my sword as I turned frowningly to confront them; when, at that moment, I perceived by their many lights, a low winding passage that branched suddenly to my right, and plunging down, fled through the long vault. Winding the mazy labyrinth—now down—now up; climbing the mouldering stairs, as the irregular gallery traversed the uneven base of the monastic pile, I thought the devious corridor would never end, and that I should fall without one blow, or a dead enemy to bear me company to the grim ferryman, for there was scarcely space to move in the close confines that I traversed with my utmost speed, groping my dark way. At length I reached a low arched door that barred all further progress. Urged to desperation by the sound of my pursuers' feet, that sounded clamorously behind, I dashed all my strength, by despair made herculean, upon the iron studded door; and as my foes approached within a dozen feet of my person, the shivered lock burst beneath my violence, and I rushed through the low wicket as they reached its broken threshold!

"Small time had I to note, or much observe, the seeming shelter I had gained; yet by a pale light that hung beneath the Virgin's shrine, casting a sickly hue, and making darkness almost palpable; and, anon, the bright stream of fifty torches held in the eager hands of the incensed mob, showed to my quick eye the convent chapel, lighted as by a stormy sunset, or the red glow of the eruptive lava. Down aisle and transept, chancel and corridor,—behind, before, on every hand, the gathering enemy poured threatening in, and with their loud exulting cries and thundering tramp, shook in their hollow tombs the bony dead! Far up the space the lofty altar peered through the ruddy shade majestically grand and indistinct. That sanctuary that to me could lend no aid! One look of hesitating doubt I cast around, such as the panting hare flings on the chase when the hounds' hot breath fans his erected fur; then, as rose high the cry of—'Yield! Secure the sacrilegious wretch!'—I bounded forward with a yell of loud defiance, right through their obstructing swords, and with a spring like the hunted deer, cleared the high altar-rail, while up its marble steps my clanging feet sounded profanely dissonant. 'In the Holy Inquisition's name yield, thou accursed heretic!' shouted the foremost of the grim familiars. Another leap placed me aloft upon the table of the sacrifice!

"A peal of horror burst from every breast at a sacrilege so full of shame and dread; and gathering like an enraged sea, their tide of anger rolled around me fast and menacing. With an insulting laugh I mocked their senseless horror, and, turning, dashed my sword through the painted oriel, showering, like

December hail, the rich emblazoned glass, till through the apostolic casement my destructive weapon had hewn an ample passage,—then, with a wild demoniac shout, plunged headlong through the gap! The fall was high, and for a moment I lay stunned and quivering on the hard pavement of the court: but little hope as yet was mine. Before me stood the outward gate, its space and access filled with turbulent and frantic foes, armed to the teeth, while foremost of the troops, and waving, comet-like, a burning torch above his head, a monk led on the band. I knew him at a glance,—his cowl was black, and his red eyes were fixed on me. It was the damned traitor to his word—my double-dyed and cursed betrayer! Confident, the plotting priest pressed forward, shouting with glee, 'Save him for the flames! Strike not, but spare the church's victim! Bind the wretch! —bind him!'

"In a moment I was on my feet, and as the hoary friar drew near, I wrenched the torch out of his nerveless hand, and dashed the pitchy fire across his blear and watery eyes,—and twice, thrice, passed my long rapier through his heart.

"Quicker than thought the deed was done; and as the foremost troopers gathered round, I hurled the lighted missle at their heads, and with my trusty sword, hewed, cut, dashed a bleeding pathway through their ranks, and half-fainting, half-distracted, fled, while after came the united foe, fast, fierce, and howling! Spent with my toil, panting for lack of breath, I reached my horse, and urging him with my sword to his utmost power, tore through the city gates, and gained, untracked, the sheltering country.

"League after league my fiery steed flew by. Night's gloomy shadows past, and gorgeous day broke loose again, filling the earth with sunshine; yet still untamed and furious went on my gallant horse. Suddenly he reared and plunged, scared by some white object laying at his feet. With hand and rein I urged him on; —backward he drove, trampling the impediment that scared him, when a child's faint cry rose loud and sharp, as, crushed and bleeding, it expired under my horse's hoofs. At that cry, so shrill and touching, a female form sprang from a copse, where in a spring she had been laving her parched lips, and with a shriek wild and unearthly piercing, rushed forth. I turned and gazed. Perdition! Hell! Senhor,—'twas Beatrice,—she who once had been my soul's idol. Shriek followed shriek in splitting cadence as she rushed on. The blood, gushing from her bursting heart, flowed over her pallid lips, as with out-stretched arms, and a reproachful look to heaven, she fell dead—dead! my lord, on the mangled body of her child!

"All hell seemed burning in my heart, and madness in my brain. The clouds shook with their thunder; lightnings flashed; earth reeled, and nature, to my fancy, shuddered! Oh God! God! Almighty God! that moment was eternity of woe! Damnation hath no equal to that drop of agony! Striking my horse with my clenched fist, I made him bound in mad career from the revolting scene! That infant's face still haunts my mind. My features there were writ, but in a character so soft in innocence,—such as we deem mankind assume in heaven,—that I can never lose their image,—never forget! I fled, and in the deepest wilds of the inhospitable Pyrenees hid my proscribed and murderous head. I was once more a beggar, powerless, impotent. The familiars of the Holy Office seized my effects, razed to the earth my gorgeous house, and rioted in the abundance of my pillaged coffers. A price was set upon my head; a fierce denouncement on my borrowed name; and to the hand that rid the world of such a dreaded wretch as I, remitted sins and special absolution was to reward the deed that cut me off.

"Life grew hateful to me. My mind, long used to excitement, grew weak, and my imagination foolish, under the rigorous solitude of my new existence; and, at times, even the Inquisition seemed preferable to my dull retreat and uncongenial cave; for I became a beast, and shared the prey of the wild wolf, and disputed with him for a den. At length I fell upon the track of a horde of French and German gipsies, who, driven from their long permitted country, had crossed the Pyrenees, in the hope to find in Spain a shelter for their persecuted and proscribed existence.

"A few pieces of coin I had about me, purchased admission, and a garb to their fraternity, with shelter and protection in my hour of need. With them I lived a tranquil and reflective life; and innocent compared to the fierce career through which I had lately passed. My vices now were small—mere paltry acts of theft, with just sufficient hazard to give a zest to plunder, and keep my acquisitive mind in play; but in my leisure hours,—and, certes, I had plenty,—I bent the natural talent of my wayward fancy to pursuits of more congenial, philosophic ends,—such as you found me busied in, and we have brought to such perfection down below. And when I took your service, I made a vow, without one reservation, to deal honestly in your work; for you promised well, and have performed more than you promised;—and I'll not deny that these doubloons you give so frely—as they will hereafter give me food for life—gave me new life to work for food. But come, my lord, I'll to my couch, the night grows dark; I've told you all my history that's worth recounting. I'm tired, and wish you, senhor, a fair good night!—good eve!—and pleasant dreams attend your sleep: adieu!"

So saying, Garcia bowed with more respect than might have been expected from the familiarity of his conversation, and the rough nature of his habits, and retired to the small oratory, leaving Almazuma still seated at the table, in the same attitude which he had preserved througout the lengthened story. A slight inclination of his haughty head, as his accomplice retired, was the only indication of courtesy that unbent the stern lord, or acknowledgement to his menial's good night; but when the last sound of his retiring feet, and the locked door informed his practised ear that Garcia had reached and secured his chamber, a change came over Almazuma's manner, and his features relaxed into a ghastly and forbidding smile, as he rose from his chair, and strode, with folded arms, across the gloomy and high arched apartment in which the solitary and now lighted lamp cast, from the scanty furniture and grotesque chairs, dim and lengthened shadows over the oak floor, giving a dungeon-like character and sombre gloom to the spacious chamber. And as the stately lord paced the vaulted room in moody silence, the picture became truthfully perfect, as he exemplified in person the caged and condemned captive of the lonely prison, striding his confined limits in bitter meditation.

"Yes!" he at length soliloquised in a subdued, complacent tone ; "yes, I am not deceived, nor have I studied these many years in vain, that dark and cunning book, that abstract of all passions, that printed volume of the heart,— man's legible face!—that title page of each life's history! 'Show me his company, and I will tell the man,' so says the wisdom adage ; but let me look upon the face, and I will read you out the soul, even to its subtlest workings. No! I am not deceived. This Garcia may be trusted for the time, but not an hour beyond. Poor fool! he little thinks I hold him in a leash, that would hurl him down, quick as the vaulted lasso, did he but make one motion to betray my compelled and needed confidence. How far was he from deeming the personality and justness of his own remark,—soul-corrupting gold? Yes, he shall feed his greedy eyes, and satisfy his hungry appetite, with the hard metal, to repletion ; he shall have his idol, till satiety is sick with feasting ; but never shall his hoard pass the boundary of these three ribbed walls,— no ; he shall riot in anticipated freedom, while every hour around his neck the tether tightens and contracts. Poor, deluded fool! I have bought him soul and body! Were not my high name's safety in the question, I might find it in my heart to let the wretch escape, and load him with substantial favours, for the consummate excellence of his work ; but no, I must not hazard one hair of my proud head by playing now the part of generous dolt. That were a folly unfit my boasted wisdom. Pshaw! what is his paltry life? No, no ; the man is only safe beneath my watchful eye. My sense o'ermates and fascinates his own ; he quails and shrinks under my cognizance ; and in my confirmed and basilisk gaze, I hold the key and magnet of his soul: he feels it—and I must keep the influence up till—ay! till the last! 'Tis strange that his presentiment of death and my resolve should jump so much together! Well, he needs time for penitence—much time;— and he shall have it—yes! he shall have time. What a blessing's ignorance! Would he had worked so well had he known all? I question not. Why, 'tis a grand idea: his own grave and fabricated coffin! And he can sleep, and jest, and laugh, while in my will his life is shrunk to days and numbered minutes. Well, 'tis destiny rules all. But stay,—to morrow I begin my part, make my first entrance on that stage where I shall win the completion of my long digested scheme. Yes, the time and tide is now arrived that bears me on with flowing sail to the accomplishment of my revenge— my great revenge! Let me to bed, to dream of my felicity."

And, taking up the lamp, Almazuma passed out of the chamber, securing the door behind him, and wending his way along the corridor, sought, in the opposite wing of the castle, the apartment that had been fitted up for his use.

CHAPTER VI.

"I HAVE brought you here, my friend, to this pleached grove, whose odorous perfume and rich fruit, ripe for the fall, shadows, in fancy's eye, my coming bliss and mellow happiness;—I have brought you here, where, from the haunts and ears of men, away from stirring life, I may, true lover like, pour into thy friendly ear all the wild tumults of my heart; make thee a partner of all the imagery that love, ever profuse in fancy as in words, moves in my expanding breast and joy-delighting soul,—here, my Almazuma, ere I present thee to my beauteous bride, to give thee all a friend's deserts, the life and history of my love. Thou art too staid, grave, and profound in knowledge, I know, my Ferdinand, to waste, as thou would'st deem it, precious hours or moments in the soft caressings of a mutual flame. Thy thoughts stray not to female excellence, and thy heart is barred to the allurements of the sex, and shut to all capacities but noble, generous friendship, and the philosophy of minds, mighty, though dead. Thus, then, excluded from the temptation of soft love, thou wilt more readily become a patient auditor to the long pent unliberated thoughts of thy sworn brother and familiar friend: I know thou wilt not grudge me audience."

So spoke Don Alonzo, as, on the following day, agreeable to the intimation conveyed in the last chapter, Almazuma visited his friend at his temporary residence at the palace of Alfendera— the abode of his purposed bride,—and where now he walked arm in arm with him, down the long vistas of the orange groves, that, like minature forests, dotted in many places the vast and luxurious pleasure grounds, that in every direction encompassed the princely dwelling of the marquis.

Here, far away from observation, the happy lover and expectant bridegroom had drawn his friend, before presenting him formally to his bride, his father, or the large assembly that had been collected by Catalina's sire to honour and augment the coming ceremony, that he might expatiate to willing ears the never-tiring —never told perfections of his enamoured mistress.

And as the two hidalgo's strayed slowly along the embowered pathway, an observant eye could not have failed to have marked the singular contrast in form, feature, mien, and feeling of the two nobles. Almazuma, tall, stately, haughty, and cold, kept on an even measured tread, and from the dullest detail, to the most impassioned burst of his friend's enthusiasm, showed no change of temperament, no efflux of feeling; on the other hand, Alonzo, gallant, graceful, pliant, with features radiant with happiness, and his frame quivering with animation, leaning on Almazuma's arm, now with eager glance looking in his face for confirmation of his speech, or approbation to his thoughts, or, with free, unchecked movement of his arm, giving an emphasis or sprightly dignity to what he said; then, pausing in his exuberant haste to meet the measured paces of his friend, as his excited thoughts ever and anon urged him before the regulated steps of the unmoved Almazuma,—thus, as they strayed through the cool sequestered labyrinths of rich Pomona's temple, two more opposite characters, more opposed to each—than each, were never before bound in the professing chains of friendship.

"I know thou wilt be patient," continued Alonzo, as he bent forward on his companion's arm, and looked inquiringly in his face, "and, in my very tediousness, find measure of forgiveness—cause of extenuation. Say I do not tire thee? Say thou art not weary?"

"Go on," replied Almazuma, in his calm, unimpassioned voice.

"Oh! if you had seen my love," continued Alonzo, "you would have eyes, sense, soul, for nothing else. She as much surpasses and outstrips all competition, as the faint, transparent moon, seen on a summer's day, when the sun rides westward, is cold and powerless to the gorgeous, vivifying king of heaven, when in his solstice eminent and unmatched."

"And does thy beauty own an equal transport? Does the same fire pervade her veins, that shoots such lightning through thine own? Can Catalina love?"

"Oh! treason to my friendship—treachery to my love to doubt it," replied Alonzo, eagerly. "I grant, my friend, that outwardly, and to common gaze, her port is cold, her manner most reserved; but as in snow there's warmth, in ice there's fire, so in her inmost heart a tide of living warmth, a spring of ample love, gushes and flows stronger and firmer for the formal barrier placed against its ebullition. Thou dost not know my Catalina."

"We have met," quietly observed Almazuma.

"Ha! they did not tell me that."

"Our acquaintance was most brief. Less than an hour would cover all the intercourse, and that, some space ago," resumed Almazuma.

"No matter," replied his friend, "I shall still have the pleasure to present you, and I will teach her noble heart to love you as a brother."

"That were too much happiness. No! yet, possibly, she may learn in time not totally to hate me," observed Don Ferdinand. "I will study to deserve her approbation."

"Be sure I will bespeak it for you. My friend must be, as myself, my wife's regard, and mine."

"I do not doubt but time, that great worker of events, will bring us more acquainted, when she will know me most thoroughly. Indeed, I wish it from my heart. I have a craving hope that she, in time, may know all my kind feelings for her; for in the brief glimpse I once enjoyed of your fair mistress, I saw enough to wake a powerful interest in her behalf. But who have we here?" inquired Almazuma, as the figure of a man crossed the open glade, and, doffing his hat, approached respectfully the spot where the two nobles waited his coming.

"Oh! I remember," exclaimed Alonzo, as the individual drew nearer. "'Tis a new servitor of mine, who joined me yesterday; a fellow of most uncommon skill and shrewdness. I never was so well attended. I have given him precedence of all my menials:—the man's a prize. How now, De Vega," cried the young nobleman, as his servant stood aside to let him pass; "what is it?"

"My lord, in his great speed to dress and hasten hither, omitted to wear his sword, and I have brought it to rectify my own neglect," replied the servant, presenting the crimson sheathed and gold handed weapon.

"Ay! my sword,—true; 'tis of no consequence—it matters not. Nay, I'll put it on. I must be full equipped, or my bride's father will think his honour is at stake. Give it me! So!" and taking the long, strait, and formidable rapier from his attendant's hands, threw the jewelled and embroidered belt across his neck, and fastening it with a diamond buckle to the bosom of his doublet, adjusted the sword to his side. "Look you, De Vega, I have lost a glove; can'st thou find it?"

"It was not in your chamber, senhor," replied the man, whom for the present we shall continue to call De Vega, as he looked up, and for an instant fixed his eye on the countenance of Almazuma with a casual, and to the uninitiated, a meaningless and idle glance. The action was brief as thought, but in its momentary survey, expressed a lengthened sentence. The most trivial elevation of the eyelids was the only reply made by Almazuma to the quick, expressive look the other cast upon him, that an observer might have thought it was more the result of surprise, that a menial should have lifted his gaze so high, than the secret telegraph of some dark plot.

"Find me another pair, good Vega. And, hark thee! a word of preparation;" and stepping aside for a moment, Alonzo conversed in secret with his servant, giving him some directions regarding his friend's accommodation. Almazuma took a few steps in advance, while a pleased, faint smile seemed to brighten in his eye and deepen the angles of his mouth, as he half whispered to himself.

"He is worth his weight in specie! It is begun; yes, I feel it is begun. The first link is dropped on which, loop by loop, slowly, but surely, I will hang and forge a chain, so strong and fettering in conclusion, that it shall manacle her very soul. Oh! I begin to breathe and live. Admirable fellow! Yes, I may trust him. He has dropped the glove where 'tis red shame to find it. Good, excellent Garcia! What a pity 'tis that thou must die! But I must—yes—I must crush him: thou will know too much, infinitely too much, to live! But I will have thy best services first; and when thou art worn dry, and my purposes achieved, I'll put my foot, and as I would a reptile, crush thee!" and as he finished his inaudible soliloquy, he placed his boot upon the ground with a firm pressure, and drew it suddenly backward along the gravelled walk, exclaiming aloud, "Yes,—crush thee!"

"Crush who?" inquired his friend, joining him, as the servant withdrew.

"Oh! 'twas a noxious vermin, that, if it lived, would hurt me;—nothing more," replied Almazuma, with a quick transition to his former even manner, as he took his friend's arm and passed down the avenue. De Vega bowed respectfully as they passed him, and stood at the mouth of a diverging alley, for a few moments watching, with apparent interest, the retreating figures as they gradually blended with the shade, and ultimately disappeared down one of the intersecting pathways.

"What a great master is that man! What

[DON GARCIA.]

consummate villany! and what a deep disguising face is Almazuma's?" observed the servant musingly, whom our readers have, no doubt, discovered to be no other than Garcia,—now ostensibly Alonzo's confidential valet, but in reality still the secret agent of Don Ferdinand, and his able abettor in all his yet unworked villanies.

"Yes—I watched him while all those feelings passed through his mind, and burst at last to that short pithy speech and most expressive gesture. Poor Don Alonzo! thou little deemest thou art the reptile that as yet he only crushed in fancy. Ay! hang upon him—tell him all thy thoughts—court thine own undoing. Poor fool! thou art the reptile—thou the deaf adder—thou the dangerous snake that stings his peace, and yet huggest thy own destruction with all the innocent confidence of a believing maid, or the incredulous folly of the blind besotted lover. Ha! ha! ha!—what a genius hast thou, Almazuma!

I glory in serving thee—taking apt lessons from the wisdom of thy deceit. Why, thou could'st almost cheat me, fool my understanding, and lead me to my own damnation. But, no!—he has no object there, and knows I am too sharp a scholar in life's academy to be hoodwinked now in my very pride of manhood, when all the sap and strength of full existence animates the pregnant brain, and makes it quick and capable, opening all avenues to personal enjoyment, and barring all access with watchful guards against surprise or treachery. No! I am too heedful—too dangerous, to be practised on: and yet that silly lover can neither see, nor hear, or yet perceive the sure net that's wound around him; but as if time had no end, no limit to his enjoyment, revels in extravagant hope upon the very mine I hold the torch to fire—dreams of years to come, when his short span is lessened to a few mean days, told in a breath; and I shall live long summers to fatten on the gold his taking of secures me. 'T is I that should be jocund—and I am happy! And yet 't is a pity so gallant, comely, and so fine a youth, should be eclipsed so soon. But I have no choice—none, where self-interest pulls so hard. Then go thy ways, thou vermin, that may do harm. Ha! ha! ha! the image was not bad! Poor dolt! poor ass! Yes, yes—we'll crush—we'll crush you!—doubt it not—doubt it not!"—and with a slow exulting chuckle, Garcia turned, and pursuing an opposite direction, sought the palace, to put in practice the orders he had just received, as at the same moment Almazuma and Alonzo re-appeared through another opening, and again trod the more spacious and now deserted avenue that they had so lately quitted.

"Felix is too like myself," resumed Alonzo, as they drew nearer; "too intent at my fair sister's feet, to be a listener to my rapture. You have now heard all the first, the progress, and the confirming hour of my happy love: how I sued and won her unwooed hand; and what mettle, purpose, and resolve the expectation put into my arm in battle, that I might win a name, and bring an honourable title home, to grace and dignify my wife. And, by my honour, friend, I never felt such genial happiness, such warmth of honest pride, as when I yesterday placed in her hand this noble mark of honour; and when again she placed it on my neck, and said it well became my name and form. Not the august praises of my liege and sovereign, when he made me knight, and fixed it on my breast, were half so pleasing, near so estimable, as the brief words and kindly glance of my true heart's affianced love, when she returned the order of my knighthood;"—and lifting from his breast the jewelled badge of St. Jago, he pressed it with glowing fervour to his lips; then, looking up, exclaimed—

"Ha! here comes my honoured father and the Marquis: let us on and meet them. There's Felix, too. Ah! we shall meet a censure—they are come to upbraid my want of courtesy in not presenting thee before. Give you good day, worthy Senhors! I have played the truant sadly, and would with timely submission disarm your anger, and mitigate your condemnation," cried Alonzo, as the two venerable noblemen approached, followed a few steps behind by Felix; "but I had so much to say to my long-lost friend, and fellowship was so congenial, that I trust for pardon, having made a full acknowledgment of my error. My honoured father, let me present, next to the love I bear yourself, my bride, and sister—my dearest, truest friend —my long-tried collegiate, Don Ferdinand de Almazuma. To you, Lord Marquis, my adopted brother is already known. And now, companion in my arms, partner of my dangers, and almost brother, let me next pledge you to a share in that esteem I prize so highly: know him, my Felix; and, Almazuma, estimate him too." Each cavalier doffed his plumed bonnet, and bowed with graceful and dignified ease, as Don Alonzo in turn presented his friend to the Condé, Marquis, and Felix. Alfendera, alone, felt some diffidence. Almazuma was one, whom rather from prejudice than formal objection, he had omitted to invite during the solemnities. He had, too, been a former suitor for his daughter's hand, and delicacy had had a share in the omission; and he had not thought it needful to inform the bridegroom that such had been the case; but as young Alvares and Almazuma had been schoolfellows, the former could not permit his earliest friend to be debarred the pleasure of sharing in his happiness, and had solicited the Marquis to be allowed to invite him in his name to take up his abode at the palace till after the marriage; and he had consequently now arrived to swell the already ample retinue who now formed the household of the pleased and happy Marquis.

"Don Ferdinand will forgive the seeming negligence of so unformal an invitation; but his long absence, and our ignorance of his return, must plead as palliatives for not with courteous embassy begging the honour of his coming. 'T was only yesterday we had the happiness to hear our neighbourhood was graced by the restoration of its highest dignity, the Lord of Almazuma."

"But now we have you, fair Senhor," added the Condé Alvares, "I trust that we shall grow so well acquainted that we shall hold you in the best embrace of friendship, and that the knowledge made to-day will only end with life. As the companion of my dear Alonzo — as the friend of all this house, and as my own particular esteem, conjoined with all the rest, I hope my poor house may henceforth be made happier by the frequent visits of my son's dear friend and mine.*

"I will endeavour to deserve so great a pleasure, and make my life a study not to undo the high opinion you honour me withal. From the noble Marquis, apology is needless," replied Almazuma, bowing; "to the worthy Condé de Alvares, the words are not in use that can express my deep sense of his considerate kindness, as the worthy father of my noble friend: I owe no less than duty to make my will obey his pleasure."

"Too much for truth—too little for sincerity," mused Alfendera, as he bowed formally and turned to depart. "'T is strange I should not like this man — the Condé seems bewitched; why should I misgive him?—he may be truth: mankind has many crusts and outward shows repugnant to our sense or prejudice, and when known, and tested to the quick, show gallant qualities, and put our first-formed thoughts and the eyes' impression to the serious blush:—so may this man of stern and gloomy front harbour beneath that chilly mail a noble heart and warm affection. Alonzo has known him long, and should be ablest judge—true, he should."

"Come, Felix, by your leave," playfully observed the Condé, passing his arm through Almazuma's, and following the Marquis. "I'll first monopolise our new-made friend: it is the privilege of years you know; your younger bloods will find more time for mutual knowledge when our stiffer limbs and lagging energies find restoration in the cool siesta. I will for the present engross Don Ferdinand's attention,—that is, if the old man's chat is not too irksome to my worthy friend. What muse you on, my noble host?" he continued, addressing the Marquis; "see, the lovers are already in deep conference—shall we go?"

"I was thinking," replied Alfendera, "that

the longer stay from our fair charges and our many guests may seem discourteous : with your leave, fair Senhors, we will repair our fault—the noonday meal is spread ;"—and ushering the way to the palace, the tall and commanding Marquis preceded the group, and conducted them to the presence of the already assembled company.

CHAPTER VII.

"I have earned of Don John a thousand ducats."
"Is it possible that any villany can be so dear?"
"Thou should'st rather ask, if any villany can be so rich; for when rich villains have need of poor ones, poor ones may make what price they will."—*Shakspeare.*

It was midnight, and the wind blew in loud fitful gusts, while the rain in occasional showers fell heavily, soaking the unhoused traveller to the skin : the moon, in her waning quarter, gave but partial glimpses of light, as struggling through the dense clouds, she sailed on her obscured voyage through the thick curtained sky. It was a night of gloom and storm, and unusually cold, and none but the necessitous would have ventured forth to brave its inclemency, unless the hired bravo, to meet his belated and unconscious victim ; or the night thief, bent on booty :—and yet was it neither necessitous, booty, or pelf, that induced Garcia, though closely muffled in the ample folds of a long Spanish cloak, and well provided against the driving rain and the chilly blast, to venture forth at such an hour. It was a craving at the heart— a restless and impatient longing—an eagerness overstepping even his accustomed prudence, to behold again his ill-got wealth—to gloat upon the aspect of his amassed treasure—to count once more his gold—to feel again the precious coin, test its reality by the tangible evidence of his sense, and to assure his mind and tranquillize his heart, that it still remained in safety and integrity, after the long absence of a tedious, slow, enduring week, that he had counted as months, since last the golden harvest blest his sight ; besides, he had acquired more in the interval to add to the already *much.* Alonzo had given him his year's wages in advance, and added a rich bonus to the sum to get him those small adjuncts to his gala dress that should become the season of festivity ;—and to keep so much upon his person, and debar the treasury of the accumulation, seemed to his imagination like bad husbandry and improvident waste ; and he had resolved to take advantage of the blusterous night, and his ended duties, to take the toilsome walk, and, unobserved by mortal eye, revisit, if but for a moment, the heaven where all his thoughts—his hopes—his joys, were centred.

The deep bell of the castle of Almazuma proclaimed with long and solemn strokes the hour of midnight, as Garcia stood by the low arched door, at the base of the building, through which we have previously seen him and Don Ferdinand pass, when habited as mendicant friars, thus returned from Madrid. Not a light was to be seen through the extent of the vast range of building—not a sound, save the moaning wind, as it sighed through the thick foliage, disturbed the air ; and all was dark and quiet as

Garcia turned the lock, and entered the low vaulted passage, securing the door hastily behind him ; then, drawing from his bosom a small lantern, with a flint and steel, he proceeded to strike a light, and ignite its wax taper ; then following the course of the passage till it terminated abruptly at what appeared to be a dead wall, and excluded all further progress, he set down his light, and inserting the point of his hanger into a crevice of the masonry, a revolving door opened in the wall, and admitted him into a lofty narrow labyrinth, divided from a wider and more spacious one by a low iron gate, which ran at a right angle from that in which he found himself. Merely stopping to re-close the entrance, and casting a hasty look to observe if the gate was still locked, as he had left it, he took up the lantern and traversed the long and circuitous passage, the sides and flooring of which were covered and carpeted with thick matting, so that the heaviest tread could make no sound in its progression. After some time, the subterranean gallery terminated at the bottom of a narrow staircase, the steps and sides of which, like the passage, were clothed in the same material. Ascending the steep flight, Garcia at length reached a small recess or landing, and pressing back an ingeniously secreted spring, pushed aside a sliding panel, and immediately entered the wainscoted oratory, which we have already described, and in which, before leaving the castle, he had been accustomed to repose. Holding the half-darkened lantern over his head, Garcia peered eagerly and cautiously around, directing his first inquiry towards the strong chest, which, with a low cry of delight, he perceived still safe. Coming forward, and replacing the panel, he proceeded hastily towards his bed, and sitting down on his rude stool, he drew the trunk as before, between his knees, and feeling for his keys with a tremulous hand, unlocked the box and threw back the lid, holding his light low down to satisfy himself that all indeed was well, and an exulting smile rose on his face as he perceived his treasure safe ; and opening the two sides of his dark lantern, that the reflectors within might cast all their light upon his idol, he set it down upon the lid, then taking from his doublet a leathern pouch, counted out its contents. Reserving one piece for necessary use, he allowed the rest to slide off his fingers into the heap below ; then thrusting down his hands, wallowed and rioted in the jumbled and commingled coins. And as the ruffian miser gloated on, and in, his wealth, his features, illumined by the concentrated and reflected light, assumed a most unearthly look of ghastly pleasure and malignant cunning ; while the long shadow from his high lamp, and the deep gloom beyond, with the one dash of light over head on the arched roof, and the indefinite outline of the stooping man on the panelled wall, gave to the dim chamber a mysterious and repugnant grandeur.

"All safe again ! and so much the richer since I last visited it !" exclaimed Garcia, still stirring up his gold, "and shall be richer yet—oh ! how much richer ! Truly thou art worth serving, Almazuma: Was not this sight worthy of six leagues' travel ? Surely yes !—Oh, yes. I shall be much richer when—ah ! true, well remembered

—let me look over my letter again—let me peruse this master-piece of double-faced and double-meaning villany. Ay! here it is—here it is—I have it: "—and he drew from a leathern case or small mail that hung round his neck, a folded paper, and opening it, held it down to the light and read aloud, making his comments as he proceeded in its perusal. "Let me see—yes—so. 'Believe me, dear A——,'—that ambiguity is good; the A stands either for Alonzo or Almazuma. Ay! and so is the caligraphy—these are Alonzo's characters to a stroke and turn—his very dots: the items are complete to make the whole perfect! 'Tis a matchless imitation! I pride myself upon it. 'Believe me, dear A——, that neither the trifling disparity in our years, or our long absence since school time, can ever diminish the fervour of my regard for my best friend; but on *that* subject,'—good again—that subject,—'do not urge me further: each man holds a reservation in his heart, not even friendship may touch correctly. She is that isolated point, in whose behalf I must decline all counsel. I grant your arguments often before, and most particularly last night, were generous, manly, noble, and in every case but the proud C——a's,'—oh! what a deal of hellish malice is there in a dash or unfinished name or word; that's good too,—' I would obey them, but I have sworn to conquer her, my friend; sworn it—dreadfully sworn it!' True, quite true, *he* has; 'and I'll not add vaccillation to my soul, not for twenty such proud beauties. Do I love her? No: I did but fool her arrogant pride with the false hope, and mocked her dignity with the illusory belief.'—That will sting sharp.—'She has wealth, and that is all that is estimable in her, except the rich pleasure I shall have, when mine, of bending that insulting scorn to the obedience of my debasing will: I'll make her crawl, and kiss the humiliating earth beneath my feet. I tell thee, friend, I will not be checked in my heart's desire; thou canst not know the burning force of my malevolence. Yes, under the profusion of my ardent love, and most impassioned words, I hid this one transport—only object of my breast. She thinks sincerity and love had never such faithful votaries, as in me her sworn, ——ha! ha!'—That break's as good as any, for it will stand for husband as well as enemies, and the short laugh, oh! it will stir—it will stir the venom.—'I must break off—I see her in the garden, and I must keep up the show, my friend—the show till she is safely mine. Preach to me no more—I'll not be moved—I swear it! She approaches. I send this by my trusty helpmate, De Vega. To-morrow you shall know the scheme I hinted at, to make her mine; to-night I put it to the test—I'll make her leap into my arms, and cry,—Hide, save me!—preserve my honour!—You shall know all—I say *shall*, or else thou art not my friend, but hers. Adieu! Yours till death, Al——.'

"I think in that epistle," continued the villain as he laid it down on his box, and apostrophised its contents, "I have succeeded to admiration, I have hit off Almazuma's feeling—that is, what I fancy he feels; for by looks only can I guess his heart's utterance. Yes, I shall be rewarded for that—I shall—I know I shall;—it is good—it is excellent, and hits the very soul and centre of her pride—it is good—yes, yes!"

"Hell could not better it!" exclaimed a deep calm voice, that seemed to issue from the recesses of the earth, as Garcia, springing to his feet, staggered back heavily against the panelling, his limbs trembling, and a livid hue suffusing his face, and giving a distorted and ghastly aspect to his features.

"Merciful God!" he at length exclaimed in acute terror. "Holy St. Francis!—Mother of heaven!—Pity, save me!"

"Cease, fool—'tis I!" cried Almazuma, as, enveloped in his monk's disguise, his figure loomed dimless in the dense shade of the vaulted room, giving a supernatural height to the tall Spaniard.

"Hell and damnation!" cried Garcia hoarsely, as terror gave way to a vague reality; and, drawing his sword, he attempted to put his quivering body in a posture of defence. "Who stands there? Speak—quick!"

"Put up your sword, fool!—'tis I. What has beset thee? Art mad with holy fears?"

"What! is it my lord? no—yes—no, impossible! My master—Don Ferdinand—ha, ha, ha, ha! ho, no, ho, ho!"—and with a spasmodic and convulsive laugh, in which fear and pleasure were blended, Garcia dropped his sword, and, staggering to his bed, sank on the mattress; then drawing his arm across his face to free his brow and eyes of the cold dew that obstructed his vision and fell in large drops from his corrugated forehead, he cried, "My God! I breathe again. How came you here, my lord? By my soul, I took you for the fiend himself—no offence, Don Almazuma, but I took you for the devil in person, come before his time—ho, ho, ho!"

"Thou art too complimentary, my good Garcia; I am not that powerful being—not the Prince you took me for, but a poor hidalgo—a subject only," replied Almazuma with scornful playfulness.

"And have you heard, Senhor, all my soliloquy,—the letter, I mean, that, agreeable to your wish, I have compiled?" inquired Garcia, as with a still unsteady hand he removed the light from its place that it might not betray to the keen glance of his master his secreted hoard.

"Nay, leave the light alone," observed Almazuma; "thou needest not fear my inspection. It pleases me to find thou art so provident: here is more to add unto thy bank, before you close your well-lined coffer. I am a week behind with thee: here is the sum," he cried, throwing him a silk purse, which Garcia caught; "and here, good fellow, for thy excellent letter, is a further guerdon,"—and he drew from his vest a precious stone, and placed it on the box, as with the other hand he removed the letter—and stooping forward, perused the lines and characters of the epistle with a steady, unmoved, but pleased and delighted eye. "Thou hast earned more than I have now upon me to bestow. You have done well—well," he continued, as Garcia, with fascinated gaze, turned over the stone in his hand, and with intense perusal studied its shape and size; then wrapping it up carefully in many folds of paper, deposited it at the bottom of his hoard. "I will not forget a further recompense;"—and taking the stool Garcia had so lately occupied, sat down by the now closed chest; and, putting up the letter, turned his full eyes on the face of his companion, as seated on the low bed, the two confronted each other. "I heard all thy comments, Garcia," continued Almazuma, in reply to his companion's former question; "and you may marvel how I came hither. Mark me! You must never more prejudice my scheme, or jeopardize my hopes, by such a risk as to desert thy post, till all 's fulfilled—never! Answer me not. You feared me—me!—thought I would debase my hands, by robbing my servant of his due—his lawful wages. I know thou did'st—deny it not. I bade thee leave it here, lest it might betray our cause, and that it was safer where it is than where thou art. But take it with thee, if thy heart will be at rest. Arise—remove it straight! Thy horse and mule—for I revoke nothing once bestowed—are at thy service: take it, then, and go thy ways—I 'll work the end alone. But if thou stay, never return hither but *the once* again, and then your task is done—your course completed. I saw thee quit the palace, and deeming truly what had led thy heart astray, I followed, and am here. Now answer—either thy unlimited confidence for the few days remaining; or, arise, take up thy gold, and leave me. Pick up your sword—come. I will hold the light myself to guide you."

"Pardon me, my lord; pardon me," cried Garcia, in a humble and deprecating tone. "I have done wrong, shameful wrong; I own it all—and you are right—it was the gold, the cursed gold, that made a traitor of me; but I did not do your dignity the wrong to think you would retake what you had so freely given. It was some damned woman's feeling, some weakness, longing, hell!—I know not what—that for the first time in my life brought on me a just rebuke. But, forgive this dereliction, Don Ferdinand, and as the saints are in the heaven!—well, then, as the fiends in hell!—a better oath for me—I swear I 'll not once think of the cursed dross till every tittle of our compact's fulfilled. Let my conduct hitherto towards you plead now in my justification."

"It shall—secure your chest, and let us talk," replied Almazuma. Garcia obeyed his master's injunction, locked his chest, and placing the light on the lid, awaited Almazuma's farther pleasure. "Tell me all that has passed since we last conferred, for we have had no time of speech of late."

"Why, first, Senhor," replied Garcia, "I stole at night, unseen, into the outward chamber of the Donna Catalina, and dropped Don Alonzo's glove upon the seat she occupies:—but first I wrote his name upon the inner leather. Next night I placed a sword-knot upon the carpet, by the door: the following one I slipped his handkerchief, marked in full characters, under the pillow of her siesta couch; and my last exploit—that was the best, most hazardous of all—I flung his lettered garter upon the toilet of her sleeping-room. That achievement cost me much difficulty; but watching well, and prudence, overcame all obstacles, and I succeeded: that ends that adventure."

"Good—very good! Proceed—admirable! Garcia."

"The next task, Senhor, was obtaining sight of Don Alonzo's papers, copying his hand, and fabricating the letter you have got: the next was to invent some idle pageant, to draw the lover once a day from out the guests, to see how I progressed in my device; and last—for I can turn my hand to any craft—was in the hours of night, to fashion me a corresponding suit to Don Alonzo's, from out the cloth and velvet I brought from Soria. The garb is now complete—and when dressed, and in the gloom of evening, I 'll defy sharper eyes than a woman's to tell the difference between the lover and myself. And now I wait your further orders."

"I 've nothing to direct, but what you know. Go on, still as begun the night following to-day—for morning 's almost broke. At the hour of eight I shall be in my accustomed walk, and then you will put the first great speaking evidence to her sight. Be careful that she sees you—remember, all, every thing, depends on the success of that device—a moment too late, or yet too soon, would ruin all—think well of that."

"I 'll not forget it, Senhor; it 's all imprinted on my mind."

"Now let us part," cried Almazuma; "and as an evidence of thy full faith and unconditional trust, depart at once, and leave me here: we must by different routes retrace our steps. Go!—yet, stay!" he suddenly exclaimed, as Garcia crossed the room;—"stay!"—and pulling from his breast a jewelled buckle, such as cavaliers used to loop their hats and secure the white ostrich plume in its circling belt, said,—"take this brooch—it is of the same fashion as that worn by Alonzo; I have carefully remarked it: your skill can trace his name on the gold setting; drop the betraying gem—where—where it shall be deep damnation to be found. Away!—marvel not how I came here—that is thy course,"—pointing to the panel Garcia had opened;—"follow its windings, and begone: show me thy instant duty and belief. Go—I have no time for further speech: thoughts are busy here—here, in arms and conflict;"—and he strode up and down the small chamber, striking his forehead with his open hand, as Garcia, having lighted the iron lamp that stood on the floor, took up the lantern, and closing all but one pane, passed through the sliding door and descended the narrow and matted staircase, and pursued his way through all the labyrinths, till he stood again without the castle. One glance of inquiring doubt he cast upwards to the turret window, but all was dark; and without another look or word, the accomplice struck into the dense shrubbery and disappeared in the surrounding darkness.

As soon as Almazuma was satisfied of Garcia's descent to the subterranean passage, he paused in his walk, and putting his foot on the lamp at his feet, extinguished the treacherous flame; then approaching the window, bent his ear with the caution of intense listening, till the slight but unusual stir in the foliage told him that Garcia had departed; then turning, groped his way to the opposite wall, and pulling down a panel that descended through the floor, entered a small closet in the thick masonry of the building, from which a trap-door conducted him to a lower chamber, and ultimately, by a back stair, to one of the intersecting passages of the grand hall, and from which he speedily found an egress into the open air and stormy night. Mounting a mule that was secured to a ring in the wall, and urging the animal down one of the vistas, Almazuma quitted his own mansion, and pursuing a path in an opposite direction to that taken by Garcia, bent his course as rapidly as the darkness would permit for the palace of Alfendora.

——

CHAPTER VIII.

"Good morrow, boy."
"Good morrow, sweet Hero."
"Why, how now? do you speak in the sick tune?"
"I am out of all tune, methinks."
"Clap us into 'Light o' love,'—that goes without burden."
"Do you sing it, and I'll dance to it."—*Shakspeare.*

"WHY, thou art as sad and melancholy to-day, my sister, as a new caged bird—thou dost not speak, and here within the counting of a week, our wedding-day; what makes thee so perverse at happiness? That which makes me glad, saddens with you. The buoyancy I feel is heaviness in thy heart—that which becomes us most, is unbecoming now in thee;—tell me whence springs this moody loneliness of thought—this sequesterment of thy tongue? Oh! shame upon thy sex, that thou should'st prison up the instrument of joy in such propitious hours—that bell and music of life's soul, that ringing, gives a harmony and charm, and paints transportingly our else dull nature and uncongenial world. Oh! what were this gardened earth, and God's own temple—Man, set in its flowery centre, did not the chime of praise—the minstrelsy of blessing converse, ring from the delighted tongue accents of endearing fellowship and love, giving a life, a purpose, and capacity to the meanest and most trivial thing sent from the laboratory of great nature's Father."

Thus spoke Amina Alvares, as seated beside Catalina in the apartment previously described, she playfully and reproachfully upbraided her now almost sister-in-law—as she had long been in heart, for the taciturnity she displayed at a time when, as Amina believed, she should have been most happy. Judging from her own feelings, and loving Don Felix with the true sincerity of her young heart, she saw no reason for reserve—no motive for sadness in others, when she, in her innocence, felt happy.

"What is it," she continued, "that distresses you, dear Catalina? Is Alonzo less kind—less true? Oh, no! it cannot be, for he is honourable—sincerity itself: you cannot doubt him—sure you cannot?"

"No, no! my lively and vivacious sister;—no! I cannot tell the motive of my sadness: and yet I am sad, I own. Remember, love, my nature is as opposite to thine, as morn and evening sunshine. Thou can'st, in very idleness of thought and paucity of cause, talk on, and find no end of needless argument; and then, in very wantonness, like early spring, laugh and weep on by turns, to show how each becomes thee best—varying, but never sad; for even in thy very grief, thy warm and sunny eyes dispel the sorrowing clouds soon as they are formed, making bright rainbows on thy tear-dropped eyelids. But I, Amina, cannot weep: my spirit knows not the ebb and flow of thine; there is no tide within my soul to swell and overpeer its

banks with the inundation of my tears: mine is an equitable and uninfluenced sea, that, never lashed to turbulence, sinks never to the monotony of calm, but, in a steady undulating wave, keeps on its course, neither too high nor low to merit censure, or deserve reproof. But yet I will confess a weakness that has crept upon the tenour of my general mind I cannot on the instant conquer. I'd rather feel my cheeks suffused with tears,—weep till my steady eyes, stiff with salt drops, turned me to Niobe, or a noviciate school-girl, home-sick and techy, from indulged caprice, than be the prey and sport of unsubstantial fear, or lose the equanimity of my familiar nature. I blush at change so opposite and dissimilar to my accustomed habit; and a weakening fear, scanning into futurity's dark womb for omens, portents, and images of supernatural and intimidating folly, has taken possession of my once strong mind. I feel as I have heard old woman say—under a spell; as if an evil eye were bent upon my peace, to uproot heart and soul, all my resolve, and wed me to perpetual pining grief and care."

"It is a momentary cloud, dear sister, on your health," cried Amina, kindly, "to which all natures at times are prone;—beneficial, though sad to bear—like frowns that gather on a sultry sky, shutting the very medicine from the earth that does the earth most good, lest, in his vertical and steady beam, the gorgeous sun undo his own great doing. Even so, upon thy soul, dearest Catalina, the mind throws out its vapoury doubts, obscuring for an hour the spirit of thy life, that it may afterwards burst refulgent from its cloud, to glad thyself, and pleasure all around. As sickness brings the mind nearer to heaven, and returning health invigorates the heart with charms life never felt before, so is it with thee; and thy present sadness shaken off, you will come forth new-born—new-made, in fuller happiness and larger measure of content. Come!—shall I sing to thee?"

"No, Amina, no! My mind's distuned, and would keep no symphony to thy soft music. This fit will leave me on the morrow,—I know it will, and I will resolve it shall. Tell me, what think you of our new guest—the gloomy Almazuma?"

"I admire him as I would a variation in an air—by contrast. When I am merry, 'tis good to look at him, and straight I'm sobered; when pensive, another glance gives back my mirth, in ridicule at his most solemn face. Oh! he is the very antithesis of joy—the most murderous enemy of pleasure that I ever saw. I saw him smile the other day; and though the ripple in his mouth was not uncomely, yet when contrasted with his unmoved eye, it seemed in him malicious mockery to laugh. How can my father and Alonzo find such merit in him? Felix regards him not, but rather shuns than courts the misanthrope."

"With me, his conduct is most reserved and cold, as though we ne'er had met before," replied Catalina.

"Nay!" exclaimed Amina, the "man's polite enough, and his greatest merit is his unfamiliar habit. Yet I have noticed that when we meet, or cross him in his walks, he bends a sorrowful and feeling eye on you, as if he either pitied you, or mourned his own rejected self?"

"I am not ignorant of the look you have observed," rejoined Catalina. "Perhaps the man believed he loved me: but I'd as soon have wooed and wed a spectre, or an Afric Goul, as mate with such a man. I have observed that, nightly, when we and our good lady-guests retire, and leave the nobles to their wine, their jests, and recreation, that moody man shrinks from the crowd, and in the avenues of the sheltering groves, with folded arms stalks up and down the silent paths, bending his eye with reading earnestness upon the barren ground—gloomy, unsociable, and alone."

"I have observed it, too, and matter more for speculation," cried Amina; "for Felix says, Alonzo also steals away, and hies him, doubtless, to more congenial company than embowering trees and smiling flowers. Dost not think so, thou unconfiding maid?"

"What meanest thou, dear Amina?" inquired Catalina, with surprise.

"Nay, never blush: is it a fault to give an audience to thy almost husband?—thy pledged and bounden lover?"

"Can'st thou suppose, or does Alonzo dare imply, that I have ever met, or secretly encountered his address; or, save in the lawful presence of my sire, or in the noon-day light, in fitting hour and proper place, listened to the alluring tales of love, though from the mouth of my affianced lord?—Never, sure—never!" replied Catalina, with a hectic glow of deep displeasure.

"Nay, why so warm, dear sister? Is there a fault in dearly loving him our parents sanction?—or had'st thou met him here, or in the arboured walks, would that be deemed unwomanly? If so, oh! then have I sinned against the credit of my sex; for I have deemed no shame to circle in my lover's arms—endure his fond caress—or plight anew my love, confident in his protecting truth and honour."

"So have not I; nor would I give my husband all my love, my duty, and my heart—but till I call him by that sanctioning name: neither familiarity of act or word shall ever give my maiden blush reproach. Nay, weep not, dearest sister," continued Catalina, in more tender tones than was her wont, folding her arms round the sensitive girl, and imprinting a kiss on her fair brow; "I did not mean to say, or to imply, thy conduct was unwomanly, or less than strictly chaste: but what in thee were innocent, backed by my nature and my pride, my known reserve, and formal courtesy, were all astray, and open to the deep-mouthed censure of the world, and, most of all, unto myself: that which becomes and sits on thee with all the grace of native beauty, would deform my head; and what would become my port, would all ill suit and disagree with thine. So in our dispositions, as in our dress—each may become, and lend a dignity to that she wears; but, if transposed, would both offend the sight and jar the contrast."

"I will believe thee—for it were wrong to doubt my sister, where she least can err," cried Amina, wiping her soft eyes, and smiling through the struggling mist, that hung like transparent vapour over her bright orbs; "but, sooth, I had no warranty for what I said—for Felix told me, under strict confidence, that Alonzo, aided by his shrewd and clever valet, Devega, is busied at those hours when he withdraws, in bringing forth some rare device or pageant, to give content and pleasure at our nuptials; and that he spends his evenings with this man, in forwarding the cunning trickery;—but this he bade me not to tell, that they might more delight you; and, look you, like a silly, idle thing, I've broke my vow, and told you all."

"I will be ignorant of thy fault, dear Amina, and be as much enchanted by what I see, as if it grew by magic unawares upon my view; and thou shalt lose no credit by thy forestalling knowledge. Come, wipe away those traces of thy tears, and we will go and note how our new clothes grow into shape under the active fingers of our women. Come, dry them up."

"I do, I do—oh! they will soon be gone. Why, how is this?" exclaimed Amina, as she inspected the handkerchief she had used to dry her eyes. "This is Alonzo's handkerchief—here is his name. I found it 'neath this cushion, and deemed it was my own."

"Alonzo's, say'st thou?"

"Look! it has his name."

"Under that cushion?" inquired Catalina, surveying the handkerchief with surprise.

"Aye, here!"—and Amina drew back one of the soft square bolsters of the ottoman on which they both reclined, and pointed to the spot from whence she drew it."

"You must have brought it here yourself, dearest Amina, mistakingly for your own," observed Catalina, after a moment's thought.

"Aye, I must; it is the only likelihood. And yet 'tis strange how I should find it. I'll take it back to him. But come, let us go and seek the millinery; I long to see how well I shall become my bridal dress, and test how far my mother's gems, and father's added gifts, enhance my sunny hair! Oh, come! why tarry you?"

"That handkerchief surprises me."

"Pshaw! what an unworthy thing to give surprise!—what is there in it worth a second thought? Alonzo has mislaid, and I have ta'en it up, and brought it here unknowingly."

"That cannot be," replied Catalina; "see! here is your own;"—and she lifted from the ground a slight embroidered handkerchief, and presented it to Amina.

"True! so it is!" observed Amina, taking it. "Why then, I must have brought Alonzo's yesterday."

"Yesterday!—why, you were not here—we went to hawk; and in the evening-time, until the hour of rest, we passed with all the donnas in the music-room."

"Why, then, it was the day before."

"The day before!" replied Catalina, as if endeavouring to recall the events of the alluded time.

"Ay!—or the day preceding that, or that. What matter if a week ago? Come, you excite my curiosity; and now, upon a trifle, less than the value of a hair, you'd baulk my expectation. Come—the dresses."

"A trifle?"

"The veriest atom of insignificance—too trite for breath. What do you muse on? You stand, and gaze, and ponder, as if life and death were wrapt in the meshes of that Cambray lawn and Malines lace; and, after all, a paltry handkerchief."

"Ay! but 'tis a man's!"

"An ogre's, if thou wilt, and stained with victims' blood—aught that you please, so that you will let me see the dresses, I 'll say Alonzo's not my brother, but some baby-eating giant, or a grim vampire on the prowl for victims—only let me view the new-made dress."

"Come thy ways, then, giddy girl. But this perplexes me. I can account for nothing, unless you brought it," replied Catalina, as she approached the door after her impatient friend.

"Oh, yes! I brought it, of course—how else could it come? Donna, your servant;"—and curtseying with mock gravity, the lively Amina threw open the door, to allow Catalina to take precedence; and then with a bound like a delighted fawn, leapt after her more stately companion.

CHAPTER IX.

> "Take hands!—A bargain;
> I give my daughter to him, and will make
> Her portion equal his."
>   "One being dead,
> I shall have more than you can dream of yet.
> Enough!—Then for your wonder. But, come on!
> Contract us 'fore these witnesses."
>   *Shakspeare.*

In a long, low arched room, lighted by four deep embayed windows, whose stained and variegated glass, richly emblazoned with the coats and quarterings of the noble house of Alfendera, sat the Marquis and the Condé De Alvares; before them was a large carved oak table, covered with a bright crimson cloth edged with deep bullion fringe. Between each compartment of the windows stood the effigy of a knight in complete armour, holding in their crossed arms the formidable lance, while over the head of each, projecting from the wall, hung the bannerette, on which was traced, on an argent field, the cognisance of the former wearer. The entire length of the opposite side was divided into carved oaken compartments, with small flying buttresses, and floridly-traced finials, the spaces being parted by shelves, and the whole entirely filled with massy tomes, elaborately bound and gilt; while from some of the divisions projected rolls of many ancient manuscripts, from which small strips of parchment, on which was neatly inscribed in German letter the name of the primitive volume, was suspended from each. At the extremity of this library, and covering the entire end of the long room, was arranged armour of all descriptions, from the pike, brownbill or battle-axe, to the Damascus and Toledo blades of high and valued price. Each species of offensive or defensive arms was adjusted by itself, and formed into quaint and singular devices; while over all, a group of time-worn and tattered pennons stood proudly out, hallowing and ennobling those savage implements of blood and death. The floor, like all the apartments of the period, was composed of oak scantling, highly polished; while up its centre, and with a diverging belt to each window, ran a narrow strip of rich Brussels carpet. A few carved chairs, like porch or cathedral seats in Gothic architecture, to correspond with the style of the room, completed the furniture; while from the rose-gilt pendants that hung from the elaborate ceiling, were suspended four antique bronze lamps, used at night to light the somewhat gloomy armorial library. The time was evening, and as the sun set full before the windows, his beams piercing the painted glass, bathed the whole chamber in a flood of soft and variegated light; while here and there, the glinted rays catching the fluted mail of the armed figures, or the spear-points of the depending Gonfolons, dyed them in gold or purple hues. And as the two nobles bent their venerable heads over the strewn table, their thin hairs and aged features, by turns influenced by the ever-changing light, were suffused in all the tints of many rainbows.

"I have taken a strict account of all my wealth, personal and hereditary, and find the first amounts to—what I hold at present—a sum something exceeding the gross of thirty thousand ducats *—great ducats of Spain," observed the Marquis, continuing a previous conversation. "This present sum I shall divide into two portions, giving a third to Catalina with thy son, which, with the Andalusian farms and vineyards, will be an annual stipend of five thousand more; that, with the winter mansion at Madrid, which we have just confirmed, and what my provident care can save 'twixt my death and now, to swell the total to a worthy dower, in which a father's yearning heart will not be found a niggard broker, must for my girl suffice."

"A very noble and princely fortune," replied Alvares, "fully beyond the measure of necessity; for, thanks to Providence, my boy shall not be found a poor or insufficient bridegroom. But I 'll speak of my intents anon, when thou hast made an end, my friend, of thy most fatherly resolve. Proceed!—I interrupt you!"

"The moiety," resumed Alfendera, "thirty thousand great ducats in ready specie, I give unto my second son, Don Felix, with thy daughter, with all my tenements and landed property in the town of Soria, held on long tenure by right worthy and substantial burghers, which, from my steward's roll, I see will yearly halve the sum he takes in hand. Then at my death, his mother's property reverts to him, the which I hold for benefit of life. Your patience for a moment—and let me make an end, good Condé. Sebastian, my eldest born, takes in reversion all my effects, the Alfendera Palace and domain, and my two mines in Mexico; the revenue from one of which I now allow him for the ample maintenance of his state and name; so that I have amply shared and well considered each, and in my conscience feel content. These deeds are all complete, wanting only attesting witnesses, and our hands to make them valid; this shall be seen to after supper. What say you, friend, to that which touches you?"

"Most amply satisfied," replied Alvares; "and to make thy Catalina's portion equal to her high desert, I 'll fix three thousand double ducats yearly on herself, and six thousand on Alonzo, till in due course of nature he inherit all the rest. And for my own dear girl—my sweet Amina, as I cannot portion out my land, nor draw from the male branch an acre of the soil, to give in dowers, I 'll lay her down upon

---

* Value of Spanish coin at the period of the story:—Pistole 7s. 9d.; Crown 8s.; Ducat, 8s. 6d.; Double Ducat 17s. 1d.; Great Ducat £1 15s.; Doubloon two Pistoles, or 15s. 6d.

her wedding morn, sixty and five thousand gold doubloons, which, with the portion Felix owns, and claims from you, shall hold them well in hand, until the death of a rich relative—you yet have little knowledge of, and whose attested will I 've read—brings her in an equal half with my son Alonzo of two hundred thousand crowns. My kinsman's old—a bachelor, and in the course of time cannot see many years; and so, my friend, I think, thus provisioned, our children will have no need to count our few grey hairs: or, as old Naso Ovid says, 'Mingle the nightshade, or inquire too curious into their fathers' years,' or grudge the morsel that our shrinking appetites and toothless gums require, but let us tread, unenvied to the grave, the few remaining days or hours allotted us in the death register of heaven. Give me thy hand, my friend,—and as we thus so cordially shake the free palm of friendship, may endless love and peace crown our dear children's lives.—Pshaw! my eyes grow very dim, and a thick rheum comes at times across my sight—that—that, will —will not be suppressed."

"Amen! to thy good wish, my noble friend," ejaculated the Marquis, with a tremulous voice; and passing his hand over his eyes in sympathetic action to the Condé's, "Why should we blush, or falsify the cause that brings this soul's dew upon the full heart's mirror? No, my brother, the tear that dims the patriot's eye who bids eternal parting with his native land, and that springs from true parental love, are noble—holy drops, and hallowed in the shedding! But see!—where, in the mellow glow of even, yon happy groups sport on the green-faced lawn. There, with her light steps, sweeping the tapering blades, gracefully waving, goes the bounding doe—the soft, gazelle-eyed fair Amina, and my gallant lad—my youthful soldier, Felix, full of blithe grace and supple action;—see how the happy pair joy in the dance, and all the spectator crowd stand hushed, admiring!—See, there are twelve couple; and the soft music—from invisible hands and lips—makes the scene enchanting."

And as he spoke, Alfendera and Alvares entered the embrasure in one of the windows, and gazed with happy delight on the peopled lawn, where proud nobles and beauteous Donnas, in all the pageantry of festive splendour, danced with the brides, or stood in many parties, applauding and admiring the bright scene — while over head, and all the air, was one warm golden medium.

"And do you mark," cried the Condé, equally charmed at the cheering prospect,—"do you observe how that swan-like queen—thy beauteous daughter, with her stately steps and sober mien, proudly treads the measure, while my boy's gloved hand just touches the taper fingers of her curved and snowy arm. How gallantly she holds her head—how regular her foot descends;—and he, to match the spirit of her soul, moves in the even pace that so becomes her form and nature. And now, as change comes o'er the dance from grave to light, and light to grave, my fawn-like girl can scarce subdue the mettle of her step to keep due measure, but would be off again to bound in joyousness: each of the two have in that dance their element. Oh! that my dear—dear wife were here! the sight would

make her young again, and drive cold cramping age from out her blood. Why, 't is a sight to make age youth, and youth perpetual. Good friend, let 's go and share at least their joy, if not their sport. Now, by St. Jago! but my limbs grow blithesome; and were it not for my white hairs, I 'd trace a measure with the bravest among them, and teach their young feet how, in the Emperor's time, Spain trod to its soft music. What say you—shall we go?"

"With my best will!—we 'll have the feast upon the lawn, and sing and dance, by turns, under the shading trees, or in the full eye of the pale moon, grouped like the mixed parties in a Flemish picture. Come——But who is yon?" he abruptly exclaimed, as about to quit the window, his eye encountered an object to which he directed his friend's observation;—"he who stands aghast and all alone, with folded arms, and contemplative brow. There—I see the figure, but cannot, through the obstructing glass, make out the man,—yonder, half hid by the low branches and thick foliage of that aged chesnut. Do you perceive? It is a noble form —and yet I know him not. Hast caught the object?"

"Oh!—'t is Don Almazuma," replied Alvares; "he takes no part in festive scenes—his mind is too deep and philosophic for our diversions. And yet, he is a noble gentleman—full of deep learning—most modest in that affluence that man too frequently parades; he bears his wisdom and his knowledge like the cold flint that, till corrected by congenial touch, emits no light: but once enchafed, the liberated sparks become a flame, and give a steady fire of deep and eloquent discourse. I have much courted him since being here; and in my comprehension, I have never met so apt a man, a scholar, and a gentleman."

"True — it is Almazuma: I might have known it by his reserve," replied Alfendera. "I 'm glad you find him such good fellowship. I will confess, I 've done him wrong in mind; for I have thought him dark and subtle."

"Oh! no—'t is habit only: the rough exterior off, or broken down, by more familiarity, and you would quickly grow to estimate him. Beneath his icy look, there are warm and noble impulses; indeed, he chides himself unmeasuredly for his uncongenial nature. He says he seeks a heart to love, in whose one bosom he could bound the world, centred in one true affection: wanting that, he is what you perceive."

"I 'm glad of this—and sorry, too: glad that I see him in a newer—better light; sad, that he cannot meet the happiness he craves. But, come—the dance is over, and the split party wander for pastime. Let us go and order forth the supper. Come, good friend—come."

So saying, the two venerable nobles quitted the apartment, and joined the guests on the lawn, giving directions to the servitors as to the arrangements of the evening, and mingling with the pleased groups, seemed, in the general happiness, to lose their years, and live their youth again.

——

6

CHAPTER X.

"But all was false and hollow, though his tongue
  Dropp'd manna; and could make the worse appear
  The better reason; to perplex and clash
  Maturest counsels, for his thoughts were low
  To vice industrious, but to nobler deeds
  Timorous and slothful."—*Milton.*

THE opening scene of our chapter lay in the rich and beautifully ornamented garden attached to the palace of the Marquis of Alfendera. It was night—a summer's night, in all its warmth of glory; the moon shone in her majesty of place, soft and calm, casting a misty veil—a vapoury shroud around remoter objects, and bathing in a flood of mellow light meadow and hill, foliage and stream; casting from the tall trees, dense shadows over the greensward and fainter shades, where their outlines fell athwart the broad white paths. Ever and anon, a stray moon-beam would penetrate the mass of shadowy foliage and, after spangling bough, leaf, and trunk with a thousand touches of scattered light, expand itself in some antique statuary, that, illumined by the ray, seemed to start out of the surrounding gloom like some phantom guardian of the glade. Parterres of the choicest flowers, and most odorous plants made the air redolent with perfume; long vistas of cork, chesnut, and oak trees threw their giant images across the living streams, that, gently murmuring, traversed the extended garden in every direction, concentrating their divided courses where six or eight lofty ashes spread their thick and emulous branches over the collected waters, giving to the deep pool below a stygian darkness, till it fell bursting over an artificial boundary, rushing and bubbling in the open moon-light like a broad sheet of silver, when its turbulent course was again silenced and engulphed in a wide tranquil lake that swallowed up the blustering stream, quenching it to repose—like unbridled youth, clamorous and arrogant, rushing headlong on the tide of life, its mighty ocean clips him in with scarce a ripple left to note the tributary bubble.

From numerous groves of olive, myrtle, and orange, the soft voice of nightingales chanted their loves, or in long-borne tremulous notes, taught the replying nest, while others from the distant trees held amorous parley, filling the still air of evening with eloquent harmony. Here on the grassy banks of the fast whimpering streams, willows gracefully bent, bathing their long tresses in the clear water, breaking its current with their pencilled leaves into a thousand brilliant gems;—while, bending over its surface, the Narcissus timidly gazed into the bright mirror, courting its nodding shadow;—or further down, where the checked rivulet flowed more sedate, the lotus spread his broad leaves, sleeping in tranquil heavings on the water's bosom, sheltering under his green fans his curtained petals. Statues of Naiades stood on the river's brink; while Fawns, Dryads, and Satyrs, in the darker nooks, or open glades, basked in the moonlight —or, half revealed, seemed coyly lurking in the cool green shade. The scene seemed fairy ground;—for all that art, or taste, or nature could supply to please the mind or captivate the sense, was centred in that small paradise, charming the beholder's eye on every turn, and filling the tranquilled memory with consonant and soft associations. But what fair thing in nature but has its dark, corroding blight, to chill felicity and neutralise the soul's success. The richest fruit holds in its seeds the deadliest poison : the brightest mead, the purest stream, secretes the wily snake and scaly foe: the noblest work of God—mankind—deforms its image! has it not the vicious heart—the cankering mind? And even here in this fair Eden stalked the destroying serpent.

With arms folded over his chest, and with a slow meditative step, a man issued from under one of the deep embowering vistas of the shadowing trees; and with a pensive and deliberate movement, passed from the darkness of the grove, and crossed the broad moon-lit lawn, bending his eyes steadfastly on the earth, and to all appearances wrapt in profoundest contemplation; though at times a quick and furtive glance would be directed towards one of the windows of the palace, which, being open, gave the gloom of the apartment a singular contrast to the rest of the building, the numerous casements of which, lit up by the full effulgence of the night, glittered and sparkled like a thousand mirrors, as the whole line of palace was bathed in the splendour of the silver beam; while from within the halls, the voice of song, the cheerful laugh, and note of music sounded softly mellow, as it floated on the still air, and died in faint repeating whispers through the adjoining groves.

As the individual who had just emerged from the shadow stood for a moment listening to the strains of mirth and harmony within, a light was suddenly seen in the chamber, to which he had directed more than one inquiring glance. At the same instant the slight and graceful form of a man was observed to quit the room, and springing off the low balcony that encompassed the window, leap over the small parapet that bordered the garden in that direction, and disappear in the dense shrubbery beyond; while, instantly after, a lady, richly attired, came forward, and leaning over the balustrade, exclaimed in an indignant voice, "What villain dares presume to violate the sanctity of my chamber?" Then as her eye fell on the individual before noted, who stood a silent and amazed spectator of the incident, she continued—"What ho! churl; stand you silent and inactive when I call? Pursue yonder audacious wretch—secure his person. Do you hear me, vassal? Must Donna Catalina command her servant twice?"

"And is it," said Almazuma, advancing nearer, and speaking in a low, soft, and melancholy tone—"and is it possible thou art the noble, beauteous Catalina! Surely—oh God!" he exclaimed with the evidence of deep intense feeling—"surely mine ears deceived my faculties—my eyes destroyed my judgment! What, that thrice outraged chamber yours? Oh lady! would to heaven that I had died before you had confessed so much;"—and as he spoke he hid his troubled features in his hands.

"What mean you, sir?" replied the imperious Catalina, while over her face and neck she felt the rushing blood that rose indignant at the surmised impeachment.—"What mean you, sir? what dare you mean, my lord?" Then, in a voice more mild and slightly tremulous with fear as she surveyed his evidence of grief she continued—"I beseech you, sir, as you are a gentleman and noble, follow that villain, and maintain my spotless honour."

"Speak calmer—lower, madam," Almazuma replied, with sorrowing accents; "pursuit is bootless now; the gallant has escaped. Had I not believed from his demeanour and his dress, he was a welcomed and expected visitor, by yonder lighted heaven I swear! I would last night have cleft him to the earth;—but, agonising thought! I knew not then that chamber was the resting-place of her I once so madly loved, still reverenced in despair."

"Last night! blessed saints, what treachery is this? Tell me—I command you, sir, tell me.—Last night!"

"No more, lady—no more! Calm this extravagant amazement—rest confident in the fidelity and secresy of my heart—a heart that aches to bursting, with its conflicting love and grief."

"Confidence, sir!" replied Catalina, with indignation; "think you my fame shall rest dependant on the possibility of scandal to denounce? No!—it shall instantly be put to the strict and searching inquisition of appeal."

"Madam! as you value your earthly peace, let me implore you be not thus wildly, madly rash!" Almazuma exclaimed, in sudden and breathless energy, "What! to the busy tongue of a wide clamour, would you intrust that fragile gem, that precious jewel, on which a breath once passed is certain ruin—your reputation? What! publish to the admiring world, that which will so soon expire with me? For, give me, lady, but the cue—and, as the saints are witness, here is my heart, and here the active hand and ready instrument that shall at once, and with my death, expunge the only record of your shame!"—and, as he spoke, he tore the silk vest and scarf back from his bosom, and with the other hand drew a long sharp poniard, and held it above his head, ready to strike, only waiting her mandate to inflict the death, that with the most compassionate grief and devoted affection he appeared anxiously to court.

"Mother of heaven!" passionately ejaculated the momentarily-terrified Catalina—as with folded hands and outstretched arms she addressed her fervent supplication: "Thou, who from thy throne of bliss, surveys the hearts and notifies the deeds of our corrupted natures—shelter me with thy wings of mercy—shroud me in thy chaste and watchful love—and, as thou knowest mine innocence, preserve me! Make evident on their guilty heads this slander that destroys me. Madonna! hear thy supplicating daughter—and in her purity of thought support her fainting strength—and in its own dark iniquity confound malevolence!"

Then, slowly dropping her arms, and bending her eyes upon the earth, she stood for a moment wrapt in inward prayer and contemplation; at length, fixing her look on Almazuma—who, motionless, and in the same attitude, remained gazing mournfully on her, she added, in a calm but scornful tone, in which all her native pride and haughtiness of soul was evident, "Sheathe your dagger, my lord—I shall not need to test your resolution. The petty thief, that we have seen escape, may possibly have robbed my cabinet of some paltry gem, some valueless device—

but you mistake the object, sir, if you believe that the fair name of Alfendera's daughter could be tainted, or the stout bulwark that shields her spotless fame could be assailed by such a puny artifice. Your alarms have marred your judgment, noble sir. Put up your steel—the dews will spoil its brightness:—besides, I must intreat your instant presence, before the guests retire, to lay with me, before a father's wisdom, this rude adventure. The timid dove, Don Ferdinand, may fly the threatening hawk—but the bold heron meets the dangerous foe; and in the conflict bravely dies, or nobly lives."

A cloud, gloomy and ominous, crossed over the features of Almazuma, giving a malignant and savage scowl to his countenance, as the taunting words of the proud beauty fell on his ear; and he bent his head, to shadow in his broad plume the workings of his face;—but, master of every dissimulation, the darkness passed from his brow in an instant, and with the same specious and earnest energy of voice and manner, he replied, as sheathing his poniard he threw himself on his knee before the now-restored and scornful Donna Catalina—

"Hear me, lady, I conjure you!—if not for yourself, for the dear fame of your noble father's house, hear me, I implore you! Nay—by my hopes of bliss, you shall!" he exclaimed vehemently, as he observed her about to withdraw from the balcony—"you must!—by the love I once bore you; I will not see you sacrificed. Blind not your judgment with the vain belief that the world will credit yon gallant was a midnight plunderer!—Banish the delusion! Pause, I beseech you—command me not to speak. I can be dumb as death—yea, will, to save your fame, put destruction betwixt my tongue and your repose—but, speaking, Almazuma's honour may not mitigate the truth. Hear me, for the love of heaven! Three nights consecutively have I beheld that figure quit your chamber; but, till this hour, held it some ignoble gallantry, beneath my notice:—but, did time permit, I could reveal so many facts damnatory to truth—your ear would curse me for the heavy fatal knowledge it received. Grant me an audience for an hour to-morrow, and if I do not prove the dangerous precipice on which you stand—the hopelessness of all appeal—the baseness of your cherished lover—and my own disinterested and painful part—oh! from that hour denounce me as accursed of heaven, unworthy God or man's belief—call me the vilest traitor, and the most debased that crawls the earth. Give not this night even to your dreams—your thoughts. Bury what's past within the closest cells of your confiding heart. Suffer me to-morrow to confer alone with you; and if I show you not a deep-laid scheme, plotted and wove to whelm you in despair, for ever let me be abhorred:—but when I have proved the sure damnation that engulphs your peace—then, lady, will you find how great the sacrifice I make to save you—without a smile to cheer my path—without a hope to bid my lonely heart rejoice—without one selfish wish to recompense my grief; for I must offer on the altar of your honour the dearest tie of man—the first acknowledgment of his soul—the sacred bond of friendship. Judge me, heaven! that to save immaculate this doubting beauty, so devotedly loved, but never to be mine—through the nearest kindred of my blood—through the hot veins of my throbbing heart—and in the belieing throat of my warm friend—this avenging steel shall execute her wrongs, and save unscathed her spotless honour!" Then, slowly rising from the ground, he took a step backward; and, after a short pause, added—"I have done. But witness for me all you powers who rule the human mind, and probe its darkest windings, that I have spoken truth. My God!" he cried, with anguish, clasping his hands, "she will not hear! she will not let me save her!"

The time—the manner—and, above all, the energy of Don Ferdinand, the disinterestedness of his own pretensions, and the tenderness with which he had still loved her in silence and in secret, could not fail in that moment to find a favourable reception in her heart for his sincerity: and then the strange coincidence of Alonzo's handkerchief, found in her room, flashed on her mind; and the half-implied belief of Amina, that he had held secret audience with her, even in her chamber; and his nightly absence from the guests—a fact of general observation—all leading to a foregone conclusion, struck on her heart with icy chill, and her very soul shrunk in dismay; and all her boasted pride and self-sufficiency of integrity deserted her before the vague and dreadful picture of disgrace that seemed to gather up to crush her. "But whence could spring Alonzo's motive?" she thought. "Were they not plighted?—would not another week make her his lawful wife?—was he not bound by honour, love, and reverence—to uphold, not stain, her honour? That 't was Alonzo who had left her chamber, she could not harbour doubt:—his height, his garb—all confirmed it. She sought in vain for motives to a deed so black and treacherous. 'T was certain Almazuma was cognisant of more than he revealed:—his look, his tone, and language, gave confirmatory evidence that to him familiarly was known the springs of this iniquity; and as the humiliating sense crept on her mind—that to him, of all men under heaven, she was exposed—she stood, shook, crushed, abashed, by a thousand fears; and like a deserted ship tossed on the troubled ocean, as the winds and waters influence her course, she either plunges down the steep side of the parted sea—or, dashed in foam over some crested wave, ploughs onward through the brine, to dive again into the hollow deep in wild successions. So tossed, so driven and impelled by the winds and waves of grief and indignation, the mind of Catalina was urged from sea to sea of doubt, mistrust, and shame. Amid such turmoil, how should she guide her course—how stem the evils latent and revealed—which way fly in her distress for succour—where, in her alarm, implore advice?"

"Merciful Providence!" she at length exclaimed, when the tumult of her excited thoughts had somewhat subsided: "whither shall I fly—where seek a refuge from this shame. Oh! blessed Mother! stoop from thy throne, and whisper counsel to thy wretched daughter,—direct me whom to trust—what enemies to shun: my pride, that was a regal mantle to my fame—that slander feared to look upon, falls powerless and discharmed before this midnight villany. You should be honest!" she cried, suddenly turning towards Almazuma: "and though rejected in your suit, should, from the very integrity of your honour, scorn to wage a conflict on a defenceful woman,—and in that veracity should be trusted. Yet so should he, still more, whose plighted vows were mine—and yet, if him, how base—how treacherous, and how despicably coward. Instruct me, heaven, what to select—whom credit; for I am lost—utterly lost in my startled and bewildered thoughts!"

"Put your unhesitating trust in me, fair lady—freely and boldly," replied Almazuma, with an earnest modesty of speech that calmed while it assured the timid hearer,—"and I will show you by what unsought means I have, against my will, been made a hearer of a vile abuse,—how thy repose struggled against my long-tried friendship, and conquered my regard, and made me vow to save you. But of this last indignity I was ignorant—though now his ambiguous letter is unravelled; and I believed—pardon me the thought—that chamber held some light Abigail, my licentious—friend I'll no longer call him—found welcome access to. And if I do not give sufficient proof to-morrow to warrant all your confidence, give to my name the foulest epithet of villain. You are betrayed—deceived—dishonoured; but you shall be yet revenged! Call up your native spirit, and let it possess your soul with noblest resolution; and when you have heard the scheme through all its vile debasing course—traced all the devilish villany of the mind that thought—the heart that plotted it,—if you can pardon and forgive, I'll bow to your intents, and lay my lifeless body at your feet; or set the widest seas between my banished tongue and your dear valued peace; but if what I shall show, you find approved by circumstance and deeds, and if you have a heart capable of vengeance, you shall find in me one sworn to aid you."

"If I have!" exclaimed Catalina, interrupting him, with a vehemence that surprised even the wily hypocrite as he heard it, "I have a heart, soul, and mind, towering as man's in my revenge—a steady purpose, and a living hate! Give me but evidence—confirmatory proof, that Don Alonzo is the wretch my fears this night presage him—make it apparent to my dispassionate view, and, by the Sainted Mother of our faith! this once rejected hand, when it has washed away this night's opprobrium, is yours for ever. I swear it! Ask not my purpose: you shall find that savage Tullia was less obdurate in her hate—less bloody in her rage, than I will be in executing my just revenge."

"Let me implore you, for your own content in fathoming this dark plot," cried Almazuma, interrupting her, "that till I lay before you all its bare details, thou wilt to no living thing breathe what I've said, or in your eagerness for more, you'll danger all. Be ruled, sweet lady."

"Fear not—fear not!" cried Catalina, with a bitter smile; "I will in this be very cool, and guided but by you. Oh! I will be prudence itself; fear not. Good night—good night! I but exist until to-morrow quiets my doubts, or gives my life a new and fearful aim. Adieu! and heaven direct us;—I go to think—to think; for I shall sleep no more."

So saying, she hastily quitted the balcony, entered the chamber, and instantly drew down the blinds of the verandah, and closed the window. For a few moments after her departure, Almazuma remained on the spot, preserving the same attitude of respectful distance, while a faint smile crept over his unmoved features ; then, repeating in a subdued but self-satisfied voice, her last words,—" I shall sleep no more," rejoined, in a congratulatory tone, " No—no : you shall sleep no more !" turned on his heel, and immediately disappeared under the now dense shadow of the trees.

CHAPTER XI.

" Is he not approved in the height a villain, that hath slandered, scorned, dishonoured my kinswoman? Oh! that I were a man !—What ! bear her in hand until they come to take hands? Oh, God !—that I were a man, I'd eat his heart in the market-place."

Shakspeare.

WHEN Catalina withdrew from the balcony, and entered her rich and elegantly-decorated apartment—once the seat of her pride—the shrine of her purity—at whose threshold the admiring world had paused in awe and admiration, a sickening of the heart—a revulsion of the brain came over her proud soul, and she sank down on the soft, luxurious cushions, abject, crushed, humiliated. The spring of life, the fountain of her incense, the hope, the aspiration, and the existing object of her very being, was annulled, dammed up, profaned ; and in the withering of her pride and eminence of fame, her heart collapsed before the agony of her fall, and drew from her fair white brow damp and heavy drops of torture. It was only now, within the solitude of her desecrated temple—no eye to mark her shame—no ear to note her woe—no tongue to rouse the dormant functions of her sufficient soul, that the full calamity of her dethronement, the complete undoing of her life, and the overwhelming misery of her annihilated honour, burst in its full unmitigated revelation upon her startled and amazed perception :—a father's honourable name profaned, his grey hairs insulted by his daughter's infamy—the proud escutcheon of a noble line defamed—disgraced ! And for herself !—Oh, agony too deep for measured words—unutterable ! Where should she fly—to what remote extremity of the wide world ? What cavern in womb of earth was far or deep enough to shut for ever out the voice of pitying scorn, that already in her ears rang pealing madness ?

Man can endure privation, poverty, all earthly woes, with some complacency, but not contempt and its twin birth—scorn. Philosophy, the coward's medicine for human ills, can never stop the breach through which the world's opinion flows contemptuously ; 'tis like the adder's sting—small, but deadly. This hydra-headed monster overleaps all compass ; defiance spreads, and chastisement inflames it. She felt the venom rankling in her soul, and groaned beneath the anguish that expressed her full.

" No, no !" she cried, wringing her hands in painful agony, " I am lost—lost for ever, and irretrievably condemned ! Creation has not left a nook so close, a grave so totally profound ; nor darkest night a canopy so black ; but malice, million-eyed, and every eye a sun, will find me out, and blaze the proclamation into day ! Oh, torture, torture ! My pride—my pride has killed me ! The modest and retiring maid who erred from love and trusting confidence, had found a balm e'en in the dregs of her affliction ; for tender pity would have held the tongue, and feeling virtue drawn oblivious veil athwart her name and fault. But I, who ever stood aloof, pre-eminent in fame—throned in strictest chastity — before whose name license and pleasure shrunk abashed ;—I, who was the pattern and the proof of spotless womanhood—who held my honour as my life, and my dear fame as the salvation of my soul ;—I, virtuous in act and thought, from nature and from habit cold and strict,—Oh, Sainted Maria ! I, to fall, to live, and henceforth breathe under the stigma and imputation of rank profligacy. Who will believe my protestations ? My father !—no, my God ! no !—he'll strike me to the earth, and trample on his child ! and the huge disgrace will break his aged heart. No—will the world credit my denial ?—It were unjust to think it. No! were my head armed with Medusa's terrors, or the brazen teraphim shielded my hot cheeks, the credulous and callous-hearted crowd would smile, and in derisive sorrow pity me. Oh, miserable me! my torture has no hope or palliative — my anguish no remission : not death, all powerful as he is, can give extenuation to my woe ; or else—else this blessed blade, that I have ever worn as the dear sister of my fame, should find an instant remedy." And as she spoke, she threw back the folds of her long robe, and drew forth from a gold sheath, a long and exquisitely chased ivory-handled dagger, on which she gazed eagerly as she apostrophised the sharp, tapering, and formidable instrument. " No," she resumed, " no !—death that to others flings the boon of peace, would on my head bring damning and confirmatory guilt, and I should live in my exulting sex's rankest memories, as harlot double-dyed—twice criminal. No, death is not for me, to leave attachment blighted—a life dishonoured. Oh, horror ! horror !—I shall go mad ! O that I could blot out my being from the world, and leave no memory or trace that such a thing had life : for what to me is the true knowledge of my innocence—of what esteem or value?" The smallest coin the most debased and abject beggar craves of hungry poverty, were of more potent value than all my boasted virtue under the ban and interdict of loathed incontinency. If so, why should I live ? Why ?—for revenge ! Ah ! what do'st thou say, my soul—let me murmur the music to my ear again. Revenge ! Yes, revenge—great heaven ! There is life, fame, honour, in the thought. Where had my fancy strayed, that I had lost my way, and in my foolish fear and weak alarm, buried my resolute and conquering soul ? A glorious thought ! I feel new made. Fresh impetus and nutrient blood transfuses in my veins, and makes me from the toe and head a new woman. Rouse thee, Catalina ! wake from this crushing somnolency ; for in that small dissyllable there is a world of living hope and ecstacy. Yes ! I will be revenged ! Ay ! such vengeance as but a woman's brain dare to conceive—a woman's outraged heart commit. What, though I wed body and soul, my mind and person, to an enduring hell of life-long torment, I'll sweeten every pang, and season after grief, by the knowledge of this great triumph! Stay! let me pause—for I must plot with cool and steadfast mind. Passion or heat would but insult the dignity of my cause. Let me think. No, none but Almazuma is yet cognisant of the scathing on my name; and I have vowed,—ay, and must purchase silence from his tongue, at the sacrifice of my hand and person. But what is that to an untarnished reputation? Nothing—as dross. 'Tis true, I loath—abominate the man; and the bare contact of his hand is as pollution to my haughty sense. But the plain, dull creature loves me—loves me with the deep devotion and timid awe of the obsequious hound; and I can model his rude passion to the fullest bent of my caprice—rule, govern, and sway the thing, and a toy I make a husband of. Once mine,—held in the potent chain of my dominion,—he dare not, for his honour, breathe a whisper, or imply by look or act, a thought against my fame : and raised upon the height of power to which this alliance sets me, backed by position, influence, and wealth, who dare asperse, who malign the Marchioness of Almazuma? I would the morn were come, that I might pour into his friendly breast all my resolves, and give a tongue to the fast wishes of my determined heart. Alonzo, thou shalt die, while I look on and glory in thy death. Oh, base man, and vile as base,—thou, whom I fondly thought worshipped the ground I trod; held my honour, dearer than this life ;—so kind, so gentle, brave, and seeming noble; the picture of all worth and excellence—one whom the world was emulous to please and flatter—never wearied in its adulation of thy virtue ;—thou, on whom my heart first opened—whom I could have loved with all the potency of true affection; proud in my love, jealous of my election; whose fame and high desert was, in secret, to my breast a world of exquisite delight—generous as day, fond, trusting and devoted ; whose very being took its light from me, and gave beneficence in every smile. What! are these tears?" she cried, hastily wiping from her eyes the bitter drops that awakened memory drew from thir source. "Unworthy woman, to debase thy cheeks with tears for such a wretch—hypocrisy's arch-fiend !—base, craven, vile—the seemer of all seeming—a huge misshapen lie !—false tongue, false face, false heart. Away! for ever quit my memory! —for ever!—Who's there ?" she exclaimed suddenly, as her attendant maiden entered the apartment, and placed the lighted tapers on the table. Why do you intrude upon my privacy, Benina, before I summon you? What want you now ?" demanded Catalina, in an angry voice, as the Abigail drew the folds of the full curtains over the windows, and adjusted the flowers that in profuse abundance filled the costly vases, that adorned the chamber of the proud and humbled beauty.

"'Tis late, my lady," replied Benina, timidly, "and past the usual time for lights. The guests have all retired. My lord, the Marquis, bade me greet you with his best good night, and Don Alonzo——"

"Well, why do you pause ?" inquired Catalina, sharply, as the attendant hesitated. "What of Don Alonzo? Go on!"

"I thought—I believed, he had been seeking you," replied Benina, with considerable trepidation.

"Where should he seek for me at such an hour as this?" asked her mistress with marked anxiety, as a dreadful fear crossed her mind—an alarm that perhaps even her servant had witnessed her false lover's visits to her chamber, and that to more than one was known the fatal secret on which more than life itself depended; and as the conviction grew momentarily stronger that she was betrayed—past all hope irretrievably exposed, a sickness fell on her heart, and her brain grew dizzy, and she pressed her hands upon her brow, and closed her eyes, as if to shut out thoughts too horrible for their view. At length recovering her self-possession by a violent effort of the will, and smoothing her troubled features, while she assumed a repose and tranquillity of speech, far from real, she arose, and resting her left arm on the high back of her chair, extended her right hand in an attitude to demand attention, and drawing her majestic stature to the full attitude of display, she continued her question to the timid and much wondering Abigail.

"Where should he seek for me at such an hour as this ?"

"Nay, my lady, I know not," stammered Benina, "I only thought—— "

"What didst thou think? Proceed !"

"Nothing !" replied the girl, alarmed at her lady's manner.

"Tell me, thou saucy minion—tell me thy thought, or on the instant quit my presence, never to visit more, me, or my father's house. Speak, girl! I command you. Think not to blind my judgment by weak evasion. My eye detects a hesitation in thy manner, and I perceive a secret knowledge in thy breast your timid tongue fears to give utterance to. If, as I know it must, and does concern myself, give me an instant information of the fact.—Speak! I again command you, or else for ever lie under the heavy burthen of my displeasure.—Speak!"

"I thought—I didn't know—I believed," replied the attendant confusedly, "that it was possible that Don Alonzo might have sought you, that is, inquired for you, my lady—here."

"Here in my chamber !" replied Catalina, in well-feigned amazement. "Dost thou dream girl? or do you dare tell me you speak from knowledge of such a thing? Hast thou ever seen my affianced lord within the purlieus of this section of the palace—set apart exclusively for the noble Donnas here invited by my sire, thee, my woman, and myself? Who ever enters this chamber but Donna Amina, my governante, and you?—who?—answer me !"

"Holy mother !—none, lady, none !" eagerly responded the interrogated menial.

"Then wherefore should he seek me here? Presume not to evade my level question.—Your reason !—quick :—answer me !"

"Pardon me, dear lady—mistress—Donna Catalina, forgive me, and I'll tell you all," cried the attendant imploringly.

"Go on," replied Catalina, in a voice that she struggled violently to render calm, though her heart beat audibly, and the pulses in her brain throbbed with the intensity of her suspense, as it trembled on her handmaid's answer;

—"go on; I'll pardon all for truth—all your knowledge, even to surmise."

"I know not how they came," resumed Benina, pausing in fear on every word she spoke; "but for many nights I have found—here, in your chamber, lady—and—and—once—in—indeed I know not how they came—once, on your bed, many articles of dress—gloves, handkerchiefs, a garter, sword-knot, and other trifles of a man's costume; and here, to-night, just as I entered at the door—as if just dropt—this jewel of Don Alonzo's: it is the buckle of his hat, and holds his plume—and I thought that he had let it fall as he left;—and that, my lady—that is all: and, oh! pardon my presumption—I meant no ill—indeed, indeed, dear madam, I had no evil thought, no wrong suspicion;"—and as she made an end of her short speech, she clasped her hands, and looked imploringly upon her lady's pallid brow and starting eyes, that gazed with wild and fascinated stare upon the diamond brooch; and as her mind took in each circumstance of the dreadful villany that seemed to rise on every side to stun and wither her beneath the load of its consummate evidence, she groaned in self-abasement at the implication that involved her, and mechanically repeated the last words of her servant's speech—"no evil thought—no wrong suspicion"—while all the time she kept her stedfast gaze upon the gem that lay sparkling in her sight: and as, one by one, the officious maid drew from a cabinet each item she had named, and spread them out before her, she never moved, and scarcely seemed to breathe, as resting on the chair, and with her white and parted lips, and glazing eye, she stood the image of a chiselled form, so marble-like was the fixed attitude and keen observance of the half rigid, half palpitating statuary — that, as Benina looked upward to her face, a sense of terror and alarm pervaded all her frame; and deprecating her mistress's anger, she fell upon her knees, and with clasped hands implored her lady's pardon.

The supplicating action brought back the blood and memory in a revulsion, sudden, stern, and grand, into the proud donna's veins and mind; and with a haughty gesture, waving her to rise, approached the table, and with a frowning calmness, a stoical resolve, and firmness almost masculine, surveyed each article, and read in letters legible as open guilt, upon the glove, garter, and sash, the word "Alonzo." Then, shaking off all semblance of timidity or fear, she grasped Benina's wrist with her convulsive fingers, and, dragging the alarmed girl to the extremity of the room, forced her upon her knees, before a golden crucifix that stood upon a shrine in a recess of the apartment; then standing over the terrified girl, with one arm folded on her bosom, and the other pointing emphatically to heaven, she cried in an imperious voice—"Swear!"

"I do—I do!" sobbed the frightened attendant—"I do swear!"

"Swear on thy knees, by all thy hopes of heaven! thou did'st not place those things where thou migh'st after seem to find them."

"By the true cross, I swear I did not!"

"That thou hast not been bribed to play or wink at this most fearful trick on thy confiding mistress—swear it!"

"Holy Mother! bear witness that I am ignorant of all knowledge of them, and that I would die before I'd plot my lady harm," cried Benina, as she clasped her hands and bent her head in reverence before the symbol of her faith, and with truthful earnestness abjured all participation in the fraud attempted on her lady. Catalina gazed long and steadily into her menial's face, as if to read the workings of her heart: at length, satisfied with the scrutiny, she said in a milder tone—"Enough—arise!"—and as the servant rose from her lowly posture, Catalina continued:—"I will find this treachery out, Benina—I will find it out. To whom hast thou divulged what thou hast told to me?"

"To not a living soul, as the saints in heaven! but hid each thing I found, and buried the acquaintance in my secret heart."

"Thou hast done well, Benina—very well." Then, in a kinder voice, added—"Pardon me, good girl, if for a moment, in my anger, I did you wrong. We will together find this traitor out. Be secret till I bid thee speak, and keep a watch and wakeful sentry on these chambers. Thou shalt in future sleep with me:—we will find the villain, Benina—our woman's wit shall yet unmask him. We will find the villain, yet —fear not—we will."

And with a smile of deadly import, she passed her attendant, and entered her bed-chamber, followed by the unsuspicious and attached Benina.

CHAPTER XII

"A woman sometimes scorns what best contents her;
Send her another, never give her o'er.
For scorn at first, makes after love the more.
If she do frown, 'tis not in hate of you,
But rather to beget more love in you.
If she do chide, 'tis not to have thee gone;
For why, the fools are mad if left alone."—*Shakspeare.*

IT is unnecessary to our story to record the meeting which the now humbled Catalina accorded on the following day to Almazuma, or explain the means—real or ambiguous—by which he seemed to open to her mind the enterprise of villany meditated against her peace and honour by her intended bridegroom, whose object in blighting her fame was to induce her to compromise all her reserve and stately bearing, and throw herself for shelter, unconditionally, into his arms; and then, having triumphed over her pride, and secured her wealth, desert her for a more congenial and less haughty mistress. All the arts that he had himself adopted with such success, step by step he recounted to her, as having been disclosed to him by the base Alonzo himself, who, far from feeling repugnance or remorse, gloried in his dishonourable purposes. And when the enormity of the confirmed whole burst on Catalina's ears, and her reason shook beneath the weight of evidence adduced, he placed in her hand the fabricated letter, forged by Garcia, which, on perusal, banished every wavering thought, and raised the last scruple from her mind, of doubt—the faintest lingerings from her heart of love; and fully impressed with the base nature of her affianced husband's scheme, and roused by the indignity contemplated on her fame, her resentment knew no limits, and her passion mounted to the furtherance of the most fearful retribution. To the speciously reluctant Almazuma, who, for a time, artfully and conditionally declined to accept her favour, the result he feared, as he told her, of sudden revulsion of feeling, she renewed the last night's proffer of her hand—seriously sealed her plighted palm with all the energy of her awoke and impassioned soul, and swore before the sainted heaven, that it should be claimed at any day, or hour, or time, or moment in the scope of his desire, when once she had vindicated to his satisfaction, and the approbation of his mind, her spotless truth—her slandered honour."

For this purpose, a meeting was arranged for the following night, in a secluded and unfrequented bower, the whereto Almazuma was pledged to conduct the traitor, and where, having confounded the miscreant by the evidence of his friend, and her own integrity, she would bury her poniard in his maligning throat, and teach mankind a bloody lesson of a proud woman's vengeance.

But even in this burst and whirlwind of her rage, Catalina's prudence did not totally desert her. She remembered that there was another evidence of her presumed guilt :—her woman servant—menial, Benina, had seen and found those serial proofs of damnatory shame, and she disclosed the fact to Almazuma, asking his counsel and advice. The nature of that counsel, and the manner in which it was put in practice, will be seen hereafter : it is sufficient for the present to say, that when Don Ferdinand and Catalina parted, she had resolved to sacrifice her life and peace for the unstained maintenance of her high name. And having broken down the first barrier to restraint—given a secret audience to a man she professed to hate, she would not pause in using subterfuge to sweep her way from all impediments that, like burs, would cling and soil her reputation. We must, for the present, leave the issue of that conference to the result of time, and conduct our readers to another part of the grounds, where, in the afternoon of the same day, Don Alonzo and his friend Almazuma, were engaged in deep conversation, taking advantage of the usual siesta, and the most retired walks, to hold a free and uninterrupted converse.

"It is the error of thy too fanciful imagination," observed Almazuma, in reply to an observation of his friend's—"the result of thy too ardent feelings."

"Possibly it is," replied the lover, dejectedly. "I am too apt to picture human feelings as my own—see every heart in the glad halo of my own perceptions."

"And thou art wrong, my friend—wrong Alonzo. No two natures yet so harmonized, that they could travel on the self-same path without divergence, though every alley or collateral branch led to the one appointed goal."

"Oh, thou art true! and speakest the collected wisdom of experience. Thy figure's just."

"Then is it not a cruelty and a sin to question the intents of those who journey with us on life's road, or the more flowery path of love. Because sometimes they court the shade when we are chill ; or bask them in the sun, when our hot bloods pant for the cooling breeze or sheltering grove. We must, my friend, in this world's pilgrimage, borrow sometimes the eyes, if not the hearts of those who form our fellow-travellers ; and so adapt our vision, as our feelings, thoughts, and acts, to the attendant influence of the way. No man to-day is, in himself, that which he owned but yesterday. This hour we are languid, dull, and food but for our own thoughts' company ; the next, are full of gaiety, and find distaste in what was late our appetite."

"Oh! very true. But yet there should be special difference in that which touches——"

"By your leave," replied Almazuma, "no special difference should hold in any case. The law is blind, and sees no path but the direct highway :—so in our natures, Reason should be the law of rule ; and what we know ourselves deficient in, we should in charity and right permit our friend. I tell thee, good Alonzo, love—thy love especially—is too imperious in exaction : thou lookest to have the same return each hour from her that thou wouldst give—when sickness, lassitude, or the many rubs of life may render irksome, at the moment, what presently 't will stretch its arms to welcome."

"But still, my counsellor—my friend, though I admit the potency of thy just conclusion—acknowledge all the truth implied in thy most graphic instances, yet——"

"Ay, yet!—that yet !" replied Almazuma, interrupting him, "was ever traitor to a precedent sentence. The judge's verdict is but half pronounced, if on the heels of grace that blighting *yet* is sequent."

"Yet, in defiance of thy just displeasure, I must reply, my friend," cried Alonzo sadly, "and say, I do not think love, when acknowledged or professed, is warranted in putting on the face of chilling coldness, or the look of sharp displeasure."

"The look and feeling was in your mind, Alonzo."

"No! Almazuma—no. I met her more than once, and every time that I approached, her brow grew darker, and her aversion more—as though I were the blackest ingrate and the most debased of traitors."

"'Tis sickness that a night's rest will conquer," remarked his friend.

"No! Her health was never more equitably true than at this hour."

"Why, then 'tis but perversity of sex—a woman's weakness."

"She's not perverse, but keeps a steady manage on her soul ; never above or yet below the level tide of just discretion. It is not so, my friend—not so !"

"'Tis nothing else, or but the phantom of your own creation. You are too constant in your wooing. A woman longs for change, as eagerly as breath to give her life. A lover once exhausted in his theme, is as a tiresome tale : believe me, however outwardly she shows a steadfast front, the weakness and the woman quality is in her soul, and sways her actions. You have been too long the ardent—be now the indifferent lover. This assumed caprice of hers will on the instant vanish, if she perceive a fear of losing thee. The counsel that I give, though a subterfuge, experience—as I have read—has found medicinable to the sex. The keenest relish will be cloyed by a repetition of the strain —and you must strike a newer bar, my friend— if but to pitch a key."

[CATALINA AND AMINA.]

"It goes against my soul, dear Ferdinand, to descend to such ignoble shifts to fix the love I deemed already anchored to my heart. But if I thought you saw the truthful source of this cold semblance that has overclouded all my joy, I would not hesitate to practise what you teach, so I might win her back to make me blest again."

"A day—nay, an hour will test its efficacy: if you find the project fail, then seek for farther motive; and if successful, throw off disguise at once. But should it seem at first to fail, be not too rash, or seek immediate reason, but leave thy remedy to work, and quit her suddenly. Remember, good Alonzo, as a friend you ask my counsel; and as a friend, much—much interested, I now advise you." And laying his hand on Alonzo's shoulder, Almazuma looked into the lover's face with a kindly, generous glance, and spoke in terms of such true friendship, that Alonzo grasped his hand, and thanked him with mute eloquence of eye and action, for his disinterested and prudent counsel.

"But how shall I proceed?" inquired his deceived companion.

"Recount to me again—for I took but little heed before—how, and in what way she greeted you—her look, her manner, and her speech; for on that depends the answer I would give," replied Almazuma, as they seated themselves in one of the alcoves.

"Last night I left her," replied the lover, "with our usual kindly greeting—affectionate, but not familiar, such as her custom has permitted, and my respectful love has ever sanctioned. This morning when we met, last of the throng was I saluted; and then with such constraint, as if her spirit loathed the action courtesy compelled. No speech—no act—no kindly gesture of the eye, such as love brings spontaneously into view: but all was stately—frigid—distant. Again I sought

7

her in the rich parterrés, my throbbing heart full in my throat—my tongue chained up, and in my looks speaking the troubles of my soul——But, no—she did not stop to hear my liberated words, or read the language of my sorrowing face, but with repugnance and disdain—yea, by my life! a loathing in her eyes, she turned, and with a scornful step quitted the spot and sought the palace gate. Tell me, what shall I think—what apprehend from this?"

"That it is momentary spleen, or waywardness, to-morrow will dispel. But for a remedy: will you adopt it, if I lay down the way?"

"Give me the means," cried Alonzo, eagerly; "and as they trench not on my honour—touch not the reputation of her I value next to heaven, I will subscribe to the full working of them."

"Neither shall be affected. Go to her. Yonder I see her through the parting trees. Assume a careless and indifferent ease; laugh—jest: show her, by outward actions as by speech, that she is too far compromised your wife to claim exemption to any humour so opposite to your repose. Let her feel, I say—feel that she is, and must be, yours, and that you hold the consummation of the rite quite as a thing of taste in you to abrogate, or yet fulfil;—let her know that obloquy will light upon her head, if you reject to ratify the contracted match. Do this, and on my life, to-morrow night will set you free from every earthly doubt—lift you to heaven in satisfaction, and nothing further injure you in her esteem. I speak advisedly. Go! and having acted skilfully your part, leave her with indifferent haste. Keep from her sight—debar yourself her company, till the stomach of her spleen is past. Away! I would be now, my friend, alone. Go to her."

"I will upon the instant put your suggested plan in force, though much against my nature. I pray it may succeed. Farewell!"

"Be confident it will; this little outrage on thy feelings shall bring thee lasting peace—I prophesy it. Adieu!"

And Alonzo, with a wave of his hand, quitted the alcove and disappeared in the winding paths, to put in practice Almazuma's devilish project.

"Yes," exclaimed Don Ferdinand, when alone,—"yes, I prophesy it shall bring lasting peace, and that to-morrow thou shalt be free. Why, my plan goes swimmingly: each wheel turns in its due and proper course, and brings in, each revolve, another spoke into my closing hand. What, ho! Art there, my Garcia?" he cried, in a subdued voice, bending his ear to listen. "Art thou at hand?"

"Ever ready, my lord," observed Garcia, as he pulled aside the jessamine boughs and tendrils that covered the arbour, and stepped out of the close underwood, where he had lain concealed, into the alcove. "Ever at hand when wanted."

"Good, faithful Garcia, the end of our long scheme's in sight: another day will liberate us all. Have you written the letter, as I suggested?"

"I have it here about me," replied the man, drawing forth a paper and handing it to Almazuma. "Ah! here it is—all as you ordered."

"I have no time now to peruse it. You have made the writing ambiguous as I wished—varied the characters, so as to make a doubt of its authentic source."

"All as directed, Senhor: some of the lines are in my natural hand, but the larger part a fac-simile of his—the purport, word for word as you advised."

"So much for that. Hast thou procured the Thebiac drug, mixed it, and made it potable for use—forgot no portion of my last desire?" inquired Almazuma, with more lively interest than he usually evinced. "Nothing omitted?"

"Nothing. I have supplied myself with every needful thing, even to the panniered mule, and muffled hoofs, the sacking, and dried leaves to such up every trace. All's ready."

"Excellent! Now, good Garcia, attend: it is my last commission. Hie thee to the deserted hut, put on thy friar's gown—make thyself old, and, thus disguised, come to the palace gate, and seek for alms. Say thou art bound for Soria; the Donna Catalina's maid will ask thy holy company, as guide unto the city: give it her, and take her where thou wilt, so that she never more revisits here, or puts the knowledge she has gleaned into the ear of man. Do you understand?—dispose of her; and return with all the expedition in your power, for work, my Garcia—stirring work is on our hands, and we must sweep our path of briars before we tread the safe and certain highway to success. To-morrow, Garcia, sets you free. Think of it, man—dream of it; but look to this—look to this."

"I'll do it instantly," replied the man, as he turned to quit the harbour: while Almazuma approached, and laying his hand on the villain's arm, said in a cautious whisper—

"She must be silenced—make that sure! Silenced! You understand?—totally silenced!' and as he spoke, he pointed with a significant gesture of his fingers to the earth. "Silenced—dumb—dumb as death!"

Garcia gave an expressive nod with his head, and hastily quitted the spot. Almazuma gazed after him for a moment with a malignant smile, and muttering between his clenched teeth "Fool—fool!" dived into the recesses of the grove, and was instantly lost to sight.

CHAPTER XIII.

"GIVE my best greeting to the Donna Amina," said Catalina, as she entered her apartment, and sank listlessly on one of the couches; "and tell her with all love, that I am troubled with a throbbing brow, and do not feel myself sufficient company to make her welcome; and that I shall go to rest anon, and wish her all good eve—that I would be alone. Say this, and then return."

Benina curtseyed when the message was delivered, and then withdrew. Catalina remained for some time gazing with vague intensity on the ground, in the deepest mental abstraction. No one definite thought was uppermost, but her mind was a chaos of conflicting agonies: she saw nothing distinct—no one terror stood bolder out than others; it was an overwhelming load that bore her down, and seemed to crush her into earth. The elasticity of mind was for the moment gone, and a powerless, feeble, soul-less apathy alone remained within that late indomitable heart and head.

Presently she seemed to wake, as stung by some quick, sharp thought; and folding her hands, she pressed their palms with straining force across her brow, as if to check the fast and rising fancies: then, in utter hopelessness, she withdrew her hands, and dropt them by her side in lifeless languor, fixing her eyes with vacant watchfulness on the blue and gold cantharides that sported in insect pastime round the chamber; and thus remained in painful silence till the returning attendant roused her to other thoughts, recalling her to remembrance of the part she had to play.

"The Donna Amina's hearty love and grief, my lady, and wishes all soft sleep, and quick return to health," observed the servant as she re-entered the apartment.

"What is the hour, Benina?" inquired Catalina, languidly.

"It has just struck three, the hour of rest, my lady: the day is very hot."

"Have I not heard thee say, Benina," rejoined Catalina, not heeding her maid's remark, "thou hast a wedded sister settled in Soria?"

"Ay! that I have, madam; my good, dear Leonora."

"And thou couldst spend the night there, if so needed?"

"Ay! and a month too, an' I list it, and had my lady's leave."

"'Tis well!—another time. I have just bethought me, Benina, that I shall need a locket, for some hair I would present to my dear sister, on our wedding day; and as I wish no one to know of this, I'll have thee go—thou 'lt reach the city long ere dark—thou 'lt go to the jeweller's near to the Trinidado. I'll write a full description of the toy I want; and having got the trifle, hie thee to thy sister's and spend the night in her protecting company, and in the morning, come thee homeward, soon after matins."

"Oh, my lady! I'll go directly," cried the delighted Abigail. "I'll take a mule, and Lopez—he shall go with me for company, and sleep at the posada, as it were not meet to journey there alone."

"Nay, Benina, that were hardly comely for a maid to go so far with such a guide—not fit at all. I met a friar even now at the gate, and questioned him—he is a brother of the neighbouring Chauntry, and is bound to Soria, and will return to-morrow: he has undertaken to see you safe there, and home again—and he were fitter company for a young maiden, than such a wild young man as Lopez."

"A friar, my lady?" replied the Abigail, in deep chagrin.

"A holy friar, an infirm and aged man."

"An old stupid friar, who can talk of nothing but Paters and Ave Marias; a stupid old man! I'm sure Lopez is a very steady youth."

"Benina, I will entrust you to none other," added Catalina, decidedly.

"As the Donna Catalina pleases," rejoined the girl, with ill-concealed vexation; muttering to herself many maledictions on the head of the intended guide, for his inopportune arrival, and wishing him every mishap she could conceive for coming purposely to thwart her, and make her journey miserable.

"Father Anselmo waits at the postern for you; do not tire him by needless stay. Go, bid the men caparison your mule, and get you quickly ready—I will write the note."

"I wish he was at the bottom of the sea, the old fool! Tire him, indeed!—won't I tire him—that's all.—I'm going my lady," she half muttered to herself, as she slowly crossed the room, delaying the time as long as possible. When she had departed, Catalina wrote a few directions regarding the trinket required; and, when after much procrastination, she returned, Catalina had completed her note, and, presenting the girl with a purse, told her to settle with the jeweller from that, and purchase herself what dress or ornament her fancy chose. A slight smile passed over the attendant's countenance as she heard the permission; but it was momentarily extinguished as the thought of her companion reverted to her recollection.

"Oh, Benina!" exclaimed her mistress, as the girl prepared to depart, "I have discovered all the secret of those articles you found: it was——"

"Yes, my lady!" cried Benina, in a strain of lively curiosity, returning into the room, while her eyes sparkled with animation at the expected secret.

"A mere jest—not worth recounting," added Catalina, coldly, while the disappointed Abigail made a curtailed obeisance, and with a moody countenance, and scarce suppressed mortification, withdrew.

"Thou art gone," she exclaimed, when once again alone; "that's one obstacle removed, never to return. Father Anselmo will conduct her to a nunnery, where under fear, and charge of heresy, she must be made to take the veil. I would not have the poor thing hurt; no—she is safe from harm: but I must be confident that I am safe. Father Anselmo is a devout and holy man, it seems, and will watch o'er and tend her through her noviciate and probationary term; and though her body must be carcerate, will not her soul be amply cared for?—It will. Then hence all void regret,—the great necessity of the cause admits no medium. She will be safe?—yes, surely—anon I'll look into 't myself, and see she's well attended: my mind is easier now she's gone. Poor Benina! there was no help: either thou or I must have kissed the correcting rod; and this seeming violence may win a soul to heaven. If so, then is my very crime a virtue! I'll think—think——" and bending her head forward, rested her brow on her hands, and mused for some time without change; at length her thoughts assumed a different course; and lifting up her head from its recumbent posture, she said, musingly:—

"Yes, he was right; 'tis all confirmed, e'en to the fraction of a doubt—made clear as noonday sunshine. And I have harboured in my breast this cankerous snake!" she exclaimed, as the remembrance woke her to indignation. "This well-painted danger, this fair beseeming, comely, deadly treachery! Oh! Almazuma—thou hast spoken truth, saved me from ruin, plucked me back from the sheer abyss over which I hovered. Yes! it is confirmed. Was not this letter," she continued, as she removed from the bosom-folds of her rich robe, the letter that Almazuma had given her, and spread it upon the table before her, "sufficient to convince my still doubting and incredulous heart—it was. But he has now set the signet of authentic truth on every circumstance. What! on the open lawn to float, insult me! tell me to my full face, my testy humour—my haughty pride, was out of character and place! That were I wise, I'd court, not chill the heart that optionally could make me blest, or most unhappy : called me coy, perverse—one blind to her own necessitous good, that might by playing with, endanger reputation. Blessed Maria!" she suddenly exclaimed, as her frame trembled at the remembered insult; and rising, traversed her chamber with hurried and uneven steps. "Blessed mother! and have I lived—I, the daughter of Alfendera—I, the once high, honoured Catalina—lived—to be branded with the seething words of a dark villain! Lived, and did not strike! No, no, no—but I will strike. Oh, yes, I will strike—revenge the foul indignity! Oh! Almazuma, thou art full of prudence—thou hast schooled me well : left to my own headstrong feelings, I should have paid at once the debt, in one wild, angry burst : but you, you, good Ferdinand, have taught me how to husband my resentment, multiply my hate, luxuriate in my revenge! Yes—I will first stab him through each sentient part with my upbraiding tongue, and then, with my executive hand, and sharp blade, bury the defaming lie in the black heart that engendered it! Yes! I will—I will perform it."

And in the intensity of her excited feeling, she moved, looked, breathed, and seemed in every inch a sworn avenger! And as she paused, and held above her head the long dagger, which, in her impassioned burst, she had plucked from its sheath, and gazed upon it with a stern denouncing frown, her knitted brows, and flashing eyes, and stately form, gave to her whole contour a sternness, dignified and terrible; while the deep folds of her sweeping garments, and the majesty of her attitude, lent an uncommon grandeur to the commanding stature.

"Hear me, and witness for me, all ye saints— that I have resolved!"—Then quickly passing to a milder mood, she replaced her poniard, and walked the room with calmer steps, continuing her soliloquy.—"Dear Amina!—Oh, thou art not false!—I dread thy grief!—If anything can touch my heart it will be that. Thy gentleness so fond—thy love so true—thy very look's infectious, whether in sorrow or in joy. Oh, how shall I combat with my resolve—wage torturing war upon my soul?—to meet thy tears—witness thy distress; while, in my hypocrisy—Judas-like, I comfort thee in the misfortune that my own hand entails on thee and thine. Poor child,— strong in fraternal love—she cannot see the viper in her brother's form—dreams not of malice in that fair case ; and to tell her of his guilt, were pure destruction to all her life and peace. No!— doubt and uncertainty, is better here than truthful knowledge ; and while hope endures, she may be happy in her ignorance :—but I shall never more know ease of mind—tranquillity of thought. I cannot blind my mental eyes, or shut out the sunlight of reproachful memory : —but hence, these weakening fears for others' woes !—I must be stern—determined—masculine in my progressive steps to safety—must know no let—no— again !—whose there?—not gone ?—ha !" she exclaimed sharply, as she turned round, and an aged female entered the apartment. Catalina instantly corrected her tone when she saw the visitor, and said in milder utterance, "Well, good Senora, thou art come to inquire after my health

—something disturbed by last night's exercise, and too late freedom in the air, and to-day's oppressive heat ; but I am better now, Bianca, and shall not need thy friendly or medicinal aid ; a night's repose will quite restore me—'t is nothing."

"Thy words and looks, dear Donna, are at variance : you speak against the thing you feel, and would make light, for others' sakes, of what I can perceive is shadowed on your brow—pain," replied the governante.

"Believe me—no, 't is better—infinitely better."

"I am bound to credit thee, my lady, though Benina said you were most ill. I have chid myself for being told—not having apprehended it myself, as in my duty I should have done."

"Be satisfied, Senora, that I improve very fast," replied Catalina ; then added aside as she turned away towards the couch,—"yes, I improve in subterfuge and evil rapidly."

"Oh, I am pleased at this," rejoined the Senora Bianca, "as you can then comply with my lord's request."

"Speak it, and I will."

"Oh, 't is a pleasing task—'t is but to ratify the marriage settlements, omitted last night by the lateness of the gala on the lawn. The Marquis and the Condé, and the two noble gentlemen—Don Alonzo and Don Felix, with all the quality of the house, are now assembled in the library, waiting your presence to sign and to attest the documents that fix the doweries and the fortunes of the brides and happy bridegrooms.— Will you go, Donna Catalina ?"

"Assuredly :—the task will not delay me long, and I must not keep my dear Amina waiting. I will follow—inform my father so. Yes," she resumed, when the governante had retired, "I must complete this further semblance of the never-to-be-completed marriage. How full of thought is Almazuma : he advised me that this scene would be required, and bade me meet it cheerfully, and greet Alonzo as if corrected by his wholesome censure, and as though no impeachment dwelt on his honour. Oh, 't is a painful act ; but I will do, and would do more, to forward my revenge. How easy and resistless is the descent to crime when the barrier is overleaped—the first false footstep made. Upon the further bank we stand amazed with fear—abashed with shame : but leaping once the stream of falsehood, we tread the hither shore, scorning the former danger—braving the coming peril : even so feel I. I am embarked, and I will mount each wave though they exceed my head, and threaten ruin in their frown."

And with a determined look and steady pace, Catalina quitted her chamber, and descended to the thronged library. As she entered the apartment, no eye could have discovered the feelings that warred within her heart; for in the semblance of calm dignity that she assumed, and was so natural to her, all outward show of resentment or hate was banished from her tranquil features, and buried for the time in the recesses of her breast. Alonzo, who had so keenly outraged his love and devotion, in his late conduct to her, and had passed intolerable moments of anguish ever since, though conscientiously believing his coldness called for and palliated by circumstances, and not doubting the wisdom of the advice that sanctioned it, had, nevertheless, experienced all the torments that an unworthy act elicits in a generous heart that has been betrayed into a fault, and bounding forward as Catalina entered, took her hand tenderly, and with a gentle pressure, looked into her face with all the ardour of his soul, saying in hurried whispers as he led her forward, "Pardon me, my dearest Catalina—pardon my late transgression."

"I am corrected, and have nothing to forgive," she replied, while a hectic flush for an instant dyed her face, as the lover lifted the small hand to his lips, and kissed it with deep devotion.

"Ah!—can'st thou blush, dear sister?" said Amina, in her ear, as they stood together. Thou did'st but feign thy illness to keep me from thy company, and play the tyrant;—but I'll be revenged—I will!"

"And so will I," replied Catalina, in a deep whisper; then added quickly, "on thee, thou disbelieving girl."

"Come, my fair daughter, seat thyself by me, and honour the old man by the proximity of so much excellence," cried Alvares, as with a courteous dignity he rose from his place by the table, and drew one of the heavy arm-chairs for her accommodation; and taking her hand from the embrace of his son's, led her forward; while all the guests, who had risen at her entrance, resumed their places as Catalina took possession of the chair allotted her. "Here sit enthroned, the queen of virtue," continued the Condé, as he raised her hand to his lips, and bowed his head in courtly reverence to the proud lady; while with a polished, but formal etiquette, the old nobleman took his seat by her side.

Amina, Felix, and Alonzo, with the Marquis and the lawyers, filled up the remaining space round the strewn board.

"Bid the servitors bear round the wine and meats, good Lopez," cried Alfendera to an attendant, who stood respectfully behind his chair.

Lopez instantly obeyed the order, and twelve servants in gorgeous liveries entered the room, each bearing a massive gold salver, half of them heaped with small Dresden plates filled with confectionary, figs, dates, pomegranates, citron, and other conserves, with small rich biscuits and frosted cakes; while the remaining half bore on their trays wines of all flavour, from Tokay to Xevey, with those exquisite tall, tapering Venetian glasses, whose sympathetic flint shivers at the touch of poison, and stained of every hue, embracing the bright purple, amethyst, topaz, and ruby. The servants divided themselves into two parties, three with the conserves and meats, proceeding up each side of the long room, followed by a like number bearing the wine and many-coloured glasses.

When the guests had all refreshed themselves with the light but luscious fare, the Marquis rose, and placing his sign-manual and signet on the parchments, presented them to Alvares, who, in like manner, attested each; then came the signatures of Alonzo and Felix; and when, last, Catalina rose, Alvares, with a graceful bow, presented her with a pen, which with a smile of thanks, and a slight tremor of the hand, she took, held it for a moment with an irresolute action, then with a hasty glance at Alonzo, put her hand to the deed, and wrote her name with an unmoved and steady countenance.

With a quick, nervous haste, the half-frightened, half-pleased Amina added hers; while in her cheeks alternate red and white was struggling for the mastery.

"My friend, Almazuma, thou shalt attest for me," cried the Condé, as he beckoned Don Ferdinand from the extremity of the library.

"And you, Don Juan de Arquillo—you shall bear witness for our house," observed Alfendera to a nobleman near him.

The two hidalgos approached, and as Almazuma confronted Catalina, he cast one quick, intelligent, and rapid glance upon her features, and with a bland smile to the Condé for the compliment, and a formal bow to the company, placed his signature to a bond he felt and knew had not one day's validity in prospect. When all had been completed, Alvares rose, and taking from a jewelled case a diamond necklace, threw it with graceful gallantry round Catalina's neck, upon whose face and brow a deep and burning blush on the instant mantled; and but her voice failed her, and the eye of Almazuma for a moment rested on hers, she would have put it back, and have refused the gift: but ere she could gain resolution to adopt her first resolve, the Marquis rose, and placing round Amina's small fair neck a chain of equal value, led her forth; while the Condé, offering his arm to Catalina, followed, as the lovers and assembled guests, in pairs, swelled out the train, which, ushered by the servitors, proceeded to the grand banquet-hall.

CHAPTER XIV.

ABOUT an hour before the meeting of the guests, as related in the last chapter, a group of young nobles, and several of the higher domestics of the establishment, was collected round the figure of an infirm and venerable monk, whose long beard, of silvery whiteness, exhibited a holy reverence as it flowed down the coarse serge of his much-worn and mended gown. That portion of his face which was visible beneath the capacious cowl was deeply furrowed with age: long straight lines diverged, as from a centre, round his eyes and mouth; while his forehead, corrugated like a fallow field, gave a stamp and character of extreme age to the stooping and paralytic form of the poor brother. A small scrip or wallet of leather, greasy and black with time and use, was suspended by a cord from his right shoulder, and rested on the opposite hip. A bat, or rough staff, nearly six feet long, lay in the hollow of his right arm, on which, as he leant his back against the wall, he placed one of his much-swollen and bandaged legs, as if to ease the pain the too great weight of his otherwise spare body occasioned him. With his left hand he took from time to time small leaden images from his satchell, and pressing them with a devout piety to his lips, presented his effigies of saints and martyrs to the by-standers, who, with an equal sanctity, suspended them, either on their breasts by silk cord, or placed them in the belts of their hats; not, however, forgetting to drop a consideration into the open and soliciting pouch of the holy father, as a slight compensation for relics so valuable.

"Whither journey you, good father?" inquired Don Felix, as with Alonzo and Almazuma they approached the spot where the old monk stood. "Methinks thou art too old to quit the shelter of thy cell, or the sunny bench of thy house's cloister. Thou art very old."

"St. Chrysostom and St. Anthony bless thee, young lord," replied the monk, in a weak and tremulous tone; while the words whistled as they passed through his shaking jaw. "I am old and weak in body, it is true; but holy St. Francis be praised, the spirit is strong, though the flesh be frail. I am bound on our poor house's benefit, to Soria, so please you, my good son, and have tarried hither on the way to eat of thy bread and drink of thy cup, and say one prayer for the noble house."

"Good father, was there none younger would take thy mission?" observed Alonzo.

"None, my son—none. Besides, it is an act of penance. We have all grievous sins, my son —grievous sins to expiate."

"Thine must be light: life's passions have long put out their fires within thy breast, and strife has done with thee. Thy faults are nothing."

"Who shall read the heart, my son?" replied the friar, as a hard convulsive cough shook his palsied frame, and seemed for a moment to extinguish the small vitality that remained to him.

"True," added Alonzo, musingly. "Who shall read the heart? Here is a ducat for thy own necessities, and to be just, two more for thy brotherhood."

"Saint Francis is merciful to his order."

"And here," cried Felix, "is an equal doit. Give me one of thy saints."

The old man, with a low reverence, took the money the two youths bestowed upon him, and in return, selected from his store two of the best figures it contained, and putting the sign of the cross on each, presented them to the two nobles.

Almazuma had stood a silent and contemptuous spectator of the scene, though his eye had more than once investigated the figure before him: the inspection, however, did not seem satisfactory; and turning round with an indifferent carelessness, looked among the group assembled, as if in search of some other object; but not finding it, a frown gathered on his brow; and as his friends were leaving, he drew forth a purse, and putting his fingers in the meshes to withdraw a piece of gold, approached the mendicant with a stern countenance, saying as he halted for a moment, "Here, old man, is a doubloon." At that instant his eye encountered the twinkling glance of the friar; and gazing for a second with a searching intelligence, the cloud passed from his brow, and dropping the whole purse into the open wallet, that with shaking hands the old man held open, exclaimed in a low voice, as he withdrew an effigy from it, "Excellent!" and passing his arm through Alonzo's, the three entered the palace, as with a deep obeisance the wandering friar folded his arms over his chest, and bent low his venerable head in speechless thanks. At the same moment, Benina, mounted on a handsome mule, and led by one of the men-servants, entered the avenue that conducted to the palace gate, and where the monk still stood, parting with his remaining saints to the eager domestics. As the servitor led up her mule to the place of her new guide, Benina drew back her mantilla, and

looking into the friar's face and scanning his unprepossessing appearance, inquired with an accent of disgust, "Art thou the monk who art to conduct me to Soria?"

"Verily, fair maiden—he, he! ugh, ugh, ugh! hoo, hoo!—the vile cough!—surely it will kill me! out on 't! how it shakes me.—Verily, maiden, I am—ugh, ugh!—that unworthy person," replied the friar between the fits of his hard cough.

"I don't doubt it," she said in sharp pique. "Can'st thou not walk?—A pretty guide, truly.— Lame old fool!"

"Nay, nay!—Madam Benina," observed a servant reproachfully; "it ill becomes thee to flout the good father on the infirmities sent by heaven upon us all."

"Hold thy peace, Pedrillo!—I did not speak to thee," retorted the indignant Abigail, as she replaced the veil, and cried in very vexation of spirit.

"Nay, rebuke her not, my son—hoo, hoo! ugh, ugh!"—responded the friar, as he rose from his leaning position against the wall, and with slow and limping pace drew near the mule, and took the bridle from the domestic's hand. "The revilings and the scoffs of the unthinking are as medicine to our flesh—it is part of our spiritual correction, and our poor despised order is doomed to suffer. Leave the maiden alone— heaven works its own cure, and at its own appointed time. Benedicite to all—Pax vobiscum." And turning round, he held up his hands and muttered for a moment a short prayer; then leaning on his staff with one hand, and grasping the bridle with the other, put the beast into motion, and tottered by its head down the avenue.

When they had at length lost sight of the palace, and reached the open country, Benina with a sudden jerk, wrenched the reins out of the palsied hands of her guide; and exclaiming, "I shall never reach Soria at this gait if I stay for you," gave the mule a fillip with a small riding-whip she held in her hand, and trotted away at a rapid pace, fast distancing her infirm companion. The monk cast a quick inquiring glance around, and finding there was no one near to help him, increased his pace gradually from a slow to a quick walk, and at length put his body into a long swinging trot—expostulating all the time, and imploring the runaway to tarry.

"Blessed Maria!—not so fast—think of my age—ugh, ugh!—my cough!—You 'll be the death of me.—Pity an old man!—Good damsel, stay—tarry my coming. St. Francis! thou 'lt murder me!—think of that, maiden.—Mercy! stop! stay! hoo! ha! hoo!—tarry for me."

But all the old man's prayers and entreaties would have been in vain, had not his own hitherto dormant energies of body aided him; for Benina kept whipping her animal, and gaining ground rapidly: when putting all his agility into action, the monk at length, spent with toil, and totally exhausted for lack of breath, sprang forward and secured the rein of the mule, and brought him to a sudden halt. Benina instantly dropped the bridle, and with an angry toss of her head, cried: —"You are not so lame as you pretend, methinks!" Her guide may no reply for several minutes, as he seemed bent, and almost suffocated with his asthma; but, at length, drawing freer breath, he took the precaution to pull the reins over the mule's head, and making a loop of them, fastened them to his arm ; then addressing the animal, exclaimed in panting breaks :—" Thou varlet, thou—thou most unmannerly brute—to run away—with the maiden—ugh ! Thou wretch ! I will anathematize thee—thou whoreson carrion—thou might'st have killed her. He might, my daughter, have killed thee,—I saw thou could'st not keep him in. They have hard mouths, these brutes ;—but never strike a runaway beast, my daughter—it only scares them more. Out on the wretch ! how skittish !—ugh ! ugh !—it has almost killed me. Thou art not hurt, art thou ?—'tis a perilous danger to escape—limbwhole. Yet thou did'st do bravely —a stranger would have thought thou wert riding for a race : thou art excellent at the saddle.— Out on the bute !—to hazard my charge." And with a feeble impotency the old man dealt the animal a few blows with his fist, which, seemingly violent, were, in effect, mere touches.

" How likest thou that correction ?" he continued ; " I'll warrant thou hast not been so maltreated since thy noviciate to the bit !—varlet, take that—ho ! ho ! ugh ! ugh !—Oh dear, oh !"

" Methink thy lameness, priest, is more pretence than real ; or thou could'st hardly have overtaken my runaway mule," added Benina, cruelly vexed ; and finding the impossibility of evading or escaping her tedious attendant "You can run fast enough."

" Thy danger, daughter, took all my ailments off for the moment, as a bed-ridden man at the cry of fire will spring to his feet and fly. Do not slander that which, under the saints, was the means of saving thee.—Ho ! ho ! oh dear !—But let us wend our way, and as we trudge along, I'll put up a thanksgiving for thy miraculous safety :" and putting the mule into a quick walk, the monk began recounting, aloud, a form of thanks.

" Don't trouble yourself, old man, with prayers for my safety—I was safe enough ; pray for yourself. I would you'd let my mule alone ; I was but practising him for my lady's use, and you must spoil my sport—and my day's pleasure too."

" Poor child ! Thou dost not know the difference between a vicious and infuriate beast, and one under the bound and manage of his master. Poor child !—but how should you ?"

" I'm not the fool you take me for," replied Benina tartly.

" I can see you walk better than you did—how comes that ? Is it a miracle, pray you ?" she asked with a sarcastic laugh, " or one of your holy cheat ?"

The monk crossed himself devoutly at the implication, and in a meek and humble voice rejoined : " Heaven forgive thee, daughter, as I do from the bottom of my soul, for thy unjust and cruel words. I didn't think that my dry eyes could ever weep again."—And the venerable father cried with hysteric and choking sobs.—" I did not think there was so much moisture left in this old and shrivelled frame, to make so full a shower. God forgive you, maiden, for thus cutting to the heart a weak poor old man—a most unworthy servant of the cross. Pardon me, good daughter that I thus give way. I am very infirm—forgive me—forgive me ! I know I am too old to live—a very dog—a worm—and in the world's highway—forgive me !"

Benina had a tender heart—she was a woman, and a young one ; and the meek words and tears of the old man, joined with the knowledge of her ill-humour, and the harsh words she had used to the unoffending priest, touched her with the liveliest shame and self-reproach ; and bursting into tears, she begged the holy father would pardon her ; confessed her cause of spleen, and asked a full forgiveness, and that she would again in no way hurt or cross his will, but bow obediently to his guidance, and not, by word or thought, reproach him, should they take a day to reach their destination.

" Thou art pardoned, fully—fully !" replied the friar, " and we will journey faster ; for I feel better, and my feet are less afflicted than they were at starting. And I do believe that my kind brother, Anastatius, hath par-boiled the peas within my sandals, knowing me old and weak ; for a verity, they do not now abrase my flesh, as at my starting—they did at first. This is why my gait is easier, my child—for this mission is one of voluntary penance ; and the brotherhood have, in kind error, practised on my tender feet a pious stratagem—I feel it is so."

" For thy sake, good father, I am right glad to hear it ; 'twas cruel to walk so far, in so much torture. But, sure, we leave the road," she cried, as they began to wind up a long steep path, that, cut out of the face of a high hill, afforded room only for one to advance at a time. " This leads not to Soria, or else I've lost remembrance of the way ; 'twas sure the highway we have left."

" I told the Donna Catalina I had a missive for a holy sisterhood, whose convent stands on the brow of this same path, where, for five minutes' rest, we may refresh us, ere we descend the other side into the city. This way saves half a league. But I'll return if thou dislike it ?" replied her guide, as he still kept her mule at a quick step up the dangerous shelf of pathway. " Ten minutes takes us to the house ; and the descent is by a broad and steady road,"—and he cast a quick glance down the declivity.

" Nay, as you list—go on. Have you travelled far, good father ?" inquired Benina, now quite reconciled to her companion.

" Ay, good daughter, I've been to Egypt— that land of grand and awful wonders,—traversed the prairies of the New World,—seen sights to stagger reason—heard things to make belief a liar !"

" Indeed ! Oh ! how I should like to see those sights in foreign parts I hear the pilgrims talk of ! But methinks your cough is better, father."

" It is, my child : the pure mountain air benefits me. I am much improved within the last few minutes—the higher I go the better. Yes, I have seen sights !—kissed the blessed sepulchre."

" Oh ! what a blessing."

" It is, my daughter. When I was in Syria, a holy bishop taught me to read and understand the stars. Holy man ! he is since canonized, and is a saint in heaven."

" Read the stars, father ?" inquired the maiden, with lively curiosity. " Can'st thou foretell events ?"

" All, but my own fate, is open to me, child ; that——" and the friar shuddered—" I cannot fathom—I would I could. Why dost thou ask ?"

" Nothing—only—oh, nothing ! I was thinking how awfully deep it is—and the broad river looks like a belt beneath," she suddenly exclaimed, as her eye wandered down the precipice on the ledge of which she was travelling.

"Thou wast thinking of thy own fortune, daughter—the next turning of the path leads us from this danger—come, I will tell it thee;" and he stopped the mule, and placed himself between the animal and the face of the rock.

"Nay, father—I—indeed—no—I have no curiosity:—oh, no! I am not at all curious—only, if you really—really could say *who*——"

"Who will be thy husband?" added the monk. "I 'll try;"—and taking from his pocket a series of cards, on which a number of figures were printed, he presented them one by one to Benina, inquiring if her age was in the list of numbers; separating those that she returned in the affirmative from the others, he arranged them on his hand, and, after a momentary glance, pronounced her years "nineteen."

"Holy father! how could you tell that?" cried the credulous girl. "I didn't say my age."

"Tarry a little, daughter," rejoined the old man, with a wave of his hand—"tarry;"—and pretending to read the figures on the cards as letters, he added—"and the name of your lover, at least, is—let me see—is it an L." Then, after a little hesitation, and wiping his eyes—while Benina watched him with intense interest, forgetting in her curiosity the dangerous path on which she stood, the monk replied by spelling the letters "L O P E z—Lopez."

"Lopez!" ejaculated Benina, with a deep blush. "Is Lopez to be my husband?" she inquired eagerly.

"Nay—that merely tells thy age and lover's name: as for your after-fortune, that is another process."

"Oh! do tell me!" cried the excited girl, now indifferent to every thing—her journey—sister—all but the gratification of the one wish; and every moment increasing her admiration for the old man beside her. "Quick!—pray tell me." But the monk was seized with another long and troublesome fit of coughing, which only added to her suspense and impatience.

"Oh! I should like to know what my first boy's name will be. Do tell me that;—come, what is the process?"

"'Tis a more serious one—thou would'st not like to hear it here; and it is only at times that my mind is clear enough to unravel them. To-morrow I may not be able—I must not speak it now."

"Oh, yes! I will hear it now, and here! What's to be done?—do tell me."

"I fear it cannot be practised now—let us go. No—not now.—Come!" replied the priest, as if about to resume his journey.

"No! no! no! Good, holy father—why not here, and now?"

"Alas! I am but a poor begging friar, and I have not about me any coins of value, nor a handkerchief, to try the potency of my sure charm. I feel the spirit's on me, too. It is a pity, for it will not last. I would have gladly told thy fortune, maid—to prove to thee that I am grateful to those who can pity and bear with the troubles of an infirm old man. It is a pity I cannot—I'm poor!"

"But I—but I have both, good father!" cried

Benina, with breathless impatience, interrupting the monk in his prosy speech. "I have plenty of gold!—here—take it!"—and he drew forth the purse Catalina had given her, and placed it in her guide's hand: "and here—here is a handkerchief. Now father—now! quick!"

"Not so hasty—not so hasty!" rejoined the other, as he undid the purse, and, taking out each piece, made a cross on it, and placing them in a row, with their medallions downwards, on a projecting piece of rock, tied the handkerchief round his eyes—and, making two or three genuflexions to the east and west, removed the bandage, and crossing himself three time, looked upon the money, and pretended to read from the initials on the coins the name of Lopez. "Lopez again!" he exclaimed in surprise. "Am I right, maiden?—know you such an one?'

"Yes—yes—yes!" blushed and stammered Benina—"but what of him? Can you tell me any thing of Lopez?"

"He shall be thy husband! But now for the great test—thy future happiness, and thy boy's name!" continued the astrologer, putting the money back into the purse, making crosses over it, and shaking it till the pieces were all mingled; then, taking from his pouch a small phial of red atramentum, he wrote with a stylus the name of Lopez on one of the gold coins; and, again shaking the purse, pronounced an unintelligible prayer, placing the money all the while under his feet; then, folding up the handkerchief till he made a narrow impervious band of it, he said— "Now, daughter—now!—not a minute to lose! You must let me bind this round your eyes; and, when blinded, put your hand in the purse and withdraw the first piece that you touch—and all your future life will be revealed to you. Be quick to secure the blessed coin, for the charm will not endure five minutes. Haste thee maiden— haste!"

Benina was too much excited, and her curiosity too intense, to require further urging: she accordingly stooped down her head, and drew her mantilla over her face to make obscurity more perfect, while the monk passed the handkerchief twice round her eyes, and firmly secured it in front. When all was completed, he bade her put her hands together, and repeat an Ave Maria for success, and then test the fortune that was waiting for her.

The infatuated girl did as he required, folded her hands and began to repeat aloud her short prayer; but scarcely had she commenced it, when the monk, having placed the gold in his pocket, fell back a few paces, as far as the narrow path would permit, and making a bound forward with his outstretched arms, hurled her off the back of her mule down the precipice. One loud shriek burst from the lips of the deluded girl, as, revolving in the air, she fell right down the abyss, into the opening waters of the fast, deep river that flowed beneath. So great was the momentum of the villain's drive, that the body cleared all the projecting dangers of the way, and escaped mangling in its descent.

For one instant the monk paused to hear if there was a reply to that shrill, piercing, terrible cry, but all was still—the elevation was too great to wake a friendly answer; then seizing the alarmed mule by the head, he strained and struggled in the long fruitless task of backing him over the edge of the cliff. At length, grasping the animal's forelegs in his arms, and lifting him by main force from the ground—to which, with an instinctive terror, the creature endeavoured to cling, he drove him backwards over the precipice : and as the brute fell rebounding from the face of the hill, cry after cry broke from his lacerated body. Not pausing to note the result of his deed, the monk fled down the path for several hundred yards, till he reached a spot where the hill shelved with a steep but inclined side from the pathway down to the river. Instantly gathering his gown around him, the monk sat down on the verge, and drawing up his feet, depressing his shoulders, and throwing back his body, shot down the declivity like a bolt from an arrow, and never stopped till immersed in the river; from the impetus of his descent he struck out, and buffetting the water regained the bank.

After a moment's rest to recover breath, the pretended monk walked searchingly about, seeking for the body of his victim; but the stream was rapid, and there was no trace on the banks, or in the waters, of the unfortunate Benina. The bleeding and disfigured carcass of the mule, still panting in its death agony, lay a short distance higher up; and that was all that remained to bear witness to a deed so heartless.

Taking off his hooded gown, the villain stepped forth in the dress of the Zingari, in which we have first seen Garcia introduced in our tale. Tearing off part of his late disguise, and scattering pieces of it along the face of the hill in the way of his descent, he enclosed some heavy stones in the rest, and plunged it into the stream.

" If they find her body," mused Garcia, " they will think that I blindfolded her because she was timid, and that the mule took fright and plunged her over the brink." He continued as he struck into the wood that began to skirt the banks of the river, and proceeded to retrace his steps to the palace—" Ay, ay !—and that, in indeavouring to save hers, lost my own life.—Ho, ho ! capital ! my gains are good to-day : six ducats from the bridegrooms—thirty doubloons from Almazuma—ha, ha, ha !—he didn't know me—that was good—didn't know me !—He pays like a king ; and all to circumvent a woman. Well, we 've all our weaknesses—all our soft points—and that is his ; and he'd spend a revenue to further it. He might do it cheaper—cheaper. Well, let me see :—two pistoles from the servants, and twenty-two great ducats from Madam Benina—ha, ha, ha ! Lord, what fools women are ! Well, she would have her fortune told, and I did it.—She was a buxom wench too. I couldn't afford to run the risk of saving her for myself.—No, I couldn't do it—no.—I must find another to-morrow ;—aye, to-morrow !—for then ends my 'prenticeship—I shall be free to-morrow. Oh, how I shall luxuriate —I 'll turn my house at Madrid into a harem, and live the life of a Bashaw. Oh ! I will enjoy my coming time !—I will be provident in my pleasure, and make them last me.—Yes, yes ! —the time 's at hand !—That fool Alonzo little dreams how near his end approaches.—Yes, that was a good application of Almazuma's—' Crush him !'—To-morrow—ha, ha !—yes, he shall be crushed to-morrow ; and I shall live, hourly to laugh at his credulity—to laugh at him—ho, ho ! —jeer at him !"

And with such soliloquies Garcia employed his thoughts as he returned to the precincts of the palace, on the day preceding a night that was to be so eventful to Alonzo and himself.

CHAPTER XV.

IMMEDIATELY in the rear of the Palace of Alfendera, and extending for many acres on every side, were the rich parterres and ornamented gardens before described ; with its lawns and walks, intersected and irrigated by various parted and uniting streams, cascades, and lakes,—giving a delicious verdure to all the vegetation, and cooling the else oppressive air. Beyond these extensive plots of garden were planted thick groves of orange, citron, figs, and myrtle, the retreat of all the southern tribes of birds, whose many throats made the perfumed woods harmonious.

These scented orchards and living aviaries were succeeded by dense woods of chestnut, cedar, sycamore, beech, and oak, which, planted in regular order, and as it were built into a vast temple with its nave, aisles, chancel, and transepts, formed a perfect labyrinth ; and though every avenue and glade was most dissimilar—yet each being arched and embowered, gave at the first glance a uniformity to the whole, which, in reality, it did not possess. Here and there, where the long vistas met or diverged, an opening in the canopy of leaves admitted the sun or moon-beams, which, like a belt of gold or silver light, illumed the green path. Statues, lions, fountains of showering water, classical altars, or honey-suckle bowers, were liberally distributed throughout this templed wood and meditative scene. And as the eye, from the palace terrace, took in the whole prospect, the effect was gorgeously beautiful : the smooth green lawn at the spectator's feet ; the garden rich in every colour, hue, or tint, of nature's floral excellence, with its cool transparent waters, edged with kissing and depending flowers ; beyond, gracefully tall and nodding with exuberant fruit, or shaking their long-fringed sprays under the pressure of many painted birds, rose the diversified groves of fruited orchards ; and further off, towering high above all, stretched out the bounding woods, displaying from their emulous branches every shade of colouring, from the silvery ash, trembling in its own bright light, through all the tints of green, sienna and purple, to the black and crowning fir and cedar ; and as their thick tops were lit by the beams of the setting sun, each leafy branch or pointed spray seemed bathed in a flood of golden fire—while below, the opening glades or caverned vistas slept, curtained in the gloomiest night.

We have been thus particular in giving a general outline of the grounds adjacent to the palace, as the scene we are about to describe is laid in one of the remote and secluded walks situated in an unfrequented portion of the extensive wood.

The palace clock had just struck ten, and the faint echoes were yet vibrating in the dense foliage around and overhead, as Almazuma and Alonzo entered a distant and neglected harbour that terminated one of the last of the many avenues. The day had been intensely hot, and though the night was dark and cloudy, and a low wind crept through the trees, shaking their tops, and gently undulating the lower foliage ; yet the air was close and sultry, and felt but little cooled by the fanning breeze that with whispering cadence sighed through the leafy boughs. The close embowered arbour which the two nobles entered was about twelve feet square, furnished with a small table and two rustic chairs. Against the mossy walls reposed a few large folios, a telescope, (a very rare article at the time) and a few astronomical instruments ; upon the table stood a small unlighted lamp, fed with naphtha from a reservoir to which it was attached : upon a bench, in one of the corners, were some stoups of wine and a few gold-brimmed beakers. Without, the alcove was rendered impervious to light by the matted and abundant tendrils and leaves of honeysuckle and jessamine, that, growing from either side, clung and embraced, and formed a net-work and complete investure of combining flowers, throwing their long pliant arms heavy with perfume, like embroidered drapery, far over the open doorway or mouth of this sylvan grotto.

"Welcome, my friend !" cried Almazuma, as he let fall the thick odoriferous branches he had withdrawn to permit Alonzo to pass,—" welcome to this retreat—this hermit's bower, and scholar's cell, where, since my sojourn here, I 've passed most of my midnight hours, reading the stars through yonder opening in the woody roof of the high trees—scanning futurity's dark calendar, and tracing from the book of life, recorded there, the passages to come. But this is the night of thy initiation to my mysteries ; and I will teach you wondrous facts—help you to knowledge vast as heaven. Stay—I will strike a light,"—and approaching a recess in the soft wall, drew forth the needful implements, and lighting the lamp on the table, took off his bonnet, and throwing it on the ground, sank into one of the rude seats, pointing out the other for the accommodation of his friend. Alonzo gazed about him with an unquiet eye, and some curiosity ; and following Almazuma's example, observed—

" 'T is strange I never observed this grotto, and I thought I knew each nook of these woods ! Why, even Felix is ignorant of this retreat."

" Did'st thou ask him, then ? " inquired Almazuma, slowly.

" Nay, not I ; but he would have led me hither had he known it. How solemn and gloomy is the place : the very birds would seem to shun its solitude. Is that De Vega ? No. How strange the human mind should harmonize with such a lonely scene ! "

" It is not strange at all. If you put life in those tall tapering stems, give them the functions that elaborate with ourselves—call the green leaves their lungs, the dews of heaven their drink, the rich salacious sap, drawn from the heterogeneous earth their hourly diet ;—those emulous branches, so many eager hands stretched to the sun for light, to fructify the food, drawn to their soft pith by the far-spreading sponges at their feet ;—those million points that hem their leaves, conductors of the latent principle of life, the lightning of the air, to give vitality and action to the whole. Look on the woody prospect thus, my friend, and you will find communion with a world of most congenial objects, as new—as varied : they grow—they live—mature, and die ; each, though of one family—as with man ;

has, to the intelligent eye, special appurtenances—difference of feature. Like mankind, all this attests to life—enjoying life. And who has yet asserted, provingly, that they want sensation ? "

" I 'll think the better, for my life to come, of the green shade," replied Alonzo ; " for you have opened to my mind a thought it never had before. 'T is true, I knew the plantings lived, bore fruit, and died : but that they claimed so near affinity and likeness to ourselves, was matter quite oblivious to my mind. Where tarries De Vega ? "

" Did you bid him come ? " asked Almazuma, indifferently.

" Oh, yes ! and bade him bring a slight refection, which, with a cup of cool wine, will make this arbour less gloomy, and our friendly chat more gladsome ; for I own I 've not the just hilarity of thought that usually attends me. There is no cause for this, and yet I 'm sad. I would that De Vega came !—There is a sort of heavy aspect on my soul—a kind of death-bed seriousness, that, without cause, oppresses me. Is he coming ?—It gains upon me against my reason, and I 'd give a fortune to be fit to laugh," cried Alonzo, dejectedly, as he passed his fingers through his long waving hair, and listened for his servant's steps. " I 'd have some wine—wine, for this hateful gloom without 's infectious."

" Does thy servant know the way—the path is something difficult to find ? "

" Oh ! he 's shrewd enough to find it blindfolded. I told him of the spot as you had pictured it to me—the ceder avenue at the extremity of the wood. He will find it, though he 's late. He went to Soria, yesterday, on a mission of his own : the knave is doubtless tired. Hark ! "

" Your ears are good—steps are coming : but they are yet far off," observed Don Ferdinand. " Have you——"

" I would he came. My heart's too low tonight—I want a cup of wine ! " cried Alonzo, interrupting Almazuma's question. " Ha !—he comes ! " he exclaimed, as Garcia—or De Vega, as Alonzo called him—stopped at the mouth of the arbour, with a closed basket on his arm. " Come in—come in, good fellow ! Come, De Vega—whither hast thou tarried ? My friend and I would sup. Come, quick to thy functions—prepare—haste thee,"—and with a restless eagerness, Alonzo rose and walked about the arbour, while Garcia busied himself in spreading the table with the contents of his well-stored basket.

" Come, my good friend," observed Almazuma, " the meal is ready. Come—give me—what is thy name, companion ? " inquired Don Ferdinand, in natural and well-affected indifference.

" De Vega, so please your excellency," replied Garcia, with consummate gravity.

" Then, worthy De Vega, fill thy master a beaker full of thy coolest wine. Thou dost not eat, Alonzo ! He is athirst—let it be good—you understand. This capon 's excellent ! Good fellow, dost thou understand the quality of vintage ? "

" Ay, worthy Senhor."

" 'Tis well. See thy lord's potation is to the purpose, fully seasoned to the palate—every way fit for the occasion. Come my friend, do justice. I tell thee 'tis thy last supper,—the last bachelor meal we shall partake of together : eat cheerily, then. Hast prepared the drink !—that beverage that lifts the soul to heaven! Come eat,—eat," urged Almazuma.

"I do, I do.—The wine, De Vega—the wine !" exclaimed Alonzo.

During the foregoing sentence, Garcia had proceeded to the rude bench on which stood the stoups of wine, and placing a beaker on a small silver salver that he had brought with him, took from his vest a phial, and turning his back on the two nobles, with one hand poured out the contents of his bottle into the measure, while with the other he filled the cup to the brim with the sparkling Xerez, and turning round with a respectful obeisance, approached his master, and presented the drugged goblet.

"Ah! most welcome," cried Alonzo taking up the gold-mounted cup. "Here's to our endless friendship !"—and putting the bowl to his lips, quaffed off the contents at a draught. Almazuma watched the process of his friend's destruction with a calm smiling eye, while Garcia drew a freer inspiration when the other replaced the beaker on the board; and stealing a glance at Almazuma, retired into the shade.

"You have omitted me! Let me have a bowl to answer such a noble wish, the same my friend partakes of. His draught is sure warranty of the juice's excellence—quick !" And as he spoke, the crafty plotter followed with inquiring and steady eye, the action of his accomplice, who filling another cup with the same liquor, brought it with obedient courtesy to his employer. "I drink this goblet to the quick completion of my dear friend's peace," cried Almazuma, with a meaning emphasis, as he carried the vessel to his lips.

"I do not know whether 'tis the error in my taste that's something vitiated; but that wine is not so good as it was wont to be,—it leaves a heaviness upon the palate, and a rank flavour on the tongue : or me, or else the wine's in fault—there's an earthiness about the taste," remarked Alonzo, as Almazuma finished his draught.

"Nay, 'tis in thy appetite. I never tasted finer, or more generous grape. Set the stoups on the table, De—— what is thy name? Ay, ay, Vega ; true—Vega. Place the wine here : give thy lord another bowl, and we will fill the beakers up ourselves ; take hence the food, and you may leave us. Come, Alonzo, taste the other—it may be in better season to thy liking—try !"

"Oh! this is better, infinitely better," cried the lover, as he helped himself to another quality, while Garcia, having removed all but the wine, bowed respectfully to the two friends, and withdrew. "Ay! this is excellent," he continued, as he filled another bumper ; "this warms you to the soul, and I feel the sadness rising like a pall from off my heart. Ha! I begin to enjoy the night. Here's quality, my friend—come."

"Nay, I will keep to this : 'tis not obnoxious to my taste as yours. 'Tis full of flavour, fruity, and bodied," replied Almazuma, declining the stoup that Alonzo pushed gently towards him. "It is against my usual habit to drink two cups, but I will exceed for once. Who knows if ever we may pass another night together! So I will lay aside austerity, and pledge thee, friend, in brimmers. Come, fill—fill! To the peerless Catalina !"

"To the peerless Catalina !" reiterated the lover,

with animation. "I will drink till my soul grows thirsty, relishing each bumper with the blest name ; for we are friends again ;—and she is all my wildest hopes imagined—my bounding heart desires. Peerless, matchless in her goodness !" exclaimed Alonzo, with heated energy.

"Another goblet to thy happy union !" cried Almazuma, filling his measure and lifting it to his lips. "Pledge me in that !"

"Ay! with the pulses of my soul! Our happy union !"

"Another to thy friend, the noble Felix," added Almazuma, still plying his infatuated victim with the wine. "Come !—to Felix !"

"I must want breath when I refuse it !" cried Alonzo, with a flushed face and bounding pulse, drinking his beaker to the dregs—while the crafty Don Ferdinand, watching a favourable opportunity, poured the contents of his measure down his neck and bosom, and watching with lynx eye every movement of his devoted friend. "How is thy sadness now ?" he inquired, jocosely. "Takes it complexion from the scenery still ? or has the cloudy fit dispelled, and let the sun shine on thy heart ?"

"Ha! ha! ha! ha! 'tis gone—'t is gone! and my freed soul steps boldly from its prison, as if it danced on life-giving air. Ha! ha! ha!—thy company, my friend—thy glorious company—has—has wrought the admirable change. Come, let us sing—sing! I will sing!"

"Let us first be courteous in our cups—fill thy bowl again. Here's health to thy sweet sister, the fair Amina !" cried Almazuma.

"Though 'twere my last gasp, I'd drink to that. Ha! ha! ha! here's fair Mina !—huzza! huzza !" shouted Alonzo, with excited action and a wild extravagant gesture, as the half-formed words parted from his impeded tongue, and, stretching out his arms, gave a deep yawn. "O, pardon—pardon! but—but—yawh! the wine's more—more potential than usual. She's a good girl—good—very—another bumper to her happiness !" he exclaimed loudly, and with a sudden burst, as if to shake off a heaviness that grew upon him, while, with an unsteady hand, he conveyed the goblet to his lips. "Come! come !" he continued, in the intervals of quick yawns, and as his voice occasionally rose and fell, as the lethargy stole on his brain, or the yet struggling reason flashed out in bursts, to break the drowsy potency of the fast conquering drug—"Come—no evas—ion, Ferdinand—yuh !—no—no—no subterfuge—no school-boy trick—trickery—to make believe. 'O, for the sparkle that gems the bright bowl,'" he attempted to sing, in a hoarse dissonant voice ; but memory failed to supply the words, and, nodding his head for an instant, as his senses became oblivious in the momentary pause of words, he began to breathe with hard prolonged suspirations ; then suddenly rousing himself, by a strong effort, he cried—"No subterfuge—drink! drink to me. Here's Mina and Felix !—Felix !—Mina !" and, with an agitated splashing action, Alonzo brought the beaker to his head, and poured the wine down his throat with a quick thirsty craving.

"I were less than friend to refuse the pledge to such a worthy nobleman," replied Almazuma, as he filled his measure, and, pressing it to his mouth, disposed of its contents, as he had done several former cups, watching with a calm smiling eye every gesture of his devoted associate, as the narcotic drink invaded every nerve of his strong frame.

"I shall grow giddy—sick—I shall, if you keep dancing—so—so—so very—very rapidly. Do—do—catch the lamp: keep it still—stop the table, Ferdinand—it whirls—whirls—whirls! Put your hand out, man—see! see! I must shut my eyes till you are quiet—or shall be gid—gid—gid—quite giddy—I shall—quite:" and as his voice gradually failed, and his words came slower and more impeded from his lips, he dropped his head upon his arms, and rested on the table, while a gradual and conquering stupor crept through his blood, each instant mounting higher to the assaulted brain, and taking the heart captive.

For full ten minutes Almazuma never moved, but, erect in his seat, and with a bright tiger glance, sat silently watching his fated victim, observing with curious interest the gradual progress of his soporific potion, and marking the loud stertorous inspirations, as they gradually subsided into the slow inaudible breathings of a deep coma. A slight rustling at the entrance, among the sweeping tendrils of the arbour, diverted Almazuma's attention; and, holding up his hand as a sign, Garcia crept cautiously into the alcove, and, gently rising to his feet, approached Alonzo, placed his hand softly on his pulse, and bending down his head, listened for a moment, with practised skill, to the steady heavings of his chest; then, standing up, spoke aloud—"He's safe my lord—no farther fear of him: he's as powerless and as speechless as a babe. We have no time to lose; the palace clock has some time struck eleven, and twelve's the hour you spoke of. I must be quick, and make the cavalier's toilet—oh! oh! He didn't think he was so near heaven, poor fool!—not he! He took your words for metaphors—ha! ha! ha! Well, well; some men may be snared with their eyes open—but they must be born fools. But let me look after my duty." And, gathering up the wine and measures, he put them hastily into a pannier he drew from some sheltering foliage, and instantly disappeared with his load. In a few minutes he returned with a large mattress made of dried leaves and sacking; and, laying it along the ground, at a little distance from the mouth of the grotto, covered it with several horsecloths that he carried under his arm for the purpose. "I thought it best to gag the mule:—those beasts will often speak, when their tongues and sweet voices are any thing but agreeable," observed Garcia, when he had completed his task.

"Thou art full of thought, and most considerate in thy practice, good Garcia," added Almazuma in a complimentary tone as he rose and drew near Alonzo, stooping his ear to catch the faintest suspiration.

"Your hand, my lord," resumed Garcia, as he grasped the lover's shoulders, and allowed the inert body to fall back in his arms. "Your aid for a moment, Senhor, and we will give him a handsome laying forth—so;—that will do. I'll straighten his limbs, my lord, and make his pillow comfortable. Silly fool! 'twas only yesterday I said to myself—'Ay, ay! we'll crush you to-morrow,'—and see how pat the thing has come to pass. To be meshed with his eyes open—why 'twas a boy's weakness,—so that will do." And

assisted by Almazuma, the two laid the body of Alonzo upon the leafy mattress that Garcia had just prepared; while the accomplice muttered his contempt or ridicule of the lover, as, kneeling, he adjusted the body along its thickly quilted couch, and while Almazuma, with a freezing smile and a subdued triumph in his eye, watched with folded arms the process of Garcia's occupation. When all had been arranged to his satisfaction, the villain rose with a chuckle, observing with a repulsive laugh:—"I'll warrant thou wilt lie soft enough—this is an honour, now, I shall never have, to lie in state—ho, ho, ho!"

"Now, good friend, haste to the pannier and bring the cloaks.—Quick, Garcia—quick!" And when the man had departed on the errand, he half whispered to himself, "Confident dolt—self-sufficient and hood-winked fool! But I must get possession of his weapon—I must have his sword: it is a very key in his cunning hands, and he prizes it as inestimable. My whole plan is baulked, unless I win his blade;—let me see—a plan—a feasible device.—Yes, yes, it will do! Ay! now the cloaks—the cloaks!" he exclaimed aloud, as Garcia returned with two large mantles. Taking one of them, Almazuma spread it over the body, covering the face and extremities in its ample folds; then throwing the other round his shoulders, cried petulantly as he boggled in adjusting it: "Curse on it—why did I wear this cumbering sword? Undo it, Garcia, undo it—quick!"

And as Garcia obeyed, and unlatched the jewelled rapier, Almazuma observed carelessly: "Put it on, good fellow, and lend me thine; 'tis short and will not incommode me as this long toledo does."

"Surely, my lord," replied the accomplice, "if you will wear it:" and unfastening his hanger, he fixed it in Don Ferdinand's belt, and buckled the other to his side;—"though for that matter," he continued, "there's not a better blade 'twixt this and Milan—'tis of my own workmanship. I tempered it with calcined hoofs and ice, and I have tested it on the stillest water from point to hilt; 'tis thorough to the centre. Just look at it, my lord," he cried drawing it forth from its sheath and holding it down to the lamp with all the gratulative pleasure of a child expatiating on his toy. "See, it has a strong broad back, serrated as a saw, and would turn off a thrust pike, or cut through a tree. It has a beautiful point, observe—double-edged, and widens, to a nicety, just two and twenty inches in the blade from guard to point—light, manageable, and strong. Then look! the handle makes a hammer, and when unsprung thus,—Oh capital!—a file, coarse and fine—feel!—and the end a screwdriver. Here, too, is a gimblet, sprung in that groove of the haft. Oh! 'tis a valuable article! With that weapon," he continued as he re-adjusted its parts and sheathed it, "I'd cut through a stone wall. It took me time—long time; but I prize it above all compensation—I hold my life and that sword together!"

"'Tis a beautiful invention," remarked Almazuma, as he replied with apparent interest to the other's eulogy; "but I trust thou wilt never use it for such a purpose. In two hours more, my trusty friend, thou shalt be on thy journey: though trust me, I am most loath to part from thee; but so it must be. I will, however, take considerate care, that thou shalt never want again.

Thou 'lt be safe in Madrid under a new name; and I'll provide against thy enemy the Inquisition. I hold a means to stop their hands from you; so thou hast nought to fear. When you return to the Capital, you shall make me such another blade as this, and the price of it shall not be limited. This traitor's sword is worth its weight in gems. But come—now to thy hiding: I must go meet my betrothed—my love. Remember, when I depart with her, be quick in thy dispatch—see that not a trace is left behind. I shall but lead her to the postern gate, and then rejoin you straight. Forget not!—The light!"

And with a hasty step and rejoicing heart, the subtle and dark-plotting Almazuma threw his mantle round him, and hastened from the spot. Garcia stayed for a few minutes to remove the table and chairs to the back of the alcove, and extinguishing the lamp, approached the body of Alonzo, and passing his hand under the cloak, withdrew a heavy purse from its vest; saying, as he rose from his stooping position, and weighing the contents in his hands, "This is my lawful booty: there 's fifty doubloons in it, for I filled it myself this morning, and did not forget the privilege of my office—to pay my own expenses; and I 've good reason to know the sum. Some people now would call me mercenary; but no such thing: these are the lawful and time-immemorial perquisites of our trade—profession, I mean,—the bonus the dead man leaves on his person for being handsomely sent out of the way; and that 's the reason your real gentleman—the true hidalgo—never goes out without a well furnished purse to pay his funeral expenses—ho, ho, ho! Well, no matter what villany breeds, the world still wags; and though the monk may preach, or the pope fulminate, there will be always employment for the unscrupulous—for such excrescences on society as myself, who carry their consciences in a leathern pouch, or a silk-beaded purse, cheek-by-jowl with their stiletto; of which fraternity I must now write myself brother, or honorary associate—he, he, he! I' faith, the trade 's not bad: the master pays us for cutting him off—and the friend pays us by will, or codicil, which you like—for doing it neatly and in a tradesman-like way. Well, then I'm Alonzo's heir by prescriptive custom—the *lex non scripta*, as my holy teacher used to say, when he gave me a smattering of jurisprudence. Well, heir or not, these are the only shoes I ever cared to take from dead men; and these delicious nightingales will buy many a new pair—ha, ha; and there 'll be no fear of a misfit. So, Don Alonzo, good even for the present: you have taken your supper, and I' ll go and finish mine." So saying, the deliberate villain stepped over the body of the young noble, and chinking the gold in the purse, left the arbour and struck into a coppice close at hand; where, sitting down by a mule that was tied to a tree, took out some wine and provisions from one of the panniers on the animal's back, and began to make a hearty meal, stopping every now and then in his agreeable task, to chip up the silver salver he had brought from the palace, and with a small knife ripping off the gold mountings and hoops from the wine-beakers, and depositing his amassed spoil in a capacious pouch by his side, leant his back to a tree, and folding his arms, remained with his ears raised and closed eyes in watchful rumination.

CHAPTER XVI.

WE must go back for about two hours in the time of our tale—from the event that has just taken place, and conduct the attentive reader to the chamber of the Donna Catalina, at the hour of ten on the same evening, and at about the same period that Almazuma and Alonzo secretly left the palace, to spend the hours of midnight in convivial and friendly harmony in the secluded arbour. Catalina, accompanied by Amina, entered that luxurious apartment, that had witnessed so many years of her proud happiness—so many bitter moments of her humiliated existence.

There was a nervous anxiety perceptible in her manner, and a restlessness of action, that could not prosecute for an instant the same subject, or permit her mind to rest for a definite space in the contemplation of one object—or follow one theme, however brief, to its conclusion. And though her power of self-control was great, and usually exerted with success, yet to-night, though she felt Amina's eye upon her disturbed gait, she could not subdue the insubordinate feelings and dreadful images that crowded to her excited mind; but with a wandering restlessness and vague inaptitude of words and act, she spoke in starts—sudden and loud, or walked the room, or took a book, or with a purposeless vacancy struck a harp-string, or turned the leaves of her illuminated missal, as if in search of some familiar or appreciated passage; then, sink upon a seat, and wring her hands, and beat the ground in nervous quickness, with her small and tapering foot—then start again in rapid walk, and speak quite from the purport of her former words.

"Nay—it grieves me, dearest sister, to behold you thus—you, so generally passive: I cannot bear to see you so disturbed," cried Amina, in kind accents, as she took a seat by Catalina, in one of her pauses, and prepared to take her hand.

"Do not observe it: it is nothing—nothing," replied Catalina, rising; and, as if shrinking from the fair girl's touch. "The night is painfully hot; and I feel as if lightning played through my veins. The heat—the heat!" she exclaimed, with restless impatience.

"I will open the windows and cool the chamber," added Amina, rising from her seat and crossing the room hastily.

"Leave them alone!" cried Catalina, almost rudely: "I'll have none of it—the cold would kill me. Sit down—sit down."

"You are ill, my sister—very ill. 'T 's a fever that has seized upon thy strong heart," replied Amina soothingly.

"Yes—yes," she rejoined with a fearful smile, "you are right—it is a fever, of the brain and heart; and I must let blood to cool it: there 's no physician," she continued, in a more musing tone,—"none, equal to the sharp instrument that bleeds the over-burdened heart, and lets forth the grumous mire that breeds rebellious thoughts, and the dark deeds of some corrupted natures, that, like the Egyptian slime, engenders snakes and pestilence. Oh! 't is a vile clot, that life-blood—full of malicious evil."

"Merciful saints! how you talk!—you terrify

me—you are very ill. Let me go call the Marquis—send for the leech."

"No—no, I am better—much better," she replied, quickly. "'T is but a gloomy humour of my mind, always the precedent of a storm. The day was hot; and there's mischief hanging in the clouds: we shall have thunder—dreadful thunder. My sympathies are so allied to it that, like the sharp-scented kite, I can understand it in the air. I shall be better—quite well, when the storm is past, believe me. It will be so."

"Oh! you ease my heart of a load. You frightened me to see you look so wild," observed Amina, as she wiped her eyes of the fast tears that her tender nature gathered on their trembling lids. "You were well even now: 'tis within the hour, you have grown thus feverish," resumed her sister. "You are too anxious about Benina."

"I am—I am—very anxious—most anxious," exclaimed Catalina, eagerly catching at the suggested cause of her perturbation.

"Oh! she is safe,—depend she is."

"Safe! oh yes, I hope so; but she should have returned ere noon: and yet she comes not—and here is night, dark, dangerous night."

"Who attended her?" inquired Amina.

"A very reverend friar, a man of age, and holy piety; else were I more unhappy," resumed Catalina.

"Then banish recollection: some giddy toy has caught her eye—some pastime stayed her; the road is safe,—she'll come to-morrow."

"I trust so. Yet he were a poor defender did danger threaten. The father was infirm and lame, and I believe they went by the Sierra road, which I have heard is dangerous."

"Oh! not to a practised guide. Besides, the chapel to our lady has sanctified the way; 'twas built upon the height to give a confidence to all who travelled; and I have never yet heard of a mischance. But you would go to bed: shall I send my maiden to assist you?" inquired Amina.

"No, love, no! Get thee to bed and sleep, as I shall do. My governante is here at hand, and will perform all that is needful. I would the storm were passed. I should be all myself again. Good night."

"Nay, I must have my kiss before I part," cried Amina, as she twined her arms round Catalina's neck, and pressed her soft mouth on the parted lips of the reluctant beauty. "Good night, dear—dear sister! beloved Catalina. Heaven bless thee with repose and health! Adieu! the saints watch over thee and guard thee! Good night."

"Amen!—good night to thee, "replied Catalina, as her friend, waving her hand, turned and quitted the apartment.

"Oh! what a Judas do I feel, to take that heart-breathed kiss, while in my breast I harbour that which shall for ever kill her peace. Merciful heaven, what a wretch am I—fallen, fallen to the very dregs of vile hypocrisy! But if he live, I am for ever lost; and in his death can only live: for what to me were life, disrobed of its sole excellence—unstained honour? How willingly would I pour my best blood out, to save her gentle heart a pang, could I, in dying, die still honoured. But no! I have inspected every shade and turn of probability—studied the

countenance of every likelihood to spare the villain's life for my sweet Amina's sake; but it cannot be. A stain—a breath—a touch would taint my being, and hang a guilty or slandered epitaph upon my tomb. Oh! you wise lawmakers and potentates of the earth, why leave from out your code the vilest guilt of all? why not heap on the malevolent tongue of slander the sharpest torments of red-handed justice? What murder steeped in iniquity's dark flood is match or equal to a slandered name? Oh! for a rod of Aaron, to strike a million plagues on the blotted soul of a calumniating coward! What is his death to the living sufferance his detested machinations have heaped on me? No!—there is no human remedy but revenge. Then let the frowning judge denounce, while every injured heart writes its own verdict in the abridgment of the villain's life, who else went scathless free! Revenge!—revenge! shall be the judgment and the record."

Catalina rose from her seat as she concluded, trembling with the intensity of her feelings; and having traversed the chamber with quick and uneven steps, she stopped before a splendid mirror, that, of an oval form, projected in its massive frame, from one of the silk embroidered walls; and gazing for an instant on her determined countenance as reflected in the Venetian glass, she drew near, and drawing a gold and ivory knob that stood from the wall, and appeared part of the frame, a soft, silvery sounding bell was heard faintly in the distance. Then tranquillising her features, she returned to her seat; while immediately after the door opened, and the governante entered the chamber.

"Place the lamp on this table, good Senhora, and give me paper and ink; I have a missive to indite ere I retire to rest. Benina's absence troubles me. Send Lopez on the swiftest horse by early dawn to Soria: let him inquire at all the religious houses—should he not find Benina at her sister's—for one Father Anselmo, a Franciscan friar—her guide; and bring me quick intelligence of his success. Place my night-gear on the bed, light my toilet lamp, and see the flame is fed before the picture of my patroness—it burnt but dimly when I last was there; and that, good Senhora, is all I need. Nay, good governante, I will not keep thee up; it is my decisive wish that you do get to bed: when I have written my letter, I will retire myself. Good night, kind Senhora—good night!" And drawing a chair to the table, Catalina addressed herself to write, while the governante, having complied with her lady's injunctions, entered the inner chamber, and after a brief absence returned; and seeing her mistress engaged, made a low courtsey, and retired for the night.

Catalina threw down her pen when left alone, and remained in silent rumination, till the heavy palace clock struck the hour of midnight; when, starting, she instantly entered her bed-chamber, and returned in a few moments closely enveloped in a wide cloak. Taking the precaution to extinguish the lamp she had left burning, Catalina cautiously opened the door, and descending a private staircase, ultimately gained the shrubbery, that on one side skirted the lawn, and disappeared in its embracing darkness.

It was a few minutes after midnight, as a cavalier, closely muffled in a large Spanish cloak, entered one of the long vistas of trees, now in complete gloom—that adjoined the orange groves, and formed the commencement of the wood. After walking once or twice to the extremity of the green and woody aisle, where the moon, partly risen, shed an occasional sheet of light, and listening attentively for a few seconds from beneath the shadow of the last tree, his ear was quickly sensible of the approach of a light, hasty step in an opposite direction; and turning round, he resumed his former position, when a tall, graceful figure, enveloped in a rich cloak and hood, suddenly emerged from the overhanging foliage that bordered the path, and stood before him.

"I have tarried," said the last comer, in a voice that was recognised as that of Catalina, "but my purpose is not changed. Am I late?" she added, as her companion turned to move.

"No!—There is no need of speed!—he will wait," replied Almazuma. "Have you read those last-sent letters?—Are there any doubts left?"

"I have," rejoined Catalina. "There is no doubt.—Lead on—my purpose cannot cool; but quick atonement will be a luxury. I feel my reason stands or falls upon its speedy execution. My sex has left me for the time; and to be again a woman, I must get this demon from my heart: and a death—his death, can alone abrogate the power that stirs me. Come!—conduct me!—haste!"

"I will: we tread the path already. But ask that heart again, that is but glossed with sternness, not of its structure, has it resolve!—Has it——"

"You little know what a proud woman dares," she replied, in scornful accents, as she interrupted him—"what deeds she can perform, when roused by black ingratitude to exert the passions nature planted in the breasts of mortals. In man, all potent—in us, smothered, and kept in bare existence by the soft humanities your tyrannous sex always compel us to evince, if not to feel; but when awoke by stabs upon our only excellence, the tigress is less deadly, though she kills, than an outraged woman, when aroused to vindicate her honour, and avenge her wrongs. I tell thee, Lord, her blood is poison to her veins, and ministers the heart to direst cruelties; and in her executing wrath her passion is a hurricane!"

As she concluded, her features worked with her emotion, and her whole frame shook with the energy of her declaration—proving how truly she felt the force of what she described. Her companion gazed on this evidence of her feelings with an ill-concealed satisfaction; and the contemplation of her sufferings gave him an inward pleasure—a malignant joy amounting to ecstacy: but he made no answer—showed no wonder; but advancing a few steps before his companion, conducted her down an avenue, and taking her hand—for the partial moon had passed behind a mass of clouds, and the path they were pursuing was wrapped in darkness—he led her down the several intersecting alleys and broad glades, till reaching a low embowered vista, they proceeded in silence along its ominous solitude. At the extremity of this arcade, and where two other broad pathways diverged from it, they approached the alcove, which, almost hid in the angle formed by the three radial branches, was not evident to observation till closely inspected; though a narrow belt of moonlight, at the moment they reached the entrance, fell from an opening in the foliage overhead, and formed the only light or relief to the sombre aspect of the neighbourhood, and served to direct them to its precincts.

"He is there," said Almazuma, pointing to the arbour, and standing on one side of the leafy entrance, as he threw back the encumbering boughs. Catalina instantly passed her conductor, and entered the gloomy recess, followed by Almazuma.

"Where," cried she, impatiently—"where is this traducer of my name?—where the base, dishonoured, and despised Alvares!—where the disgraced Alonzo?"

"At your feet, fair lady—where such a villain should be," replied Don Ferdinand, as he directed her attention to the ground, where, enveloped in Almazuma's mantle, lay the body of the apparently dead Alonzo. "Tread on his corpse, as I do—the deceived companion—injured friend—and thy avenger!" And, as he spoke, Almazuma set his foot on the body, and raised his hand aloft in an attitude of commanding sternness.

"Ha!" cried Catalina, with flashing eyes and angry speech, "you have deceived me! Was this well, my lord? You have anticipated my revenge!—robbed me of my purpose!—taken from the lioness her prey!—from the relentless wolf her savage banquet!—robbed me!"

"I have," replied Almazuma, calmly. "I would have saved him for your special vengeance, but he was presumptuous, and deprived me of the power. And I am glad it is so. I would not have had your hand stained with his disloyal blood: the thought, in after-life, when thy just rage is gone, would have made your every hour a hell:—'t is better so. Yet here—kneel with me beside his body; and, as you swore, again attest your promise to be mine!—to hide from man, from church, and heaven itself, even in whispers, this night's consequence:—here, over his body, swear it! and, as you pledge the oath, draw forth your dagger, and together let us bury our edges in his heart: the act will give your hatred vent—smooth, without remorseful agony, your indignation—and conscience-quit you of a guilty deed. Will you perform?—and will you swear?"

"I will!" replied Catalina. "Speak the oath—I am ready—and, to bind it firmer, I will seal the covenant with this;"—and she drew from her zone a long, sharp ivory-handled poniard, and held it above her head; while, sinking on one knee beside the body, she awaited the propounded oath—as Almazuma, standing erect on the other side of the muffled figure, threw back his mantle, unsheathed his dagger, and with both hands raised, said in a deep, slow, and solemn voice—

"By your eternal hopes of heaven!—by all that's binding on the soul of man!—by God's dread wrath, you swear—to give your person, and your hand—your mind, and every action of your life, to Almazuma's will, as a devoted wife:—that you will keep this night's deed, and all its consequence, before and after, for ever hidden from the world: never, by word or implication, to reveal in prayers, in penitence, confessional, or to mortal ears—by tongue, by sign, or hand, this dreadful secret!—or, if you should, let curses light upon your perjured head, and heaven for ever shut you from its grace, and seal its indignation and its anger thus——"

"Record the oath and attestation, heaven!—I swear!" replied Catalina, with solemn energy, as the long blade flashed in its descent through the obscurity, and with unerring aim entered the heart of the prostrate body at her feet. A gush of blood—a sudden contraction of every limb and muscle—a deep groan—then a convulsive tremor of the frame—and the body settled into final repose.

"Merciful God!" shrieked Catalina, relinquishing her hold of the dagger, and leaving it standing in the body, while her voice was almost choked with superstitious horror—"*He was alive!*"—and she gazed inquiringly, and with distracted looks, into Almazuma's face, on which a hideous triumph and savage exultation was depicted, in all the fearful characters of deformity.

"It was the last spasm of lingering life," he said. "The victim was young, and the tenacity for breath with such is marvellous. It were pity the fair youth should linger : I thought him dead. 'T is said, the mind retains the anguish of the flesh, and full intelligence of thought, even when the heart has ceased, and the spirit of utterance flits over the convulsive ongue : if so, we will be merciful, and annihilate this obstinate vitality. 'T were pity he should linger,"—and, as he spoke, Almazuma gazed for a brief space with a malicious satisfaction at the workings of her tortured countenance, as writhing under the horrid thoughts his words called forth, she seemed lost in a chaos of stupifying wonder ; then, slowly kneeling opposite his still amazed and awe-struck companion, he drove his broad dagger deliberately to the hilt in the breast of the now passive body—then flinging back the folds of the mantle, that had hitherto enveloped the head and upper part of the figure, exposed to view the pale, yet nobly handsome face of Don Alonzo Alvares. At that instant, the moon entirely disappeared behind a mass of clouds, casting, as it passed, for one moment, a sickly beam upon the features of the corpse, leaving the night, and all around, in profound darkness.

It would be impossible to picture the wild and ghastly features of Catalina, as she still knelt in awful wonderment by the side of her late affianced husband. Her mouth was open—her eyes dilated, and rivetted on the pale face of her lover ; and as she bent forward, one hand stretched before, with the fingers parted as if to repel some fearful object, and the other raised above her head, her dark robe and black hair contrasting with the deadly white of her bare arms and bust, she seemed like a sculptured form, of an embodied horror—mute, terrible, and grand ; while opposite, with his arms folded on his chest, and an erect bearing, stood Almazuma, like the great enemy of souls, gazing with malign pleasure, and a fiendish smile, on the completed picture at his feet. At length, breaking the painful silence of the dreadful scene, Almazuma exclaimed—

"Arise, Donna Catalina—the deed is done! I swore to save your honour—and witness, I have performed my oath ! Henceforth, thou wilt live in peace. The villain, to the last, gloried in his work. Come—rejoice !—give me your hand, my bride, and let me lead you forth : the night's unwholesome, and the disappearing moon has somewhat damped your spirit. Come, my newfound love—my wife, that is to be—come ! "—

and taking her unresisting hand, Almazuma raised her from the ground, led her in silence and in darkness from the fatal spot, and conducted her to the palace, whence, by an unfrequented door, she at length, exhausted, speechless, and bewildered, found her way to her solitary chamber ; her companion, before parting, having whispered a few inaudible words in her ear, returned to the garden, and ultimately to the arbour.

When Almazuma returned to the spot of the late connived murder, he found every trace of the deed removed, and by the obscure light of a clouded moon, he was enabled to observe that the arbour had all the appearance of complete desertion. Entering the gloomy recess, he struck a light, and lighting his lamp, investigated every foot of the mossy ground ; but not the slightest evidence remained to reward the strictest scrutiny—not a stain was on the elastic carpet at his feet—not a symptom to denote a deed so full of treachery and horror that had been so lately perpetrated on its heathy bosom. While still busied in the necessary investigation, he was joined by Garcia, who observed, as he noticed Almazuma's eager inquiry to ascertain if all precaution had been taken : "It's all right, my lord. There's not a blade of grass awry—not a drop of blood spilt : I have carried bed and body altogether, and placed it on the mule across the panniers. Come, my lord—we had better start ; we have a way to go already, and I'll stake my head there's not a jot of evidence left. There's a blind alley beyond, through which I can force the mule, and it will rain anon and wash even that faint trace away. Come, we've given him his last supper —ho! ho!"

"It is all admirably managed,—let us hence, for I must return ere morning. Quick, Garcia, quick!" And the two instantly disappeared in the wood ; and in about two hours afterwards Don Ferdinand and Garcia—one leading and the other following the burthened mule — stopped at the low gate in the shrubbery at the base of Almazuma's castle. Opening the secret door and lighting a torch, Almazuma proceeded with the flambeau along the subterranean vault followed by Garcia, bearing in his arms the body of the young Alvares. When they had reached the iron wicket that divided the more spacious passage from the long tortuous one that led to the stairs, Almazuma took out a key, and unlocking the gate, proceeded forward for a considerable distance, and opening a recess in the wall, entered a secret chamber, holding his light high to enable Garcia to enter the door-way with his burthen.

After a few minutes' stay, the accomplice returned alone in the dark, and taking off the panniers from the mule, reclosed the door, and returned to the gloomy chamber. For about half an hour all remained silent within that aweinspiring and mysterious apartment : the door had been closed, and not the slightest intimation of life existed within. At the expiration of that time a sudden sharp clash was heard, like the closing of many powerful springs, and then a smothered voice, as if issuing from the bowels of the earth, exclaimed in a cry of frightful horror : "Merciful God! I am betrayed! Christ have mercy on me !—Eternal villain !—Black fiend ! Hell !—curses !—damnation ! But in a moment after, all was as still as the grave, and in about

A. MILES

ten minutes later, Almazuma re-entered the passage with the flambeau—his face ghastly pale, but a triumphant wildness sparkling in his eye. Securing all the doors, he extinguished his torch, and leading the mule down the avenue into the open road, mounted him, and goading the animal with his dagger, galloped at full speed in the direction of the Alfendera Palace.

CHAPTER XVII.

THE night, which had been long threatening, broke towards dawn in a tempest of rain and thunder, such as had seldom visited that neighbourhood. Trees were torn up by the wind, others shivered by the lightning, the river overflowed its banks, and inundated large tracts of country; and, for the few hours the storm continued, it seemed to mock in its terrible grandeur the fatal scenes so lately enacted in its vicinity by the devastating agency of corrupted and remorseless man. But, about matins, the sun burst out in all its splendour, dragging the mist and fog from the earth upward like a curtain, and smiling in all benignity on the refreshed and laughing world, that through its yet glistening tears seemed rejoicing in the glad change.

The guests and inhabitants of the palace were aroused on the morning succeeding a night of so much storm and crime, by a concert of most inspiring music; and, as in different bands the musicians circled the extensive building, their rich deep voices harmonizing with the blended melody of their guitars, harps, flutes, and hautboys,—the dulcet strains or liquid notes of each as they rose in symphony with the

9

vocal organ, constituted a serenade of most ravishing sweetness and skilful excellence.

All the company had assembled in the great hall of the palace, and the morning refection was prepared, when, for the first time, the absence of Alonzo and Catalina was observed; but as Amina informed the anxious marquis that his daughter had, the previous evening, complained of slight indisposition from the excessive heat, her absence at so early a meal was not regarded with more attention than a passing regret, and the ceremony of dispatching a servant to inquire of her women into the state of her health; but for Alonzo's non-appearance there was no assignable reason, unless in his morning's walk he had extended his ramble too far to return in time to partake of the repast. His room, Felix said, was empty, for he had called on him, that they might stroll together, and note what devastation the storm had committed, but the early riser had flown, nor could he find his servant to inquire in what direction; and he had as yet, searched for him in vain,— though he doubted not, he continued, laughing, to find the truant in some far nook inditing sonnets to his mistress, or wounding the smooth bark with her endeared name;—but I will search for him anon, and bring the penitent to strictest shriving, exclaimed the gay friend and lover, as he left the board, and proceeded in quest of Don Alonzo.

It was mid-day when Felix returned to the palace, after a long and unsuccessful search after his friend, hoping that he had in the interim found his way back to the mansion. Great then was the surprise and alarm of all present, when Felix entered an apartment in which most of the company were assembled, to find that no tidings had yet been received of him. A general gloom settled on every brow, and apprehension appeared on every face. The general anxiety that was creeping on all, was increased by the information conveyed by the marquis, that Catalina's indisposition had assumed a serious character, demanding the instant presence of a leech;—and to heighten the growing uneasiness, the return of Lopez from Soria added consternation to their alarm, when he reported the result of his mission:—that receiving no intelligence in the city of either friar or maiden, he had, with some friends, searched the road, and lastly the convent path, and there found conclusive evidence of a fearful accident. They had descended to the stream, and, on examining the banks, discovered the mangled carcass of the mule, fragments of the friar's dress, his staff and cowl, and half a league farther down the stream, attached to a projecting spray, the mantilla and handkerchief of the unfortunate Benina,—but no trace of either body was anywhere to be found.

"Merciful saints!" exclaimed the marquis, when he heard the tale that the sorrowing Lopez recounted, "some fearful calamity seems impending over my house. Call up the servants. Let us make a strict inquiry, senhors. Gentlemen, aid me."

"Where is Don Ferdinand?—where is my friend?" cried the nearly distracted Condé. "He has wit, he has judgment—he will find my boy. Almazuma! Almazuma! aid me,—aid me, my friend," he exclaimed, as wringing his hands,

he paced the large apartment, looking into each face and calling on his friend. "Where is he? Where art thou Almazuma?"

"Speak! senhors, speak!" cried the marquis. "Know you, any one, where the Don Almazuma is?"

"The Don Ferdinand, with four mounted servants, has been on the search this hour, your excellency, and has not yet returned," replied an attendant, who entered at the moment.

"I knew it, I knew it—I was sure he would be up and doing: a father's blessing and an old man's prayers shall reward his kindly zeal!" replied the anxious Alvares. "But let us lose no time in aiding him. To horse, to horse, cavaliers! —some of you on foot," he cried, as a host of servants entered the room, obedient to a former summons. "Search the woods—examine every spot, I'll give a fortune to the man who brings me tidings of my son. Haste, gentlemen, haste!"

The marquis, however, checked this hasty order to arrange more sober plans, dividing the company into equal parts, and assigning to each body its proper guides and directions, so as to secure certainty with dispatch in their inquiry. He then dismissed them on their various ways; and none but women and the two disconsolate parents were left in that lately crowded mansion. The female visitors having retired to the opposite wing of the palace with Donna Amina, who, on the tidings of her brother's presumed danger, had been borne insensible to her chamber, the rest of that weary day was spent in fruitless search; and when at length evening closed, and the various groups returned fatigued and disappointed, each guest was interrogated anew: the servants questioned, but all in vain. The house—the grounds—the country had been explored, and midnight only suspended the investigation, till light and morning enabled the alarmed and wondering visitors, and weary vassals, to resume the inquiry with increased vigilance, but hopeless aim. Hour followed hour in profitless succession, and hope at last gave way to the certain belief of danger. From the first intelligence of Alonzo's absence, Almazuma evinced the liveliest surprise:—and as the hours stole on, his solicitude became more eager—his grief more poignant; and even after midnight, attended by one or two friends, and a few domestics with torches, he continued the harassing search through all the woods, defiles, and plains for many miles around the mansion: nor did mid-day find him exhausted in his anxious task. Again he led his party through all the mazes of the palace grounds: stream, river, lake, grotto, and grove were inspected with all the scrutiny of plodding and unwearied watchfulness. The first to start the vain pursuit, Almazuma was the last who would relinquish hope,—the very latest who would resign the fruitless task;—and when at last, despairingly and sad, on the following afternoon Almazuma returned, and sank exhausted and pale from fatigue into a chair, the unhappy father gave way at once to uncontrolled despair; and, like a sudden deluge from the sky, the flood gates of his soul were opened, and tears in bitter agony suffused his venerable face.

"Some villain has cut him off!" exclaimed

Alvares, in accents of heart-rending grief; "some bravo's hand has robbed me of my son, and left me in my perished age to creep in sorrow to the grave: the stay, the prop, the honour of my house, the joy,—the comfort of my years, the glory of my white hairs!—my son! my son! my son!—my noble, gallant, handsome boy! Oh! I shall never see thee more—never behold thy hope-inspiring face, or hear the music of thy voice and step, that used to ring so glad a welcome in my heart: never—never see thee more! Destroyed in the lusty manhood of thy prime, when, like becoming scars on a bright buckler, thick honours marked thy front, and gave a dignity to the very quality that so became thee:—to lose thee thus! I, who lived but in thy fame, whose nourishment and blood was all digested from thy excellence. Oh! my God! my God! thy chastisement is too heavy for an infirm, old man to bear, and strikes me pitiless to the earth!"

And in the bitterness of his lamentation Alvares tore out the thin filaments of his white hair, and in distracted agony, and a burst of uncontrollable grief, he cast himself upon the ground, and beat the floor with his clenched hands, weeping in long drawn sobs of sharpest misery.

"Santa Maria!—holy mother, have pity on me, the glory and the comfort of our house is turned to mourning," cried Alfendera, as he sank into a chair, and buried his face in his hands.

"Arise, my worthy lord, arise!" said Almazuma, in a voice of deepest sympathy, as he approached Alvares, and knelt by the old man. "Arise! and husband this excess of grief; give not thus way to thy full sorrow, we have yet no evidence of certain danger. I will search the land but I will bring thee tidings of thy son. Arise! let not one flood of grief destroy what nature and kind heaven has spared so lengthily: live for the prospect of his return. Come, mitigate this punishing and killing grief. Rise, be comforted! and let God's great boon to suffering mortals—hope, cheer thee, or sober thy else killing grief: embrace it—believe it."

"Oh! thou art a friend indeed, my excellent, kind Almazuma!" cried Alvares, as he partly rose from the ground, and rested his head on the shoulder of his professing friend. "You too loved him, and sorrow has writ on thy tranquil brow deep anguish. There's comfort even in thy sympathy. He was so kind, so gentle, so true in all relations of his life—so—so—so——" and the unfinished sentence stuck in his throat, and half articulated sobs concluded the brief speech.

"Where is his servant, De Vega?" suddenly exclaimed Felix: "he must know most of Alonzo's movements. Why have we not thought of him before? Let him be sent for."

"It has been thought of," replied the marquis; "but the man is no where to be found. He has not been seen since Alonzo's disappearance: they must be gone together, for neither bed was lain in that night. 'Tis mystery all—painful mystery!"

"Ha! indeed!" cried Felix. "I fear some treachery. I ever did misdoubt that man,—he was too canning—dark, for truth."

"Haste! let us search the fellow's room," replied Almazuma eagerly, as he placed the Condé in one of the seats. "And 'twere not amiss to inspect Alonzo's chamber. Don Felix, with some friends examine that, while the marquis and myself inspect the other. Take comfort, senhor, take comfort," he added to Alvares, as with the rest he withdrew to make farther investigation.

The examination, however, was unsatisfactory, and in a short time Almazuma returned There was no evidence in De Vega's apartment to warrant any conclusion that he had been privy to his master's movements, further than the fact, that neither chambers had been tenanted on the night of the storm, and that his absence confirmed a suspicion, that they were in life or death together;—but the general distress was soon augmented by the hasty entrance of Felix and his companions, with a letter, found in Alonzo's chamber, directed to the Condé, and in the hand-writing of the young Alvares.

With trembling eagerness the excited father broke the seal; but a sudden mist covered his eyes, and a sickening giddiness deprived him of the power to see or understand the purpose of the letter, and putting it into Almazuma's hand, Alvares cried, in a faint and faltering voice, "Read—read, my friend, I cannot see—my faculties are all at variance—I pray you read;" and sinking back in the chair, he hid his face in his hands, while Don Ferdinand read in a steady voice the following letter, which it will be remembered had been artfully fabricated by the villain Garcia, under the tuition of Almazuma himself:—

"To THE CONDE DE ALVARES.

"My ever honoured father,

"What anguish will rack your affectionate heart, when this fatal letter reaches your hand! what agony shake your noble nature, to hear that your once valued son is alike unworthy to live as he is unfit to die. I dare not look again upon your face in life—nor meet the just displeasure of my insulted bride; but haste to hide in——for ever, my unworthy head and ruined name. I dare not put on record my offences. Do not hope or wish ever again to view me; it would be unjust, and I must make it incapable——In my deceived, and long tried friend, you will find a better son, and had I influence with the angel I have left, and am unworthy of, I would use my last words in begging her to direct that love to him I was unfit to claim. I quit the world less miserable in the knowledge that in Almazuma you will find a better son, a wiser heir, than in the much offending and disgraced—ALONZO."

Almazuma dropped the letter from his hand and, starting to his feet, walked the room with perturbed and hasty strides; then quickly returning, as if under the influence of a sudden thought, snatched up the paper, and looking over it for a moment, exclaimed in a well assumed and tremulous voice, "This is too much—I'm not deserving of this kind regard. Alas! my noble friend! what delusion hast thou laboured under, what——" then, pausing and scrutinising the letter more closely, continued in an altered voice,—"It is so long since I have seen Alonzo's writing—that—no! and yet, these are his characters—or were; and yet here is a strange difference of form;—look, senhors,—

look my Lord Alvares! Surely this is not Alonzo's hand: it is some foul villany,—some dark device. Behold! am I not right? are not these letters distinct in length and shape, in total form from these ? " and he held the letter down for the inspection of all present as he pointed to the difference which he had planned, for the very purpose of creating doubt, and now pretended to have just discovered.

"As opposite as two men's characters can be," remarked the marquis: "but what can be the object? "

"Let me look—let me see!" cried Alvares, as with a tremulous hand he took the paper. "The upper lines, the last two, and the signature, are in my boy's writing: 'tis his—'tis his,—but not the others."

"Is there any sequence in the matter if we omit the doubtful parts? " inquired Felix. "Let us peruse the lines again."

"None, none,—'tis all amiss,—vague, and purposeless, together or divided, all torturing suspense and doubt,—nothing assigned—no object specified," resumed the father, as he re-read the letter.

"There is treachery here!" cried Felix, with a stern brow and hasty glance at Almazuma, "and I will spend my life to find it."

"You are right! I am convinced there's villany in this," replied Don Ferdinand, with a steady glance and tranquil countenance, as he looked boldly at Felix; "and as his friend I swear I will lose no moment of my time until I find a clue to this most hellish mischief! This De Vega must be found——"

"He shall!" abruptly exclaimed Felix, with emphasis.

"He shall," quietly rejoined Almazuma. "I'll to Madrid and make a strict inquiry: the hound will kennel there."

"And I will join you," added Felix, "on the instant."

"Agreed!—this moment," replied the other; and, taking a hasty leave of the disconsolate Alvares and the sorrowing marquis, the two, attended by their servants, took horse and quitted the palace: while on the following day the remaining guests departed, leaving a house of mourning where so lately all had been pleasure and rejoicing.

Poor Amina mourned her brother's loss with all the anguish of her sensitive and feeling nature, striving to subdue her own deep grief, that she might minister to the misery of her sorrowing father,—soothing with gentle words and kind solicitude, the woe that bent him to the earth; and then in turns watching her sister's couch, and through her flowing tears, gazing on the dry, bright eyes of the suffering Catalina.

We must now revert for a brief space to Catalina, who, on that fatal night of crime, returned, as we have seen, to her chamber, and though bewildered and almost lost in her conflicting and excited thoughts, preserved a methodical and mechanical species of prudence and secresy in her actions, more like an automaton than a living being. She disrobed her majestic form, and bound in broad braids her luxuriant hair,—and having adopted all precautions to avoid the supposition of her absence,—like a sleep-walker with her eyes open

but her senses closed, she went through all the forms of her usual toilette; and as the heavy tongue of the palace bell struck the solitary and dreary blow of one, the prolonged and swinging echo seemed to awake, as with electric force, the bound up mind from its lethargic dream, and liberate her imprisoned faculties; and falling on her knees by the side of the bed, she clasped her hands with a spasmodic force, and poured out a burst of supplicating prayers in pardon for the guilt in which she had so largely participated. But neither prayer nor penitence, or holy rite, could, as heretofore, relieve her oppressed heart. A heavy load was on her soul that crushed the elasticity of life, and, like a waking nightmare, haggard her thoughts, and chained the healthy utterance of her mind; and at length, worn out with bodily endurance and exhausted with mental toil, she sank upon her pillow, a prey to every passion but remorse. Through the weary hours that remained of that long night—through all the grandeur of the storm, she never closed her hot and throbbing eyes, but in distracted watchfulness experienced, for the first time, her own foreboding fear, "that she should sleep no more." And when the calm and sunny morning broke, gladdening the earth with its warm beams, and the soft-tongued instruments and mellow voices of the serenaders, roused the household with rejoicing music, it fell upon her ear with jarring discord and maddening clangour, while the tempered sunbeams, through the curtained windows, seemed in their intensity to blind her; and when, at length, the governante arrived to dress her mistress for the morning meal, she found her ill, too weak to rise, too powerless to converse,—pale, haggard, and disturbed.

Messengers were instantly dispatched to Soria for physicians, and the anxious marquis beheld with fear the sudden change in his beloved child's condition—from health to dangerous sickness;—and believing it the result of his own imprudence in permitting the evening pastime to be prolonged so late, he reproached himself in bitter terms for his inconsiderate folly, and ordering a strict seclusion and silence to be observed, rejoined his guests with a foreboding heart and melancholy countenance, to hear and mingle in the general consternation that every hour became more fearful, as to Alonzo's fate. Strict orders were given that no one should breathe to Catalina, in her present state, the doubts that were distracting all with regard to her bridegroom, lest the knowledge should render useless the remedial means, and aggravate the already formidable symptoms: and until her physician pronounced her convalescent, even Amina did not break the fatal news. On the first reported information of her lover's disappearance, Donna Catalina gave way to feelings too acute for utterance. The horror of that fatal night, the revulsion of her feelings, the dreadful compact, sealed so ominously, preyed on her heart in secret, and showed the terrible ravages in her face and mien. Closely closeted in her chamber, she brooded in mournful solitude, the weary weeks in which suspense was kept alive, in thoughts too deep for fellowship; and when at length conjecture settled into certainly, and rumour took the substance of authentic fact, and it was by all believed that he had fallen by some assassin's blade, who in the guise of a domestic had gained an easy access to his person. Then when Alonzo's fate had ceased to be a tale, and flagging interest grew weary of the theme, then it was that Catalina once again came forth in weeds of solemn sorrow; but no more the proud, the haughty, and the bold:—that aspect had deserted her, Calm, indeed, and resigned she seemed, though suffering. Her very gait, that once drew admiration for its majesty of step, had left her, and a languid motion now usurped its former dignity. Alvares marked the change, and wept in the very bitterness of regret to see her widowed loveliness; and his heart was almost bursting at the contemplation of the ruin of his hope, his joy, and love; and as he bade the sorrowing maid farewell, his stifled sobs were the sad adieus that graced his speech and compliment.

Calamity, that never single-handed, touches our suffering nature, but comes in hosts, as if to paralyzed the soul, and kill the greater grief, in newer woes, seemed bent on filling to the brim the cup of sharp affliction. A month had passed from the departure of Almazuma and Felix, when news reached the marquis that his son had been seized with a dangerous fever; and though the best kill of Madrid, and the unwearied attention of Don Ferdinand was directed to his condition, yet his life was held in the most critical danger, and the instant presence of Alfendera was called for, that he might be at hand to take a final leave of his fast sinking son. The same hour that conveyed this heavy news to the marquis, brought a courier to the Condé Alvares, with tidings of the death of his long-afflicted and aged partner. A rude and unguarded account of her beloved Alonzo's death had reached her,—and in her then enfeebled state, the sudden shock had proved instantly fatal. A deep groan, as she clasped her hands in mute agony, followed by a stream of blood from the overcharged heart, was all that passed, and served to separate the weary soul from its frail tenement.

On the same day, and at the same hour, the two sorrowing parents parted and left the palace,—Alfendera to journey to the capital, as he believed, to take the parting breath of his youngest son,—Alvares and his weeping daughter to their hereditary home, to perform the last rite to a beloved wife and mother; while the restored Catalina remained with the domestics, sole occupant of that mansion so late the scene of such joy, tranquillity, and happiness; there in secret to brood over the rash pledge she had made to Almazuma, and contemplate the devastation that her overweening pride had entailed upon herself and father, friend, and all concerned.

CHAPTER XVIII.

IT was towards the end of the year 1591, and about three years subsequent to the disasters recorded in the two last chapters, that Don Sebastian de Alfendera, governor of the province of Quito, was roused from his morning slumbers by the distant boom of artillery, and the quick replying salute from the fort of St. Francisco, when hastily attiring himself, and attended by a few officers of his household, the young nobleman proceeded to the platform of the citadel, from whence he might have a better view of the now fast-approaching ship. A matter in those days of no inconsiderable interest to each individual, and to the colony at large, when it is remembered that an annual intercourse with the mother country, and that by a solitary ship, or galleon, as the heavy laden vessels of the time were called, was all the communication, except in cases of declared war or sudden danger, that was deemed necessary for the convenience or comfort of the inhabitants in their traffic or relations with Europe.

As a deep laden and cumbrous galleon, with her quaint and towering poop, and bristling guns, entered the offing, and signalled for a pilot, every foot of shore was crowded with eager and expectant hearts,—roof tops, trees, steeples, every eminence was filled with gay multitudes, while chaunting monks and surpliced priests sang hymns of praise for her safe arrival, and each convent bell and cathedral peal, rang out rejoicing music, as every minute the deep-mouthed cannon from the fort and battery, gave a soldier-like and war-inspiring welcome to the long-travelled argosy, who, as she kept her course due for the long-wished harbour, spoke out her thanks in answering guns; while over head the gorgeous sun, gilding a thousand streamers, banners, and ensigns, lent to the view of sea and land a vast and sparkling beauty.

"By St. Jago! my lord governor," exclaimed one of the staff, to Don Sebastian, "she carries the royal standard on her foretop;"

"Indeed!" replied Sebastian. Art sure?"

"Ay! by my faith! I've not fought under its inspiring folds so long not to know my master's symbol at a good sea league."

"Then attend us to the hall of state my lords and senhors, to receive our royal master's mandate, and surrender to new hands our borrowed dignity. Let a guard of honour be ready to conduct his coming Excellency to the palace. Your company, fair sirs," cried Don Sebastian, with a dignified and graceful presence, as attended by his officers, he descended the steps of the platform, and traversed the battery on his way to the hall of audience, the assembled troops presenting arms, and dropping their ensigns at his feet, as he passed slowly forward, and proceeded to the spacious reception-room.

On a dais at the extremity of the lofty apartment, was seated Don Sebastian, in a chair of state, richly attired in a purple mantle, with a jewelled hat, and a plume of white feathers on his head, and a gemmed sword, in a richly embroidered belt, clasped with a diamond fibula, or buckle, around his waist. A long covered table, at which sat ten or twelve venerable nobles stood below the dais, while all the space behind the chair, and down the sides of the chamber, was filled with guards, officers of the household, functionaries, and messengers,—all with the exception of the governor being bare-headed. As soon as all had taken their places, the folding-doors at the lower end of the hall, were thrown open, and the newly-landed viceroy, attended by several ecclesiastics in their robes, and gentlemen of his suite, entered, and advancing to the table uncovered, made a respectful obeisance to the seated authority, and then presenting a packet, sealed with the royal arms, to one of the attendants to deliver to Don Sebastian, he laid his own credentials on the table, and waited in silence the governor's perusal of his missive.

Sebastian rose to receive his soverign's letter, and pressing it reverently to his heart, brow, and lips, broke the seal, and read the brief lines that intimated his recall, and proclaimed his success in office, and then resumed his seat, as the new viceroy, with a bow to the council and the chief, said,—

"Don Sebastian de Alfendera, late Governor of the Province of Quito, I, Don Manuel Gonsalez, from my sovereign lord his most Catholic Majesty, Philip King of Spain, Arragon, Navarre, Sicily, and all the Indies, Duke of Portugal and Prince of Flanders, Holland, and Brabant, greet thee well, and am commissioned in my august master's name to say to thee in this Assembly, here convened, that for no fault committed, but for high honours yet in store, art thou recalled, and to express his pleasure at the delegated power here held by you in Quito; and that his grace has been moved to this proceeding, partly by the strong petition of thy right trusty and valiant father, the most noble Marquis of Alfendera, and partly that his liege may confer on thy worthy honour high and ennobling marks of royal satisfaction! Let every ear hear the message of our King!" And as he concluded, the president of the council rose from the table, and, taking up the credentials the other had laid down, and in the same form that the governor had observed, pressed the paper to his lips, and opening the document, read aloud the warrant. As soon as he had finished the reading of the commission, Don Sebastian stood up, and taking off his plumed hat and jewelled sword, removed the regal mantle from his shoulders, and delivered the ensignia of his office to one of the attendant nobles, then descending from the chair of state, bowed to the company and took his place by the table. At the same time Gonsalez, conducted by two councillors, proceeded up the opposite side, where, being robed in the mantle and sword, and placing the bonnet on his head, he ascended the steps of the dais, and amidst a loud flourish of trumpets and discharge of artillery, took his seat, as all the company rose and bowed respectfully to the installed functionary.

"We relieve you of all trust and functions, Don Sebastian," cried the governor, when the tumult had ceased, and the council had resumed their seats. "My secretary bears despatches from thy noble father of pressing import; and to facilitate thy quick return we here absolve you from all attendance at our court, and grant you instant absence."

"I humbly thank your Excellency, and so permitted, with all due reverence, will take my leave;" and bowing with dignity to the viceroy and all around, Don Sebastian quitted the presence, and hastened to his private residence to peruse the letters from Spain, marvelling what mischance or object could have induced his father to petition for his recall. Shortly after reaching his apartment, a servant entered with a packet from the new secretary, and opening it with eager curiosity, Sebastian found within, letters from Felix and his father. Glancing hastily at the formal and lengthy superscription of the marquis's epistle, he broke the seal and read as follows:—

"My truly beloved and very estimable son Sebastian,

"It is only within this month (of the accompanying date) that we have received certain intelligence that my last despatch by the good galleon, St. Salvador, had miscarried,—that stout ship with all her convoy having fallen into the hands of those piratical and cruel heretics—the English.

"I must therefore repeat the sum and substance of that communication, hoping in the name of the Blessed Trinity, that this may reach you safe, and find you in the enjoyment of as much health as honour, grace as glory, and in all commendation. Amen!

"It is three years, worthy Sebastian, since I indited a previous letter to thy hand, wherein I fully told the great calamity it had pleased the saints to visit us with: in the death or mysterious abduction of that valiant and noble youth, Don Alonzo Alvares; the dissolution of our double marriage; the grief, the misery that befell us; my beloved Catalina's grievous illness, and the strange malady of thy worthy brother Felix,—likewise the death of that estimable lady, the Condé's wife; my good friend's distracted grief, and all, in fine, of those misfortunes that turned our mirth to sadness, our rejoicing into mourning. That letter was written by the couch of my almost dying Felix,—that missive too, was indited in haste, to go with Lopez and the king's commission, that confirmed thee in thine elected governorship, and while thy brother yet lay 'in extremes:' I must therefore take up my record from that date, and thus proceed:—

"I courteously dismissed Don Almazuma, who had, forsooth, with every look of kindness, tended him with deep solicitude;—and yet it was strange, that day by day,—nay, hourly, my dear boy improved when that dark man had left us. His youth, and otherwise good health, aided by interceding prayers and hourly masses, under heaven's goodness, restored my Felix once again to my sorrowing heart,—and in a month later we journeyed homewards, where to my joy, I found my Catalina much recovered in her body's health;—but, Oh! Sebastian! how changed! I never thought till then how deeply she had loved Alonzo; for nothing else could make such woful havoc. Cheer, pastime, music,—no one thing could rouse her from the deep abstraction and corroding grief her lover's untimely fate had brought her to. A year elapsed, and then I hoped her mind would change its pall-like hue, and put a healthier vesture on; but no, it kept its wonted tenour, and daily gave me greater cause to wonder and regret. It seemed as if a deadly load weighed on her soul, and kept her spirit in perpetual penance away from wholesome recreation.

"Even Felix and Amina's nuptials, which were solemnized after the due probation of allotted grief, failed to rouse or interest her; and when the happy couple left me, I felt a solitude creep on my heart,—a loneliness of soul. The chambers echoed to my solitary step—my peopled mansion was a wilderness, and I the miserable Cain that stalked the desolation. 'Tis true my Catalina still was kind and loving; did all I wished, answered when spoke to, smiled when I laughed, or played her harp when I was sad; but all was manner, all precision, all duty;—there was no spontaneous act, no impulse in what she said or did,—and if I dropped a theme, she never took it up or broke the tedious silence of my reserve, till questioned to reply.

"I found at length, 'twas hopeless to contend, and I resolved to take my final residence in Madrid; for my life was one long dull Sabbath, —nothing relieved, but each the prototype of that to follow. When on the heels of this intent, Don Almazuma visited me,—and though I liked him not, yet for many acts of kindness performed in our affliction, I could but bid him welcome. But scarcely had his dark presence shadowed my house a day, when more distress awaited me. He asked a second time the honour of my daughter's hand! and, oh, Sebastian! she who had reviled him to my hearing, treated him with contumely and scorn,—she, my son! before my eyes tendered her hand, and in my open presence accepted him her husband, —and that with such resolve, that no gainsaying might distract her from its purpose, or save me from this hateful match.

"I was amazed—bewildered. Had he given her philters, or dealt in devilish arts, to conquer thus her stubborn hatred of him? With all authority I disallowed the choice, and told the sullen Don a father's prejudice should rule his child. He smiled and said, I did him wrong. Oh, Sebastian! there is a lurking serpent in that man's smile—a killing coldness in his look, and such malignity in his freezing glance, that joy is withered under its steady beam!

"But my surprise was not yet ended: with a calm, unruffled but determined brow, your sister thus addressed me: 'Father, my honoured lord, I have plighted to Don Almazuma my hand in solemn compact, and but two alternatives shall ever make me break it,—one must depend on his release,—when I will take the veil, —the other is here in my zone,'—and she touched the hilt of her poniard;—'for your daughter shall never disgrace her name or hesitate in selecting death before breaking her oath or ratified word. Here is my future husband, give your sanction, my noble father, or lose your daughter.'

"What could I do, Sebastian? how act? She was dear to me as life—dearer!—twined round the cords that bound my heart; and though I did not think she loved him, I deemed she might possibly be happy; and I strove hard to think him all Alvares thought and good Alonzo pictured him. But still—but still, wild fears would rise, and scrupulous alarms distract me. Yet at length, reluctantly,—God knows how most reluctantly!—I gave consent;—and with shorn honours, privately, with no ostent or show,—for so they willed it,—and mid the tears of a doating father, who despaired to alter her resolve, I gave away her hand: and they were wedded in our palace chapel,—and within a week my visitor departed as my son, and took the last remaining crutch from my enfeebled hand!

"But I have never slept since then, Sebastian. A dreadful fear is on me—my mind is full of images of dread—I cannot give the hideous phantoms words, or to thy sense delineate what I apprehend. My remorse is ceaseless, and I want a friend, a counsellor, perhaps—oh God!—I must give the thought an utterance—perhaps, an avenger!

"I have seen my beloved, my darling child, but twice: I dare not trust myself again to view her features. Imagine a change terrible and great, that scares a father from his child— a doating father from his only daughter,—I, who held my being bound up and closeted in hers—I cannot pursue the theme. Come to me, —lose not a breath of wind that blows to Europe after the receipt of this. I have addressed the throne, seen our most gracious King, and got thy quick recall. His grace is full of commendation, and ripe to give thee honour;—thou hast done enough for thy country, for a season's rest,—then return I pray you—your father begs it.

"Good Felix and his dear wife are blest and happy. She has a noble boy, beautiful and gladsome to contemplate. His duty keeps him still in our revolted provinces; and with his other functions, holds a place of trust in Brussels under the court. She, the dear Amina, is a blessing to him, and their days are full of happiness. For my good friend, Alvares, I cannot speak; his sorrow touches too near my own— trenches so close upon my heart, I have not words to say. He lives, or rather I should say exists, the victim of a visionary hope. The air he breathes, the very food and drink that ministers to his life, is seasoned with that unsubstantial aliment—that life delusive dream—Hope! Even from the grave and the impacted sod that covers him, he builds the airy fantasies of his dear boy's return, that I am fain to weep from very anguish of his distress.

"And now, my son, God have thee in his holy keeping, and send thee with the quickest speed to the companionship of thy fast-failing and life-weary, but ever-loving father,

"ALFENDERA."

A dark and ominous cloud gathered on Don Sebastian's brow when he laid down his father's letter, and he compressed his lips, clenched his teeth, and remained for some minutes in a gloomy meditation. "I would have thee wedded as soon to the arch fiend himself, my sister," he at length exclaimed, "as to that repulsive villain!" then with a menacing smile he continued, "Oh! but I will give an utterance to your thoughts, my father, and it shall be a bloody speech indeed. Who had such interest in Alonzo's death as he—the despised suitor? Who so great a cause to wish and have him dead as this dark caitiff—this peace-loving craven—this fireside soldier—this world-valiant Almazuma? Oh! I will bring thy unfleshed sword to such account, that I will do thee grace in death, and take the coward stigma from thy hated name.

Within a month of that day, the late viceroy, having disposed of his large estate in Peru, and made all necessary arrangements for the conveyance home of his ample fortune, by many vessels,—a precaution that privateering, and the sweeping fleets of the English, rendered necessary,—Don Sebastian, with a few selected domestics, embarked on board the homeward-bound galleon, and bade farewell to the scene of his late regal splendour, and long military sojourn.

<hr>

CHAPTER XIX.

WE must return again to the two principal characters of our tale, and request the reader to follow us once more to the Castle of Almazuma, and to that suite of apartments which he will remember we stated to be the only portion of the mansion that had not at that time been furnished, when every other part of its extensive pile had undergone a thorough decoration. The reader will be enabled to form a tolerable guess at the motive that induced Don Ferdinand to neglect these three chambers, and not till some months prior to his demanding for the second time, the hand of Catalina, as referred to in the letter of Alfendera to his son Sebastian had he thought it necessary to issue orders for their costly furniture and sumptuous appurtenances.

At the period that we now revisit them, these apartments had undergone a very marked and agreeable change, from their former cheerless and deserted appearance. The first and most spacious had been fitted up as nearly as possible —from the hasty sketch that Garcia in his surreptitious visits to the original had been able to bear in mind, in the same luxurious and elegant style of Catalina's boudoir : for Almazuma had noted down from his accomplice's description, every feature ; and in his subsequent directions to the furnishers, had each article arranged as nearly as possible after the fashion of that most elegant chamber of Catalina's pride, and Amina's admiration.

Costly mirrors, sumptuous carpets, articles of *vertú*, and ornaments of taste and luxury were scattered in excessive profusion around this exquisite apartment.

The second, which we have observed was something smaller than the first, was fitted up as a bed-chamber, which, as nearly as Garcia's one glance at that sanctuary in the palace enabled him to describe, had also been carefully copied, at least in its principal details. Passing from this room, the reader will remember was the small oak-panelled oratory, in which Almazuma's companion had slept, and secured his ill-gotten wealth.

Covering the walls of this small vaulted chamber hung a subdued and sombre tapestry, representing the passions of our Saviour ; dependent from the cornice, and forming a kind of border to the worked picture, were deep festoons of plain arras looped up by dead gold cord and tassels, hanging in many places to within reach of the hand. A covered table, with two silver candlesticks, a crucifix, a skull, and a missal, with one richly ornamented hassock, constituted the entire furniture of this chamber of penance.

It may at first seem strange that Almazuma should have taken such pains to decorate two at least of these rooms to so near a resemblance to those in which his now wife, had passed so many proud and happy hours : or that having once been assured of the possession of the prize for which, in his villany he had plotted so long, and, as it has been seen, successfully, he should longer care about studying either the comfort or gratification of his unhappy victim.

But in truth, though outwardly, and to the world such forethought and attention to his wife's enjoyment merited the praise it seemingly deserved ; yet very different was the motive of the calculating villain who planned it, and which the miserable Catalina alone could duly appreciate. No, it was neither regard, feeling, or the shadow of respect that induced the deep-thinking Almazuma to adorn those chambers so much like the happy home she had deserted, and rendered miserable. No—it was an artful cruelty, a kindly torture, perpetually to remind her of her once blissful state by the contrast that surrounded her : and while the world commended the act, she only, who felt the motive, could in secret despise the malignity of the deed, and shudder at the artifice that condemned her to a life of torture in the midst of wealth, and the admired excellence of her abode.

Seated on one of the soft ottomans in the first chamber, her feet resting on a rich embroidered footstool while her hands mechanically turned over the leaves of a romance that lay on a small, quaint, inlaid table beside her, as if the mind took no part in the tale of chivalry she had been perusing, sat Catalina ; her eminently beautiful features showing, perhaps, to greater advantage from the almost deadly whiteness that characterised her face and bust.

The only change that three years had produced on her outward form was the deadly pallor of the skin, and a languid anxiousness of eye, that betrayed in all its movements evidence of a deep-seated misery within—a dreadful care that seemed to sit upon her soul, suppressing every hope of life, and keeping down the very wish to shake the absorbing mischief from her heart.

The strong mind and powerful resolution of Catalina had hitherto kept the traces of her anguish from evincing themselves further in her countenance and her form, save when she spoke or the keen feelings at her heart were moved to utterance ; and then the lines and delicately traced muscles of her features grew eloquently powerful, with the expression of the torture that pressed in secret on her soul ; and the beholder read in one brief glance the slow, sure misery that consumed her life. But, in repose, nothing but the cold whiteness that pervaded all her face and brow gave indication of the disquietude she suffered.

The meshing net was thrown around her every action—her very thoughts seemed trammelled to her husband's will : she could have borne indifference, open hostility, harshness, contempt, consistent anger ; but the loathed hypocrisy of even outward kindness, the studious phrase, the endearing epithet, the hateful civility of assiduous care, and the repulsive horror of his professing love—these were the plague-spots to her hourly peace—these were the homely torments that she alone could apprehend or feel : for to all others' eyes he claimed the title of a most devoted husband, making his law appear her own most ardent wish ; so figuring each performance of her life, that it should bear the stamp of her unfettered choice dictating to her unborn thoughts the form and dress that they should wear, that whether in presence or removed, she felt the dragging chain, the almost prescience of his detested rule.

She strove, in vain, to follow out the thread of the high-wrought tale before her, but futile and impossible: her own reflections were too paramount to give vacuity for others' thoughts or images; and with a sad despair at conquering them she threw the book aside, and, with a heavy sigh, looked up from the unconned page. The long absent blood mounted on the instant to her head, and died the pallid skin of crimson, as her eye encountered the bright and rooted glance of Almazuma, as from the opposite extremity of the apartment he stood silently surveying her.

"I was not aware of Don Ferdinand's presence, or I would have sooner bade him welcome to these seldom-honoured chambers," observed Catalina, as she rose for an instant, and motioned her hand to a chair.

"'Tis I, most beloved, from whom apology is due," replied Almazuma in a tone of polite but studied irony, "I, the transgressor. 'Tis true, the onerous functions of my estate and place have for some time kept me excluded from that commingling of our hearts, so much the bliss of wedded life; but I will anon repair that grievous error which, I perceive, has troubled you. Let the assurance satisfy thy soul—my power, but not my will, has failed."

"I do not doubt I have your sole regard," added Catalina, as he paused, and with a meaning emphasis on the concluding words.

"Oh! most assuredly! Thou art my thought through night, my subject in the day,—thy image never quits me."

"My lord, I do believe it. May I be honoured with the motive of your present condescension?"

"I live but in satisfying your desire. I had two themes for visiting thus your privacy—disturbing your repose."

"I am ready, Don Ferdinand, to hear them both."

"Thou hast, my dearest wife, constituted in me thy living calendar wherein especial days and circumstances are writ for record; lest in the business of our daily life the hustled incidents should be forgot. I, as your organ, then, or second memory detatched from self, am bound by duty to your own repose, exclusive of the happiness it gives me, to be thy useful slave—to point those rubric days to your remembrance that business habit brings so aptly to my own."

"My lord, there are so few events for me in life, of any interest, that I may well remember every point that has a lawful claim upon my duty," replied Catalina, mournfully.

"And yet the mind is treacherous, even in what concerns the soul's salvation; our most religious duties sometimes become dead letters to our will—lost in the bustle of our busy thoughts, and we are sinners thus from accident, and not intent."

"Most true, such may be so to those who, in the living scenes of live, hold emulous distinction: the present business fills the foregone resolve; but true piety will overtake its error, and in after-holiness make up the fault of its omission. But I, my lord, have naught to do but think and pray, and am not conscious of meriting Don Ferdinand's solicitude."

"It glads me to the heart to hear as much;

for I had feared—you might—possibly have forgotten——"

"What, my lord?"

"Simply how far the moon hath run into the month," he replied, in slow, deliberate accents, as he fixed his searching eye full on Catalina's face. "The *living* world, you say, may breed omission in our minds: the *dead* should not," he continued, with a slight downward gesture of his gloved hand. "This is the *fifteenth* day——Oh! you remember!" he suddenly exclaimed, with a horrid smile, as her face grew instantly livid from the blood that rushed upwards, and for a few seconds stagnated in the lacing veins; while her eyes, with a ghastly intensity, were fixed with fascinated stare on the sparkling orbs of her husband. "I am very—very thankful," he resumed, unheeding the agony of his wife's distress, "that I did remind you; for what would your regret have been, had you forgotten this night's vigils? Alas! I should have grieved for you, too; from my soul I should have mourned. I know, anon, you will be grateful for my considerate care. I see your looks already thank me. Believe me, love—my dear heart's best, devoted——"

"I do implore you by the living heaven! no more," cried Catalina, as with a desperate effort, she regained her speech, and her countenance assumed an ashy hue; and as she wiped off the drops that gathered on her wide forehead. "I do beseech you, by your best hopes! no more. I—I will not forget,"—and a cold shudder ran through her frame, which for a moment convulsed her fine form, as she sank back on the couch, and buried her face in the folds of her handkerchief.

"Strong-handed piety will often, in his correcting gripe, shake the weak body thus; but 't is a heavenly perturbation, common to sinning, as to the canonized flesh," replied Almazuma, as if musing on the effect his words had produced on Catalina, and regardless of the torture his speech inflicted. "But I had another theme, my soul's delight! more temporal in its bearing—more of life in it. Will it please you to hear the second motive of my coming?" inquired Don Ferdinand, approaching a few steps nearer his wife.

"I am prepared to hear—ready, my lord, to listen," replied Catalina, as she endeavoured to tranquillize her feelings, and sitting in an attitude of attention, while her lip still quivered, and a dark circle round the tremulous eye-lid showed that the blood had not yet regained its wonted channels. Proceed—go on!" she faltered, as Almazuma, drawing a letter from under his sword-belt, opened, and laid it on the table. "I have here received a missive from that worthy lord, thy father, wherein he begs the honour of our company to rejoice with him in the re-union of his family: for, as he says, couriers have reached him from Don Felix, bringing intelligence of the near approach of his son and daughter, with their child. Also from Don Sebastian, who has already landed, and is upon his journey home."

"Aught else, my lord?" asked Catalina.

"Merely the mention of a further friend, already coming, if age delay him not upon the way, who longs to greet you—the dead Alonzo's father, nothing more—the good old Condé de Alvarez, thy special favourite."

"My God!—Oh! my God!" ejaculated Catalina, clasping her hands. "I—I cannot meet him, dare not look upon his face."

"You apprehend too much. 'tis true the fates forbade your union with his son; but now thou art another's. Your delicacy is misapplied—unnecessary; the Fates have ruled it otherwise."

"The Fates!" she cried, reproachfully. "Say rather, my own ungoverned act—my wilful homicide, robbed him——"

"Peace!" exclaimed Almazuma, sternly; then, resuming, in a calmer tone, said—"You are too sensitive: your feeling nature makes you cruel to yourself—unjust to your own virtue. Say, do you not long to bid them welcome home, and to invite your happy friends back with you here, to this abode of peace and love?"

"To say I were not glad to see my brothers once again would but belie my heart; but I must leave to you all formal invitation."

"That cannot be."

"Indeed!—for why?"

"I shall not go myself."

"Not go?" she cried, with a faint feeling of pleasure.

"Not go. I see how keenly you regret the disappointment," he replied, with a slight intonation, as his quick eye detected the momentary relief his wife felt in the prospect of his absence. "I shall find ample scope for all my time in seeing that my house be fit to welcome back its mistress and her friends. Your present stay must needs be brief."

"Brief, my lord?"

"Alas! I fear thy memory is not so apprehensive as thy pious life should render it. Ah! I perceive, your quick mind has brought your truant thoughts back where all your earthly joys are centred," he continued, as her face was again suffused, and a sharp tremor passed through her body. "All bliss bound up in the strict fulfilment of thy religious duties—thy monthly fast, vigil, and penitence, thou shalt depart to-morrow, love, and will return, in due season, to perform those rites so needful to thy soul's rest. The next revolving cycle of the moon will bring about the anniversary you spend so holily."

"Unutterable misery! But, oh! 'tis hopeless to appeal to thee—I must submit. Mother of heaven, strengthen me!"

"Report speaks highly of thy brother's son," resumed Almazuma, not heeding her remark. "This young Alonzo, they say he pictures to the life, as far as childhood may with man compare, the every feature of the dead Alonzo. Your reverend father marvels why nature has been so partial in her gifts—and, out of two, presented but one grandchild to his age."

"Do you dare insult me to my face—false, black-hearted villain?" cried Catalina, with indignation, all her native haughtiness for a moment mantling to her look, her cheeks suffused, and her eyes flashing with insulted pride, as she rose from her seat, and, with a majestic and angry step, crossed the room and drew the tassel of a bell, to summon one of her attendants. "Presume to taunt the woman you have grossly outraged? Is this a Spaniard's nobility?—is this another worthy proof of Don Almazuma's honour?—is this another part of your living torments? Base!—dishonourable! But beware you do not wake again the sleeping tiger in my heart! Attend me to my room, Maria," she added, as a female entered the apartment; but Almazuma instantly interposed, and addressing the servant in an unmoved voice, said—

"The Donna Catalina desires that her mules and carriage, with a becoming escort, be ready by nine of the clock to-morrow, to convey her to the palace of Alfendera. Instruct the household steward to this effect—and when your message is performed, return hither to your lady. I will myself, dearest wife, look to the further ordering of your train," he rejoined, turning to Catalina, with a bland smile, as the maid curtseyed and retired: then, in a graver voice, resumed—"I leave you; but ere I go, attend one word—Beware! Thou wilt, my love, whither thou art going, have many eyes upon thee—many tongues in busy eloquence to lift thy thoughts—and many pregnant minds to read thy heart. I bid thee wear a guard of prudence—bid thee remember thy contracted oath. I, Almazuma, bid thee again beware!"—and, crossing the room, he turned again at the door, and added in a deep, low whisper—"To-night, beloved one—to-night thou'lt not omit thine orisons:—think of your soul. Perjury to God is a most deadly crime. Thou wilt not endanger thine everlasting peace by maimed and hasty prayers:—oh! that were foul slovenliness. No! get you ready love: I will pray with you in thought—thought!—Farewell! I shall count the minutes, till I *know* you are on your knees. In all humility address thee to thy vigils; and—remember!" he added, with a peculiar deep emphasis on the word, as he repeated "Remember!" and, opening the door, passed noiselessly from the apartment.

When left alone, Catalina sank back on the couch, as if overwhelmed by the very strength that for a moment had imbued her with the courage to brave his resentment; and, folding her hands on her knees, she remained for some time speechless, the image of vague terror, with her eyes bent on the ground, and her features contracted with painful frowns, as if to exclude the quick growing phantoms that her mind threw up before her mental gaze. At last, shaking off the oppressive burthen, she raised her head, and, as if holding an inward colloquy, repeated one of Almazuma's phrases—"Till I know you are on your knees." "Ay!" she exclaimed, "how in that dark and noxious charnel-house—how has he the power to watch my acts?—how, when beside that fearful bier"—and she shuddered as she spoke, —"does this fearful man find eyes or ears to note my process, stay, or supplication?—and though I am assured he is not by, yet dare I not evade the smallest particle of the set duty. Merciful God! Santa Maria! I am chained, body and soul, to the dominant will of this hell fiend! Torture! torture! torture! No way to break the bond, till cold lethargic death cancels my servitude. That awful horrid oath fetters my tongue, and prisons in my dungeon heart, and to my own corroding breast, the dreadful secret; that, liberated once, I feel would give me quiet—ah, me! but never—never peace! How shall I meet Amina's love—my brother's pitying looks—my father's wistful eyes—and, oh! more dreadful still—the ceaseless sorrow of that kind old man? My brain begins to throb. Oh! that just heaven would send distraction to my aid—that worst of human ills—and I would hug it with delight; for life, the sense of consciousness, my vile hypocrisy, and my guilt, makes my existence an eternal hell! woe miserable! Who's there?" she exclaimed, with agitation, as the maid re-entered the room. "Take lights into my chamber—look out my wardrobe—and place what needful things my short journey calls for, in readiness for the morning's use. I shall not want thy services to-night; it is the period of my monthly vigil, and I must spend the hours in prayer," she added, in a more tranquil tone, subduing her voice to the level of her words.

"Alas! my lady," replied the servant, "you do yourself much harm by such close and devotional restraint. Surely, my lady, no sins women can commit need such unwearied penitence."

"Each mortal deems his burthen heaviest; and my offences, to my own perception, are too monstrous for even prayers to wash away."

"Father Jeronimo says we are not to judge of our own demerits, but obey the church's ordinances in the punishment of our errors; as none can judge of his true self but by another's eyes."

"He is a young physician of the soul, and speaks indulgently. Light the tapers in the oratory, and perform the task I bid you," replied Catalina, as she pointed to the door.

"Oh! my lady, that gloomy chamber always makes me sad. I wonder you can bear that dead man's skull so near your pillow. Alas! I should not sleep a wink with such a horrid neighbour. Faugh! a skull!"

"A skull, weak girl!—the fraction of the human rafters on which the flesh is built? What is that to the horror of the complete and perfect semblance that I—— Maria!" she continued, in a displeased and altered voice, as she checked her indiscretion, "I bade thee look to my wardrobe. Light me the candles—and when you have done, retire."

The maid passed into the other room, to fulfil her lady's directions; and Catalina for a time relapsed into her previous abstracted misery, and remained in painful thought till the servant had finally retired, when she arose, and with a beating heart and death-like countenance, crossed the bed-room, and, entering the oratory, secured the door with a spring behind her.

CHAPTER XX

It was towards evening on the following day, that Sebastian, followed by Lopez, rode briskly up the main avenue that led to the Castle of Almazuma; having in the early part of the morning first directed their steps to Soria, and then by a wide circuit proceeding in the direction of their present aim, the residence of his sister. The chief and indeed the only object in taking such an unnecessary round and delaying the time of his visit to so late an hour, was in the first instance to prevent suspicion from rising in any of his family, as to the real direction or object of his journey, and in the second that he might more reasonably expect to find his sister alone at such an hour, as he did not wish to meet her husband, Don Ferdinand, until he had previously held some conversation with Catalina.

Desiring Lopez to keep the horses saddled, and himself in readiness to attend at a moment's warning, Sebastian ascended the steps of the main entrance, and desiring one of the lacqueys to conduct him to the apartment of the Donna Catalina, he threw off his hat and cloak, while the man with evident trepidation obeyed the imperious order and conducted the visitor over the marble hall, and up the spacious staircase to the corridor, on which the only portal of the three chambers opened, then bowed, and respectfully took his leave, informing Alfendera that his duty permitted him to go no further; but those were the Donna's private apartments, and that his Excellency would find her within, or he would else seek one of the maidens and send her to announce his presence. With a haughty wave of the hand Sebastian dismissed the servant, and opening the door, entered the first chamber, but finding it untenanted, he crossed the second apartment, and pushing back the door of the third that stood partially open, entered the oratory.

Kneeling on the soft cushion before the crucifix on the table, with her hands held up in an attitude of deep supplication, Sebastian beheld Catalina in silent, but by the workings of her face, in agonised devotion, which, by its fervency seemed too eager and too strong for purest piety, too worldly for sincerity. Shocked and grieved at the picture before him, ashamed of his abrupt intrusion, Alfendera would have withdrawn: but as he attempted to retire, a slight noise, as if from beneath the arras, attracted Catalina's attention, and reverting her eyes from the cross, they encountered the person of her brother. Rising to her feet with dignity, and with a mild reproachful look, she said, while extending her hand to him, "Was this well, Sebastian, to steal upon my privacy?"

"By my honour, I had that moment entered, and was about to leave—when——"

"There was another sound," cried Catalina, crossing the room, and grasping one of the bullion tassels that hung from the cornice. "I thought I heard a motion here," she observed, musingly, as she drew the fringed rope, and the pictured tapestry rose for some feet from before the panelled wall, like a looped curtain by the action of the cord in her hand. "I was deceived," she resumed after a moment's listening, and allowing the arras to fall back into its place.

"What is the meaning—what the use of this device?" inquired Sebastian, as he drew near the opposite wall, and, pulling a corresponding cord, exposed the oak lining of the room.

"Why is this, my sister?"

"I am told it is to cool the chamber, when made too hot by summer—nothing else," replied Catalina, evasively. "But let us remove to another apartment; this is too sad for converse, and has no convenience for our stay: pass, my brother."

"Nay—stay," cried Sebastian grasping her wrist, and detaining her as she endeavoured to cross to the door. "Stay, I desire you; this spot will better suit my mood and what I have to say, than any else within the range of the house."

"What mean you, brother!" cried Catalina, with surprise and some alarm, as she gazed on his darkened countenance, and angry bending eye. "What would you have?"

"Thy full, secret, and unburthened confidence," rejoined Sebastian as he led her forward to the table; and placing his disengaged hand upon the skull that lay on the rich cloth, released her arm, and raising the other hand, said emphatically : " By this ghastly emblem of our unsubstantial selves ! and this devout and blessed sign of our redemption, and God's dread passion ! " laying his finger reverentially on the effigy of the crucifixion, " and by thy soul's beatitude in heaven or awful punishment in hell ! I do command you to divulge the crime or fatal knowledge that weighs upon your heart. By all the saints !—in the reverend and honoured name of thy woe-stricken father !—by my own great right as his upholder !—by the ties of brotherhood, honour, duty, love, and reverence ! I do entreat, command, you do at once reveal this dark, forbidding mystery. Speak !—either by compliance be my sister ; or, from this hour, henceforth for ever, stand aloof an alien from our blood and house, unknown, deserted, and condemned ! "

" Pity me, brother, pity me ! " she cried wildly, as she sunk at his feet imploringly ; while a vague alarm and quivering terror sat in her face, as the solemn and denouncing words of Sebastian rang in her ears. " Pity me—pardon me ! but I cannot. Oh ! my God !—Father of Mercies ! I dare not speak,—urge me no more ! " and she clasped her hands in supplicating earnestness.

" What law impedes the revelation of thy tongue ?—what potency chains up the utterance of thy heart ?—answer me—what ? " he demanded sternly. " Answer me ! "

" An oath—an oath ! Great heaven ! a dreadful, horrid oath ! "—and she covered her face, and shuddered at the recollection of the binding contract.

" By whom administered, and for what ? " he continued ; then, after a pause, in which Catalina seemed lost in painful thought, he added : " Do not patter with me, sister—do not attempt the damned hypocrisy of a base subterfuge—give me not cause to hate my father's child. Speak !—by whom propounded ? Answer ! "

" By myself, brother, and to my own heart applied," she answered, as a burning flush mantled her cheek at the prevarication she was guilty of. A scornful smile passed over Alfendera's face as he heard the answer.

" For what purpose was this self-abnegation, this voluntary record made to heaven ? " he resumed contemptuously. " What grievous sin hadst thou to bury in the bosom of thy God alone—denied to church and man ? Answer me ! "

" No more—no more ! I must not—dare not speak ! Press me no more—it is impossible ! " she cried in bitter anguish, " desist, my brother, I implore ! In mercy leave me."

" Answer me on the welfare of thy soul, where is my friend—where is thy plighted husband—where the gallant Don Alonzo ?—Where ? "

With a gasping and almost suffocating effort, while her features grew livid from the agony of her feelings, Catalina exclaimed hoarsely as she fell at her brother's feet :

" In—in his grave ! "

" I doubt it not. Tell me further, Catalina, I command you," he resumed, as he raised her from the floor, " by what fascination or devilish artifice this dark and sullen fiend has gained this influence over thee ? How thou couldst wed or ere be wived to one thou didst detest, and from my soul I think thou dost abhor ? "

" Spare me—spare me ! " she cried. " It was a voluntary act—I freely gave my hand. The *why*, oh, ask me not ! "

" I will not add a sharper sting to what I say, or so far insult your taste as to deem you ever loved the man who calls you wife."

" Love ! oh horrible thought ! repulsive loathing !—No, no, no !—never—oh, never ! " she exclaimed, shuddering.

" Yet you could marry one so loathsome ? "

" I did. But pray—no more. I cannot speak—"

" You could wed a man your mind and soul abhors ! " continued Sebastian, musing on the strange anomaly : " unite your being and your spotless honour with one so stained ; and to become, perchance, the mother of a line——"

" No—no ! " shrieked Catalina, as she sank on the footstool, and buried her face in her robe. " No—the church's union is the sole rite that bound or keeps me to his will, — no further wedded."

" What ! " cried Sebastian, fiercely, as his face grew purple with the indignant passion at his heart. " Has the vile caitiff dared to insult my noble father's daughter—the sister of my blood, by such profaning, damned, impeaching villany ? Make thee but wife in name—a ghostly, not a legal one ? Arch-villain ! thou shalt answer for this indignity. I will not question further, sister, or say the dark surmises in my mind, or for the present give to speech all the corroborative fears I feel. But I will liberate thee from this galling yoke—free thee from this guilt-weighing oath that fetters up your tongue, and locks you from the sunshine of repose and life. Oh ! I will emancipate you from this deadly viper—this killing thraldom. I go——"

" Stay, I implore you ! " cried Catalina, rising, and clinging to her brother's arm. " Stay—you know not what you do : that which I hold the greatest bliss, you deem the head affront. Seek him not, my brother—quarrel not with him, dear Sebastian. Oh ! you know him not : his power —his art—his matchless skill ; thy arm were futile poised with his—thy judgment nothing in the cope of his strong capacity. Nay, do not smile so scornfully, or think that coward fear is prompting now the counsel that I give. You do not know, and cannot estimate, the villany that lurks in every thought and word. Do not expose thy life in profitless assault, that never—never can enhance or benefit my ease. Leave me to my fate, and him to——"

" Away ! " cried Sebastian indignantly :— " away ! If this huge vice were the embodied hell, with all its dark and devilish attributes, for eyes, hands, and sense, I would wage battle against the grizzly fiend, and, single-handed, cope in such a cause a legion of such incarnate traitors. Let me go, Catalina : my father's honour speaks in my blood for vindication ; and by the holy saints and the just God ! it shall not plead in vain ! Away—let go my arm. By hell ! I 'll seek him instantly." And shaking off her light hold, Sebastian hastened from the nearly darkened chamber ; and traversing the other apartments, and descending the grand staircase, desired one of the servants to conduct him to the presence of his master. The man, with respectful alacrity, obeyed ; and marshalling the visitor over the hall, proceeded to the centre of the large room, and bowing with low humility to his stern master, was about to announce the visitor, but Sebastian, with a proud and dignified step, passed the servitor, and with a haughty gesture of his raised arm, as he motioned him to retire, said—" Don Alfendera needs no herald to proclaim his coming—he can declare himself." And striding up to the table, he laid his hand on the rich cover, and gazed with an angry and imperious glance on Almazuma, who, rising with a bland smile and gracious declension of the head, pointed to a vacant seat by his side, as the servant retired and closed the folding-door.

" I hope my worthy friend and right noble brother will pardon my uncourteous negligence, in not before bidding him a prosperous welcome to his native land. My fault, brave sir, is more in seeming than in fact; for which offence, perplexity of weighty business, brooking no interval of rest, must plead extenuation. It had been my hope, to-morrow, to repair so far my neglected pleasure, by paying, in my person, that respectful due which custom claims as right, and worthy natures take felicity in rendering—my cordial greetings and assurances of love."

" My lord will waive all compliment, and terms of idle courtesy," replied Sebastian. " I would speak with you. Are we alone? " he inquired, casting a hasty glance round the apartment.

" Perfectly," added Almazuma calmly, and not observing the other's impatience of tone and manner; and before Sebastian could make a reply, he continued with a saddened brow, and in the deep musical notes, natural to his voice, which lent such power to all his words, and gave a pleasing beauty to his eloquence, as he said—

" I trust your welcomed visit to my beloved but suffering wife may act remedially. My Catalina's mental health—as your wisdom doubtless has perceived—is sadly out of time and harmony, afflicting my very soul with keen solicitude and fears. Alas! she finds no joy on earth, but in that deep abstracted piety, that, like a festering wound, consumes the part that gives it life. Her rosary and crucifix, missal and prayer, with all the adjuncts of strict holiness, have in her sweet nature ta'en the place of husband, father, brother, sister, and the dear converse of familiar friends. Your happy coming I have looked for with impatient haste, trusting to the all-powerful influence of thy friendly aid and brotherly regard, to work a healthier tone through those rich chambers of her well-stored, but much distuned mind."

During this long sorrowing speech, which Almazuma pronounced with all the serious gravity and corresponding action that could denote a sensitive and faithful heart, Sebastian struggled hard to preserve an even temper and dignity in his swelling resentment; and though his eyes flashed and his contracted brows met in furrows, as each false word and deceitful accent fell from his lips, he succeeded in mastering his impatience till Almazuma had concluded; when taking a few steps nearer, till he almost touched the tall figure of the unmoved lord, he bent his head forward, and exclaimed between his clenched teeth, in a hard, deep voice: " Don Ferdinand, you are a villain !—a false, base liar! and a dishonoured caitiff! You have my defiance : take thy indignity,"—and with a slight backward stroke of the fingers of his hand he struck Almazuma on the breast of his doublet, and drawing up his person to its full height, stood with a frowning look confronting his enemy.

For an instant the blood rushed in an impetuous flood to Almazuma's face, and a dark, deadly, and threatening scowl gathered on his features, as the first exclamation of Sebastian fell on his ear; but when the profaning fingers touched his body, with one hand he grasped his sword, and with the other unsheathed the blade for the space of a few inches, and throwing his left leg back, stood for a moment in an attitude of stern indignant defiance. In another second, the sword dropped in its scabbard, and the weapon fell by his side; and recovering his former position, with a quiet cold smile, from which every semblance of passion was removed, and in a voice in which no evidence of emotion could be traced, said—

" You have, Senhor, thought fit to put disgrace upon my person, dishonour to my name : there is but one way left to write the mischief out. The pen is in my sheath—the ink within thy heart !"

" Thou art too confident, civilian ! and presume upon the scholarship and holiday tuition of your foil to speak so arrogantly to a tried and practised soldier," replied Alfendera, with contemptuous phrase and gesture, taunting Don Ferdinand for his unmilitary life, and home-fencing.

" Oh, very true! But will it please you to specify a time when you may teach correctingly my inexperienced self in that warlike pastime? The practice must be excellent if it savour of the humility of the experienced giver."

Sebastian bit his lip, but replied instantly, " The insult lies with you. Select your time—let it be brief."

" Nay, it was courtesy that made me ask."

" Doubtless! I am ready, always ready," replied Sebastian.

" I did not know that thou hadst been so lately shrived !" sarcastically rejoined Almazuma.

" Insulting devil !" cried Sebastian, fiercely ! " Prepare thee! Every moment that I let thee live, heaven and my conscience reproach me for my folly. 'Tis night; but our warm bloods of Spain have found a means to counteract the gloom, where honour calls for instant surgery ;—do you understand me—can you guess my drift ?"

" Tarry a moment, Don Alfendera,—tarry a moment," answered Almazuma, with the same calm voice, and undisturbed action, as he unfastened a case near that which contained the weapons, and took out two hand lamps, or small lanterns, with bright steel reflectors, all being darkened, but one long forward pane of plate glass : these instruments, when lighted, sending out a strong, brilliant, and dazzling sheet of reflected flame. As Don Ferdinand returned to the table, and ignited the wicks of the two lamps, he continued :—

" Tarry an instant :—we shall need them for a double use : the night is dark, and they must serve as guides as well as beacons ; for we must tread where nothing mortal can intrude, and then this bout of ours shall have a sharp and bloody accomplishment. Pray make your choice," he added, as he courteously offered the lamps for his inspection. " Are these the toys your meaning touched on ?"

" Either will suit :—this, then—come !" replied Sebastian as he took one of the lanterns and darkened its pane, much surprised that a man of Almazuma's peaceful habits should be supplied with such articles of the duello.

Almazuma having put on his hat, and thrown his mantle round his shoulders, hid the other lamp under its ample folds, and passing Alfendera, proceeded to the door, as he observed tauntingly—

"You are impatient, Senhor: follow me, and school your heat to prudence—for I would have thee acquit thyself manfully."

"Lead on! and keep thine admonition for thine own defence. Proceed!" retorted Sebastian, with impatient anger."

Don Ferdinand led the way to the hall, now deserted by the servants; and Alfendera having equipped himself in his hat and cloak, followed his guide, who by an unfrequented passage conducted his enemy to that part of the building, where we have before seen Almazuma mount the mule on the occasion of his following Garcia from the palace.

CHAPTER XXI.

THE night was dark, starless, and sullen, as the two nobles issued from the stately pile, and threaded their way through the avenues; and under the dense foliage of the well-wooded park, seldom had two men, bent on a deadly purpose, been so contrasted. Almazuma, calm, malignant, haughty, and full of guile and crafty cunning, his firm features unmoved, impassive, and devoid of every show or tendency to feeling; his step deliberate, steady, and unvarying, as if it formed a part, and played spontaneously with the obdurate heart and the inflexible mind, that jointly governed every muscle, nerve, and motion of his commanding frame. And, as with a show of assiduous care, he occasionally held low his light to warn his companion of the obstructions in his way, or, by a brief and gracious direction, teaching the spots to turn, or impediments to avoid, it would have been impossible for an unacquainted eye or ear to have believed that such a being could be bent on any hostile object, or dream of the strong tide of passion that flowed within his tranquil breast, or even credit that the man he so carefully conducted was—next to the *one* being on earth—the thing he held in deadliest hatred.

Sebastian, on the other hand, though proud, was noble, more from inherent virtue and integrity of soul than by dignity of birth. Open, generous, but quick of passion, though in his deepest hatred honourable and just; despising from his soul, all artifice or low dissembling; quick in resentment, tenacious of his high birth and privileges: and exacting in all the punctilios that appertained to the then strict school of honour: but his anger once appeased, or his own errors proved, affable, forgiving, eager to make the reparation due for his own remission, and forgetful to acknowledge wrongs and past disunions. Brave to a fault; and holding in contempt that cold assumption to all danger, that puts an icy look or freezing mien upon the hot blood and swelling heart beneath. Eager for the present encounter, all the indignation that he felt glowed in his face, and showed a corresponding tremor in his frame, as, with hasty and unruly

steps, he sometimes followed, and occasionally preceded, his deliberate guide, showing in the uneven gait he kept, all the influences at work within his heart.

A low, creeping breeze moaned through the wood, and sighed in mournful cadences, as the two duellists moved along, each bent upon revenge—one for a sister's wrongs, the other for an insulted person, and a deadly hatred to the man who gave it. Sometimes a startled hare sprang forward from their feet; or the watchful lark, roused before his time by their close tread, spread his wings upward to the obscured skies; or occasionally the screaming heron, from the tall elms, split the stillness with his discordant noise; while the prowling fox, or bounding squirrel, rustling the dried leaves, gave proof that life still dwelt around them, though all eager to escape their common enemy—destroying man; but both were too much employed in their own thoughts to heed the timid things that strove so swiftly to avoid them.

At length they reached the open country, and turning down an obscure lane found themselves at its termination in a low, gloomy valley, surrounded on every side by high fir-clad hills, through whose gloomy foliage the night wind sang in harsh, sharp gusts, imparting a cheerless wintery feeling to the seclusion on which they entered. After proceeding a few furlongs down the dark gorge, they reached the low earth wall of a neglected cemetery, in the centre of which dimly loomed out the crumbling walls of a ruined chapel. Desolation had sat on the place for years, man's memory could not trace the last dead occupant of that lonely sepulchre; the windows and frame-work of the doors had years past mouldered away, and rude, irregular gaps alone indicated where light or ingress had been admitted into the ancient and now roofless tenement.

The bat, the owl, and slimy lizard, its only living inhabitants, had for ages made it their dwelling. Ivy, long waving yew, nightshade, and rank herbage, hung on the outward walls, inserted their wild luxuriance in the green and mossy stones, and waved their wide arms like feathery banners over the rugged breaches, where once the painted glass poured its rich warm sunshine, or the light and graceful arch pointed its florid tracery over the bared head of the suppliant devotee.

With difficult and unsteady steps Sebastian followed his conductor over the half-sunk trenches of buried mortality, or extricated his feet from the tangling briars and matted weeds that interlaced and carpeted the forgotten church-yard. At length, passing under the low arch of the fallen porch, and entering the broken door-way that with projecting and rugged mouth seemed to yawn ominously and drear on the passer by, the two Spaniards stood within the unroofed walls of the once sacred pile.

The pavement, for many yards around the crumbling altar, was covered with a thick sward of long grass, that springing from the green fen that covered the broad flags, looked like the miniature of a deserted lawn. Not a stone or impediment obstructed this unnatural flooring; it seemed, in truth, a fit arena for such a strife as each meditated to enact.

Proceeding up the centre of the chapel, Almazuma, who had previously darkened his lantern, approached the altar; and drawing back the shade of his lamp, placed it on the dilapidated table of the sacrifice. As the brilliant sheet of the reflected light revealed the scene around, playing on empty niches, green-wreathed pillars, mouldering tombs, buttress, pinnacle, and deep-cut crucifix, the effect was grandly solemn : the bright light and broad masses of shadow, giving by their contrast a stern feature to the bold outlines they disclosed or dimly hid ; while here and there the straggling rays expended themselves on the cold dead walls, or the dense foliage that, like a pall, hung loose from the rifted masonry ; and as the tendril boughs undulated in solemn motion with the night air, they looked like nodding plumage on the dead.

Sebastian started back with horror, while every feature seemed alive with the amaze and sacriligious terror that pervaded them as gazing wildly around, he beheld the fearful place and desecrated sanctuary.

A malicious and exulting smile sat triumphantly in Almazuma's eyes, as he surveyed the alarm and reverential fear that pervaded his companion ; and throwing contemptuously his hat and cloak upon the altar, unfastened his sword from its belt, and drawing the bright rapier from its sheath, flung the empty scabbard disdainfully beside them, and exclaimed in a voice of calm defiance—

"Prepare !"

"Not here ! my God ! not here !" cried Alfendera, in a hoarse suppressed emotion, as he instinctively withdrew a step from the profaned shrine of his religion.

"Nay, you ill repay my most considerate care," replied Ferdinand sarcastically, as he dropped the point of his blade on the pavement, " for I had deemed you would prefer to rest on holy ground. Behold, this is the temple of your faith—decayed —but, oh ! how sainted."

"Sacrilegious monster !—not here !—away !— not here !" continued Sebastian, as he withdrew further from the altar—"I dare not draw my weapon here."

"Thou art too dainty, methinks, brave lord, for a tried and practised soldier," rejoined the other, in his companion's former words. " I stand upon my privilege for ground and time. I am the challenged."

"I'll fight thee, devil, in thy native home— the jaws of hell ;—on horse or foot, with knife, blade, axe, or lance—on the sharp edge of the most dizzy cliff—on the unsteady footing of a drifting plank—on earth, sea, in fire or air—to the last pant of my strong heart—but not here ! —not in the household of my God !—not by the altars of my sires ! Remove thy ground, and, though the courtesy unroot my tongue and lacerate my heart, I'll say thee thanks, and cry— 'twas nobly done !"

"Beneath these stones rest the long dead of my illustrious house," replied Almazuma, "and I would have their ghosts peer from their mouldered shrouds, to witness how the last of their long line requites an insult to the name he bears : —and thus returns the damned indignity !" and, lifting up his sword, he struck Sebastian with the flat of his blade upon the shoulders, as he added —" We are now, my lord, even. Come on, thou tardy valiant soldier !"

"Hell fires ! death ! A blow from thee—accursed of God and man ! Have at thee, then.

Heaven will forgive my sacrilege, if I can rid the world of such a stalking fiend. Prepare thyself, and ask of heaven, not me, for mercy !"—and, like a goaded lion roused from his slumbering lair, Sebastian tore the mantle from his neck, threw down his hat, and, taking off his sword and belt, drew forth his weapon, then hurling away the scabbard, fell on one knee—and holding his hands and rapier up to the dark sky, cried with holy emotion—

"God of my fathers !—eternal Spirit of Truth ! sit on my chastising sword, as in thy name I draw it :—give to its edge a heavenly temper—that like a scourge divine it may confound, and in his guilt destroy this dread blasphemer of thy name ! And if I fall in this just battle, Jesu have mercy on my soul !" Then, signing the cross on his breast, and kissing the crucial hilt of his blade, Sebastian sprang to his feet like an agile deer ; and seizing the lamp that he had previously placed on the earth in his left hand, and throwing his graceful person in the attitude of defence and guard, beat the alarm on the ground with his firm foot, and cried—

"Come on ! I am for you."

Almazuma instantly obeyed the summons, and, taking his lamp from off the altar, approached his antagonist and measured the permitted distance, each eye being bent for a moment to the green floor on which they stood, to see their feet had a firm hold of the grassy pavement ; then throwing back their ample chests, poising their bodies on their well-set limbs, and throwing up their left arms, that the light of their raised lamps might fall parallel with their heads, they crossed their swords, and fixing a steady glance on each other's eye, stood with a slight and graceful play of body, watching with a prescient intelligence for the assailant's motion. At the same instant both beat the assault with a rapid action of the right foot, and instantly closed in quick and deadly conflict.

During the previous colloquy and all through the subsequent engagement, Lopez stood like one entranced, gazing through the leafy curtain that descended over the wide rent in the wall to the base of the building, his eyes distended, his mouth open, and his hair bristling on end, keeping up a perpetual crossing of his person, by touching his brow, breast, left and right shoulder with the forefinger of his right hand, while by the other he steadied his shaking limbs by grasping the projection of a buttress that ran up the fissure by which he stood.

For more than half an hour the well-matched combatants had employed each *finesse* that characterized the singular species of duel they were adopting, but as yet without effect on either ; though copious perspiration stood on each brow, and the accelerated blood tinged their cheeks with crimson from the violent action of the springing muscles. Now in a quick retreat or rapid circle, preserving to a nicety the exact and measured distance. Lunge after lunge, thrust on thrust, over and under in carte, tierce, seconde : defence on every quarter, parry, and drive, followed with rapidity of thought and flashing lightning : each artifice the art permits, was practised in rapid sequence—the flanconnade, the beat, the volté, the appeal, glizade was given and returned in instant change ; and as each antagonist by turns threw forward his powerful chest in the home drive of his rapier forming a straight line from head to heel, the action was so quick, the eye could hardly define the posture, ere the lithesome limbs sprung with elastic bound back to their agile and defensive guard, so that each attitude and recovery seemed spontaneous motion.*

Sometimes they hid their lamps behind their backs and fought in total darkness; then as the broad chest and weighty shoulder was thrown in the lunge, the full blaze was shot under the sword arm, right on the confronter's face, dazzling the eye, hiding the coming point, and baffling the just parry: now, over the head, anon held before the breast, and then eclipsed behind the back, the flitting and unsteady lights shot here and there like brilliant meteors, perplexing and confounding alternately the aim and guard of both; and as the flashing blaze fell on the long bright swords that in perpetual action revolved in the quick hand, they seemed like rods of flame in their swift and ceaseless passage.

With red and flashing eyes, the two incensed duellists clenched their teeth, and threw the whole strength and impetus of their bodies, and the deadly passions of their souls in each thrust and drive, parade and circle, of their tempered blades, and beat the ground, with the advanced foot, like two fierce bulls defying each other with insulting stamp. Again driven backward, but to advance in turn, the two hidalgos, with unabated power, kept up the clashing fight, both inwardly resolved to die, but never yield; and every instant more malignant thoughts and savage purposes possessing each, till in aspect, bearing, and resolve, they seemed like two incarnate fiends battling for empire.

For some seconds Sebastian had obscured his light, and though nearly blinded by the sunflashes of his enemy's lamp, maintained the unequal combat with consummate skill, till, at a favourable guard, he drew his person up, and with a sudden desperate pass, revealing at the same instant his bright light in the direction of his arm, lunged home, exclaiming in an oppressed and panting voice, "This, traitor, for Don Alonzo!" but his foot slipped in the long grass, and Almazuma's sword dashed the rapier from his hand, as Sebastian fell at full length at his antagonist's feet, and rolled over on his back.

For one moment Almazuma gazed upon his foe with a look of unutterable triumph; then setting his foot on the prostrate Alfendera, cried with a discordant laugh, "This through thy heart. To hell, intruder!"

But at that moment, Lopez, whose fear and horror of the scene, the act, and place, had given way to alarm for his master's safety, sprang from his concealment through the gap, and drawing his sword, rushed forward; and as Almazuma's long-pointed blade descended on the breast of Sebastian, he dashed it aside with such force, that the weapon flew high in the air, and after a few turnings, fell at its owner's feet.

"Damnation!—Base miscreant, hence to perdition!" exclaimed Ferdinand, drawing his

dagger and approaching Lopez, who had placed himself across his master's body. "Die, dog!" but checking himself before his arm descended, he re-sheathed his poniard, and with a savage scowl, turned, and taking up his fallen sword, broke it across his knee, and hurling the fragments in the air, cried, "Hence, dishonoured steel;" and striding to the altar, threw round his shoulders his cloak, and putting on his hat, stood with folded arms, gazing on his rescued foe.

"Here, good master—here is your sword," cried Lopez, reaching Sebastian's weapon, and putting it into his hand. "Let me help you," he continued, as Alfendera sprang to his feet. "Now, Senhor, now give it him: I'll attack him behind and you in front; and I'll warrant we'll make worm's meat of him. Lord, I'm so savage and courageous I could kill a giant!"

"Thank your base hireling for your life, Don Sebastian: when next we meet, there shall be no possibility of an interruption. We shall meet again, where heaven itself shall not save you."

"We shall meet—doubt it not," replied Alfendera, as Almazuma with a proud step and insulting smile strode out of the chapel; while Sebastian, chagrined and mortified at his defeat and his enemy's prowess, bent his steps in the direction of the castle to obtain his horses and return to the palace.

———

CHAPTER XXII.

"I HAVE apprised you both, my sons, of all the apprehensions and the darkening fears that have of late so much afflicted me—nay, that from the hour she wedded him, have racked me with suspense, doubt, grief, and care; suppressed the natural joy that should attend a parent on the union of his child; heaped, in the lapse of months, the gravity of years upon my head; made cold and desolate my heart, bent my aged limbs yet nearer to the grave, and placed my sorrowing spirit in closer commune with my God:—in fine, has taken the prop from my infirmities, and left me stricken to the soul—deprived of every consolation that, from my abounding love, should spring to cheer my age, and make my life a sweet declension of unbroken harmony."

Such was the observation that Alfendera addressed to his sons Sebastian and Felix, as, seated in the often-mentioned library, the father continued a subject, for the discussion of which he had expressly called them together.

"Let me hear all my father has to say touching this painful theme, before I make reply or comment," added Sebastian, as the Marquis paused, and reclined sorrowfully in his chair.

"'T is fitting that I should," resumed Alfendera; "and after I have made an end, each one can give his free opinion. Yet is my knowledge, at the best, but doubt—my facts but dark surmises; though both of such distressing feature—such unkind complexion, as keeps my spirit in perpetual anarchy! No—give me a tangible distress—a certain grief, and I will meet it as a man, struggle, and conquer it, or die in the endeavour, though it be huge enough to threaten life in its engagement: but against the unknown ill that wars upon my soul, by stealth—that saps, in secret, at my heart, I am but as an infant in

---

* The author believes he has taken a liberty with the laws of duelling, in making both characters use the lamp, the combat being generally with but one; the adversary having a folded cloak on his left arm, as a counterpoise to the advantage of the light.

the enterprise; and can but judge the greatness of the harm by the result it leaves behind—the aching mischief here——" and he laid his hand upon his breast, and thus continued :—

"In the last letter which I sent to you, when in Peru, wherein I told you of our Catalina's nuptials——"

"Curses on the caitiff wretch who bore her from your aged arms!" interrupted Sebastian, with looks of maddened rage—gnashing his teeth, as his thoughts reverted to his late encounter with Almazuma—"would I had succeeded in inflicting——"

"Peace! my son!" resumed Alfendera, "peace, till I shall have given utterance to my thoughts. You may remember I said there was a fear upon my heart I dared not give a likeness to—told you how *he* had rendered kindness to our house in tending Felix in his illness like a brother: how he had lingered till all the guests were gone —and with what seeming regret he at length took leave :— how Catalina, with determined look approached you, and in these words begged Don Almazuma's hand :—'*Father, I have plighted to Don Almazuma my hand in solemn compact, and but two alternatives shall ever make me break it : one must depend on his release—when I will take the veil : the other is here in my zone—for your daughter shall never disgrace her name, or hesitate in selecting death, before breaking her oath or ratified word!*' I told you likewise how much I was averse to her betrothment—and how remarkable and quick a change had overshadowed her; and, like a sudden gloom upon a summer's sky, turned all its warmth to chill, serenity to frowns, and gladsome day to cloudy evening. I said 'twas such a change, that, doting father as I was, I dared not look upon it; and found it greater tax of courage to drag a parent to a daughter's arms, than erst it would have been to stay aloof, and never see her more."

"And did you tell him, worthy Senhor," asked Felix, the younger brother of Catalina,— "did you tell him also how fast my health improved when this gloomy fiend had taken his departure?"

"I did, I did—and more, much more. Sebastian must remember that I said——"

"Most noble father, I well remember *all* you said—no part of it is lost to me; and to the last trump will it remain indelibly fixed upon my memory, a deathless record. God! how the lines seared my brain, and almost dried each petty artery up. To think that the peerless Catalina —who, in times gone by, would have spurned his love, had his riches been piled Olympus high before her, and he transformed from a mortal man to an immortal god :—to think that she, my sister, of the noble house of Alfendera—whose ancestors have mated with the highest and most virtuous Spanish Dons, should have descended so vilely low as to accept—nay, sue for the hand she had despised. Farther," he continued, turning and looking his venerable parent in the face, "you also said——"

"I did. I said moreover that I required a friend, a counsellor—and, perhaps——"

And the aged nobleman here paused for a moment, and looked inquiringly into the features of his son, who, with the utmost anxiety depicted on that index of the mind, exclaimed—

"And what?"

"Be calm, my son, and let not thy feelings o'ermaster reason. And yet, wherefore——"

"Oh! speak!"

"I said that I also required *an avenger!*" replied the Marquis, with peculiarly slow and measured emphasis in the utterance of those words.

"And you have two avengers in your sons, dear father," exclaimed Felix, "who will never see the noble house of which they form a part brought into contumely or contempt."

And, as if awaking from a reverie, he exclaimed with increased vehemence—

"Never!—no! never!"

"Felix," said the aged Marquis, "you are my youngest son: 'tis to your brother the world will look to avenge any insult intended to our house : he is the next after myself, and I, alas! am now too old and feeble to meet our wary enemy; to him therefore, I look; and may the God of our ancestors be his shield and buckler in the contest."

"But, dearest father," resumed Felix, "not only in Sebastian is our house represented, but in all its sons : and I were coward indeed to stand tamely by and witness aught derogatory to the honour of a Spanish Hidalgo.

"True, my son—true," replied Alfendera. "The unsullied honour of our house may rest securely in your hands; and chastisement on a foe, even from its meanest member, will add fresh glories to its name."

"But Felix," began Sebastian, "your wife has claims——"

"So also has mine honour," interrupted Felix, his eyes dilating and the colour mounting to his cheeks—"both thine and mine—our sisters too— all cry aloud for retribution on the craven's head."

"Alas! your sister," bitterly exclaimed the Marquis, "will never see her father more. Never again shall I behold that form—once the joy and solace of mine eyes. Heaven knows how fondly I did love her. My future hopes were centred in her prosperity—in her wedded fate. The greatest nobles of the land had asked her as their bride; but I denied them all—all : reserved her for Alvares' son—my oldest—best of friends. He, alas! when in the bloom and vigour of his life, was by some foul treachery cut off, leaving my Catalina's heart a prey to wild despair. How fondly did she love my choice—the noble Don Alonzo. No prayers, entreaties—no, nor all the pleasures Alfendera's palace could afford would help to chase one tear from her fond sorrowing eyes. My dear Sebastian, much I wonder that delay——"

"Dear father," with all the duteous haste of love," resumed his son, "the urgent call of honour—I have hastened my return : left to commissioned hands important trusts that claimed my own revision—that not one object might stand between my father's wish and my performance, or give the name of laggard to my impatient spirit : nay, so exceeding was my impetuous haste, it would not be subdued to wait the course of settled winds and favourable tides; but had my heavy barrack towed with sweeping oars far on the bosom of the wide Pacific; nor threw I off this dull progression, till, under clouded canvass and a fresh sea breeze, my bounding caraval had washed her whitened decks down to the waist in showering foam. So far my wish outstepped accomplishment."

"And knowing this, pardon me, my son, if I have marvelled that thou hast been in Spain some time, and not yet seen thy sister's husband," replied the Marquis, as Sebastian concluded ; "if I have wondered that thou should'st leave to me the mooting such a subject, or have delayed till now—until I myself have specially invited it—the very mention of a theme so near our hearts—nay, that trenches so neighbourly on the sanctity of our house's honour."

"By your good leave, my father," cried Felix, eagerly, "you do Sebastian much injustice, and, in your lack of information, greatly wrong him. From the first moment that he set his returning foot in Spain, down to the present——"

"I pray thee, Felix, by thy love and brotherhood, no more," exclaimed Sebastian, interrupting his brother's defence of his conduct, as in a tone of wounded pride, and with a slightly flushed cheek at his father's imputation of tardiness, he continued, gradually assuming, as he proceeded, a more calm and deferential voice and manner :

"To you, my lord, my conduct may seem strange and opposite—my late proceeding in no ways squaring with my former haste ; but I must beg you for the present time (a few days longer) to permit me to keep concealed that which your place, relation, years, might justly claim a title to be told, and not too harshly censure me for what may but appear omission. You would as soon, my lord, pluck down the honoured scutcheon from your house, and trample it beneath your feet, as entertain the possibility that in the blood of our high line there lurked one drop less lively than the rest, that could endure the breath of insult, or unavenge a wrong committed to the heart it warmed. The purple stream of the Byzantium line flows unpolluted in our veins ; nor shall the sanguine tide, from emperors derived to us, ever inhabit craven heart or dastard mind. Be satisfied, my father, then ;—be certain that I but abide my time ; am hourly laying up a store of facts to solve this misery that our sister suffers —and, while she suffers, heaping disgrace on Alfendera's daughter, and my father's child. Within two days you shall be fully satisfied on every point that bears on Catalina's fate and her dark husband's purpose. Till then, govern your amazement ; and if at the expiration of that time I do not lay before your view the progress of my research, my brother, Felix, the partner in my counsel as my intention, will strictly execute that duty for me, and, in all particulars, afford you satisfactory content."

"I understand you, son : I comprehend, Sebastian, what you purpose. I will not say you nay. God yield the right ! I will be patient. I felt assured thou had'st not met this man ; for either I had never seen my son again in life, or Almazuma's death ere this had been recorded. I was most certain that you had not encountered each, as but *one* result could possibly accrue from such a strife—a death."

"We *shall* meet, sir—assuredly we shall !" replied Sebastian, as he ground his teeth and spoke deliberately and hard, while a deadly pallor, from the remembrance of his defeat, spread over his face, and the sense of humiliation from the subterfuge he adopted ; and his father's confi-

dence that success or death could be the only alternative in such an encounter, shook him to the soul ; and, but for the timely interposition of Felix, who acutely shared in his distress, and averted the Marquis's attention from his brother's altered look and actual agony of conscience, the old man would have discovered the motive of his distemperature, and have overwhelmed him with the self-torments of his defeat.

"This I may tell my father," observed Don Felix,—"that the day on which we pay our formal visit at the castle (now so near at hand), we have resolved, Sebastian and myself, to watch him closely, and gather from Almazuma's manner, speech, and act, much needed knowledge. But, though we had abundant facts, could bring them home, and prove him guilty—as we but suspect him so—of Don Alonzo's murder, and other black offences, there is but one way left to save our sister from his power and basilisk influence—and that only way, my father, is by the sword—and we will bring him, doubt it not, to the strict arbitrament and judgment of our steel."

"I nothing doubt your prowess, my brave sons," replied the Marquis ; "and 'tis the consciousness that there is no other way to save my beloved one from this tyrannous master, that made me marvel. You had no sooner seen the clear necessity of this needful measure :—for while he lives, my child, my Catalina, my idol, and my hope, is dead to us for ever ; her life can be but purchased in his swift death. So fully am I satisfied of this—but that I am old, stiff in my joints, and out of all familiar practice that makes stout soldiership—I would, myself, have set his youth aside, defied him in his hold, and foot to foot, and hand to hand advanced my person against his skill and lustier manhood ; but with ill-kept prudence I have smothered my desire, till thou, my eldest should return, and with the authority of a father on thy side, and the vigour of brotherly affection in thine arm, defy him to the efficient proof of skill and courage. Nay, should'st thou fall, I have another son, and then myself, to bring against his more successful point ; for in our honour's right, all tenderness of blood, and influences of nature must give way to the clear upholding of our house's fame."

"Heaven shield my brother in his just assault !" cried Felix. "But if my sword is needed, the treble motive that will urge me on—sister, friend, and brother—will give my blade such edge and temper, that Ajax' shield should be but as a fence of glass against my heated passion and resolve."

"I see you are reserved, Sebastian, and from considerate care, avoid to tell me when you meet this plague-spot on our peace," observed the Marquis. "Well, so be it ! I will not seek to know thy secret. Only this remember, he is a shrewd and skilful swordsman, for so his friend Alonzo told me. Waste not your time and breath to find his weakness out ; for he is practised in all finesse, and will mislead you to your undoing : rather deceive him with assumed unskilfulness—for stratagem in this is lawful honour ; and when he blindly takes advantage of your fault, put in your quick passado through his heart, Sebastian—through his malicious heart," cried the old man with energy ; while a dark frown gathered on his wrinkled brow, and a severe sternness sat on his bold features.

"I will not forget your injunction, Sir," replied Sebastian, mortified that such advice should come so late; for he felt how much of his energy he had before needlessly expended in attempting to discover his antagonist's weakness; and that, to the contempt he had previously entertained of Almazuma's proficiency, had been in a great measure, the cause of his signal defeat; for it had led him into an unnecessary waste and profusion of physical ability, which would have been more providently husbanded, had he been earlier apprised of the consummate master he had to deal with. "I will observe your instruction to the letter. Has your lordship aught else, touching our previous conference?" resumed Sebastian.

"No, Sebastian—no, my son; I have nothing further to observe: for all my say and comment would have merged at last, to what I find you had resolved to do; and therefore I will leave unsaid my motives, fears, and apprehensions. Two days hence I shall expect your confidence: till then I am silenced; so of that, enough."

CHAPTER XXIII.

"There was a laughing devil in his sneer,
That raised emotions both of rage and fear.
And where his frown of hatred darkly fell,
Hope withering fled, and mercy sighed farewell."
BYRON.

THE period at which we raise the curtain on the present scene was about four hours before midnight, on the fifteenth of June, in the year of grace, 1592. The day had been unusually overcast, sultry, and oppressive; and as the sun set, his beams cast a dull and angry red over the skirts of the high-packed and dense clouds that, from the east up to the vault, covered the sky with an ominous pall, foretelling a night of storm and danger; while the low moaning of the rising wind sounded hollow and portentous as it swept round the deep angles, or lofty turrets, of the castellated mansion, and spacious courts, and died in fitful pantings, or trembled in whispered cadence through the wide arms of the tall trees that encompassed the lordly dwelling of the stern Almazuma.

The castle clock had scarcely ceased vibrating, as its heavy tongue and deep clamour proclaimed the hour of eight, when the loud summons, by some eager hand, at the great entrance, sounded hollow and reverberating through the vast mansion, calling a troop of servants from their retreat to answer the quick appeal, and unusual application for admission to that seldom visited and austere abode.

An infirm and aged nobleman descended from a carriage drawn by four mules, and leaning on the arm of a confidential attendant, slowly mounted the broad steps that led to the vestibule of the castle, and, preceded by the obsequious servants, was conducted over the marble hall to the presence of their lord.

The arrival of an unexpected guest, at so late an hour, created for a brief space some show of bustle in the residence of Don Almazuma; but in less than half an hour every thing had resumed its wonted order and monotony in that punctually regulated abode. Such refreshment as the way-worn and debilitated traveller stood in need of,

from his enfeebled condition and tedious journey, had been supplied; and the host and hostess, attended by their visitor, repaired to another apartment, where, relieved from the formality of restraint imposed by the presence of attendants, they might hold uninterrupted commune on subjects most congenial to their thoughts and several dispositions. One servant alone followed; and having lighted the branches of a silver sconce, and placed a small bronze lamp or cruse upon the table, bowed lowly to the company and withdrew.

The chamber into which we beg the reader to follow us was spacious and lofty: the carved and pendant ceiling, florid with ornament and brilliant with emblazonry, revealed, in many compartments, and from projecting shields, the lordly escutcheons of the ancient house, and the gorgeous heraldry of its collateral branches. Thick quilted tapestry, on which was worked the life of the first Brutus, through all its stages, hung from the deep cornice and frieze, covering to the ground the panelled walls of the room. A lofty fireplace, of the darkest oak, stood boldly out from one side of the chamber; while two grotesquely carved and hideous figures—half-wolf, half-man, supported on their gaunt shoulders the high and overhanging mantel. A large square table stood in the centre, covered with a crimson cloth, bordered with gold fringe that swept the floor; a tall crucifix, the figure of finely carved silver, in a cross and stand of ebony, was placed on the table, and beside it lay the open pages of an illuminated missal. A capacious arm-chair, padded, and covered with Spanish leather, stood near; while ten or a dozen high square stools, clothed in the same drapery as the table, were arranged round the apartment: a few foot-stools and hassocks, placed without order, completed the furniture.

The floor, composed of long, narrow scantlings of hardest oak, by time almost black, and bearing a polish like glass, was uncovered to its whole extent, except near the great chair, where a huge tiger's skin was spread for the feet. From the four tall and deep-bayed windows, that comprised one side of the apartment, hung massy curtains, corresponding in colour to the predominant threads of the elaborate tapestry. An old painting of a martyred saint, enclosed in a dark panel, hung high over the mantel, and formed the only relief or ornament—if so sombre a subject might be so called—to the general monotony of the whole. Yet, though the prevailing tones of the chamber were warm, the room, especially at night, had a solemn aspect—cold, and severe, partly derived from the great height and spaciousness of the interior, and partly from the absence of all those domestic elegancies that, while they impart comfort even to grandeur, inspire always a feeling of cheerfulness and domesticity.

Before we proceed farther in the description of the scene on which we have entered, we must beg the reader's permission to retrace our steps for a few moments, to give a brief account of the condition of two of the personages who constitute part of the small party to which we shall quickly return.

It would be impossible to describe the state of grief and misery experienced by the wretched Catalina, when a definitive, but courteous message from her stern husband apprised her of the unexpected visit of the Condé de Alvares, and the necessity of her instant presence to render due honour to the noble guest.

To avoid this dreaded interview, and postpone the day of meeting, was the chief object that had induced her to quit so abruptly her father's presence and sacrifice the affectionate companionship of brothers, kindred, and all that yet held a dear or sacred place within her heart, to leave the only glimpse of peace she had known for years, and voluntarily to return to that society most hateful to her life—her dreaded lord and torturing husband.

Yes, to escape the white hairs and sorrowing looks of a kind old man, one, who next to the close neighbourhood of his sorrowing child, held her in most affectionate regard, had she abruptly fled from freedom, friends, and home, to find in gloomy converse with her reproachful thoughts, and the calm tyranny, and perpetual malice of him, whose empire ruled her every act, undying misery.

And with that flattering hope that springs delusive to the crushed and suffering heart, she lived from hour to hour upon the vague expectancy and illusory belief, that some kind accident—some unseen, remote contingency might yet transpire to abrogate, if not preclude, the possibility of a meeting. Nay, should the Condé's death put the barrier to the likelihood, she would, unsinfully, she thought, have blessed the casualty that rid her of one torture less. But time kept creeping on in stealthy, certain pace; and minutes, hours, and days went by, and no relief sprang up to cheer her further with sickening and procrastinating hope; and darker thoughts grew stronger in her breast, mounting to resolve :—then she had contemplated the fearful deed she meditated in all its bearings, till the image grew familiar to her mind; and one by one the scruples that had stayed her hand, grew fainter, less repulsive, and, by degrees, the sin and deep perdition of the crime faded before the strengthening purpose—till at last, the immolation that she plotted lost all outward guise of fear, and to her excited mind and feverish eye, assumed the semblance of a meritorious sacrifice and an ennobling act.

There was but one way left to break the chain of dreadful tyranny that made her daily life a living hell—his death or hers; and it was less guilt to sacrifice herself than him. She had been spared—as she believed, by a strange act of mercy in the man who hated her—the crime of murder, when her blood was roused, and her indignation fixed by fierce revenge; and now in calmer mood —no, she would not harbour such a thought—she would triumph greater over her fell persecutor by abridging that life, the perpetual misery of which, was his great felicity—free herself from the infliction of his hatred, and the dreadful obligation of her oath—escape the searching eyes and keen intelligence of her solicitous friends, and, oh! most desired of all, preclude the possibility of meeting Don Alonzo's father.

Such were the feelings—such the ruminations that engrossed the mind of Catalina, when her servant announced the message of Almazuma, and the intelligence of the Condé's arrival. The assumed tranquillity and painful lull that the specious reasoning she had cogitated, to extenuate her crime, was in an instant broken—ruined— utterly annihilated by this unlooked-for circum-

stance—this great mischance. Her limbs shook, her courage failed her, and a deadly agony took possession of her soul, and bowed her to the earth ; while her quick mind, as if to make distress intolerable, apprised her of the day, and the fast-coming hour of midnight-penance and harrowing vigil. "It is the anniversary," she muttered to herself when left alone—"the anniversary of *his* death—the yearly revolution of that fatal night. Unlike my monthly orisons of an hour, in that still grave, I must, oh, God! spend the livelong night beside—— Jesu, save me!—and I must bear this torture too—meet father and son—oh, horror, horror!—no way left—no flight—no remedy! Yet stay—one hope yet whispers faintly to my heart a likely comfort. Yes, Alvares will sit late—I will meet him—hold him in lengthened talk—delay the time till early morning, and so evade one terror. No—he will not exact the fulfilment of the oath to-night—no, not before the victim's father—no, no, I shall escape for once. Aye, let me go—one misery I can meet, but, oh, not two!—Yes, I will go at once, lest my delay excite the memory of my friendly guard, who, in Alvares' presence, will forget both day and hour. Strengthen me, heaven, in the encounter!—Support and aid me, blessed Maria!" And hiding, as far as possible, the turmoil of her feelings, Catalina descended, and with a faltering step and sinking heart entered the chamber, and stood before the father of her murdered lover ; and while the venerable and grief-bowed noble paid her the courteous salutation of pure affection, her reproachful conscience probed her to the soul, and for an instant her pale cheek grew flushed from the sense of shame, and the conviction of her own hypocrisy ; and in self-abasement, tongue-tied—abashed—incapable to thank or answer the kind greeting and paternal tenderness of the benevolent and sorrowing father.

The few years that have elapsed since we last beheld the Condé had made a fearful change in the figure of the aged nobleman. No longer able to bear the slight weight of his attenuated body, his limbs shook as he walked ; and he was necessitated to support his bent frame on the assistant help of a handed stick. His hair, still of a perfect white, hung down his emaciated cheeks like threads of silver,—while his costume of deepest mourning, made the sad and care-worn features of the old man appear more woe-begone and melancholy : there was, too, a touching sorrow in his whole demeanour—an utter loneliness of heart depicted on his furrowed cheeks, and in his tear-dimmed eye, that impressed all who beheld him with reverence and respect, and woke the liveliest sympathy for a grief so settled and so deep ; for in the filmy eye, the pale, cold cheek, and wrinkled brow, a tale of blighted hope and bankrupt heart was centred,—that extremity of suffering that finds no fellowship in life, and apprehends no comfort but in death.

Such was now the Condé de Alvares, the mourning father of the once brave and gallant Alonzo, the affianced husband of Catalina, now his hostess, and Don Ferdinand's wife.

Upon Almazuma, his professing friend, the Condé's eye could note but little change : the cold stern features, which to Alvares' mind were but the index of a steady and a worthy gravity, were more confirmed by time ; and only figured forth the strict integrity and purposed conduct of the matured and steadfast man,—and the Condé found in the very characters that made him shunned by all the world, a congeniality and brotherhood, soothing to his still unblunted feelings, and in his taciturnity of mood and speech, found all the requisites to sympathy and friendship. But when he gazed on the mute partner of his life—that prize his son thought happiness itself,—the old man was moved almost to tears. Still nobly beautiful she was indeed, but oh, how changed! The Catalina of his gallant boy had passed away, and in her place there stood, 'tis true, the form, the feature, mould, and dignity and grace of former days; but the thought, the soul that gave capacity to every lineament,—the pride that lit the eye, and breathed a regal impulse in the frame, was gone for ever. The faultless figure, the chiselled face, the rounded arm, and fair small hand, still marked the matchless beauty: but the pale and marble features, the anxious look, and the unmeasured gait, conjointly showed some dark corroding mischief at the heart that had destroyed all happiness, and left a breathing statue in its place. Nature's excelling art indeed remained—life—cold, passive life, devoid of speculation.

Time had made no inroad on the physical development of her frame, more than the marked and general pallor we have before described. No, it was not outwardly the fell destroyer worked,—his ravage was within—the wasting of the mind: there, and in her heart, the four long weary years had written terrible disfigurement; and the external loss was but the reflection of the inward woe. Her beauty was of that definite and powerful mould that outlives the anarchy of mortal grief and wasting time,—bold to the last, and noble in its ruin.

Alvares gazed long and mournfully on the blanched countenance of Catalina, striving in vain to fathom the cause of her altered mien and looks, much marvelling what could have weighed down that spirit once so ascendant. It was not regretful love for his lost Alonzo; for she had early dried affection's tears, and with her own free will and choice married that lover's friend: this, from his heart the old man freely forgave, —excused. What then could cause this latent grief—this sorrow of the mind? Was she not rich, honoured, noble—loved! Perhaps not loved, he thought; and then ashamed of his long musing and unworthy apprehension, his own more immediate melancholy usurping all other cogitations, he turned to Almazuma, and said—

"You marvel, my good friend, and you, dear daughter, for such in pity let me call you,—what weighty business brings an infirm old man so far from his proper solitude at such a time to seek your hospitality: and why unadvertised, and with such frugal state, I seek your roof and your society."

"Too happy, if to be useful, will my poor house be made by such an honoured guest—most happy any way to bid my good Alonzo's father welcome," replied Don Ferdinand; then turning to his wife, and addressing her in the bland, soft accents he could at times assume, he continued: "For you, dear partner of my life, I leave to speak your own approving welcomes, knowing intuitively your deepest thoughts,"—and he spoke with a pointed emphasis. "I will not mar your better grace of compliment, by my rude manner,

knowing how sweetly free reception sounds from woman's soft persuasive lips, giving the heartfelt welcome to our friends. Speak, love! Dearest Catalina greet him well."

"Let it appear, most honoured sir," replied his wife, in a faint voice, to which an impressive emotion gave an earnest pathos, "more in my acts, and ever studious deeds, than in my words, how much my heart acknowledges the welcome that it gives. My tongue is truant to my will, and my desire to prove it more, beggars me in both, and only will permit the cordial repetition, welcome!"

"Dear friends," rejoined Alvares, "my thanks are rendered to you both with equal measure: yet I have sorrows petulant, and griefs so selfish, that your good and honourable natures must compassionate the waywardness of my distress."

"I see, my reverend lord and worthy friend, the traces of a deep sorrow yet reveal themselves in thy furrowed cheek, and prematurely wasted frame. These habiliments of woe, so long posterior to the cause for which you donned the sober vestment, proclaims your grief still green —the wounded heart uncicatrized. Has life no savour left?—no beam of sunshine to give a transitory smile to your sick soul. Is there no balm, no comfort in ameliorating time?"

"None, Almazuma, none," responded the mournful father. "Each day my sorrow wakes, and clamours 'gainst my heart with all the fresh and vivid memories of its first bereavement; and I am come again—(that is my errand here, before I visit daughter, son, grandchild or friend: so restless is my life, so full of doubt and vague surmise)—to look into the evidence of the past— question each witness o'er again—seek out for clues—unravel all dark hints, and strive 'gainst probability for satisfaction. For now my mind is full of floating images, sometimes of prosperous issue, and then of crushing certainty—that I would give, my friend, my worldly wealth, and the few drops that still trickle in these shrunk veins, even to the murderer's knife, for the blest consciousness of certainty,—the confirmation of Alonzo's death. It is suspense, my friend, cruel uncertainty that kills me in endless lingering." And as Alvares spoke in tremulous earnestness, the cold drops stood on his wrinkled brow, and tears of anguish fell fast from his dim eyes, and made him pause for utterance.

Nor was Catalina's emotion less acute than that of the old man's, though not so outwardly evinced; and turning up the spacious room to hide the struggle in her breast, she strove by violent efforts to school and quell the rebel conscience in her soul, that rose at every word Alvares spoke, to threaten and betray her.

"Oh, he was my hope, my joy, my consolation," resumed the Condé, as he wiped the heavy moisture from his brow with trembling hand— "the last tie that bound my widowhood to earth and life: so brave, so noble too, that in his fame I felt I had another son, twin-born with him,— and to be bereft of both! The blow was sharp for a poor weak old man to bear. I tell thee, Almazuma, the wound is in my soul, past remedy of any hand but the great God's! whom I do night and morning pray to succour me with that sweet medicine—death!" And with pious reverence, meekly, and with eyes suffused, Alvares raised the black-plumed bonnet from his head, and bent his looks to heaven in most beseeching supplication, as in his throat the final sentence of his speech faded in half-expressed articulation.

"Have better cheer, my noble friend. Calamities with resignation borne, are heaven's correcting rods to chasten us for bliss."

"I know my grief is selfish, good Almazuma, —bear with it. Oh, you may converse on what possession gives, the blessings held in hand : for they are yours. But I—I have nothing—no stay left—no prop to rest exhausted age upon. Nay, no further business here—treading the blooming earth that never, never more can blossom joy for me !"

"Say not so," replied Almazuma: "you have a worthy daughter, a valiant son, and, as I hear—for so my dearest wife reports—a grandchild, who so puts on the semblance of your lost son, that, years apart, you would believe it was Alonzo's self. Here then is comfort—large room for gratitude."

"No, no : dear as I love my girl, she cannot fill the void of him. The son grows up as part, and appertaining to the household of the sire :— not so the fragile branch of womanhood : they from their homes depart, and make new kindred, hearths, and loves, around the rooftree of their lords."

"Think better of it, worthy sir : nature has left you still one tie."

"No compensation ! No ! no ! no ! Lost to me—lost to me—dead ! Yet, had he died as should befit his name, my lamentations would have had some season in their woes : I could have drawn out life penuriously, living from day to day, and hour to hour, upon my brave boy's deeds :—but so cut off—sacrificed in his ripening honour—murdered by some base hireling's steel! —oh, friend ! the thought is madness. And you, fair excellence, who should have been his bride," he continued, turning towards Catalina, "so young, so beautiful, so loving, and so much happiness in store ;—so affluent in our future hopes, that opulent expectation could not calculate on ruin :—and then to be of life, expectancy, and joy, deprived, annulled—bankrupt in an hour— the turning of a sand. Nay, now, pardon me, fair creature," he exclaimed, as he beheld Catalina's distress, and the agony of her ungovernable feelings, "for my tell-tale and loquacious age makes me unmannerly: forgive me—for I see that I have touched you to the quick. Why should I shadow your happiness in grieving over what is dead—dead ! Oh ! fatal syllable—period of fate. Nay, pry'thee pardon me."

During this heartfelt, painful speech of Alvares, Catalina stood like a statue, rooted to the ground, while the distracted play of her convulsed features gave to her pale and flushing face, and swelling veins, an aspect less than earthly ; and, but for the calm fixed gaze of her husband, whose eye bent upon her like the snake's, watching and probing every impulse of her heart, chilled and subdued her voice to silence, her excited feelings had broke the spell with cries of mercy and forgiveness. Her inmost soul revolted at the savage despicable part she played ; and the bereaved parent's grief shot through her frame a pang so keen, that every word fell with a scorching blight upon her brain, as if each syllable that dropped from the despairing father was lightning, sent to wither and consume.

"Give your griefs way—stint not your tears," cried Almazuma, addressing the Condé ; "there's closer brotherhood in sorrow than any tie or friendship else. Yet, for your brave Alonzo, I do believe it not impossible, but, that nameless in the ranks of his victorious country, he has found a soldier's grave—honourable, though obscure. Say, dearest love," he added, turning to Catalina, "is it, think you, probable ?" And he bent his dark and lustrous eyes full on her countenance, and planted his keen gaze with such a fixity of purpose, as he would read the very birth-springs of her mind—while a slight and scarcely perceptible curl near the angle of his mouth, gave a cold, treacherous, and malignant cast to the dark features. Twice the fascinated wife essayed to speak—but the rebellious tongue refused its function, and the faint answer died in whispered accents in her throat.

"Your heart's too full for utterance," the Condé kindly interposed. "Your mute sufferings, dearest lady, touches me with gratitude. Yes— that thought, Almazuma, were a comfort to my age," he resumed, turning to Ferdinand, in reference to his last remark. "Yea, I could hug it to my heart, had it a lineament of likelihood."

"Be sure it has," responded his specious host ; and let regret grow mellow in the certainty. My loving and my gentle wife holds frequent memory of him ; nay, she has almost daily reminiscence of his fate :— say I not sooth, sweet wife ?— *monthly* she holds a solemn vigil on the day we lost him. Do you shudder ?" he added, in a low, clear whisper, that reached her ear alone, as her frame, shook by the dreadful memory, trembled in every fibre with a cold convulsive shudder ; and as she felt the withering of the slight hope on which she had leant with confidence, that this night she would be free ;—but now, e'en that belief was gone—for too well her mind presaged the mandate that would follow—the hated penance yet reserved for her.

"See !" continued the tyrannous and torturing husband, "what a poor dissembler of her heart she is : her soft and eloquent soul speaks in the anguish of her face. Be calm, my love ;—suppress this evidence of woe—your life is very precious to me."

"Heaven bless thee, Signora, for this tender feeling to my misery. This is a day on which I bid it flow unchecked—for 'tis the mournful anniversary of his loss. Nay—you must permit my sorrows way—and let me sit me down, think over all my woe, and ruminate on my affliction." And, as Alvares concluded, he slowly crossed the room, seated his weary limbs in the antique chair, and burying his tearful face in his attenuated hands, reclined his head on the table before him, and gave way to long and painful memories.

"And we have registered the date in deathless recollection," replied Almazuma, as the Condé took his seat ; then, approaching his wife, who had removed to the extremity of the apartment, and stood the picture of despair, continued in the same calm, deep, malicious tone, that outwardly had all the semblance of meek piety and honourable truth, "go, fair mistress !—remember you, dear wife—my heart's true fellow—this is the night on which you hold your stern and pious orisons. I am loath to lose your dear companionship, but should be still more keenly grieved to rob thy heart of gentle, holy consolation. The Condé will forgive thine absence: nay—I will plead your cause. You are impatient to be gone; I read it in your eyes, my sainted excellence!"

With a desperate effort Catalina essayed to speak; and, at length, conquering the spell that bound her tongue, she said, in a voice full of anguish, and subdued to meet his ear, with a supplicating look and action of intense beseeching—

"Spare me to-night!"

But Almazuma, as if not hearing what she said, continued in a strain of self-regret, as if his duty warred against his inclination, as he replied—"I must sacrifice my own contentment to the claims of heaven! Alas! I must not stop you."

"Mercy, this once!" she cried imploringly; "mercy!"

"Impossible!"

"I cannot—dare not go!" she added, in utter misery.

"Omitted vows," he replied with sternness, "are registered as sins. Think of your everlasting soul."

"Mercy! husband, mercy!"

"The bright jewel in the crown of heaven."

"Take pity on my distraction," she cried, with imploring earnestness.

"Your soul!" repeated Almazuma, with solemn emphasis,—"your soul!"

"As you will pray before the seat of God for mercy, grant it to me. Relent, and save me."

"Away!—the hour! the hour!"

"Oh! by the frown and threatening visage——"

"Peace!—remember!"

"Here at your feet," she exclaimed, as falling on her knees and clasping her hands, "I throw my tortured heart in supplication. Pity my terrors; feel for my distress! This night, not for my soul's salvation, would I go!"

"Your oath."

"Lo, to the earth I sink. Mercy!" she cried, as bending lower in deep humility at her imperious husband's feet, she preferred her earnest petition.

"Look up!" was the only answer he deigned to her fervent prayer. "Look up!" he repeated, as she continued, unheeding his remark—

"The horrid scene will drive me mad—spare me that dread affliction. Even now my reason totters! Spare me—or give me instant death. By your remorseless hate, I do conjure you, kill me!—be merciful for once, and kill me!"

"Look up—arise!" replied Almazuma, in a low, firm whisper, that sounded audibly distinct on the ear of the bending Catalina, while he drew his stately person to its full altitude as he proceeded. "As soon expect the marble ribs of this strong dome to tremble at your breath—as soon believe it capable to split the foundered world with exclamations — stop nature's course, arrest the raging tide—or bid creation drop her pendent spheres, as move my firm-set soul from its avowed and purposed course. See!" he added, pointing to the Condé, who had for an instant raised his head,—"see, our friend marvels." But Catalina, regardless of all admonition, continued with vehemence to beseech his pity; and as Alvares again buried his face, she resumed—

"Oh! once more, by your eternal hopes of bliss! and by those awful fears imagination plants in the dark hereafter! forgive me now. Thine

own sins will one day need the cleansing hand of God; and what shall work thy verdict there so soon as mercy to the wretched here—charity to the unfortunate? Oh! then, by our Redeemer's love! hear me!"

With a scornful smile, and bitter intonation, Almazuma replied—"Arise!—not know me yet? Arise! 'Tis marvellous, weak thing. Would you to deep perdition hurl thy perjured soul? Go to thy vigils—go: the hour is come. Look thou to heaven, for earth yields thee nothing."

"Iron-hearted man, relent!"

"Fool—fool!" retorted Almazuma, with a disdainful smile.

"Then hear me, thou Just God!" she cried, with grave solemnity, as, turning from her husband, she extended her hands and eyes to heaven; but the stern voice of Don Ferdinand arrested her exclamation, as he replied, in slow, subdued, but deliberate accents—

"Thy oath! What, body and soul! Would'st thou, rash woman, before the face of heaven, propound a lie—unsay attested vows—recant a covenant, by dreadful rites—by fearful oaths recorded there?" He paused; and there was an awful sternness in his look, as he pointed upwards, that chilled the suppliant to the heart, as he concluded—"Shut the gates of promise on your hopes, to live accursed, and by the Merciful of all Mercies be utterly cast down. Oh! it is terrible. Bethink you of your soul—your soul!"

"Inexorable monster—fiend!"

"Beware—beware!"

"I go—I go!" she added, hastily rising. "I—I will obey,"—and as she spoke, with agitated and unsteady steps she endeavoured to leave the apartment; but ere she had reached the door, the voice of her husband checked her intent; at the same time, the Condé rose from his recumbent position at the table, on which he had been so deeply musing, and came forward to meet her.

"Stay, dearest!" cried Almazuma, in a mild and altered voice. "Tarry a moment, love: thy pious haste makes thee uncourteous. What! leave this loving friend—this cherished sire, with ne'er good night. Take his thin hand, palsied with grief—with years made cold, and by misfortune, tremulous; press it to your holy lips. See—his heart speaks in his teeming eyes. Speak comfort to his age—cheer his desolation; and let him deem himself thy father—thou, his dear Alonzo."

"What means this perturbation, dearest lady?" inquired the old man, as he fondly pressed her trembling hand to his lips:—"whence this sorrowing look—this tremor of thy frame?"

"'Tis I, my friend, I fear, who caused it—I, who wrought the mournful aspect that you see, and wondering, comment on," interposed Almazuma. "So strict and punctual is she in the purposes of her faith—so much the business of her life—her holy contemplations, that I can scarcely win an hour of her prized company. And even now, I have, with all authority of gentleness, besought—commanded, even against her kneeling importunities, that this night's vigil shall not exceed the time and limit which my former prudence defined and set, though, in the selfishness that urges the command, heaven pardon me!"

"Be ruled, dear madam," added Alvares, meekly,—"be ruled in this by your true and loving husband, whose tenderness and piety are fighting now within his breast. Give not all your thoughts to heaven: the Great Giver asks but an earnest part; that paid, affection flows in double force to the great centre of our love and duty. Let me beseech you, tarry not; and in your orisons, cast one look—one thought upon my son. Give his freed soul a portion of thy prayer. Great heaven! you are ill, Senora. Lady, what have I done?"

"'Tis nothing," replied Almazuma, in answer to Alvares' exclamation of surprise at Catalina's agitation. "'Tis nothing," he added, crossing the floor and taking his wife's hand: "she is often thus. Let me conduct you, love: come, soul of my life—come."

"Dark devil—torturer!" she replied in a suppressed whisper, as he led her across the wide apartment: "to split my heart, and on the rack of agonised remorse thus stretch my suffering soul. Will nought appease the fiend within your breast—nothing assuage thy black hypocrisy?"

"Nothing, night homicide!" he added, in the same low whisper. The faint pressure of Catalina's hand was instantly converted into a powerful and convulsive grasp, as she endeavoured to steady her tottering frame; and, but for the support of Almazuma's arm, she would have fallen on the threshold. Recovering herself, she replied, faintly:—

"Husband—master—fiend, thy slave obeys!" and, throwing off the hateful hand that held her, as something loathsome, she resumed in a moment all her wonted energy, and, turning round, made a profound courtsey to the Condé and her husband, and with graceful dignity quitted the chamber.

Fatigued by his journey, and oppressed by the many recollections of his son, conjured up by the presence of Almazuma, and the company of her he had so ardently believed his own daughter, Alvares, harassed in mind, and weakened in body, soon after retired to rest, endeavouring to bury in sleep remembrances so painful, and grief so freshly awakened and torturing.

The household had long retired to repose; and the stern master, as he paced with gloomy brow and steady steps the large apartment, seemed the only living being awake within that now silent mansion.

The evening which had been hung with dark ragged clouds—sultry and still—as midnight approached, concentrated their ominous frowns, and bursting, cast their broad and vivid sheets of lightning around the castle; while the thunder rose, in each peal, louder and more prolonged, shaking chamber and vaulted passage with its deep reverberations. Frequently, as the lightning flashed through the curtained windows, and played round the sombre tapestry, Almazuma would pause in his walk, and with straining ear, endeavour to catch some sound in the momentary silence of the thunder: then, as the deafening crash broke overhead and shook the castle, and echo magnified the rumbling tumult around him, he would stamp his foot and resume his former steady pace, at times exclaiming half audibly, "She is late: or does she think, in this turmoil, I shall not hear? Yes—to-night she shall know all—all. I'll probe her to the quick. Is this the proud beauty, who, in her arrogance of place and virtue, dared despise me?—'Has Spain no gentle suitors left?'—Oh! a life of agony is too short for that moment's scorn!—I would that she could live again.—Peace, clamorous elements! and let me hear the summons to my revenge!" he exclaimed, as he again bent his head forward in an attitude of eager listening; then with an impatient wave of his hand, resumed his gloomy walk; and as another thought rose in his mind, he continued in a subdued voice to soliloquise.

"Ha!—well remembered—to-morrow this meddling fool—this prying brother seeks his fate. Perchance, he may be fortunate, and I may fall. Well—I have lived sufficient length after to-night. Yes—I will leave a sting behind that shall defy the potency of a priest or heaven to cure—living remorse and guilt. Oh, 'tis a rich legacy to bequeath a wife! I will yet make her suffering——"

At that moment, the deep-toned solemn notes, as of some powerful bell, trembled in smothered accents round the chamber. Eight—nine—ten —prolonged and hollow tones followed in measured distance, sounding from beneath the dense tapestry, distinct, mournful and sad, even amidst the loud burst of thunder, that, at the same instant, with fearful grandeur, shook the massive frame-work of the huge pile to its foundation.

"Ha!" he exclaimed, as the last note fainted in whispering tremors round the walls—my matchless mechanism is at work—the curtains are withdrawn—and she looks—she looks upon—— Oh, Satan never planned so sweet—so excellent a villany! Why does she pause?—Why not illume her altar and ascend the holy steps?— Why delay——"

But while he spoke, a slow succession of heavy hollow sounds, more intense and grand than even the preceding notes, boomed on the air, and filled the apartment with deep sepulchral intonations of rolling music—solemn, grand, and mysterious.

As Almazuma stood anxiously counting each stroke of that harmonious clangour, a flash of lightning, more intense than any previous, lit every object round as by a blaze of fire, revealing the darkest obscurity, and rendering the pale lights that burnt on the table almost inevident; and as it gleamed over the countenance of the stately lord, it exhibited his morose features lighted with the smile of a triumphant demon.

"She is at her prayers," he cried aloud, with a sarcastic laugh, that sounded dread and unearthly—"her prayers! The time is apt—the coincidence most opportune—to end this masterly conception. I come, proud Senora, to crown the rich felicity of my hate—to deal the last and conquering stab to earthly peace and rest!—I come, I come!"

And taking up the lamp from the table, and extinguishing the tapers in the sconce, slowly, cautiously, and without a sound, Almazuma quitted the dark and solitary apartment.

CHAPTER XXIV.

WHEN Almazuma left the apartment, as described in the last chapter, he threaded his way across the spacious hall—upon whose marble floor his stealthy footsteps awoke no echo — ascended the grand staircase, explored the long corridor, and entered the deserted chambers of his lady : two wax tapers burnt before a Madonna's shrine, in the second room, and showed by their dim light that the fair tenant had not yet retired to rest, or, to appearance, visited her apartment.

Opening by a hidden spring, the door that led from the bed-chamber, Almazuma entered the small oratory used exclusively by the Donna Catalina ; here, setting down his lamp, and carefully closing the door behind him, Don Ferdinand paused for a moment, and scrupulously surveyed each object around him ; and having satisfied himself of the entire privacy of the place, approached one side of the room, and drew a silk tassel that hung from the festooned tapestry, when instantly a part of the rich arras gave way, and was drawn back like a parted curtain, revealing the dark wainscot that lined the walls.

Inserting the point of his dagger into a small crevice in the woodwork, and pushing back a long panel, exposed the narrow, dark, and winding stair before referred to ; then, returning, took up the lamp, trimmed the long wick, and passed under the drapery, which directly fell into its former position. The faint click of a closing spring was then heard, as he replaced the panel, and the chamber retained no evidence that a living being had so lately crossed it.

The stairs that Almazuma now descended, and down which we must request the reader to accompany us—wound to the base of the turret in which the room he had just left was situated : the steps were narrow, high, and numerous ; while the walls on either side and along all the passages were padded with the thickest matting,— a needless precaution if used to deaden sound ; as the whole labyrinth was between the outer and inner walls of the castle.

Having reached the bottom of the steep descent, Almazuma directed his course along an extensive corridor, that from the inequality of its level, seemed to traverse the entire range of the irregular mansion,—sometimes by steps, ascending acclivities, at others, by inclined planes gradually declining from their abrupt ascents.

The explorer was at length arrested by the low iron door, or wicket, that we have more than once made mention of, as separating the narrow passage from the shorter, but more lofty gallery, that diverged at a right angle from the one in which he stood. Somewhat surprised to find this obstacle closed, he set down his lamp, and by the dexterous use of his dagger, was enabled to lift the heavy bolt, and force open the portal ; turning to the right, Almazuma entered the other passage, that immediately assumed a higher pitch, and greater width.

One side was composed of the rough rock that formed the basis of the castellated structure above : the other a massive wall of huge unhewn stones, placed pile over pile with rude art, without cement, block upon block—the relics of a Gothic age ; forming a ponderous Cyclopean wall : on which, as Nature's own primeval seat, later generations had built their heavy, but, to this, fragile, superstructure. After threading about a hundred feet of this long, wide, and gloomy gallery, the passage was abruptly terminated by what appeared the perpendicular face of the granite rock. Through a natural fissure at its base, Garcia's art had constructed a doorway, and an oak wicket, so adapted to the opening, and painted of a corresponding tone with the rock itself, as to deceive the unacquainted eye, and give the whole a uniform unbroken character of primitive simplicity and natural ruggedness.

Touching a small projecting spring, the noiseless portal revolved on its easy hinges and admitted the lordly master into this recess of nature. Closing the door, and pulling aside the black drapery within, Almazuma, with a measured, noiseless step, cautiously entered the cavern, and stood in the centre of this subterranean crypt.

The vault was lofty and square, and hung entirely with black cloth ; four groined beams of oak crossed, diagonally, the arched roof, springing from gaunt heads in the rocky wall, and at their junction, forming a single carved pendant from which was suspended a large bronze lamp with four burning wicks. A carpet of rich Flemish matting covered the larger extent of the floor ; a carved table, a footstool, and a quaint arm-chair, completed the secular furniture, if we except writing materials that lay on the table. In a recess, at the upper extremity, was erected an altar elaborately carved and decorated, and on which burnt six tall wax candles in heavy silver sconces, that threw a pale and ghostly light over the object on which their beams entirely fell ; for stretched on the table of the altar, beneath the tabernacle and cross, lay the body of the murdered Don Alonzo Alvares, Catalina's dagger still in his heart.

Mortality's corrupting hand had made no inroad on the manly beauty, that perfect, as if just slain, lay in the tranquil sleep of death, mocking, in horrid outrage, the pageantry of Christ's belief, the tokens of our faith, the symbols of redemption.

Another wound, the tardy stroke of Almazuma, showed its position in his breast by the dark stain and congealed blood that still surrounded the spot. In every respect, save the absence of its cloak, the body lay just as it died. The gloved hand, the plumed hat, the festive sword, and bridegroom-trim of the happy, joyous, gallant youth, cut off by treachery in the hour of blossoming felicity.

Seated in the carved chair with her fair white neck gracefully bent, while the small delicate hand guided the pen, sat Catalina, writing on the table before her. The broad light that fell from the lamp suspended above her head, threw half the graceful outline into shade, while it revealed the commanding profile of her expressive face, and made the pallor of her neck, arms, and brow, stand out from the sombre drapery around, in soft, subdued, but exquisite contrast.

As she wrote, the moving fingers and the working features formed the only indication of existence, so calm her attitude—so death-like was the silence of the scene.

Almazuma stood for some moments in the centre of that dreary chamber with his arms folded over his chest, and a malign smile playing round his lips and flashing in his eye, as he surveyed, in silence and surprise, the employment of his wife.

"Your prayers have been most speedy—are your sins so few ? " he at length said, breaking the oppressive silence with his deep, steady, and equable voice, while the words came from his chest, and the unmoved features and rigid action he preserved, gave him the aspect of an endowed statue. At the first sound of his abrupt voice, Catalina started from her seat and dropped the pen from her trembling grasp, while the startled blood forsook the heart, and mantling in her brow and cheek, dyed the marble countenance with the ruddy glow of sunset, and for a moment imparting a sense of pain and wild alarm to her fine features. With an assumed calmness, however, she turned to her husband, and replied faintly as the transitory flush faded, and was succeeded by her natural paleness,—

"My sins are many, and I have prayed; but I had hoped this dreary vault might have ensured my privacy: the picture's not too cheering. May I possess the company of my own thoughts?"

"I am come," replied her husband, "not to intrude upon your pious meditations, but, as thy stern confessor, inexorable in his duty, that you may think, being probed of all thy sins, and in the general sum, ask pardon for the omitted and particular."

"What more than those too sorrowfully known have I to answer for? Methinks yonder reproachful form," she said meekly, "that ever bleeding to my eyes, would keep remembrance watchful,"—and she pointed to the dead body on the altar. "That is a monitor stronger than you have power to conjure. I pray thee, Senhor, what new misfortune waits me?"

"Misfortune!" cried Almazuma; "you wrong the application: "why 'tis life's sole, best monitor—the nurse and very mother of our wisdom."

"I dread the wisdom your misfortune brings."

"I come to touch your heart—to give your sorrow aim and voice."

"My heart," replied Catalina, "is a solemn court, where sorrow holds paramount seat—a frowning judge of sighs and tears, and bosom-piercing groans. Pry'thee what is your purpose?—to torture me, I know. Pray let me have it, then: it cannot fill the measure higher of my woes."

"My purpose," added her husband, "has reference to your *lover*."

"More mockery!—go on. Oh! it befits a man who calls himself honourable, thus to insult a life-sick miserable wretch. I do not weep, my lord. Heaven, in its anger, has dried the fountain of my tears. I cannot please your hate with such an evidence of my sex's misery. Proceed, Don Ferdinand, in your ennobling. baseness;—your victim's but a woman: double your sport—since she's your wife."

"The camp, the cabinet, the cowl, the pen," resumed Almazuma, with more than usual severity of manner, "may, to weak minds, appear the potent gradients to ambition, fit for the meaner selfish souls of plodding clay; but I had a nobler flight, a loftier aim:—to crush thy haughty spirit, and trample on thy pride!"

"It was a gallant purpose to war on a defenceless woman—a worthy object for your high chivalry!" she retorted, with bitter sarcasm.

"The object elevates the act: 'tis in the mind nobility of purpose lies. But I digress. I came to tell thee the mystery of thy lover's death:—nay, tremble not; this chamber has no ears—our secrets are our own. Art thou not curious? 'tis worth the knowledge: mark! and let your soul join in the hearing. Skilled in the art and use of potent herbs, I mixed a potion in thy lover's

drink, in which he pledged your health—the health of his expected bride! All unsuspiciously he drank the drugged and dangerous bowl—drained it of the Lethean draught, whose subtle juice but simulates mortality. Life still beat in his slow veins, and the responsive heart held with the sympathetic mind warm intelligence: nature lay dormant under the efficient drink, quenched for the hour in heavy slumber. 'Twas then that we, two plighted lovers, stole on his sleep—and thou, eager in action, unfastened life's strong cage, and gave the bounding spirit wing!—'twas then——"

From the commencement of this speech Catalina had stood motionless, with her figure slightly bent, the head thrown forward, the eyes dilated, and the orbs themselves protruding, as though they would leap from their sockets; her mouth was open, and the beautiful features of her face painfully distorted—while the small passive ear, from the intensity of the straining sense, stood forward to catch the faintest syllable of the treacherous discovery. One foot and arm was advanced, while the raised palm and outstretched fingers of the white hand denoted eager curiosity and revolting fear; but, ere Almazuma could conclude the sentence, she interrupted him with a wild, shrill, and piercing cry, exclaiming while she clasped her hands in terror—

"Great God! he was not dead?"

"No!" replied her husband, almost choked with exultation, "no! he was alive!"

"Sainted Mother of Heaven!" she groaned; "and I slew him!"

"Murdered him in his sleep," added Almazuma, calmly.

"Horrid monster! but thine own hand shared in the guilty deed—the act was not all mine, though the remorse be so. Not all the guilt, just heaven! not all!"

"Prevaricating fool!" contemptuously replied her husband, "it was all thine own—thine own sharp and avenging weapon, that through his heart let forth the fountain of his life. Look yonder, and behold!" as he pointed to the evidence still in the body; "thine own quick deed that sent his soul to heaven unshrived. I tarried till the ebbing stream flowed faint—and when I struck, I drove my dagger in his corpse! and, thanks to the ambrosial flesh-preserving odours, that from the bounteous womb of this dark cave distil and fill the air with rich embalming qualities, that bleeding witness shall appear against your peace, perfect and uncorrupted, even to the resurrection! No, thy lover shall not rot in loathsome festering, like common clay. No! we will keep him daintily preserved, like Memphian lovers for their heavenly brides!"

"Cold, horrible villain!" cried Catalina, shuddering, "and did your own black heart, and fouler brain, conceive and fructify this base device? Had'st thou no aid, no counsel, no devilish minister to succour you?—nothing to mitigate your own great crime and overloaded soul?"

"Oh, yes! I had a trusted and a valued confidant—one to whom thou art indebted much, did'st thou know all;—a ready and a willing tool—one schooled in noble villany."

"One, who will yet divulge your guilty course, and beat your proud confidence to the earth—expose, and crush you!"

"You are deceived—mistaken."

"What! do you think you're safe? Will not your base, corrupted hireling, when remorse begins to gnaw his heart, denounce you?—yes! and you will yet meet from the hand of earthly justice the branded doom, the hatred that your crimes so justly merit. Oh! live in fear, and be most certain of it."

"Impossible!" replied Almazuma, confidently.

"Not so—not so!" cried Catalina, warmly; "his craven heart will yet relent, and publish your misdeeds. Of such base wretches God makes atoning scourges, to lash the lofty execrable!"

"Do you think I am so poor in my device?" replied Don Ferdinand, while his lip curled with insulting scorn at his implied danger; "so weak in intellect, as to leave my bosom open to a reptile's sting? No—my foundation is as stedfast as the earth:—*you* dare not—man *cannot* touch me!"

"False confidence—the trust of guilty compact—the hope of cowardice alone!" rejoined Catalina.

"Judge for yourself!" retorted her husband, as he strode haughtily past her, and ascended the steps of the altar.

"Behold!"—and, striking the oak slab, on which lay the body of Alvares, fiercely with his clenched hand, the carved panel that comprised the entire front of the edifice, fell with a loud crash, and exposed to view a long narrow recess, in which lay the emaciated form of a man, wa ted by hunger to the bones. The face still bore the traces of agony with which anguish and suffering nature had marked his visage; and he lay contracted, shrivelled, and drawn into the smallest space.

"Spoke I truth?" he resumed, while a ghastly smile lit his features, and with a sardonic laugh he cried, pointing to the body :—

"Behold my instrument! thy lover's valet—Benina's murderer!—the soldier—gipsy—priest—and my accomplice, Garcia!"

Catalina gave a loud involuntary shriek at this new and startling evidence of his cruelty, and exclaimed, burying her face in her hands to shut out the frightful picture—

"Hide me, my God!—hide me from this human wolf—this monster demon! Thy punishment, avenging heaven is too great—too terrible for erring nature. Hide me!—hide me!"

Almazuma stood for some moments surveying her torture with malicious pleasure: then closing the panel, descended the steps, saying, as he passed his still shrinking wife—

"Are you satisfied?"

"And you have murdered him! Poor miserable wretch—unhappy and deluded victim—murdered him!" she replied, removing her hands from her deadly countenance.

"No!" continued Almazuma, no. Do you believe that I would stain my hand with the dark mire of such plebeian blood! no—you mistake. Listen! Yon slave had more than ordinary wit, which in a loftier mould would have been genius. His cunning skill fashioned this altar, and all the hidden works that make this labyrinth perfect. More too: I made him for the time my bosom confidant; his art it was that executed all my plans—assumed your lover's dress! Nay, start not—you shall hear it all. 'Twas he invaded the privacy of your chamber! Wring not your hands, but mark me. Pass we his minor services, and come we to his end. After we brought your lover hither, upon that night—I perceive you do remember well—I questioned in my mind whether to place the bridegroom within that spacious coffin, so amply holy, or on the altar where it now reposes. To satisfy my doubts as to its fitness for the nobler dust, the ready and obsequious fool agreed to try its measurement with his willing carcass; and then——why then I clasped the ponderous springs, and bound him in his own made tomb, a living grave! At first the jilted villain laughed, but with a doubting and convulsive mirth: then something petulant, he cried—''Twould do!' I knew it would, and bade him rest content, and recommended him to prayer. But when I placed Alvares' body over head, the shriek of horror and the cry of utter misery he gave, would have corrupted other blood than mine to stagnant ice: for 'twas of every death the one he dreaded ; and when I left, his smothreed groans followed my retreating steps in harrowing cadence. He did not implore, beseech, or pray: he knew that such appeals to me were hopeless ; and he despaired at once, for ever, and at once!"

No pen could adequately describe the conflicting feelings in the breast of Catalina, during the cold-blooded, fiendish recital of her husband. Disgust and horror, anguish and despair, took by turns possession of her mind, and a dread sickening—a repulsive loathing crept through her veins, and her whole frame shuddered when she remembered that this monster held her very soul in chains, and usurped upon her person the fearful right of husband. She felt, too, that mentally she had long been guilty of her lover's death, for she had meditated the accomplishment ; but soothed hitherto by the specious hypocrite's false words, she had begun to think the bloody act was not all hers : but now reft of this hope it stood with all its bleeding, damnatory truth fixed on her soul, a black, indelible, and eternal blot. Her mind, too, wavered ; she had thought the murderous act a virtuous deed in retribution for a dishonoured name ; but now strange fears pervaded her. It was not Alonzo, then, who like a night thief entered her chamber, but this accomplice, who had paid so fatally for his corrupted part. Might not—and the thought was torture worse than death—might not the statements, and the letters too—all the startling evidence that had confirmed at once her mind and purpose—all—all that made her what she was, be false! But oh, how specious, regular, and sequent was the tale. The fearful doubt shook her frame with such remorseful agony, that cold drops bedewed her face, and an unearthly hue spread its ashy character over her features ; but summoning her resolution to the highest stretch of firm endurance, she addressed her husband in a voice tremulous with emotion, as she said—

"Don Alonzo died, and I—you tell me now I murdered——" her speech failed, and she could proceed no further ; but Almazuma completed the sentence, by saying—

"You did. Murdered him in his sleep!"

"And—and——" she continued, regaining strength, "it was not him whom I was made believe entered my chamber. It was not Alonzo?"

"Yonder starved slave, dressed in a suit made after your lover's fashion, for the especial purpose," added Almazuma, filling up the pause in her inquiry.

"And the letters?" she asked, with trembling interest.

"Were false!" he cried,—"forged in the fertile brain of my remorseless hate, and written by the skilful Garcia ; and you were caught, snared, damned by the very instrument that, rightly read, had saved you from perdition."

"Merciful saints! but you have told me," continued Catalina, with painful difficulty, and panting eagerness, "that he was false, traduced my fame, defamed my honour, and asserted——" she could articulate no more—her voice failed her, and she abruptly ceased, chilled by the withering smile upon her husband's lips, as he exultingly replied—

"There, too, I lied—immeasurably lied ! He loved you doatingly, honourably, madly loved: loved you with all the tender, watchful, holy truth of virtuous passion. That knowledge was my greatest triumph."

"Heaven's vengeance light on you !" she shrieked, in a tone of wildness that might have appalled the dead ; and falling on her knees, she buried her agitated face in her shaking hands ; while Almazuma strode up to where she knelt, and in a transport of choking joy exclaimed—

"This is the ecstacy of success ! I have avenged thy taunting scorn—have triumphed o'er thy pride—trampled on thy heart ! Arise ! —do you attend—arise ! Your lover's father claims your domestic care. Arise, and honour him : the sire expects it at the daughter's hand. Morning draws near, and he will desire his child. Go, and let him kiss the hand which robbed him of his son ; he is too old to smell the carnage on it. Arise—go forth, and bid him trebly welcome ! "

Catalina rose slowly at his bidding, and confronted her husband, but with an eye so fierce, a look so bold and resolute that, for a moment, his steady and exulting look quailed before her threatening glance, as she said, in hollow and deliberate accents, " And I have been deceived."

"Most completely," rejoined Almazuma, with a low laugh.

"Deceived !" resumed his wife ; "and by a fiendish lie ! Made life-long wretched—wrecked in my hopes—blighted in heart, and ruined in my eternal peace. A course that promised happiness, content, and love—years full of bliss and living joy, withered—destroyed by a malignant devil ! These tears,"—for she wept in very bitterness of thought, — "madness, not sorrow, wrings from my outraged heart. Pity, tenderness, and all soft attributes of woman, hence. Resentment rises in my soul ; and passion now usurps the throne on which duty, honour, love, were once enshrined, and prompts my indignation to overleap all barriers to reach the summit of my just revenge. Stand thou aghast, presumptuous fiend !—shake like the seared leaf tossed by December's angry wind ; for here, confronting thee, no timid woman stands, but an avenger, springing on her prey ! "

While speaking, Catalina had gradually approached the altar, and, ascending the steps, drew from the body of Alonzo the fatal dagger, still dimmed and clotted with blood ; then, with one bound, sprang upon the smiling Almazuma, who, with arms folded over his breast, stood scornfully gazing on her passion. So quick—so sudden was her action and her speech, that escape or opposition was alike in vain, as she cried hoarsely—"To death, thou fiend !—to death ! "—and drove the long-bladed poniard to the hilt, obliquely, in his throat ; then, staggering back, exhausted with conflicting energies, sank insensible on the ground.

A deep and gurgling groan, followed by a stream of frothy blood, that poured from the divided arteries, was the only sound returned in that dreary vault. The hand involuntarily grasped the fatal weapon, and withdrew it from the wound ; the head dropped on the chest; the limbs lost their tension—bent under the frame ; and with a heavy sound the body of Almazuma fell dead upon the earth.

The swoon that succeeded the fall of Catalina was but of short duration. A few spasmodic actions of the limbs equalised the circulation, and freed the plethoric heart and head of their unnatural load ; and she awoke to all the fearful terror of the scene—her former guilt, her husband's baseness, and this latest act of desperate vengeance.

Taking up the lamp that Almazuma had placed on the table when he entered, she approached the bleeding body, and stooping down, surveyed, by the thin flame, the now tranquil and bloodless features.

"Thy form was noble," she said, apostrophising the body ; "but, oh ! how much deformed thy soul ! This deed touches me not: thou wer't unfit to live. But thou ! " she cried, turning and ascending the altar, "noble in heart—generous in soul, I am thy murderer, too ! Oh ! did I believe that thou could'st harbour fraud,—did I give up the rich possession of this heart—endless love, for guilt—for penitence, and life-corroding cares ? Accursed pride ! — horrible credulity ! whither—oh ! my God !—whither has it driven me ? Terrible, remorseless thought ! Hide me, ye saints, in death—shroud me in instant darkness—annihilate at once, and crush my being, that I may think no more ; for memory kills too slow——But yet, I will not tarry," she exclaimed with sudden wildness,—" I will not stay. Alonzo, open your dead embrace to pardon me before I die. My friend — companion—murdered love, clasp me to your icy heart, and let me perish thus,"—and throwing herself on the body of Alonzo, she wept long and bitterly, kissing the cold and stony lips with all the fervour of devotion. "But, stay ! " she cried, suddenly rising from the body: "I have a task that must be first fulfilled ; I dare not die till then. I will not procrastinate, my love, but join thee soon."

And as she spoke she descended from the altar, and tranquilly seating herself at the table, completed the writing in which she had been interrupted by the abrupt presence of her husband. Having folded, arranged, and superscribed the papers she had written, she arose, and taking from the bosom-folds of her robe a small phial, knelt before the crucifix, and addressed her supplication to heaven.

"Oh, God ! and Thou Emaculate, whose pure faith and holy symbol I have so transgressed—so awfully profaned, forgive the further sin I meditate, as expiation for my crimes. And thou, beloved—too lately prized, look from your heaven of place, and in my death receive atonement for thy blood so blindly—madly shed. Alonzo—friend—lover—husband—thy Catalina comes, true at last in death,—never—Oh, never more to part."

Then slowly rising from the ground, she placed the phial to her lips, and drained off its deadly compound; and with a calm mien and steady step crossed the floor, paused for a moment by the body of Almazuma, and resuming her seat by the table, awaited with tranquil patience the slow but certain poison.

Presently her eyes became suffused and red—a feverish heat pervaded all her frame—and the propelling heart sent the hot blood profusely to her brain—her features worked with violent gestures and grew fearfully distorted—delirium took possession of her mind, and a horrid fear—a supernatural dread diffused its terror through her excited brain. The hour—the place—the dreadful witnesses around, and the dead silence, joined to her conscious guilt, drove her distracted.

"The poison will not work," she cried, with harsh, cracked utterance; "and memory—memory murders me!—Horrible shadows flit before me, and mock me as they stalk along Death, death, death!" she shrieked in shrill discordant accents, "why com'st thou not? I call in vain, and this dread charnel-house smells of its rank mortality to stifle me! Lie still, Alvares—rest ye still, my love, and I will come, Alonzo. Hideous monster, keep on the earth!—Approach me not, Almazuma!—Detested fiend, avaunt! come not near me, and I swear to follow! See—see the gaunt, starved wretch creeps from his closet; his fleshless bones rattle as he crawls along. Avoid me, horrors, and I will obey you all!—See with what energy I strive to come, and break from life to follow you. Stand back, dark fiend—stand back!—back——" she exclaimed; and rising from her chair, ran wildly round the vault, as if escaping from the pursuit of imaginary and horrid forms; till tearing down the corded tassel that hung from the drapery over the secret entrance, she threw it fiercely round her neck, and drew both ends with the force of desperation, till the tense ligature nearly severed her small white throat.

The face and head grew suddenly black, swollen, and hideous—the eyes leaped forward—the mouth gaped—the tongue protruded—and a stream of dark blood gushed from the distended nostrils, as the liberated soul took wing from its earthly tenement. So powerful was the contraction of every muscle—so rigid the whole frame, that it was several minutes after death before the body lost its equilibrium, and fell prone, and in the same exact position to the ground.

One by one the wax tapers expired in their sockets—the light of the lamp by degrees grew fainter—cast a dimmer beam on the scene of woe—flickered—fell—gave one quick sudden flash—then sank in utter darkness.

The sun rose warm and glorious on the following morning; and nature rousing from the previous night of battling turmoil, shook her wet tresses in the new-born light, and with a thousand glittering tears, smiled in dimpled joyfulness in the bright transition; while overhead, high in the heavens, and all around, far as the sense could hear, the air seemed one glad chorus with rejoicing throats.

The matin-singing lark—the ring-dove from the wood—the thrush—the nightingale and blackbird from the grove and spray—the stalking heron—and the plover from the fen and stream—all joined in concert to the giver of all bliss for the rich sunshine, that from the drenched earth brought forth new life, and gave another day of boundless happiness.

The soft odour wafted from the blossoming trees—the fragrant scent distilled from the opening flowers, mingled with the perfume from the new-mown meadows, filled the surrounding space with luscious incense, invigorating the breathing frame with healthy pleasure and delightful sweetness; while through the perfumed atmosphere, the flocking bees hummed their delight in idle pastime, drinking the honied nectar from the air, and, in inebriate pleasure, neglecting their sweet task of thrifty toil. A fairer scene, a brighter morn, man never witnessed: earth and heaven conspired to make the picture blissful, crowning the whole in soft repose.

The Condé de Alvares rose betimes, and sought the fragrant lawn, to recompense an ill-spent night. The strife of elements, and the awakened gush of memories, rendered the hours of sleep a painful vigil; and, with heavy eyes and unrefreshed infirmity, aided by his long-tried domestic, he descended from his chamber, and, basking in the warm sunshine of the bright morning, awaited his host's summons to the matin meal.

The castle clock had struck the advanced hour of nine, when Almazuma's steward, with looks of consternation, approached with reverential gesture the seat on the lawn, where the Condé, attended by his servant, was reposing; and, in a few hasty words, informed Alvares that neither Don Ferdinand or his lady were to be found;—that neither couch had been slept on—nor was there the slightest evidence to denote whither they had gone, or when they had departed. Each gate and wicket had remained secured, as the seneschal over-night had fastened them, and yet each chamber of the extensive mansion had been searched, and neither clue or reference could be found in any to indicate a knowledge of their whereabout.

"My God!" exclaimed the Condé, raising his emaciated hands, when the steward had concluded his brief intelligence.

"Holy mother! is there another scene of misery in store for me—another dark impenetrable mystery to fill the last few hours of my sad life with newer-kindled terrors? What fatality, great heaven! is this, that blights my kindred and my friends! To horse—to horse!" he cried, addressing a large group of servants, who, with looks of wild and superstitious alarm, gathered around him, as if dreading the precincts of the castle.

"To horse, good sirs, I pray you! Some of you to horse—haste—summon the Marquis hither and his sons. Hence to the palace, bear my greeting to the worthy lord, and bid him hasten hither, straight—away! But on your lives, good fellows, let not my daughter hear this fatal news. Oh! be cautious, I beseech—I pray you! and now away—go—quick! I will, myself, with the steward's aid, investigate the house. Come, lead me in, and let me scrutinise this awful judgment of the Lord's," he continued, as two of the domestics mounted their horses, and dashed off in the direction of Alfendera's palace; and the Condé, resting on the arm of his servant, followed the steward into the castle, while the terrified menials, in low mysterious whisperings slunk in groups to their several departments.

Before mid-day, the Marquis and his sons had arrived at the scene of confusion and alarm, and another strict investigation of the whole house was instantly instituted, but, like the former examinations, all in vain: nothing was discovered, no light revealed to explain or guide the mystery or research.

Sebastian's first suspicion was directed to the oratory, and repairing at once to the spot, tore down the arras, inspected, minutely, the floor, and sounded the panels; but being assured by the steward and seneschal that there was no egress beyond, and that the hollow reverberation was solely the result of the wainscot being detached from the walls, and that the turret in which the apartment stood, was completely detached from the building, he relinquished pursuit; and proceeding to the base of the castle, began afresh to explore each nook, chamber, and passage of the entire range of the extensive mansion.

For hours, with plodding and unwearied industry, Sebastian and Felix investigated the castle, courts, offices, and grounds, and were only diverted from their fruitless task, by a message from their father and the Condé, who had in the interval carefully examined each of the domestics but without eliciting the faintest information to solve the thickening mystery.

The servants of Almazuma's household refused in a body to remain after dark in a place so signally visited by the wrath of heaven. Dreadful sounds and solemn music of unearthly depth and grandeur had been heard at the dead hour of night, trembling through the stone walls with slow and awful intonation; and last night several of the more hardy had listened and heard the pealing notes, even during the loud crashing of the thunder; and they felt no doubt but that the Enemy of Souls had borne off both Almazuma and his wife, during the tempest, which the arch-tempter had stirred up to drown their cries, and stifle their appeals; and they begged that they might be instantly permitted to quit a place so pregnant with calamity and horror.

In vain did Sebastian command, or Felix argue: the importunities of the sorrowing Marquis, or the beseeching Condé failed in effect to change their rooted resolve; and, with the exception of the steward, as the shades of evening closed around, the troop of affrighted domestics departed, with all the expedition that supernatural fear could excite in their wildly-heated imaginations.

*   *   *   *   *

Days passed and weeks succeeded into years. Amazement settled into grief, and mournful sorrow: but never from that hour a smile lighted on Alfendera's face, or earthly joy or pleasure touched his heart. One constant theme was on his tongue, one only image pictured on his soul—his lost, his sacrificed, and blighted daughter: his peerless child—his noble Catalina. But of her fate, and Almazuma's end, whether they died by bowl or steel—by wrath of Heaven, or craft of man, to him was never known: and for a hundred years the curtain of oblivion fell across those stately chambers and deserted halls, and shrouded in its dark, mysterious folds, the published record and the buried crime.

THE END

www.ingramcontent.com/pod-product-compliance
Lightning Source LLC
Chambersburg PA
CBHW081211170626
46811CB00010B/3243